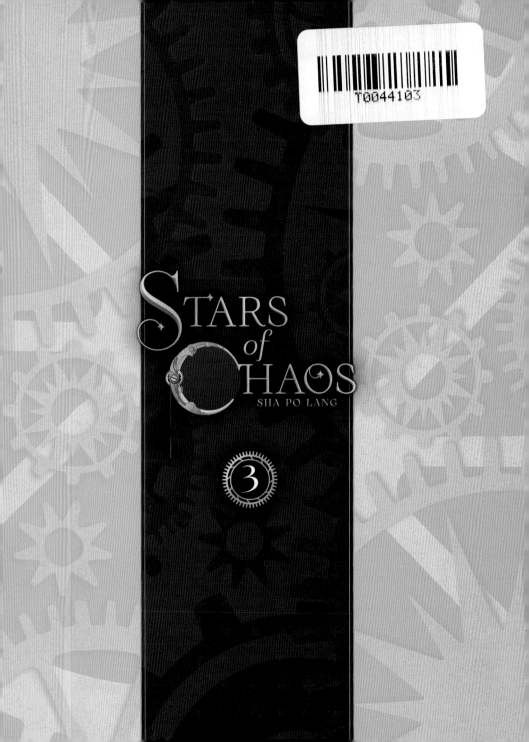

STARS of CHAOS

SHA PO LANG

3

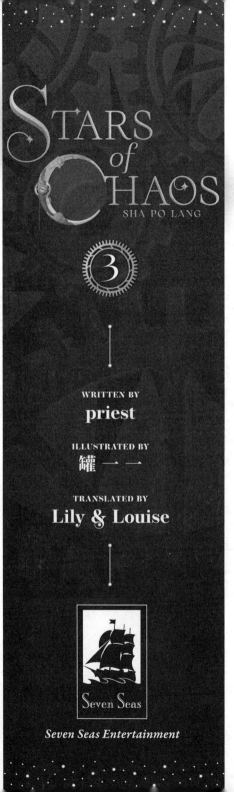

STARS of CHAOS

SHA PO LANG

3

WRITTEN BY

priest

ILLUSTRATED BY

罐一一

TRANSLATED BY

Lily & Louise

Seven Seas

Seven Seas Entertainment

STARS OF CHAOS:
SHA PO LANG VOL. 3

Published originally under the title of 《杀破狼》(Sha Po Lang)
Author © priest
English edition rights under license granted by 北京晋江原创网络科技有限公司
(Beijing Jinjiang Original Network Technology Co., Ltd.)
English edition copyright © 2024 Seven Seas Entertainment, Inc.
Arranged through JS Agency Co., Ltd
All rights reserved

Cover and Interior Illustrations by 罐一一 (eleven small jars)

Seven Seas press and purchase enquiries can be sent
to Marketing Manager Lauren Hill at press@gomanga.com.
Information regarding the distribution and purchase of digital editions
is available from Digital Manager CK Russell at digital@gomanga.com.

Seven Seas and the Seven Seas logo are trademarks of
Seven Seas Entertainment. All rights reserved.

Follow Seven Seas Entertainment online at
sevenseasentertainment.com.

TRANSLATION: Lily, Louise
COVER DESIGN: M. A. Lewife
INTERIOR DESIGN & LAYOUT: Clay Gardner
PROOFREADER: Stephanie Cohen, Hnä
COPY EDITOR: Jehanne Bell
EDITOR: Kelly Quinn Chiu
PREPRESS TECHNICIAN: Melanie Ujimori, Jules Valera
MANAGING EDITOR: Alyssa Scavetta
EDITOR-IN-CHIEF: Julie Davis
PUBLISHER: Lianne Sentar
VICE PRESIDENT: Adam Arnold
PRESIDENT: Jason DeAngelis

ISBN: 978-1-63858-938-9
Printed in Canada
First Printing: May 2024
10 9 8 7 6 5 4 3 2 1

T A B L E   O F
CONTENTS

ARC 8

BATTLE HYMN

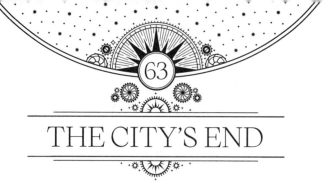

THE CITY'S END

WESTERN ENVOY had come with offers of peace.

This single envoy caused the day's morning court session to spiral into a headache-inducing argument. The instant court was dismissed, Chang Geng took Master Fenghan's arm and made a beeline for the palace gates, ignoring the crowd of officials attempting to solicit his opinions, each weighed down by their own worries. Anxiety hung heavy over the capital, and the streets were near deserted. Gu Yun usually instructed Huo Dan to wait for Chang Geng outside the palace with his horse at the ready, but today, Huo Dan seemed to have been held up and was nowhere in sight.

Chang Geng didn't think much of it. Strolling shoulder to shoulder with the old director of the Lingshu Institute, he made his way back to the Marquis Estate.

These days, Master Fenghan hardly left the Lingshu Institute for a moment from dawn till dusk. His eyes had become sunken, and his entire person resembled nothing so much as a dried-out radish. Only his eyes were bright with a wily gleam—as if one would chip their teeth if they tried to take a bite of him.

"Thank you, Your Highness, for your patience in accompanying an old geezer like me with my feeble legs," Master Fenghan sighed. "Is there any news of our reinforcements? When will they arrive?"

"The chaos on all four borders is hampering the movements of the five military regions," said Chang Geng. "You know the present state of the regional garrisons. Military budgets and violet gold allocations have shrunk again and again in every region. Most can scarcely support a couple suits of heavy armor, so they're almost uniformly composed of light-pelt cavalrymen. Light-pelt cavalry are fast on the march, flexible, and easy to deploy—but they are also easy to stall. The enemy need only set up a blockade of heavy-armor infantrymen or war chariots, and any less-experienced commander will find their forces quickly surrounded. The Westerners can hold up our forces with very few of their own troops."

"Your Highness, this leaves me too ashamed to show my face. The Lingshu Institute hasn't produced anything presentable in years." Zhang Fenghan shook his head in self-ridicule. "And here I am, a useless ancient who refuses to die, enjoying the privileges of my office without doing a lick of work. I'd intended to inform His Majesty of my retirement after the turn of the year, only for the nation to fall into this crisis. At this rate, I won't pass peacefully in my bed."

"Master Fenghan is laying the foundations on which we will build a thousand years of prosperity," Chang Geng said warmly. "You must not belittle yourself."

"A thousand years... In a thousand years, will there still be a Great Liang?" Zhang Fenghan pressed his lips together. "I'd always imagined that after I joined the Lingshu Institute, I could turn away from the affairs outside my window and spend the rest of my life surrounded by steam-powered engines and steel armor, focusing on nothing but excellence in my trade. But this world is such a hive of activity. Even if gentlemen and miscreants stick to their own roads, their paths will eventually collide. The less you wish to mingle—the more you wish to stand above the crowd and achieve a little greatness—the more you shall find you can achieve nothing at all, even if your goal was only to be a lowly mechanic with your hands covered in engine oil."

Chang Geng understood that Master Fenghan was venting his inner turmoil and had no real interest in his response. He offered a soft chuckle but said no more.

The two-generation-long conflict between imperial and military power was the catalyst that had precipitated Great Liang's slide to its current precarious state, yet it wasn't the most fundamental reason for its decline. The chronic ailments of the nation had sealed its tragic fate the moment the contents of the national treasury began to shrink by the year.

"The hidden mechanisms of the aerial defense field controlled from Kite's Flight Pavilion are adjusted every day," said Zhang Fenghan. "Those Westerners are afraid to deploy large formations of armored hawks and only dare advance toward the city by chariot. Even so, there's a limit to what the aerial defense field can do. I hear the Westerners have been flying wooden kites on strings beyond the city walls—after a few more days of this, I'm afraid the stockpiles of iron arrows within the hidden mechanisms will run low. What will we do then? Does Marshal Gu have a plan?"

Even if they included in the count those missing an arm or a leg, the suits of Black Hawk armor in the Northern Camp now numbered less than a hundred. The failure of the aerial defense field would likely signal the city's end.

Chang Geng placidly hummed in answer. "He knows. He's thinking."

Zhang Fenghan, burdened with a heart full of worries, was torn between laughter and tears. He didn't know whether he should laud this Prince Yanbei for displaying such heroic character at his young age or be concerned that there was something deeply wrong with his head. Master Fenghan thought that even if the sky should collapse in front of his nose, the young prince would only offer a detached "Understood."

Lowering his voice, Zhang Fenghan said, "Your Highness, did you notice Captain Han missing from court today? A rumor is spreading that although His Majesty made a show of fury toward the Western envoy, he is making plans to move the capital even now."

Chang Geng chuckled, seemingly unsurprised. "His Majesty is planning no such thing. We have not been maneuvered into a corner just yet. I see the carriage from the Lingshu Institute now; allow me to help you up—oh, Uncle Huo is here?"

Huo Dan was hurrying in their direction, unease writ clearly across his face. "This servant has arrived late. Please forgive me, Your Highness," he said, striding up to Chang Geng.

"It's no matter." Chang Geng waved aside his apology. "Uncle Huo, were you delayed by some business?"

Huo Dan eyed Chang Geng warily as he spoke. "Last night, the marquis was wounded by a Western arrow. I only found out this morning and had just gone to—Your Highness!"

Under Huo Dan and Zhang Fenghan's open-mouthed stares, a transformation came over Chang Geng's face. The prince, who had been strolling casually seconds ago, leapt onto his horse and disappeared like a gust of wind.

Outside the nine gates, the gunpowder smoke had yet to disperse. The Western forces had made a dejected retreat shortly after daybreak, and Gu Yun had finally gotten a moment to breathe. A dent marred one of his black-iron pauldrons. The arrowhead had already been extracted, but two medics were still orbiting him with forceps and scissors, carefully prying the deformed armor off his shoulder. Beneath lay a mess of fabric plastered to bloody flesh.

Chang Geng charged inside, but no sooner had he laid eyes on Gu Yun than he had to avert his gaze. The look on his face was bleaker than that of the injured party.

"Can the two of you get this over with?" Gu Yun hissed in pain. "Are you doing embroidery here?" He turned to Chang Geng. "What is it?"

Chang Geng didn't immediately reply. He took a deep breath and stepped over to Gu Yun, waving the two medics away. Bending down, he carefully examined the piece of armor embedded in Gu Yun's shoulder. Then, he pulled out a pair of shears the length of a finger, wrapped an arm around Gu Yun's shoulder, and began to cut from the other side. Chang Geng worked with swift movements, and the sharp blades of the shears carved through iron as if scraping away mud, prying away shards of the pauldron. Blood rushed out and coated his hand. Chang Geng's entire face was pinched, and for a moment, he could scarcely breathe. "You were injured this badly—why didn't you tell me?"

Gu Yun had been grimacing in pain as the medics worked, but now, he forced every trace of it from his features. "This is nothing," he said through a clenched jaw. "What did the Western envoy say in court?"

"What do you expect? He was there to blow hot air before the throne, of course." Chang Geng shook out his faintly trembling hands before continuing to remove the shattered bits of armor glued to Gu Yun's body with drying blood. "He demanded we cease our 'persecution and exploitation' of the nations in the Western Regions, concede all territory beyond Jiayu Pass for use as an international trade zone within which the laws of their own nation would be enforced, and..."

The entire deformed pauldron was at last removed. Chang Geng sucked in a breath at the sight of Gu Yun's injury, then struggled to his feet to gather himself.

"What else?" Gu Yun shivered; cold sweat had drenched his body. "My esteemed doctor, don't tell me you faint at the sight of blood."

Chang Geng was as stiff as an iron rod. "I faint at the sight of *your* blood." He snatched Gu Yun's wine flask and swallowed two large gulps, his head spinning so violently he thought he might puke. He forced himself to take two more steadying breaths, then plucked up a pair of scissors and began to cut away Gu Yun's clothes, which were so stained with blood he could no longer discern their original color.

"...And concede the thirty-six commanderies along the northern border to the eighteen tribes," he finally continued. "Everything north of the line stretching from the old western capital to Zhili and You Prefecture. On top of that, they are demanding that Great Liang's seat of government be moved to the old eastern capital in the Central Plains—and Princess Hening is to be handed over to the eighteen tribes as a hostage. Henceforth, our government is to declare allegiance to the eighteen tribes and offer a yearly tribute..."

Hening was Li Feng's only daughter. She was just seven years old.

"Bullshit!" Gu Yun spat in rage. Blood began pouring from his shoulder.

"Don't move!" Chang Geng snapped, unable to bear much more of the gory sight.

The two stared at each other, a turbulent expression in Gu Yun's eyes. A long moment later, he finally broke the silence. "Continue."

"They're also demanding Li Feng order Shen Yi's Southern Border Army to retreat from the islands in the South Sea. The Westerners wish to set up a separate territory bordered by the East Sea Canal; they're demanding that the Jiangnan Navy retreat inland of the canal, and that the land beyond the canal all the way to the East Sea be ceded to them as a 'Far Eastern District' under Western control." The look in Chang Geng's eyes was gloomy, but his hands were surpassingly gentle as he wiped the blood from Gu Yun's wounds. He paused for a beat, then went on. "Then there're the reparations..."

Gu Yun's body tensed.

"At morning court, Li Feng wanted to execute the envoy on the spot, but the officials managed to persuade him to leave the man alive." Chang Geng placed a hand on Gu Yun's uninjured shoulder. "I need to clean the wound. Yifu, may I give you something to put you under?"

Gu Yun shook his head no.

"Just a little bit of medicine," Chang Geng coaxed. "You have a high tolerance, so you won't be asleep for long. If anything happens outside the city gates, I'll guard them for you..."

"Just clean it," Gu Yun interrupted. "Enough with the chatter."

Chang Geng leveled him with a long look. Trying to reason with this person was useless.

At that moment, Tan Hongfei ran inside. "Sir..."

Gu Yun had just turned toward him when he detected a strange fragrance in the air. Caught off guard, he breathed it in and immediately went weak. The wise and powerful Marquis of Order had never expected His Highness the Commandery Prince to know a jianghu trick like hiding secret drugs up his sleeves—much less that he would use them on him!

"You..."

Chang Geng didn't so much as blink as he rapidly inserted thin needles into Gu Yun's acupoints, then caught his godfather's limp body. Having witnessed his own marshal taken down before his eyes, Tan Hongfei froze in the doorway and stared blankly at the commandery prince.

Chang Geng gestured for him to hold his tongue, then lifted Gu Yun and laid him on his back to begin carefully cleaning the arrow wound.

Tan Hongfei's eyes nearly popped out of his head. "This...uh..."

"Don't worry—let him get some sleep and suffer a bit less."

Tan Hongfei blinked. Some time ago, he had seen Prince Yanbei as an amicable scholar. Later, he had discovered this prince was capable both on and off the battlefield and came to respect him, feeling that he was a kindred spirit... It was only now that Commander Tan felt the first spark of a burning reverence for this man. Tan Hongfei's hand came up to touch his own cheek, where the scar from Gu Yun's whip had yet to fade. *His Highness has got some serious guts,* he thought.

Chang Geng turned to face him. "Ah, what were you going to say?"

Tan Hongfei recovered his wits and said in a rush, "Your Highness, His Majesty is here. His carriage is out back now. What should we..."

Li Feng arrived while they were speaking, his face haggard. He was dressed in casual clothes and was accompanied only by Zhu Xiaojiao. The emperor peered down at the unconscious Gu Yun and reached out to feel his forehead. "Is Uncle well?"

"Just a flesh wound." Chang Geng finished bandaging the injury, then wrapped a thin silk outer robe around Gu Yun's body and tidied away his acupuncture needles. "I administered some anesthetic, so he won't wake for some time. I hope Brother will take no offense."

With that, Chang Geng rose, picked up Gu Yun's windslasher, and turned to walk out the door without donning a single piece of armor.

"Where are you going?" Li Feng called after him.

"I'll guard the city gates in Yifu's stead," Chang Geng said. "Even if their envoy is in the capital, the Westerners aren't to be trusted. They may yet attack while our guard is down; we can never be too careful."

Li Feng stood stiffly in place for a moment, then grabbed a sword and made to follow Chang Geng. Zhu Xiaojiao was shocked. "Your Majesty!"

Li Feng ignored him and climbed to the top of the city wall alone. The Longan Emperor lifted his field scope and saw the tents of the Western army lined up not far away. The fertile soil of the capital's surroundings was pitted with scars. The roads beyond the city gates, which had so recently flowed with rivers of horses and carriages, were now deserted. A collapsed corner of the city wall was held up by broken pieces of black-iron armor; as he watched, it teetered precariously, yet obstinately remained standing.

The rank-and-file soldiers of the Northern Camp all knew Chang Geng and stepped forward to greet him, but none recognized Li Feng. When they saw his refined dress and noble bearing, they took him for a civil official and murmured a greeting of "my lord" in chorus. The Li brothers, whose harmonious relationship was skin-deep at best, stood shoulder to shoulder atop the city wall. From their faces to their figures, they were alike in not a single aspect; their familial bond was as thin as a paper window that could be torn by a finger.

"Han Qi should be back by the afternoon," Li Feng said suddenly. "Relay the message to Uncle; tell him to have someone he trusts receive him."

Chang Geng didn't inquire after his intentions, as if he wasn't the least bit curious. He assented briefly to the request.

"Why aren't you asking where we sent Han Qi?"

Chang Geng cast his eyes down to the stone bricks that made up the city wall. After a moment of silence, he said, "Lately, I've been reallocating violet gold and other military necessities with the Ministry of Revenue. I discovered a few discrepancies in the figures for violet gold acquired and dispensed by the court...but perhaps Brother has been making his own arrangements."

When the Longan Emperor heard this, he knew Chang Geng had long noticed the violet gold he had been stockpiling in secret.

"Ah," Li Feng began, a bit awkwardly. "Inside the Gate of Virtuous Triumph, there's a secret passage that leads to the Sunlight Palace. We ordered Han Qi to take some troops, exit the city through this passage, and open the secret warehouse in the Sunlight Palace, which contains..." He coughed, then continued, "Eighty thousand kilograms of violet gold that we have not yet gotten around to allocating. Keep this to yourself. The court is losing their resolve, and if they learn of the secret passage, I'm afraid they will waver."

Chang Geng nodded but showed no sign of surprise. Li Feng was emptying his coffers. Someone as headstrong as the Longan Emperor would never bring shame upon his nation by pledging allegiance to another. He would rather be buried below these nine gates.

Once Chang Geng fell silent, the conversation stuttered to an end. Actually, this was always the way with these two. Aside from political debate in court and hollow niceties exchanged when Chang Geng came to pay his respects, the Li brothers truly had nothing to say to each other.

Li Feng finally hit upon a topic: "How old were you when you met Uncle Shiliu?"

A pause. "Twelve."

Li Feng hummed in acknowledgment. "He has yet to marry and spends long stretches of time leading troops in the northwest. He must have been rather neglectful when it came to your care?"

Chang Geng's eyes flashed. "No, he's very good at doting on people."

Li Feng squinted into the faint traces of light on the horizon and recalled how he, too, had grown up with Gu Yun. In his youth, he had felt the occasional sting of jealousy over his imperial father's treatment of Gu Yun; he was better to him, gentler to him. But by and large, Li Feng had still retained a good opinion of his young imperial uncle, even if the boy didn't often play with the rest of them.

He had once thought these youthful sentiments could persist for a lifetime. Yet within the span of a few decades, their relationship had deteriorated to this point.

"A-Min," Li Feng said, "if the city falls, we will abdicate the throne in your favor. Take the harem and the officials, make your departure through the secret tunnels, and establish a new capital in Luoyang... The rest can be taken one step at a time. A day when we can once again rally our forces will come."

Chang Geng finally spared him a glance.

"And if it does," Li Feng said, staring calm-eyed into the distance, "you need not return the throne to the crown prince, as long as you provide your nieces and nephews a place of refuge."

Chang Geng was silent. After a beat, he said, calm and unmoved, "Brother, you are getting ahead of yourself. Our circumstances are not yet so dire."

Li Feng gazed at his youngest brother. A faint recollection rose in his mind, something his empress mother had told him when he was young: All northern barbarian women were enchantresses, adept at using poison and casting spells on people's hearts. Their vile spawn were beasts who polluted the imperial bloodline of Great Liang. Later, after the Marquis of Anding retrieved this fourth prince who had been lost among the commoners and fetched him back to the palace, Li Feng had allowed the boy to stay as a concession to the late emperor's final wishes and an attestation to his own reputation of benevolent virtue. It cost him nothing save an extra allowance from the Department of the Imperial Household, and the little prince normally stayed out of sight and out of mind.

It wasn't until this moment that the Longan Emperor discovered he couldn't read this young man at all. He remained composed in the face of national peril and a great enemy army. Even the prospect of sitting on the imperial throne did not move him. He seemed to be dressed in last year's clothes—the hems of his sleeves had grown thin from wear—yet he didn't change them out for a fresh set. He was more of a puzzle than even Great Master Liao Chi of the National Temple; he showed no partiality toward anything, as if nothing on earth could move him.

Li Feng had just opened his mouth to say more when Zhu Xiaojiao quietly reminded him from where he stood on the side, "Your Majesty, it is time to return to the palace." The emperor came back to himself and handed his sword to a nearby soldier. He patted Chang Geng's shoulder without a word. With a last glance at the young man's ruler-straight back, he turned to leave.

After Li Feng left, a travel-worn monk ascended the city wall. Liao Ran.

All the monks of the National Temple had retreated inside the city. By day, Liao Ran recited scriptures with the abbot in prayer for the nation. By night, he liaised with his informants investigating Li Feng's servants.

Chang Geng cast him a questioning glance.

Liao Ran shook his head. "I went down the whole list, but all His Majesty's servants are clean. None had close dealings with the shamaness of the eighteen tribes or her entourage."

For a moment, Chang Geng considered. "His Majesty is paranoid by nature and is not a man incapable of guarding his own secrets. The leak on our side has been continuous, so the traitor *must* be one of his closest confidantes. Have you looked into Zhu-gonggong?"

Liao Ran shook his head again, his expression grim—he had, but found nothing out of place.

Chang Geng frowned.

It was at this instant that Gu Yun finally awoke after being knocked out with both medicine and acupuncture. He'd fallen so deeply asleep that he hardly knew what day it was when he opened his eyes. Not until he felt the ache in his shoulder did he belatedly recall what had transpired.

Gu Yun crawled out of bed and pulled on his clothes, prepared to get even with Chang Geng. Yet no sooner had he stepped outside than he heard a loud *boom* that shook the entire capital. Gu Yun put a hand on the city wall for support. *An earthquake?*

Atop the wall, Chang Geng's head whipped around, a vicious look flashing across his face. He had always thought the traitor within the capital was among Li Feng's servants. But Li Feng was cautious and paranoid—how could he have revealed the secret of the Sunlight Palace to a mere servant?

"What was that?" Gu Yun asked.

"I don't know." Chang Geng took the stairs down in rapid steps. "Li Feng was just here. He said he ordered Han Qi to exit the city through a secret passage and transport violet gold from the Sunlight Palace... Did that sound like it came from the west?"

With a start, Gu Yun found that he was now fully awake.

On the ninth day of the fifth month, the secret buried within the Sunlight Palace was blown sky-high. The Far Westerners' offer of peace was indeed a ruse, but they hadn't planned to use the opportunity to attack the city directly. Instead, they'd sent troops to circle around to the west and intercept Han Qi.

After a bitter struggle with the Western troops, the tides had turned against Han Qi. He made a snap decision and set the tens of thousands of kilograms of violet gold alight, detonating the secret passage and ensuring not a drop of fuel was left behind.

Raging like a prairie fire, the great blaze devoured the entire western outskirts. Li Feng's bottomless well of violet gold burned like karmic fire summoned from deep within the earth, sending the imperial guards who'd been sent to escort the violet gold, the surprised Far Westerners, and even the exquisite scenery and elegant architecture of the Sunlight Palace up in flames. The telltale purple fumes glowed across half the heavens like an auspicious omen, as if a vividly painted dawn ascended from the horizon.

The heart of the earth was burning, and the capital trembled in its wake.

A wall of heat expanded dozens of kilometers in every direction, until it gradually seeped through even the rock-solid capital gates from the west. The capital's mild early summer submitted to a heat rivaling the furnace of the southern border. The scent of violet gold, ordinarily indiscernible, billowed in on the westerly wind, and the citizens of the capital at last experienced that unique aroma. It was in fact a clean sort of fragrance, difficult to describe. Like sharp pine rosin, mixed with a hint of grassy roundness.

Gu Yun deployed every suit of heavy armor that remained to him and drew taut the string of every parhelion bow. Yet as he expected, the main body of the Western army made its move to counter. Gu Yun knew not how many of the Western army's men had been incinerated in the fire, nor did he know how long the pope could last at this high rate of attrition. The siege had been long, and both sides were at their limit.

The first frenzied wave of attack came in the middle of the afternoon. Heavy armor and war chariots advanced in turns, and shot after shot roared from cannons and parhelion bows in a seamless, violent cacophony.

64

IN DESPERATE
STRAITS

C LOUDS OF DUST and the clamor of war surged on all sides. The air grew hot and sere in the wake of the great conflagration to the west of the city, and sweat rolled down the soldiers' backs. The screech of an armored hawk taking flight sounded from afar. Though the aerial defense field had yet to fail completely, the Far Westerners had lost their patience—they sent countless armored hawks to challenge the defenses with their very lives.

This Western army had been stalled by Gu Yun for over a month, then routed by the capital's forces at the city gates and stymied by the aerial defense field. Every day, they suffered unimaginable losses, and each day they spent in fruitless labor chipped away at the patience their faraway Western masters had for this eastern expedition over a decade in the making.

Under the city walls, Chang Geng grabbed Liao Ran. "Listen to me," he said quickly. "There's no way the person we're looking for is a palace servant, and we've investigated all of Li Feng's closest advisors more than once. The previous dynasty fell at the hands of sycophants and flatterers; our dynasty has never allowed eunuchs to hold power. No matter what else His Majesty has done, he wouldn't be so absurd as to have eunuchs handle the Sunlight Palace...nor could that person be one of the court officials. Han Qi's departure had the whole court in a state of anxiety with everyone speculating that His Majesty planned to flee, yet Li Feng kept his cool and didn't say a thing. He intended to abdicate the throne in my favor, yet he only offered me the information in person once Han Qi was nearly back..."

Liao Ran stared at him blankly.

"This imperial brother of mine distrusts generals in times of peace and civil officials in times of war," Chang Geng muttered. "Who could it be? Who else is there?"

Liao Ran's fingers froze on the prayer beads he had been unconsciously turning, and he drew in a cold breath. This eminent monk, who so resembled the reincarnation of a Buddhist lotus, suddenly wore an expression so grave he looked like a corpse.

Chang Geng's heavy gaze turned on him. Slowly enunciating every word, he said, "The National Temple is to the west of the city."

A stray explosive landed near the two of them, and both Chang Geng and Liao Ran were knocked off their feet by the force of the blast. Chang Geng staggered upright, but the prayer beads around the monk's neck burst off their string at the impact.

The aged wooden beads scattered into the wretched mortal dust.

Chang Geng dragged Liao Ran up by the collar, helping him stumble to a standing position. "Get up, let's go. If we kill the wrong man, count it on my head!"

Liao Ran shook his head as if on reflex. He had thought that, after his many years of cultivation, he had already seen through the joy and sorrow of the human world. But in this moment, like encountering demons in the Latter Day of the Dharma,[1] he finally discovered that any pretensions he had of transcending the physical world were mere overconfident illusions.

---

1 The Latter Day of the Dharma is the last of the three ages of Buddhism in East Asian Buddhist beliefs, a ten-thousand-year period in which society falls into chaos and the teachings of Shakyamuni Buddha lose their effect.

Chang Geng pushed Liao Ran and stared into the pale-faced monk's frightened eyes. "I'm not afraid of karmic retribution. I'll take care of it. Great Master, don't stop me; don't blame me either." When Chang Geng had still been young and innocent, he had already suffered the full gamut of every frightful retribution the world had to offer. There was nothing in this world or the next that could give him pause.

"I'm going to borrow some men from Yifu," Chang Geng said.

Liao Ran was still frozen in place. The young commandery prince made a peculiar gesture—he curled his thumb in and pressed his palm down slightly. The wide sleeves of his court robes sliced through the air with his movements, and the metallic embroidery flashed like silver dragon-fish darting over the surface of a river— *When times are prosperous, we are content to till the land, to study our books, and to roam the depths of the jianghu.*

Liao Ran's entire body was shaking. After a long interval, he raised trembling hands to press his palms together and bow in Chang Geng's direction—*When chaos is imminent and the abyss looms near, we shall die a thousand deaths to save the people. This path is called "Linyuan"—to approach the abyss.*

Chang Geng chuckled lowly. "Fake monk." With that, he turned and ran toward the city gate.

Tears poured down Liao Ran's face.

Those who have not known suffering believe in no god nor Buddha.

What few Black Hawks survived were all in the air. Gu Yun had gathered every remaining scrap of firepower in the capital and now sent it pelting down from the city walls in a last desperate struggle. Within the city gate, heavy armor infantry lined up at the ready, and for the first time, Chang Geng saw Gu Yun abandon his light pelt for a suit of heavy armor. His bloodless face seemed to take on some of the boundless, rock-solid color of the black iron around him.

When his personal guard reported Prince Yanbei's arrival, Gu Yun's head snapped around, his expression darker than when he was getting an arrow extracted from his shoulder. He strode forward and grabbed Chang Geng's arm in his iron gauntlets. "What are you doing back here?"

"How's it looking?" Chang Geng asked. "The Far Westerners are losing their patience. What are your plans?"

Gu Yun said nothing as he dragged Chang Geng down from the city wall. His answer was clear in his silence—*What else is there to do but defend our position to the end?*

"The attack on Captain Han Qi was no coincidence. There is a traitor near Li Feng," Chang Geng said. "Yifu, lend me a squadron of guards. I will resolve the hidden danger that lurks in the city. Elsewise, if our enemies remain able to coordinate from within and without, it will be only a matter of time until the city falls..."

"Chang Geng." Gu Yun wiped his habitual irreverence from his face. "Your Highness, I will send a squadron of guards to escort you away. Look after yourself on your journey, and don't come back again."

Traitor or no, it was likely only a matter of time until the city fell.

Chang Geng's eyebrow jumped. He had a feeling Gu Yun didn't mean solely "away" from the capital's gates and into the city proper.

An enormous crash came from behind. A heavy artillery strike from the Westerners had slammed into the city wall, leaving the gate that had stood impregnable for centuries trembling in its wake. The mottled outer surface of the wall crumbled pitifully away, exposing the black-iron beams and interlocking iron gears within. The face of the city wall was peeled back, revealing the fearsome flesh and blood beneath.

The headless corpse of a Black Hawk plummeted to the ground nearby. Gu Yun pulled Chang Geng into the safety of his heavy-armored embrace as a giant chunk of falling stone smashed down behind him, loose debris tapping out a discordant cacophony against black iron. The two were mere centimeters apart, practically breathing the same air. They hadn't been this close since Chang Geng had begun deliberately keeping his distance. Gu Yun's breath was searing—perhaps he was running a fever—yet his gaze was sharp and bright as ever.

"What else did His Majesty say when he was here?" Gu Yun asked, his words rapid-fire in Chang Geng's ear. "Do as he said, go!"

When Li Feng had come, Gu Yun was unconscious. The two hadn't even laid eyes on each other. This lord and subject had continuously speculated on each other's motivations, always suspicious and on guard beneath a veneer of affected harmony. But in the nation's time of extremity, both understood what the other was thinking.

Chang Geng's pupils contracted. He reached into the heavy armor to pull Gu Yun down by the neck and, throwing all caution to the wind, pressed a kiss to those wind-chapped lips.

It was the first time he had tasted Gu Yun while they were both sober. The kiss burned, as if he were about to self-combust, and carried the faint tang of blood. Chang Geng's heart pounded so hard in his chest, he felt it would crack—not because of some phony sense of honeyed joy as written in tales of romance. Instead, a wildfire capable of engulfing heaven and earth roared to life in his heart, a raging inferno entrapped within mortal flesh, on the verge of bursting from its confines and devouring the present and future of this nation teetering on the brink of destruction.

The moment felt as long as hundreds of centuries, yet shorter than the blink of an eye.

Gu Yun dragged Chang Geng off himself. Human strength was no match for the power of the black-iron heavy armor. But he didn't lose his temper, nor did he toss Chang Geng indiscriminately to the side. He gently opened his iron gauntlets, treating Chang Geng as if he were something precious as he set him down a few paces away.

Without a thousand different fetters and barriers of etiquette, could burning devotion in desperate straits melt even Gu Yun's iron heart? If he was prepared to die upon these city walls, would the last person whose lips he felt upon his own in this lifetime spare him from feeling he had left absolutely nothing precious behind when he set off down the road to the Yellow Springs?[2]

Would it offer comfort?

Or would it...merely seem absurd?

At that moment, there was no one in the world who could read a single one of Gu Yun's thoughts from his handsome face.

Chang Geng fixed his gaze on him and spoke in tones as calm as still water. "Zixi, I need to intercept the traitor in the city, so I can't keep you company here any longer. If anything happens to you today..." A faint smile appeared on his face. He shook his head, deciding that words like *I swear I won't live on alone* would make him appear too weak. Gu Yun would laugh at him. But it wouldn't have been an empty promise—or was he supposed to drag out a meaningless existence with the wu'ergu as his closest companion?

He didn't hate himself that much.

Gu Yun sucked in a deep breath. "Old Tan!" A Black Hawk screeched down from above—Tan Hongfei. Gu Yun gave his orders: "Assemble a squadron of light-pelt cavalrymen. You will personally

---

2 黄泉, huangquan, the Yellow Springs, also called the Nine Springs, form the underworld in traditional Chinese mythology.

escort His Highness." He climbed back up the city wall without a backward glance.

Firebrand arrows loaded onto parhelion bows sped through the air in neat arcs, meeting the attacking Western hawks midair in a violent clash—this was the final batch of firebrand arrows delivered by the Lingshu Institute.

Their enemy built a ladder from human flesh, a bridge from sunken corpses, throwing themselves forward in endless waves, a reckless onslaught. A Western hawk used a comrade's mangled remains as cover to brashly swoop past the line of parhelion bows atop the wall and launch a cannon blast toward the center of the city, striking Kite's Flight Pavilion. A Black Hawk collided with the Western assailant. One of the Black Hawk's iron wings was malfunctioning, and thick, dark smoke poured from the back of his armor. He had not a single remaining weapon and could only cling to his enemy by the shoulders, dragging them both tumbling from the sky. Before they could hit the ground, the hawk's overloaded gold tank exploded, and the brief flash of the resultant flames engulfed both the Black Hawk and his Western foe.

Mutual destruction.

After suffering the cannon strike, the Moon-Shot Platform of Kite's Flight Pavilion listed to and fro before collapsing with a great rumble. Now, all that could be seen from the Great Yunmeng Outlook was its crumbling ruins. That grand capital that had seen a hundred years of prosperity, those glorious dreams of eternity floating above the red walls and golden tiles, now collapsed to the ground amid the shattering of colored glass and turned to dust.

Pandemonium reigned in the great audience hall. Zhu Xiaojiao stumbled over and threw himself at Li Feng's feet, choking his words out through sobs. "Your Majesty, the nine gates are about to fall; please relocate! This servant has already ordered his yizi³ to prepare a carriage and commoners' clothes and wait by the north gate. A hundred and thirty imperial guards remain inside the palace. They would give their lives to allow Your Majesty to break through the siege..."

Li Feng raised a foot and kicked him to the ground. "How dare a servant make decisions on his master's behalf! Get out!" He turned back toward the rest of the room. "Bring us the Shangfang Sword!"

When Wang Guo heard this, he sank to the floor in a bow. "Your Majesty, you must think this through! As long as our lord and ruler is well, the foundations of the state remain. In the future, there will..."

As he spoke, an imperial guard presented the Shangfang Sword to the emperor with both hands. Li Feng drew it and knocked Imperial Uncle Wang's black gauze official's hat from his head with one thrust, then strode toward the door.

Zhu Xiaojiao scrambled after him. Like a herd of sheep that had found a bellwether to lead them, the terrified ministers and officials trailed after Li Feng in single file. Outside the north gate, the imperial guards had pushed Zhu Xiaojiao's pair of powder-faced godsons to the side, where they were calling out to Zhu Xiaojiao in a panic.

"Impudent!" Zhu Xiaojiao shouted in his high-pitched voice. "How dare you!" This eunuch was a favorite of the emperor, after all. The imperial guards hesitated and accidentally let the two kept men slip by them to charge inside. At the same time, Great Master Liao Chi of the National Temple appeared on his way to meet them, leading a crowd of monks in warrior attire. He stopped before Li Feng.

Li Feng's severe features relaxed, but as he made to greet Great Master Liao Chi, one of Zhu Xiaojiao's powder-faced godsons

---

3   义子, yizi, "godson."

suddenly raised his head, a mask of bloodlust on his previously sub-servient face. From his position at Zhu Xiaojiao's heels, five steps from the Longan Emperor, he blew a blow dart from his opened mouth.

For an instant, everyone was too shocked to react.

At the most critical moment, Zhu Xiaojiao lunged forward with a shout. His broad frame crashed into Li Feng's back as he blocked the fatal blow with his own body. Li Feng staggered and nearly fell into Liao Chi's arms. He turned, a mixture of shock and fury surging through him. Zhu Xiaojiao's eyes were wide, as if still in disbelief that his docile godson had transformed into an assassin. The old eunuch's body twitched like a wooden puppet on strings, and he breathed his last without uttering a single word more.

Li Feng's breath caught in his throat. But at the same instant, he heard an "Amitabha Buddha" from behind him. Before the Longan Emperor could begin to grieve, an icy hand was pressed against his throat. Hidden within his sleeve, Great Master Liao Chi was wearing an iron claw. This monstrous hand which could crush stone with ease gripped the Longan Emperor's fragile neck, and the Shangfang Sword clattered to the ground.

The officials and Imperial Guard were all struck dumb. Jiang Chong, a frail scholar who hadn't the strength to subdue a chicken, somehow found the guts to step forward and confront Liao Chi. "Abbot, have you gone mad?"

Liao Chi raised his head to look at him, still wearing the melan-choly expression that never left his face. He chuckled. "Amitabha Buddha, this humble monk has not gone mad. Justice Jiang, you may not have even been born when Emperor Wu recklessly exhausted the strength of his military to whet his black-iron sword warring against his neighbors on all four borders."

"What..."

One of Liao Chi's "warrior monks" stepped forward and uttered a string of syllables to Liao Chi in a language Jiang Chong didn't understand. Moments later, several heavy-armor infantrymen emerged from all directions and fell into formation behind the monks. The Minister of State Ceremonial cried out in shock: "A Dongying man!"

Liao Chi laughed again. "After Emperor Wu's Gold Consolidation Decree, all sixteen members of my family died at the hands of his black crows; I was left alone to drag out a pointless existence. I found myself in your esteemed state, and thanks to the general pardon granted at the time of the former Marquis Gu's marriage to the eldest princess, I became a free man. I cut all ties with the secular world and took endless study by lamplight as my constant companion. After forty-six years of painstaking effort, this day has finally come."

Li Feng spoke haltingly through the cold grip around his throat. "You...are a descendant of those condemnable violet gold smugglers!"

"Smugglers," Liao Chi echoed with a smile that didn't reach his eyes. "That's right. It's all the fault of violet gold. Your Majesty, your tongue is sharp and your heart is stone, but are your bones the same? Please relocate with me to the red-headed kite."

"We—" Li Feng began.

"Your Majesty believes in my Buddha," Liao Chi said. "If you believe in the Buddha, then you believe in this humble monk. There is little difference."

Liao Chi shoved Li Feng onto a red-headed kite and ordered his subordinates to take the coiling dragon banner from the imperial carriage and hang it from the vessel's stern.

"Cut the ropes and release the kite," Liao Chi said. "Spread the news: His Majesty plans to abandon the city and escape by air!"

"How dare you, you miscreant!" Jiang Chong yelled.

Liao Chi laughed out loud. "Anyone who would like to commit regicide, please be my guest and step forward!"

Just then, a great roar tore itself from someone's throat a short distance away. Liao Chi started and turned. Atop the rubble of Moon-Shot Platform stood Liao Ran. The mute monk's throat had been malformed since birth. Even exerting all his strength, he could produce only a wordless cry. It was a rather inelegant noise, and accordingly, no one who knew Great Master Liao Ran had ever heard him make a sound. His image before all was graceful as the cool breeze, an expression of compassion ever present on his face.

The previous abbot of the National Temple had taken him in as an abandoned infant, but it had been his shixiong Liao Chi who raised him. He had been an unruly child who didn't seem much like a proper monk, and had begun slipping out of the temple to wander the jianghu at scarcely more than ten years old, even going on to join the Linyuan Pavilion. Yet even so... His youthful affections for his shixiong may have faded over time, but they had never left him entirely.

"Shixiong," Liao Ran signed at him, "it's not too late to come back to shore."

Liao Chi stared at the shidi he had raised from childhood with a complicated expression; he, too, failed to resist the tug of nostalgia. After a brief moment of distraction, he muttered in reply, "The river has already dried up, where is the..."

Before the word *shore* could leave his mouth, in the brief instant Liao Chi lowered his guard, a bolt the length of a palm flew out from an impossible angle and buried itself neatly in his throat.

Everyone cried out in shock. A Black Hawk bore down on them, flying low through the air. Standing on the hawk's back, Chang Geng held a crossbow, the string still vibrating. With his windslasher in hand, the Black Hawk—Tan Hongfei—blocked two more attacks from the Dongying warrior monks with a wave of his iron arm.

"What are you all waiting for?" Jiang Chong yelled. "Protect His Majesty!"

The imperial guards swarmed forward, and a squadron of light-pelt cavalry in black-iron armor charged in through a narrow alleyway. Li Feng shoved Liao Chi away, and the body of the most eminent monk of his generation tumbled from the deck of the red-headed kite.

Liao Ran knelt, devastated, in the rubble.

Nowhere in this nation, nowhere in this world, bounded by oceans to the east and west and extending endlessly to the north and south…was there room for a single tiny shrine, far from mortal dust.

The Dongying warrior monks and the imperial guard were soon embroiled in a chaotic battle. A heavy-armor infantryman who had come with Liao Chi fired his cannon into the sky, and Tan Hongfei made a steep vertical descent. Chang Geng leapt nimbly from his back to land on one knee, and the two parted ways as debris flew through the air.

Chang Geng briefly met Li Feng's eyes as he unslung his parhelion longbow, pressed his back to a wall, and drew the iron bowstring to its limit, the bow curving like the full moon—

With a sharp screech that vibrated through the teeth of all present, his arrow punched through the heavy armor's gold tank. He jumped back out of range, and the gold tank exploded. The red-headed kite heaved from the blast of hot air.

Li Feng grabbed the railing. "Tan Hongfei, get this damned thing started and take us to the city gates!"

Startled, Tan Hongfei glanced hesitantly toward Chang Geng. Chang Geng's gaze was dark, but his silence constituted tacit permission.

The red-headed kite conveyed the emperor toward the city gates with over a hundred imperial guards and every important official following on foot behind it in a winding procession. There were six kilometers of bluestone road between Kite's Flight Pavilion and the city gates. As they advanced, more and more local citizens and refugees who had fled to the capital poured in from both sides of the road to join their ranks, like rivers meeting the sea.

At the same time, the defense of the city walls was finally beginning to falter. The aerial defense field had gone mute, and the capital's forces had fired the last of their firebrand arrows.

From atop the city wall, Gu Yun called out an order to open the gates.

Ranks of Black Iron heavy-armor infantrymen who had long waited for this moment marched through. Gu Yun, in the lead, turned to give a hand signal to the injured soldiers who had stepped up to man the mechanisms atop the wall, and the gate slowly ground shut behind the heavy armor formation.

Gu Yun lowered his iron visor. One by one, every heavy-armor infantryman behind him followed suit.

SURVIVAL IS FOUND

THE HEAVY ARMOR FORMATION moved out.

The battered city walls trembled with the thunder of their locked-step footfalls. Submerged in a cloud of snow-white steam impervious to any breeze, a dark front of black-iron armor swam against the torrential current of the enemy army's cannon fire.

The first wave of heavy armor swept across the battlefield like an anti-cavalry saber, advancing straight toward the heart of the enemy formation. Heads and limbs detached in the repeated blasts lay scattered over the earth, but raging fire couldn't melt black iron. As long as the gold tanks of their armor hadn't exploded, those corpses who had failed to complete their quest in life could yet stand. The flesh and blood soldiers within the iron had already perished, but mechanical gears still turned, continuing their forward charge as if the lingering spirits of their operators had returned to the battlefield.

Only when their legs failed to move would later waves of soldiers pry open the gold tanks on their backs and ignite the fuses encased within.

Hidden beneath iron visors, each soldier was indistinguishable, merely one of the unidentifiable thousands. There was no difference between a marquis with a fiefdom of ten thousand households or a fresh recruit from the Northern Camp—they either charged through cannon fire, windslashers in hand, leaping over the severed heads of their enemies, or disappeared in an anonymous firework of purple flame.

Li Feng stood on the deck of the red-headed kite, hands clasped behind his back. He turned to Tan Hongfei, who stood at attention beside him. "Where is A-Min?"

Tan Hongfei was startled to be called on out of the blue. After a brief pause, he said, "His Highness the Commandery Prince went to the city wall."

A hot wind blew away the anger on Li Feng's face. He rescued his calm amid his battle-torn surroundings and tossed the newly retrieved Shangfang Sword to Tan Hongfei, who was still in his Black Hawk armor. "Deliver our verbal edict: In this time of national emergency, the crown prince is young and unsuited for heavy responsibility. Our lack of ability and virtue has left the nation and its people in dire straits, and we have disappointed our ancestors. We shall abdicate in favor of Prince Yanbei—we don't have time to draft a proper edict. Bring this to him, and escort him from the city."

Tan Hongfei fumbled to catch the heavy sword and snuck a glance at the imperial visage. His eyes snagged on the gray streaking the Longan Emperor's temples.

Li Feng waved him off without another word.

Chang Geng had climbed the city wall with bow in hand and taken command of the aerial front. Tan Hongfei touched down next to Chang Geng amid the roar of parhelion bows, holding the Shangfang Sword like a hot potato. "Your Highness!"

With a single glance from the corner of his eye, Chang Geng knew what he was about to say.

"Your Highness, His Majesty said..."

Just then, an injured soldier who had lost a leg hobbled over on his remaining foot. "Your Highness, the firebrand arrows have run out!"

"If we run out of firebrand arrows, use iron ones. If we run out of iron arrows, load the masterless windslashers. What's there to panic over? We will make our stand here until this city wall crumbles to dust." Chang Geng didn't even blink, but his next words were extremely blunt: "Commander Tan, take that thing back and tell Li Feng that I owe him nothing, and I will not become the solitary ruler of a conquered nation in his place! He is currently a living banner of command. In a standoff between two armies, the banner cannot be allowed to fall—it is this banner that gives our brothers the courage to lay down their lives. Keep an eye on him; don't let him go off and die."

At this moment, as far as Commander Tan was concerned, even ten Li Fengs giving him orders wouldn't hold the same weight as a word from Chang Geng. He ejected the emperor's verbal edict from his mind without a word of protest.

Commander Tan whistled a long note, and several Black Hawks swooped in, ready to defend the emperor's red-headed kite to the last.

Beneath the city walls, the heavy armor formation carved a path through their enemies with wave upon wave of human flesh. Once the heavy armor broke the enemy formation, there was no more use for the rumbling cannons and roaring parhelion bows. The ground became the site of a desperate life-or-death struggle. Caught in a temporary bind down below, the Western army had no choice but to throw more force behind its attacks up above.

Countless windslashers, now ownerless, were loaded onto parhelion bows. At Prince Yanbei's command, these legendary weapons were launched over the walls like the most disposable of iron arrows.

Their blades spun like dandelions blooming in midair, rending the wind itself with their passage, carrying the names of the fallen as they pelted toward the incoming waves of Western hawks.

Chang Geng hastily swiped his fingers across his dust-covered field scope and reaffixed it to the high bridge of his nose. "Load the second batch of windslashers."

A young soldier had taken up the role of his impromptu personal guard. When Chang Geng spoke, he raised his voice that had yet to crack and relayed the order: "Load the windslashers!" He turned to Chang Geng and quietly asked, "Your Highness, what happens when the windslashers are gone too? Do we throw rocks from the wall?"

Chang Geng cast him a glance, and the ghost of a smile seemed to appear on his face. "Our ammunition and supplies may be depleted, but thanks to the foresight of our emperor, there is still some violet gold in the city. If it really comes down to it, we'll emulate General Han Qi; we'll pour violet gold down the city walls and set the capital ablaze. The Westerners won't find a solitary coin to loot."

The young soldier shuddered at Chang Geng's indifferent tone.

"How old are you?" asked Chang Geng.

The young soldier started in surprise. He said shyly, "Ei-eighteen."

Chang Geng smiled. "Don't try that with me."

The young soldier rubbed his head. "Fifteen." It wasn't unheard of for poor families with too many children to send half-grown kids into the army to live off military provisions. Afraid the army wouldn't take them if they were too young, these stripling boys would commonly fudge their ages.

"Fifteen," Chang Geng said softly. "When I was fifteen, I followed Marshal Gu to investigate Prince Wei's insurrection in Jiangnan, but I understood nothing at all. You're doing better than I was."

Far off in the distance, the remaining Western hawks rose into the air at the pope's command. They were gearing up for a desperate final salvo.

The Western hawks hefted their ordnance into the air and barraged the city with fire. The long cannons they carried, which ought properly to have been mounted on the iron arms of war chariots, had a horribly strong recoil. Once the artillery fire exploded from one end, the person holding the cannon barrel would inevitably be flung backward to crash to their death. This swarm of Western hawks rained cannon fire both inside and outside the city ramparts in a suicide mission. Within minutes, half the wall had collapsed under their onslaught.

Buffeted by a wave of hot air, the red-headed kite teetered on the verge of capsizing. Screaming for his mother, Imperial Uncle Wang latched onto the mast, but was shoved aside by Zhang Fenghan, who was huffing and puffing after having climbed up to the ship.

"Your Majesty!" Zhang Fenghan had removed his formal court robes. He held a fish maw sack, heavy with blackish-purple violet gold. The swaying of the deck nearly sent him sprawling, and a nearby imperial guard hurried to take the dangerous object from him in a dreadful fright.

"Your Majesty," Zhang Fenghan continued, "we have run out of ammunition. This old subject has delivered the remaining violet gold stores in the city to the gate at Prince Yanbei's request. My subordinates have divided it into..."

"Your Majesty, watch out!"

"Protect the emperor!"

A cannon blast interrupted Master Fenghan's accounting. The shot brushed the side of Li Feng's red-headed kite and blasted off a corner of the ship, which began to list to the side with a creaking

groan. A second shot followed close on the heels of the first, striking the red-headed kite dead center. The already damaged ship
spun out of control. Amid the shouting and screaming all around,
Li Feng's pupils contracted into needle points, the light of cannon
fire reflected in his eyes.

With a roar, Tan Hongfei spread his wings and launched himself
toward the attacker, black iron feathers blotting out the sky. The
instant he made contact with the cannon, he pushed the hawk armor to its top speed. The extreme heat and the force of collision
sparked an explosion that blew that former member of the Black
Iron Battalion, a man who had stewed in his resentment for twenty
years, sky-high. He and the cannon became a firework blasting off
on a one-way journey.

But fortunately, Tan Hongfei had not failed in his mission.

Atop the city walls, the windslashers that had reaped the lives
of innumerable Far Westerners finally ran dry. Chang Geng turned
to behold the capital city. This place wasn't especially dear to him,
though it was a pity—he couldn't see the Marquis Estate from
here. He once again raised his bow, dipped the tip of his iron
arrow in kerosene, and launched a shot toward the enemy forces.
As the kerosene whipped through the air at top speed, a flame lit at
the arrow's tip, streaking through the sky like a shooting star—this
was a signal.

Master Fenghan rolled up his sleeves. "Ready the red-headed
kites!"

Aside from the one on which Li Feng still stood, the last dozen
red-headed kites in the capital floated into the air like a troupe of
dancers in festive brocade, twirling with delicate steps toward their
marks high above flashing blades and roaring flame. They were laden

with violet gold, and they collided with the Western hawk suicide fighters midair.

The heavens themselves changed hue.

Standing on the city wall, Chang Geng took the full brunt of the explosion. The bit of light armor he had equipped for makeshift protection was no use against this crushing shock wave. The enormous force of the blast crashed against his chest; he spat blood, and his vision flickered. For a brief moment, the world went black. The youth who had relayed his orders launched himself toward Chang Geng with a cry, attempting to shield the prince with his own body.

The city wall finally collapsed entirely.

Chang Geng didn't know how much time had passed when he woke again. It was some minutes before he gradually regained sensation and found that his leg had been caught between two wrecked gears. All that remained of the young soldier who had protected him was a pair of arms, torn off above the shoulders—the boy himself was nowhere to be seen. The ardent young man had turned into a courageous and loyal pair of short capes dangling from Chang Geng's shoulders.

Chang Geng gritted his teeth. The pain lancing through his body was bearable; at least, it was nowhere near as bad as a wu'ergu attack. He must have been bleeding from his ears because he couldn't clearly hear a single sound, near or far. All was a chaotic, blurry mess.

Out of nowhere, Chang Geng had the thought: *Is this what it's like for Zixi when he doesn't take his medicine? It's...rather peaceful.*

The city wall had collapsed. Had the capital been subjugated?

Did Li Feng still live?

Oh right, and Gu Yun...

Chang Geng's courage faltered when he attempted to think past Gu Yun's name, fearing those two syllables would siphon away all his mettle. He cleanly severed that line of thought and curled his body inward, groping for the seam of his greaves to pry open the series of eight clasps and extricate himself.

He had one last iron arrow in the quiver strapped to his back, and his bow was miraculously uncrushed. If he could kill one more enemy; so long as he still had one last breath in his lungs...

Just as Chang Geng extricated his leg but before he could stand, a dark silhouette swept across his field of vision. Chang Geng had no time to dodge and instinctively leaned his head back, lashing out with his iron bow on pure reflex.

A tiny wooden bird clattered to the ground in front of him. The iron bow had cleaved it in two in midair, leaving the wad of billow paper it carried in its belly to tumble out.

Chang Geng stared blankly for a long moment. The Prince Yanbei who had maintained a frightening degree of calm all this time began to tremble all over. The airy sheet of billow paper spread across the ground, and he failed twice to pick it up; he was shaking so hard his fingers could scarcely close around it. Only then did Chang Geng notice he had lost his vambraces and dislocated two fingers, leaving them deaf to his commands.

Through the cotton in his ears, he heard someone cry out, "Reinforcements have arrived!" This was the piece of good news everyone had been waiting for. But before Chang Geng could summon a mote of joy, his shock was replaced by an unspeakable terror. It was solely by focusing all his resolve on fighting to the last that he had temporarily put aside the real possibility that Gu Yun might have already perished within a pool of molten iron.

Their intended journey down the Yellow Springs road had seen a sudden change of plan, and it looked as if he would be forcibly detained on this side of the crossing. Chang Geng didn't know what to think.

"Dage!" He heard the muffled sounds of someone calling to him. A light-pelt cavalryman dashed over to his location—the newcomer was Ge Chen, with whom he had last parted a number of months ago.

Ge Chen leapt off his horse and lifted the battered Chang Geng from the ground. He began to explain in a great rush, "Dage, wh-wh-when I got your letter, I was with General Shen, but the southern border..."

Chang Geng didn't register a word of it. He cut him off, speaking as if possessed: "Where is Zixi?"

His voice was slurred, and at first, Ge Chen didn't understand him. "What?"

Chang Geng waved his proffered arm away and struggled to his feet, ignoring all else as he dragged himself from the city's ruined walls. His back had been wounded at some point, and a large patch of blood seeped through the fabric of his clothes, yet the man himself noticed not at all.

Ge Chen was dumbstruck. "D-Dage? Your Highness!"

Chang Geng ignored him. Ge Chen watched as a stray arrow flew straight for Chang Geng, yet Chang Geng made no move to dodge. Ge Chen darted forward to pull him aside in a great panic. Within the space of a few steps, Chang Geng's eyes had become so red they looked as if they might drip blood. Ge Chen sucked in a cold breath. *Shit. Nothing's happened to the marquis, right?*

Ge Chen had never struggled with indecision. Without further ado, he flattened his hand into a blade and struck Chang Geng in the back of his neck, knocking him out cold.

That day was the bloodiest battle the imperial capital had seen in all its many years of peaceful history. The Son of Heaven personally served as the banner of command, generals perished in the flames of war, and their forces were committed to fight to the bitter end. Moments before the city wall collapsed, reinforcements arrived at last. These troops were a motley crew in both their makeup and history. At their head was Shen Yi, the commander in chief of the Southwest Army, and old General Zhong had emerged from his long seclusion to bolster Shen Yi's authority. Among them were even a small number of Jiangnan Navy sailors—remnants collected by Yao Zhen after the navy's defeat in the East Sea.

Seeing that they had lost the momentum, the Western army was forced to retreat.

Nearly half of the appointed officials of the court had perished beneath the crumbling city wall. Li Feng's red-headed kite had lost steering completely, and Shen Yi had no hawks. Sweating with nerves, he had no choice but to use parhelion bows to shoot iron cables at the railings, then deploy several dozen heavy armor infantrymen to haul them in. It was the middle of the night before they managed to rescue the Longan Emperor from where he had been stranded in midair.

Nearly all of the Northern Camp had perished alongside their commander.

Gu Yun had been excavated from beneath a Western war chariot. Several of his ribs were cracked, and he was rattling out his last breaths, bleeding at the lightest touch and in such a state that no one dared to move him. Finally, old General Zhong personally arrived on the scene. After declaring, "He won't die that easily; I'll take responsibility if he does," he assigned a few medics to secure Gu Yun onto a wooden frame and convey him back to the city.

The medics combed the entire imperial palace for a few pieces of thousand-year-old ginseng and kept Gu Yun's life hanging by a thread for three days. He was nearly reunited with the old marquis several times, but in the end, he hung on until Chen Qingxu was able to rush back from beyond the pass, over endless mountains and rivers. Chen Qingxu ran several horses to death along the way, and, upon reaching the capital, spent a sleepless night at Gu Yun's side before finally snatching the Marquis of Anding from the jaws of death.

It was dusk when Gu Yun awoke. He could vaguely perceive a haze of light filtering through the window but hadn't yet gathered the strength to open his eyes when he felt the stab of agonizing pain.

I'm not dead. Gu Yun didn't feel like celebrating. What hit him first was apprehension—*Has the city fallen? Where am I?*

He thrashed once in his half-conscious state before someone took hold of his hand. That person leaned down to speak quietly into his ear. They seemed to sense his worries and said, "Reinforcements have arrived, everything's fine...the capital stands." Enveloped in the familiar scent of pacifying fragrance, Gu Yun's consciousness fluttered for a mere moment before he sank back under.

After a number of days drifting in and out of such a semi-conscious daze, Gu Yun finally struggled to full awareness. The effects of his medicine had long faded, and he once again woke as a deaf-blind man without the faculties to appreciate what was right beneath his nose.

Gu Yun blinked his eyes with some difficulty. A blurry figure hovered at the side of his bed, which he determined was Chang Geng by scent. His head was a mess, and a stream of questions poured in all at once: *How many soldiers are left in the Northern Camp? Where did the reinforcements come from? Whose troops are they? How far has the Western army retreated? How is His Majesty?*

Chang Geng carefully helped him take a sip of water. Gu Yun reached up for his hand on instinct and accidentally strained one of his many wounds. His vision flashed dark with the pain.

"It's all right," Chang Geng said into his ear, "General Shen is back, and Shifu is here to oversee everything. Quit worrying and get some rest."

Gu Yun sucked in a breath, feeling as if every one of his organs was aching.

In days past, whenever he was idle, the Marquis of Anding would bemoan to Shen Yi that no one in three generations of the Gu family had been afforded longevity. He felt that such a beset upon, sickly person as himself would also have a beauty's fragile tether to the mortal plane. He had never expected that not only was this crappy tether of his not fragile, it was in fact rather sturdy. All this, and he still hadn't kicked the bucket.

Gu Yun opened his mouth and tried to call Chang Geng's name, but after suffering such heavy injuries and spending so many days unconscious, he was unable to make a sound. Suddenly, there was a touch on his face. Gu Yun felt a hand lift his chin and calloused fingers sweep lightly across his lips, a gesture indescribably intimate and tender.

If Gu Yun could have seen Chang Geng sitting at his bedside at this moment, he would have found that Chang Geng had only draped a robe loosely around himself. His hair was down, and his shoulders, neck, arms, and even head were covered with needles, the very image of an elegant and graceful hedgehog. He sat beside the bed, stiff as a board, and struggled to so much as turn his head. Every expression of joy, rage, or sorrow had been sealed off his face by acupuncture needles, and he could neither cry nor laugh. He could only maintain a blank expression, like a handsome wooden puppet.

Even so, red still lingered in his eyes.

Over the past few days, while Gu Yun had floated between life and death, Chang Geng had suffered several wu'ergu attacks. Chen Qingxu had been forced to use acupuncture to suppress the poison, stabbing into him like a straw man. The straw man lowered his voice, and at a volume inaudible to the half-deaf man before him, murmured, "If something like this happens again, Zixi, I really will go mad."

Gu Yun was silent. Although he couldn't hear Chang Geng's words, that touch against his lips had reminded him of the disaster that had occurred at the city walls. Gu Yun desperately wanted to wail in misery—who would have thought he'd still be alive to deal with this!

Struck by his predicament, Marshal Gu froze into a majestic and imposing human pillar from the neck down.

66

TIMES OF CHAOS

SUBMITTING TO A MOMENTARY impulse was easy, but dealing with the aftermath was an entirely different matter.

If not for the great calamity that had befallen the capital, Chang Geng would never have done something so outrageous. Before this war, he had never clung to any unrealistic hopes about Gu Yun, or he wouldn't have gone off and hid for almost five years. Gu Yun was his lifelong source of solace, but under normal circumstances, their relationship never would have developed into anything more for the rest of his life. Chang Geng had confessed and laid his heart bare, and Gu Yun had resorted to the most gentle and tactful methods he had used in all his life to make clear his stance. Chang Geng had his self-respect; he never would have made another sincere attempt to persuade him.

What he did for Gu Yun and what sort of path he chose to walk were his own business. Prince Yanbei had a belly full of schemes, but he was unwilling to deploy any of them against Gu Yun. Any results achieved by such methods would be worthless.

With time, perhaps the two of them could have buried these ill-fated affections, this awkward secret, and allowed it to persist in that manner indefinitely, until with gradual practice Chang Geng trained himself to casually joke about his past feelings. Perhaps, as time went on, someone as thoughtless as Gu Yun might've even forgotten the whole affair.

Chang Geng was accustomed to restraint. As long as he hadn't lost his mind completely, he would restrain himself to the bitter end.

Holding desire within one's heart, especially desire of such an unrealistic kind, was an extremely painful thing. Whether it was desire for wealth, for power, or for something else—all were fetters around one's body. The deeper one sank, the tighter these bonds would dig into one's flesh. Chang Geng grasped the principle behind this all too well, and thus had never dared allow his desires to run wild.

Unfortunately, no matter how thoroughly his rational mind understood, it was no use. And either way, it was too late. A brief slip beneath the city wall had propelled him to take this step, and Gu Yun's lack of response counted as a response in itself... Setting aside the question of whether Chang Geng could let go as easily now as he had when he'd no reason to hope, could *Gu Yun* pretend none of it had ever happened?

As for Marshal Gu, who was currently racked by injury and illness, his head was about to burst from this headache.

He felt that, this time, the larger portion of the responsibility was his—he was compelled to guiltily admit that, under normal circumstances, Chang Geng never would have been able to lay a hand on him without his tacit permission. And even if an "accident" had occurred and he was caught off-guard, he shouldn't have been so lenient after the fact.

Even Gu Yun couldn't explain what he'd been thinking at the time. Perhaps he hadn't been thinking anything at all. Whenever he closed his eyes, he could practically see the look in Chang Geng's eyes, gazing deeply at him as the enemy army approached the city, cannon fire echoing in their ears—it was as if, in all the world, that pair of eyes contained only him.

No one could remain unmoved under that kind of gaze.

Gu Yun had one nose and two eyes like anyone else; there was nothing particularly special about him. He also possessed emotions and desires; he felt joy, rage, and sorrow. There was no way he could return to purely viewing Chang Geng as a junior he was close with as he did before. But after raising him as a son for so many years, it was difficult for him to accept so suddenly such a shift in the nature of their relationship.

Chang Geng slowly leaned down and covered Gu Yun's rather useless eyes with one hand, preventing Gu Yun from gazing upon his honorable visage. Not a single part of Gu Yun's body was under his control. He couldn't hear, couldn't see, and didn't yet have the strength to speak. For the first time in his life, he was helpless as another took advantage of him. Utterly shocked, he thought to himself, *He would even bully an invalid? Is there no justice in this world?!*

He felt a faint brush of breath across his face, and another person's aura drew so close as to be impossible to ignore.

Gu Yun was speechless. *Fucking hell, this brat really would!*

His throat bobbed inadvertently, but Chang Geng didn't do anything egregious. He paused there for a moment, then lightly brushed the corner of Gu Yun's lips with his own. Gu Yun's eyes were covered, so he couldn't help but draw out all sorts of vivid and delusional implications from that subtle touch. He imagined Chang Geng as a pitiful little creature throwing itself into his arms to seek comfort after surviving a terrible calamity, giving him a lick with its damp pink tongue.

His heart melted. Gu Yun hadn't gotten around to asking about casualty numbers, but he already had a rough estimate in mind. Even this brief consideration spurred a wave of sorrow—yet Chang Geng was here, in one piece, sitting at his bedside. To Gu Yun, it felt like he'd reunited with someone he thought he had lost forever.

Suddenly he didn't want to fuss over trifles. He wanted to embrace Chang Geng, but alas, he hadn't the strength to lift his arms.

Tender affections and unspeakable frustrations mixed together in a tangled snarl. He couldn't bear to blame Chang Geng, so he could only blame himself. He wished to return to that moment when the enemy bore down on the city walls and slap his past self across the face—*Look what you've done!*

Chang Geng sighed. Gu Yun's lashes fluttered across his palm. Right then, Chang Geng felt as if only sobbing and wailing with this man in his arms could vent even an ounce of the constant, gnawing fear inside him. But he was powerless to make good on those desires—Miss Chen had sealed all his violent emotions and rendered his face entirely paralyzed with her needles, such that he would have to strain with all his might to form even the faintest smile. All Chang Geng could do was cut a tiny hole for his worries and let them flow out in a gentle trickle.

Gu Yun's injuries were severe, and his constitution had taken a major hit. His body was weak, so struggle as he might to stay awake, he drifted off before long into a fitful slumber. Chang Geng quietly pulled the blanket over Gu Yun and, reluctant to leave, lingered to stare at him a while longer, until his joints popped sharply in objection to their mistreatment. Only then did he slowly rise, clutching the bedpost for support, and walk away on steps as stiff as a reanimated corpse.

Upon opening the door, Chang Geng was met with the sight of Chen Qingxu, who had been waiting there for who knows how long, pacing back and forth before Gu Yun's room. A whole patch of green grass had been trampled flat beneath her feet.

Chang Geng pretended not to notice the casualties strewn all over the ground and made a polite greeting, seeming all the more dignified and earnest for the stiffness of his expression. "I have troubled Miss Chen. Had you not made this treacherous journey, I truly don't know what I would have done."

Chen Qingxu waved his courtesies off, distracted. "I'm just doing my job. Um, Your Highness, wait a moment for me, I'll perform acupuncture on you in a bit...and, uh, one other thing..."

The tongue of this Chen clan member who was accustomed to seeing every kind of spectacle tied itself into a knot, and a hint of hesitation appeared on that face customarily as dignified as that of a clay statue.

Chang Geng's wu'ergu attacks could not be revealed to outsiders, so the two had pretended he was still recovering from severe injuries to give Chen Qingxu an excuse to come suppress the poison in his body. This was a task Chen Qingxu wouldn't entrust to a single other soul, so she had personally stayed by his side and listened to every word he muttered in his sleep. Unfortunately for her, she had puzzled together the pieces of a terrifying truth, one which left her unable to sleep at night and nearly left wrinkles on her face.

Chang Geng wanted to nod, but he was unable to bend his neck. Thus, he could only bow at the waist, seeming ever so polite. "There's no need. I can reach all the locations myself. I must also visit the palace shortly, so I won't trouble you."

Though they had lost a section of the city wall, they had temporarily broken the siege. However, the cleanup work was yet another headache. Aside from those like Marshal Gu who truly couldn't rise from their beds, no one dared relax just yet. The city was holding its breath for the next disaster. Chen Qingxu nodded at his response, worries heavy on her mind, and swallowed back the question that had been on the tip of her tongue.

"But," Chang Geng suddenly spoke again. "If you were going to ask..." He paused, then cast a sideways glance at Gu Yun's tightly shut door. Chen Qingxu's breath caught in her throat. With his immobile coffin-board face, he admitted calmly, "It's true. I do indeed harbor improper intentions toward my yifu."

Chen Qingxu was speechless. These words... To hear them spoken in such a calm and confident tone was quite the discomfiting experience.

"He knows too," Chang Geng said. "If Miss Chen would—"

"I won't say anything!" Chen Qingxu responded on pure instinct.

Chang Geng cupped his hands toward her in thanks. The outer robe he had draped over his body floated airily in the wind as he stepped elegantly past Chen Qingxu like a graceful immortal striding through the sky... It was quite impossible to tell that he was essentially a hedgehog underneath.

If Gu Yun had cause to feel gratitude toward Li Feng one time in his life, it would have been the next day, when he heard that Li Feng had requested Chang Geng remain within the palace.

This was a great relief. Gu Yun was sorely tempted to submit a memorial to the emperor and request he clear out a room for the fourth prince next to the western Warm Pavilion so he could move in and never come out again.

Injuries on the battlefield were common, and Gu Yun had long grown used to convalescence. If he was awake, that meant the worst had passed. After recuperating in bed for another day, he regained the energy to speak and take visitors.

His first caller was Shen Yi.

Because Chen Qingxu had refused to let Gu Yun take his medicine, he had no choice but to wear his glass monocle in his deaf-blind state and communicate with the man via screaming and gestures.

After being separated for over half a year, both men had undergone a complete transformation. When they had parted off to different ends of the earth, both were in their prime and full of vigor; but upon their reunion, one was a bandaged mummy confined to his bed and on the verge of breathing his last, while the other had run himself ragged for months until he looked like an old and withered radish.

The old radish Shen Yi bellowed his laments to Gu Yun. "We thought we'd only arrive in time to collect your corpse; we never thought we'd see the Marquis of Anding alive and breathing again. Sir, having survived this catastrophe, you must have a reward of good fortune on the way!"

Gu Yun, face covered in spittle from Shen Yi's howling, immediately began to fret again at these words. Where his reward was, he had no idea, but he sure had a basketful of regrets. He flew into a rage. "You have some nerve saying that to me! Those hairy foreigners made landfall at Dagu Harbor over a month ago and lit up the Sunlight Palace like a goddamn stove! Where the hell were you, you useless clod? Are you planning to be late to your own funeral?"

Shen Yi didn't dignify this with a response.

"Get up, get away from me; is there a leak in your mouth?! You got spit all over my face!"

"I didn't want to bring this up because I was afraid it would upset you." Shen Yi sighed and rolled up his sleeves, plopping down next to Gu Yun without a trace of manners. "But I never laid eyes on the envoy sent by the Ministry of War to notify us that the Marching Orders Decree had been repealed. The envoy was intercepted shortly after they left the city. Those scattered-sheep-droppings nations in the south took advantage of the chaos. Who knows how they discovered those secret passages left behind by the bandits, but they well-nigh descended from the skies overnight. I was caught flat-footed, and they managed to blow up the Southwest Supply Depot."

There was no way a commander like Shen Yi, who had just dropped from the skies himself, could mobilize the Southern Border Army without a marching orders decree.

"We were running ourselves ragged putting out fires left and right. Xiao-Ge happened to be looking for me with a message from the little prince—I knew it was going to be a catastrophe the moment I saw that message, but I couldn't be in two places at once." Shen Yi shook his head. "Later, a wooden bird arrived with a Black Iron Tiger Tally and a war beacon decree bearing your personal signature. I hadn't realized the situation in the capital was so dire; I managed to muster half our forces and violet gold stores and personally brought reinforcements."

There was no need to go into detail about the rest. Gu Yun could already tell from this brief explanation that the problem was the violet gold.

With tigers and wolves attacking from the northwest, neither the Black Iron Battalion nor the Northern Border Defense Corps dared move a centimeter. If they did, putting aside the question of whether they could still defend the borders, they could very well end up chased down and surrounded themselves. At that point, the capital would be besieged by the Western navy from the south and the iron-armored wolves from the north. At the same time, Shen Yi had yet to resolve the unrest in the southwest. The most troubling piece was the destruction of the Southwest Supply Depot—the violet gold stores of the Southern Border Garrison were limited in the first place, and what remained wouldn't have been enough to support a long-distance strike.

"We had to veer north first to sponge off Cai Bin's army." Shen Yi sighed. "But we encountered untold obstacles along the way. Do you know who was so successful in holding up the Central Plains Army?"

Gu Yun's face went dark.

"It was a rebel army made up of refugees," Shen Yi said. "The majority of Old Cai's forces had marched out to support the Black Iron Battalion and the Northern Border Defense Corps. The handful that remained in the Central Plains were running themselves ragged dealing with that bunch. They were all our own down-and-out citizens, so it would look ill to deal with them too harshly, but they couldn't just not fight. Old Cai's hair has gone gray from the stress."

Gu Yun leaned back against the headboard. "How did everything become such a mess?"

"The idle vagrants in the area between the Central Plains and Central Shu have been a problem for years, but they were never able to gather much momentum," Shen Yi said. "Someone took advantage of the chaos to goad those men into organizing themselves into discrete armed forces. They saw the nation on the verge of tipping into chaos—saw that even the Black Iron Battalion could lose half its number overnight—and their courage was bolstered. Zixi, lately, I've felt it's not good for the Black Iron Battalion to stand out so much. We don't want to make the emperor nervous, and the people also tell too many tall tales. Certainly our reputation has deterred some interests harboring evil intentions over the past few years, but at the same time, it's too easy for the hearts of the army and the people to falter at the slightest show of weakness from the Black Iron Battalion, even if it's just a false alarm."

The two looked at each other for a moment until Gu Yun broke the silence. "Enough about all that. What's the current situation? How many of our brothers from the Northern Camp live?"

Shen Yi's face turned grim, and he didn't respond right away.

Gu Yun's heart chilled. "Where's Old Tan?"

Shen Yi produced a windslasher from beneath his light armor, which he silently placed beside Gu Yun's pillow. Gu Yun froze, accidentally tugging on one of his injuries. He gritted his teeth without a sound, quietly curling in on himself in pain.

Shen Yi hurried to catch him. "Don't, Zixi... Zixi!"

Gu Yun waved away his hand. Voice hoarse, he asked, "How far have the Westerners retreated?"

Shen Yi cautiously studied his expression. "After the Westerners routed the Jiangnan Navy, they split their forces in two. One portion, under their pope's personal command, made landfall at Dagu Harbor and advanced straight toward the capital city. The other was mostly composed of hired Dongying suicide fighters. They drove heavy-armored war chariots north along the canal, up through Shandong and Zhili prefectures. The local garrisons had never seen such intense combat, and they scattered near instantly. We traded blows with them once on our march here, and I'll tell you, they were no easy opponent. Later, old General Zhong Chan showed up in Jiangnan and helped Yao Chongze reorganize the fragmented remains of the Jiangnan Army and Navy to march north and lend us a hand. The Westerners were forced to retreat to Shandong. Now, the two halves of the Western army have rejoined and pulled back to the East Sea, using the islands of Dongying as their base of operations. I'm afraid this is far from over."

Gu Yun hummed in acknowledgment, a deep frown furrowing his brow.

After spending so long yelling his report, Shen Yi's mouth was dry. He poured himself a cup of herbal tea and drained it, then sighed, "Don't overthink. Your priority should be recovering from your injuries. We can't lose you now."

Gu Yun lowered his lashes and didn't say anything.

Shen Yi changed the topic in an effort to lighten the mood. "That little highness of yours is practically a whole new person. He kept a low profile before, but at such a time of crisis, he stepped up to take responsibility. I barely recognized him... Did you know His Majesty removed the 'bei' from his title?"

From Prince Yanbei to Prince Yan—although it was a difference of a syllable, it symbolized a promotion from a commandery prince to a prince of the first rank.

Gu Yun shook off his distraction and muttered wearily, "How is it a good thing to be promoted at a time like this..."

Shen Yi continued to prod at Gu Yun's sore spots in a misguided attempt to cheer him up. "I saw him leaving the palace with Chongze on my way here; I imagine he'll be arriving soon."

Gu Yun went mute.

"What is it this time?" Shen Yi asked, mystified by the dark expression on his face.

After spending so much time cooped up in bed, Gu Yun ached all over. He wanted to change positions but had a hard time shifting himself. That old maid Shen was quite oblivious; despite seeing Gu Yun struggling at the head of the bed, he made no move to help, but continued to blather on: "While you were busy playing weiqi with the king of hell, the little prince has been forgoing sleep and rest to remain at your side day and night, heedless of his own injuries. He's covered in acupuncture needles and can't even bend his neck; I feel awful just looking at him. He really is more devoted than a blood-related..."

"Blood-related, my ass!" Unable to bear it any longer, Gu Yun exploded. "Where are you coming up with this stuff?! Get out!"

Shen Yi was not intimidated in the least. He impudently pressed closer to Gu Yun's face and asked, "What, have you done something stupid and offended him again? I'm telling you, Zixi, His Highness isn't that little kid anymore whom you could tease however you pleased. Don't push..."

Gu Yun groaned. "Jiping-xiong, on account of my great service in nearly martyring myself for the nation, I'm begging you, *get out*."

Shen Yi, keen for once in his life, read the words *I have some unspeakable secret* plain as day on his face.

General Shen had suffered Gu Yun's bullying for years. He could defeat him in neither physical nor verbal combat and had held his grudges all this time. Having finally grasped an opportunity to poke fun at him, there was no way he'd be willing to let it go so easily. Shen Yi was practically bursting from curiosity. "Oh, come on, the entire court is living under a cloud of misery, let's hear about your bad luck to lighten the mood..."

Gu Yun shut his mouth. The room went silent, and the two who had originally been conversing by screaming into each other's ears switched to rapid sign language.

After enough time to burn a stick of incense, Shen Yi floated out of Gu Yun's room, a thunderstruck expression on his face and all four limbs swinging out of sync as he attempted to walk. Speak of the devil—it was at this very moment that Prince Yan returned, striding in Shen Yi's direction.

"General Shen is here?" Chang Geng greeted him. "How is my yifu doing?"

Shen Yi couldn't summon a single word.

General Shen, commander in chief of the Southwest Army, faced Chang Geng. A complicated series of changes came over his expression. In the end, he failed to make so much as a squeak before he shrank back against the wall and fled, a look of petrifaction on his face.

A LIBATION OF WINE

WHEN CHANG GENG walked through the door, he saw Gu Yun leaning against the headboard, a windslasher mottled with grime laid across his lap and an expression of indescribable desolation on his pale face.

Although he couldn't hear the creak of the door opening, the instant Gu Yun felt the breeze blowing in through the doorway, he wiped the look of melancholy from his mien. "What'd you come back for—"

He had thought Shen Yi had returned. But when he peered through his glass monocle and saw who it was that had arrived, the words caught in his throat. Gu Yun's fingers swept lightly across General Tan's windslasher as he thought to himself, *Oh no.* In his panic, he wondered, *Is it too late for me to pretend to be asleep?*

Honest-to-goodness, this was the first time in his life Marshal Gu had been so terrified he wanted to outright flee from a confrontation—it was indeed a pity that the world had no "goodness" in store for Gu Yun.

Chang Geng walked straight over and picked up one of Gu Yun's paws as if naught were amiss. He laid his fingertips over Gu Yun's inner wrist and quietly read his pulse. This time, with the assistance of his monocle, Gu Yun could see him clearly. Chang Geng had lost a visible amount of weight in the past few days, and his lips were tinged with blue—the blue of someone who couldn't breathe, or who was afflicted with poison. The air he gave off was of someone forcibly summoning every ounce of energy to paper over the empty shell beneath.

Gu Yun felt his awkwardness begin to fade. He frowned. "Where are you hurt? Come here and let me see."

"It's nothing serious. Although Miss Chen claims she hasn't finished her apprenticeship, she is truly a master of her generation." Chang Geng paused, then added, "I'll be all right as long as you're okay."

Chang Geng would never fill his lungs, extend his neck, and howl to be heard like Shen Yi. His fingertips were still on Gu Yun's wrist, so he didn't sign either. Gu Yun heard scarcely a word of his speech, but experienced in full the near solid weight of his gaze.

Gu Yun eyed him. *Kid, what are you saying?*

Chang Geng's fingers slipped from his wrist, and, as if it were the most natural thing in the world, took hold of Gu Yun's hand.

It was common for people to be deficient in blood and qi after severe injury or illness, leaving their hands and feet ice-cold even in the summer months. Chang Geng cupped Gu Yun's hand and rubbed it between his palms, his features earnest in the extreme. Not only did he cover each acupoint on Gu Yun's hand, he also attended to the most sensitive spots between the fingers, occasionally sweeping them with his fingertips in the course of his ministrations. This was a bold-faced reminder directed at Gu Yun—*I'm not honoring my filial obligations to you, I'm doting on you. Don't lie to yourself.*

Gu Yun awkwardly choked out, "Haven't taken enough advantage of your yifu yet?"

Chang Geng looked up at him and smiled. He had a very handsome face, a unique kind of handsomeness that came of his half-foreign blood. His features were sharp, almost harsh, but his aura was so calm that were he to simply don a kasaya, he could impersonate an eminent monk and go about scamming people. This placidity was contradictory, yet neatly suppressed that trace of edge he'd had since birth. When he smiled, he even looked a bit sweet.

Gazing through his glass monocle, Gu Yun was briefly dazzled by the sight.

When a person's attitude toward someone began to change, they began to see the other in a different light as well. Gu Yun had to admit that for a split second, he felt a brief and indescribable flash of attraction.

Gu Yun was no monk; he could feel attraction at any time. He wasn't some philanderer who took his pleasure in the face of all moral convention, but he was self-aware enough to know that this was mostly because he usually wasn't in a position to, not because he had no desire to. Thus, he couldn't be too sanctimonious.

But...this wasn't just anyone. It was his little Chang Geng. Gu Yun couldn't bring himself to take this first step.

As all the bits and pieces of his meager conscience lined up to harangue him, Chang Geng reached over and began to pull Gu Yun's clothes open without the slightest warning. Guilty at heart, Gu Yun instinctively ducked back out of the way and gritted his teeth in pain.

Chang Geng, whose mind had obviously not joined Gu Yun's in the gutter, retrieved some medicinal salve from nearby. He managed to convey a mocking tone even in sign language as he clarified, "Let's change your bandages—I'm not a beast."

Gu Yun was actually more worried that he himself was the beast. When he came back to his senses, he didn't know whether he should laugh or cry. He chuckled at the irony of it, wondering to himself,

How did things end up like this? But laughing tugged at the broken bones in his chest and abdomen. He couldn't laugh, and he couldn't hold it in; there was simply no cure for this complicated emotion.

"Okay, okay, I'll stop teasing you," Chang Geng coaxed. "Don't squirm around."

He was afraid to agitate Gu Yun again, so he assumed his strict physician's composure to complete his examination. He carefully worked open Gu Yun's clothes and reapplied the salve, both men working up a light sweat with the exertion. Chang Geng used a fine silk cloth to wipe Gu Yun's body, his motions as smooth and practiced as if he'd done the same countless times. Recalling Shen Yi's words, Gu Yun summoned a more serious expression and asked quietly, "Why are you doing this sort of work yourself? It's improper."

Chang Geng's eyes darkened. He leaned in close to Gu Yun and said, "There's nothing improper about it. I would do anything if it meant having you here to speak to me right now."

He was too close, as if they were lovers whispering intimately in each other's ears. The skin beneath Gu Yun's ear tingled, but there was nothing he could do about it—if he flinched away, he wouldn't be able to hear.

Gu Yun sighed. "About that day..."

"Don't." Chang Geng interrupted him, his voice a bit muffled, "Don't make me think about it. Zixi, take pity on me."

Gu Yun was still unused to Chang Geng addressing him this way. But even as he opened his mouth to protest, he felt he had no right to ask Chang Geng to call him *Yifu*, either. For a moment, Gu Yun had thought to follow the flow of conversation and broach the topic of what had transpired beneath the city wall. Surrendering to impulse was one thing, but what came next?

Was he just to allow Chang Geng to go down this incorrect path and give up any chance of begetting heirs?

Even if an army rascal like Gu Yun was willing to be so shameless as to ignore their former relationship as father and son, how would the court and the jianghu look upon this Prince Yan who submitted himself to another man? He couldn't do it. Even if Chang Geng weren't an imperial scion but an ordinary commoner, how could Gu Yun allow him—someone with the talent, intelligence, and bravery to turn the tide in their moment of desperation—to suffer such humiliation for his sake?

Alas, Chang Geng shoved the speech Gu Yun had steeled himself to prepare right back into his mouth, and Gu Yun lost yet another opportunity to extract himself before it was too late.

Carefully avoiding Gu Yun's injuries, Chang Geng leaned his head against Gu Yun's shoulder and held him for a time. A long while passed before he managed to suppress the anxiety bubbling in his heart. He felt he ought to find Miss Chen and ask her to administer another round of acupuncture. These past few days, the wu'ergu had been getting harder and harder to suppress. If it kept progressing like this, eventually, he'd do something regrettable.

Chang Geng steadied himself and reluctantly pulled away. "It's not too hot out today, and the sun is pleasant. Would you like to sit outside for a while? It'll be good for your recovery."

A pause. "What?"

Chang Geng repeated himself in sign language.

Gu Yun thought about it, then resolutely replied, "No." He had no objections to enjoying the sun, but he knew he wouldn't be able to walk outside on his own two legs for another day or so—Gu Yun had no desire to find out how Chang Geng planned to get him there.

"Don't you dislike being cooped up inside?"

"I changed my mind," Gu Yun deadpanned.

As if helpless to force him, Chang Geng put away the salve and rose to leave. Yet right when Gu Yun thought he had successfully dismissed him, Chang Geng turned around, picked up a thin blanket, and wrapped it around Gu Yun's body without so much as a by-your-leave. Then, he scooped up his helpless little yifu in both arms and carried him steadily out the door.

Gu Yun was speechless. *Outright rebellion!*

The pair ran smack into Shen Yi, who had fought with himself the whole way out after fleeing in a panic and, still worried, finally resolved to return. Caught off guard by such a scene, Shen Yi sucked in a smoke ring's worth of cold air, tripped over the threshold, and sprawled face-first onto the ground.

Chang Geng started in surprise. "General Shen, did you forget something?" he asked without the faintest blush or tiniest tremor in his voice.

Shen Yi laughed awkwardly, then crawled to his feet and began to dust himself off, conspicuously scuffing away the half-footprint he'd left when he slipped. "It's nothing urgent, I accidentally dirtied the floor...ha ha, uhh...I uhh, I won't disturb you any longer." With that, the traitorous eccentric turned and ran, terrified that Gu Yun would murder him to seal his mouth.

A lounge chair had already been arranged in the courtyard. Chang Geng set the furious Gu Yun down, then tugged General Tan's windslasher out of his hands and placed it on the nearby tea table. He flashed Gu Yun an easy smile. "What? That year I didn't want to go out on New Year's Eve because of all the people, didn't you haul me outside in front of everyone just like this?"

"So," Gu Yun said expressionlessly, "having experienced a reversal of fortune, you're all lining up to get revenge on me today?"

Chang Geng chuckled. When he was done laughing, he produced something from his sleeve and pressed it into Gu Yun's hands. "Here."

The object was cold against Gu Yun's palms. He pushed up the glass monocle perched atop his nose and saw that it was a short flute fashioned from white jade. Every centimeter of it was as lustrous as mutton fat, and it was carved from a single piece of stone. The jade was of exquisite quality, and the whole was shaped like a miniature windslasher. The handle, relief, and even the blade slots at the tip were replicated in fine detail, and the character *Gu* was engraved at the end.

At first glance, Gu Yun almost thought he had carved that character himself. The handwriting was nearly alike enough to pass for the real thing.

"You should get rid of the old bamboo one," Chang Geng said. "The air in the capital is dry; it will crack over time. I told you I'd make you a better one."

Gu Yun ran his fingers lightly over the jade flute and murmured, distracted, "I actually don't have a windslasher engraved with my name."

Chang Geng sat across from him and began to meticulously brew a pot of tea. Steam swirled from the vent in the earthenware vessel as he rinsed three cups: one for Gu Yun, one for himself, and one to place beside Tan Hongfei's windslasher. Gu Yun continued, his voice subdued: "Even Shen Yi has one. I'm the only one who doesn't. When I was young, I always felt that the Black Iron Battalion was a set of shackles the old marquis had forced onto me; that it was to blame for every freedom I lacked in life."

Later, when he'd grown up, he'd felt that these black-iron sticks carved with their owner's names were like so many silent final testaments. But he, Gu Yun, had no father, mother, wife, or child, nor any other mortal ties. In all the vastness of the world, he didn't know who should receive his final testament. Even holding such a thing in his hand would have made him feel unspeakably lonely and chip away at his resolve. For Chang Geng's sake, Gu Yun kept this last part to himself. He went on simply, "Those were my petty resentments from before I grew up and understood the bigger picture. Just forget it, and don't repeat it anywhere else; don't weaken the army's morale—Old Tan was a wild ox who didn't drink tea, do you have any wine?"

"Mm, I've already forgotten," Chang Geng signed. "There's no wine. General Tan gets tea and you get plain water; I hope you two gentlemen can both make do."

Gu Yun fell silent. Chang Geng was getting increasingly impertinent with him!

"Over the last few days, I've been tallying up our remaining resources with the Ministry of Revenue." Chang Geng poured two cups of tea and one cup of water, then continued to sign. "Captain Han sent all the stores in the western outskirts up in flames. Our expenditures from defending the city are also astonishing, and our supply chain from the north has been cut off. If we continue to fight like this, we may rapidly find ourselves unable to afford the expense. Li Feng wanted me to ask you if you have any ideas."

How marvelous. After fighting a single battle, such a grand court was out of both money and fuel.

"Don't look at me for ideas. All we can do is call for a ceasefire." Gu Yun rotated his cup in his hands. "The Westerners actually took more losses than we did. Not only did they supply an army and navy to besiege the capital, they also provided engines and armor to the eighteen tribes on our northern border and various nations in the Western Regions. Returning empty-handed won't bring them any honor; they may not be able to hold out much longer than us."

"The Western army just retreated offshore; they won't stop at this," Chang Geng said. "How will the Western pope explain himself to those behind him if he goes to such expense for nothing? They'll have to make a last stand. They have retreated to the Dongying archipelago to regroup. If they dispatch troops to take Jiangnan and confront our nation's forces from the south, we will end up in a disadvantageous position."

Great Liang was too large, and the court too desperately poor. It was indeed easy to attend to one thing and lose sight of another.

"Mm...if it comes down to it, we can send people to the Western Regions. Our Loulan allies haven't turned against us yet. As long as we're not fully at odds, we can try to smuggle some supplies through there," Gu Yun said. He casually raised his small teacup, holding it with three fingers, and clinked it against General Tan's in a toast. "Brother, Prince Yan isn't providing wine and wants us to make do. I'm not the boss of him, so you'll have to settle for this."

Chang Geng silently raised his tea toward the masterless wind-slasher in a toast, drained his cup, then emptied Tan Hongfei's cup across the ground.

A libation for peaceful rest, with tea in place of wine.

Chang Geng's words were a tragic prophecy: ten days later, the Western army gave up their attack on the capital and reorganized themselves to make landfall in Jiangnan. Cutting down their opposition as easily as stalks of bamboo, they charged into Lin'an city after two days and one night. This fertile land of fish and rice that had enjoyed generations of wealth fell to foreign hands. The noble families residing there were shocked; some had long gathered their belongings and fled, while others mounted a futile resistance. When that failed, the captured committed suicide in defense of their honor.

Li Feng reinstated old General Zhong Chan, who once again donned his armor and rode out to battle, rushing to the front lines with Yao Zhen and an army of hastily pieced together troops. Gu Yun struggled out of bed for a brief meeting with his old teacher whom he hadn't seen in many years. But there was no time for a long reminiscence about the old days. After downing a cup of unfiltered wine to send off the army on their southern expedition, he watched as the old general, his hair peppered with white, mounted his horse and set off.

The next day, the Marquis of Anding and Shen Yi rode for the northwest.

Prince Yan, Li Min, revamped the capital's defenses and took up the reins of the Six Ministries. Thus he began his career as a pillar of the court: shuffling scarce resources to meet endless demands, proverbially demolishing the east wall to repair the west.

ARC 9

WESTERN CAMPAIGN

68

POISONED

G U YUN sat upright on the back of his horse. "He's still there?"
Shen Yi lifted the field scope and turned to look back.
"Yes."

Gu Yun left the capital on a rare clear day, the sun shining brightly overhead. The Longan Emperor had led a contingent of court officials beyond the city gate to escort the solemn cavalcade of soldiers disappearing into the distance. This group had dispersed, leaving only His Highness Prince Yan. Standing alone on one of the few remaining watchtowers over the collapsed city gate, Prince Yan gazed after the Black Iron general without moving, as if he meant to remain there until the end of time.

Gu Yun didn't glance back. "We've ridden so far already—there's no way you can see him clearly, even with the field scope. Don't be ridiculous."

"If you think I'm blind then look for yourself," Shen Yi snapped. "Ordering me about again and again. At this rate, people are going to think there's something inappropriate going on between me and the prince."

Gu Yun had a mouthful of excuses ready and waiting. "Why don't you try nailing a bunch of steel panels all over your body and see if you can turn your head. Why are you so full of crap?"

Shen Yi sneered but didn't bother to expose him.

"Would I look at him?" Gu Yun paused, then made himself seem all the more suspicious by responding to his own question. "Hardly. Don't assume the meager heart of an old maid like you can take the measure of a great general like me, with a heart large enough to contain a fleet of a hundred dragons."

It was said that it took a hundred days to recover from an injury to ligaments or bones. Gu Yun had been dug out from a pile of corpses and dragged back to the land of the living less than half a month ago. Forget a flesh and blood person; under ordinary circumstances, even a suit of steel armor would be difficult to repair after sustaining that degree of damage. When Gu Yun had submitted his request to return to the northwest, Prince Yan had grown so upset he nearly started a row with him before the entire imperial court. Even the lousy emperor Li Feng, who believed in forcing an ox to work but didn't see the need to feed it, felt a tug on his conscience.

But the situation being what it was, it was of critical importance that someone step up to rally the Black Iron Battalion.

After failing to lay siege to the capital, the exhausted Westerners had solidified their occupation of all territories south of the Yangtze River. There was no way they had attention to spare for their poverty-stricken allies in the north and west. The allied armies of the Western Regions were a hideous tangle, and together with the eighteen northern barbarian tribes, these forces couldn't be considered a monolithic iron wall. If they could turn the tide on the northwestern front and thereby resolve their most pressing issue—the lack of violet gold—it would be only a matter of time before they beat the foreigners back to their homeland.

An army of thousands is easy to raise, but one good general is hard to find. Gu Yun had no choice but to go himself.

In the end, it was Chen Qingxu who came forward with a solution. In an absurd stroke of genius, she delivered a rush order to the Lingshu Institute, prevailing upon them to construct a suit of specially made steel panels that fit flush against Gu Yun's body and held his yet-unhealed bones in place. Thus, an artificial body, powerful as steel, was created for his use. Though wearing it wasn't a particularly comfortable experience, at the very least it allowed Gu Yun to create the impression that he could come and go like the wind, just as always.

Shen Yi sighed. "Honestly, sir, it's high time you took this seriously. What are you going to do about this?"

Gu Yun very pointedly busied himself with his own thoughts and played deaf.

Seeing him feign ignorance again, Shen Yi responded by sucking in a huge breath and hollering at the top of his lungs, "*Honestly, sir, Prince Ya*—hey!"

Gu Yun lashed out with his horsewhip. Shen Yi raised his windslasher and narrowly blocked the whip from striking his face, going almost cross-eyed as he patted himself repeatedly on the chest. "How terrifying; I was nearly disfigured—ay, sir, I merely said a few words and you flew off the handle in embarrassment. The way I see it, although that Great Master Liao Chi was a Dongying spy, the sandalwood-scented nonsense he farted out wasn't wholly off the mark. Your fate really is too tenacious. The Red Luan star's[4] been so stifled by your fate that the poor bird can barely fly, and when it finally manages to get off the ground, instead of the fresh blooms of love, all it encounters are rotten peach blossoms. Sir, your luck in love stinks."

---

4   In Zi Wei Dou Shu, there are four stars that measure an individual's romantic fortunes. The Red Luan Star is the one among them that presides over marriage and festivities. The luan is a mythical bird and an auspicious symbol in Chinese culture. Peach blossoms are also a symbol of romantic love.

Gu Yun didn't know what to say.

Shen Yi smacked his lips. Gu Yun, he mused, really must be struggling to turn his head. Otherwise, he'd long have thrown himself over at Shen Yi to beat him to a pulp.

Gu Yun withdrew his whip and fell silent for a spell. He shook his head and said, "The country was nearly lost—what else can I do? I'll muddle along a day at a time. Who knows, perhaps one of these days, I'll breathe my last on the battlefield. What's the point in getting worked up over it?"

Shen Yi frowned. He understood Gu Yun—if this man had absolutely no inclinations in that direction, he would say so outright without a hint of ambiguity. Given what he had just said, Gu Yun wasn't hesitating over his next move. Rather, he already knew what he wanted to do, but had chosen to hold off due to certain misgivings.

"Wait, Zixi. Don't tell me you're—"

"I don't want to talk about it."

"But he's your son!"

"As if I need you to remind me!" Gu Yun snapped. He looked away from Shen Yi's shocked face in irritation.

Gu Yun missed this old maid terribly when he wasn't around, yet the moment he saw him again, he found him unbearably irritating. He spurred his horse forward with a squeeze of his legs and galloped away from Shen Yi's side. Producing a white jade flute from his lapels, he began to play a whimpering tune.

It was impossible for any instrument that fell into Gu Yun's hands to produce a pleasing sound. Encased as he was in steel panels that rendered him half a living suit of armor, Gu Yun was soon out of breath, and the notes he played quavered. Meanwhile, his fingers pressed against the instrument's holes in a manner as free and unrestrained as an unbridled horse, so that the melody he played seemed to meander almost comically around the whole of Great Liang. Yet as the strains of the flute rippled on the wind, the melody was wrapped in the sighs of those traveling westward through Yang Pass, taking on a shade of indescribable desolation so fitting that those who heard it couldn't seem to laugh at all.

Thanks to Miss Chen's steel panels, Gu Yun's waist and back were forced perfectly upright. He looked like a pillar that would never fall. Two distinctly defective windslashers were strapped to his back... neither of which was his own.

Chen Qingxu had ridden out with the military retinue. As the sound of the flute drew closer, a thought stirred in the back of her mind. She murmured quietly, "Speak no more of glory and fame..."[5]

"Speak no more of glory and fame," Gu Yun cut in impishly as he sped past on horseback, "like ice held in jade, I remain pure and unstained,[6] ha ha ha!"

Chen Qingxu was speechless. After such an incongruous rejoinder, she could no longer remember how the second half of the couplet went!

Gu Yun marched like the wind. The legendary miracle doctor Miss Chen marched with him, so he wasn't at all afraid of the steel panels coming apart. Swiftly leaving the capital behind them, the army advanced northward.

They had no sooner stepped beyond the borders of Zhili Province than they suffered two waves of attacks from vagrants. The attacks

5   A line from the poem 己亥岁二首, "Two Poems in the Year 879," by Cao Song, which laments the countless soldiers that must be sacrificed for a great general to be awarded his accolades.
6   A line from the poem 芙蓉楼送辛渐二首, "Two Poems to Bid Farewell to Xin Jian at Lotus Tower," by Wang Changling, in which the author declares his unwavering morality and virtue in the face of such temptations as rank, fame, and fortune.

didn't amount to much—the miscreants retreated after striking once, fleeing at the slightest touch like a wily pack of feral dogs nosing at them in curiosity.

"They started following us right after we left the capital," Shen Yi told Gu Yun. "I've crossed swords with them before. They're crafty, and they know the terrain. They'd flee the moment they realized they were outmatched, but in no time at all, they'd go right back to hounding us. It's incredibly annoying. This is about where we were when we received news of the siege on the capital. It was infuriating to have to contend with them during our forced march."

Gu Yun hummed in response and handed the field scope to Shen Yi. "It would seem some incompetent military strategist among them has read a book or two."

"What do you mean?"

"It's said that by affecting an appearance of total defeat, one can dupe their adversaries with a feigned retreat and lure them into giving chase," Gu Yun mused. "A pity that common foot soldiers do not understand the essence of this tactic. They chopped down their commander's banner themselves; I saw it just a second ago."

Shen Yi stared at him.

Gu Yun frowned. "Why are these people revolting, anyway? Have they no other way to make a living?"

"Hardly," Shen Yi sneered. "You think much too kindly of these miscreants. Even if they have no land to farm, most ordinary folk will find ways to engage in business or learn a new trade. It's unlikely they would end up so desperate that they find it impossible to scrape by. These vagrants roaming between the Central Plains and Central Shu are idlers who were organized by someone with ulterior motives. Aside from harassing General Cai, they specialize in the business of pillage and plunder. They go to ground whenever General Cai runs after them, then return once things have settled down. I've heard that they rob everyone they come across, but they have this rule: families who send grown men to join the bandits' rebellion are spared their vicious attacks. This way, their wives, sisters, and daughters are protected and needn't live in constant fear of abduction."

"Wait," Gu Yun said after a long silence. "This policy sounds rather familiar. Is this not the same as Great Liang's conscripted labor system? Military families don't pay taxes."

Shen Yi was at the end of his patience. "Sir, whose side are you on here?"

"All right, all right, calm down," Gu Yun said. "In that case, aren't there just going to be more and more bandits? Not only can they avoid taxes, if they join up, they can avoid the worst of the chaos of war. Who's their leader?"

"Apparently they're led by a scary-looking old bandit who's been in the business for years. They say he's covered in scars, and even has a burn scar on his face. He calls himself Fire Dragon." Shen Yi sighed. "What should we do? Pick up our pace, ride hard for a few days to bypass this mob, and head directly for Cai Bin's reinforcements encamped in the northwest?"

Gu Yun paced back and forth with his hands clasped behind his back for several minutes before speaking. "With trouble brewing both at home and abroad, any bit of unrest we can quell matters. Tigers and wolves prowl at our gates—we cannot afford to fear trouble from within them. Draft a memorial. Report to the Grand Council that we will remain in the area for a few days."

In the aftermath of the capital siege, Li Feng had eliminated the twin sinecures of the Grand Chancellors of the Left and Right and established the Grand Council to lead the Six Ministries, bringing into service a group of capable civil officials who pulled no punches in a crisis. The Grand Council's offices were invariably brightly lit well into the night. When Jiang Chong walked through their doors, it was already past midnight. The room was as bright as day from the glow of the gas lamps, yet Prince Yan had fallen asleep on the table with a brush in hand.

Jiang Chong had no wish to disturb him. After personally accepting the stack of memorials that had been delivered by palace attendants, he dismissed the servants and stepped as quietly as he could into the office. But he was, after all, a civil official with no real notion of how to conceal his presence; despite his caution, Chang Geng was startled awake. In the moment the eyes of the ever-poised Prince Yan fluttered open, an ominous red glint flickered through their depths, like a surge of killing intent rushing toward the man standing before him.

In an instant, Jiang Chong's back was drenched in a sheen of cold sweat. Like a rabbit frozen by the murderous aura of a ferocious beast, he took an involuntary step back. His long sleeve caught on Chang Geng's brush stand, and the whole affair promptly fell over with a clatter.

Only then did Chang Geng wake completely. He tucked away his killing intent in a blink, like a gust of wind scattering clouds, and rose to his feet. "It's okay, I can clean that up."

Jiang Chong looked at him, scared witless. He wondered whether he was seeing things in his exhaustion. "Did Your Highness have a nightmare?" he probed cautiously.

"It's nothing," Chang Geng said easily. "It's because I fell asleep with something pressing against my chest... I must have frightened you with my unpleasant expression. I tend to wake up cranky. Just now, I was a bit disoriented, so for a moment I couldn't figure out where I was."

It wouldn't do for Jiang Chong to pry any further...though he couldn't help but feel that Prince Yan's sleep-induced crankiness was rather excessive.

Chang Geng set the fallen brush stand back to rights. "Is there something I can help you with, Hanshi-xiong?"

Jiang Chong quickly regathered his wits and took a seat across from him. "It's about what Your Highness proposed in court yesterday—that the government issue these so-called 'war beacon tickets' to the masses. It's raised quite a stir among the court officials. To begin with, the government borrowing money from the common people is completely unprecedented. Doesn't this amount to an open declaration that the national treasury is empty? Would that not be a great humiliation for the court?"

Chang Geng still seemed groggy as he sat up in his chair and kneaded at the space between his brows. But at Jiang Chong's question, he smiled. "Half the country has been lost—what humiliation could be greater?"

"Others asked what to do if the bonds come due and the government cannot repay the loan," Jiang Chong continued. "Your Highness knows as well as I do the present state of the treasury."

"Split the payment into installments to be repaid at different times. We can issue second or even third batches of war beacon tickets later. As long as we raise enough money at the start, we should be able to keep them in circulation," Chang Geng said. "Buyers of the first batch of war beacon tickets ought to receive some suitable material benefit—titles of nobility, nominal positions in court, specially chartered concessions—anything is fine. Ideally, if we commit fully to this scheme, our citizens will be able to use war beacon tickets the same as silver."

"But in that case," Jiang Chong said, hesitant, "won't the tickets flood the market? Eventually, they'll be completely worthless."

"Once the government has recovered, we can buy the bonds back," Chang Geng said. "Whether we buy back all the bonds or continue with the policy, whether we set up a special agency to deal with the program or issue a new set of laws and decrees—we can decide all this once our circumstances have improved."

Jiang Chong nodded. "Some are also asking what we'll do if people create counterfeit tickets and use them to demand money from the government down the line."

Chang Geng broke into incredulous laughter. "Such a question should be relayed to the Lingshu Institute. Must such trifling details be addressed by the Grand Council? Shall we have a discussion on the standardization of toilets next?"

Jiang Chong grimaced. "Your Highness's reasoning is sound, but you know how it is with the Imperial Censorate... They have no real work other than picking fights. As I've heard it, they've been burning the midnight oil drafting memorials accusing you of all manner of evil deeds."

Chang Geng sighed. "I could give a thousand more reasons. At this point, this is but a stopgap measure to ameliorate a desperate situation in times of war. What else can we do? Levy heavy taxes on the refugees taking shelter in the city? Or perhaps we should tear down His Majesty's palace and sell it for parts? If the officials have concerns, they may raise them in court. I'll answer what questions I can then and there, and as for the ones I can't, I'll come back here and consider them fully before responding. These people..."

That was the way of this government. A small group of individuals were responsible for doing the actual work, while the greater majority were responsible for nitpicking and dragging the doers down. If everything worked out, the nitpickers would boast of their circumspection and discernment. Should plans fail, however, they wouldn't hesitate to demand, *Why didn't you listen?* This was to say nothing of those who muddied the waters and set up stumbling blocks in order to further their own interests and schemes. To get something *done* was no less difficult than climbing to the heavens... Everyone knew the purported wisdom of "attaining enlightenment by listening to both sides," but it was little wonder that most of the individuals whose glorious names were inked in the annals of history were dictatorial sovereigns or officials capable of overwhelming the quibbling of the court.

"It's no reflection on you, Hanshi-xiong, so please take no offense." Chang Geng waved a hand. "I've spent so much of my breath arguing with these people lately that I've grown rather short-tempered."

"Speaking of the Lingshu Institute," said Jiang Chong, "Master Fenghan submitted another pair of memorials yesterday. I took the liberty of holding them back for the time being. Perhaps Your Highness can take a look and determine whether or not it's wise to submit them to His Majesty."

Chang Geng poured himself a cup of the cold tea that had been left out from earlier in the day. "Hm. What does he have to say?"

"The first requests that His Majesty repeal the Token of Mastery Law and lift the prohibition on civilian artificers. The second asks that His Majesty terminate the ban on civilian trade of violet gold. Master Fenghan asserts that the rich merchants within our borders most certainly have their own connections for the trade of this substance. With the nation in crisis, he claims, it would be better to leverage them and secure whatever additional internal sources of violet gold we can."

Chang Geng hesitated a moment, then shook his head. "Master Fenghan... Oh, Master Fenghan."

The elderly gentleman's stalwart integrity had left a deep impression on Li Feng. He hadn't hesitated to fight with everything he had during the capital siege. Although the old coot had an awful temper and was stubborn as a mule, his loyalty was unimpeachable. Thus it was that in recent days, Li Feng did his best to tolerate the man when he occasionally lapsed into such impolitic blather.

"Have the rest of the council review the memorial on the repeal of the Token of Mastery Law. If there are no glaring issues, we can submit it to His Majesty," Chang Geng said. "As for the one on violet gold, forget about it. Does it amuse him to provoke the emperor like this? Draft a tactful summary on Master Fenghan's behalf for submission. Send the original back."

Feeling rather helpless, Jiang Chong murmured his assent. Yet as he was rising to leave, he remembered another matter. He turned back and said, "That's right, a memorial has also come from the Marquis of Anding..."

Chang Geng's head snapped up.

Li Feng had returned the Black Iron Tiger Tally to Gu Yun, thereby granting the marquis the authority to deploy troops throughout the nation and prepare in all ways for war. At this point, there was no need for Gu Yun to report every one of his moves, big or small and regardless of importance, back to his superior. Yet Gu Yun didn't seem to appreciate this kindness. He followed procedure to the letter and sent regular memorials back to the court: the places he'd been, the state of the battlefield, his subsequent plans and the reasons therefore—everything was laid out in exacting detail.

"The Marquis of Anding has arrived in the Central Plains," Jiang Chong said. "He made no mention of anything requiring urgent action; only that they had encountered a disorderly mob of bandits. He's planning on cleaning house there before continuing on but claims it oughtn't take more than a few days."

Chang Geng hummed in acknowledgment. "Leave it here; I'll take a look."

Jiang Chong sighed, deeply moved. "All matters large and small cross Your Highness's desk. You listen to a cursory briefing when it comes to the rest but read Marshal Gu's memorials with care from top to bottom. Your Highness's affection for the marshal truly is profound."

After saying his goodbyes, Jiang Chong made to take his leave. Just as he reached the door, however, Chang Geng called him to a stop once more. "Hanshi-xiong."

Jiang Chong turned back, puzzled. "Yes, Your Highness?"

Chang Geng placed a palm over Gu Yun's memorial, absently smoothing the paper. After a long silence, he finally asked, features serene as a still pond, "Could I please trouble you to collect the objections voiced in court regarding the war beacon tickets? Mark down who said what, and when. I will take their concerns under advisement and revise my proposal."

Jiang Chong started in surprise. What did such factors as "who" and "when" have to do with revising a proposal? He couldn't help but study Prince Yan under the light of those gas lamps that burned through the night. This prince's face was young, but his eyes held none of the immaturity of youth. At first glance, he appeared to be an elegant young master of noble birth. Upon further examination, however, his gaze was not invigorating like a warm spring breeze, but gave off a subtle chill. He recalled hearing that the late emperor had entrusted the fourth prince to Gu Yun on his deathbed, and that the boy had grown up sequestered within the Marquis of Anding's estate. Now Jiang Chong was surprised to find that the prince was actually nothing like the marquis who raised him.

"Yes, Your Highness," Jiang Chong finally responded after a beat.

Chang Geng inclined his head slightly. They were both clever men; there was no need to elaborate.

Not until Jiang Chong finally left with a heart full of misgivings did Chang Geng let out a soft sigh. He slept poorly to begin with, and when he had finally managed to fall into a fitful and unpleasant nap, it was interrupted by more court business. At this rate, he was likely to be up the entire night. Chang Geng stood and changed the room's incense, switching it out for Miss Chen's pacifying fragrance.

Chang Geng stood silently before the pacifying fragrance for a spell, letting the scent wash over him. Just now, a nightmare had whipped through his mind. He could barely remember it, but it had caused his chest to flare with pain, as if it were being stabbed by needles. He'd managed to suppress his discomfort while in Jiang Chong's presence, but the feeling was familiar: it was much like the handful of wu'ergu attacks he had experienced.

Miss Chen had marched with the army to keep an eye on Gu Yun's injuries. Before leaving, she had pulled Chang Geng aside and instructed him to increase his dosage of pacifying fragrance and to rest and recuperate as much as possible. The great emotional up-heaval Chang Geng had suffered in the past days had utterly toppled the foundation of disciplined equanimity he had built over many years. From here on out, suppressing his condition would become increasingly difficult. When it came to fighting the wu'ergu, the worst things one could do were to fret and overthink; these were particularly damaging to one's peace of mind.

But what choice did he have?

LIFE HISTORY

C AI BIN FOUND HIMSELF deeply vexed by the bandit mob rampaging throughout the Central Plains. The old general was getting along in years, and although the massive military force under his command seemed mighty and majestic, it was in reality known as the "Retiree Army." The garrison was situated in the middle of nowhere in a region characterized by safety and stability. Aside from putting down the occasional bout of civil unrest, the Central Plains Army primarily served as a bank of reinforcements for the border garrisons.

At present, the two battlefronts in the northwest had requisitioned the majority of Cai Bin's active troops. His forces included no armored hawks, and he was a cautious man by nature; he didn't dare take too many risks. Thus, this mob had harassed him beyond endurance.

Gu Yun spent several days verifying the origins and habits of the mob, examining the map, and familiarizing himself with the terrain. When he was satisfied, he dispatched a messenger to contact General Cai with a plan to make potstickers.

The bandit rebels hadn't the least idea who was leading the contingent from the capital. But after sounding these newcomers out several times, they had determined this party to be even weaker than Cai Bin's forces. Their heavy armor and cannons looked intimidating, but they never opened fire; at most, they fielded some light caval-rymen who would give chase for a few kilometers before being re-called. Thus, they determined that this group of soldiers was a band of impressive-looking but useless idiots. Yet just as the bandits had resolved to surround their prey once and for all, Cai Bin seemed to suddenly lose his mind. He abandoned his previous style of combat, which consisted of solely defending and never pursuing, and turned out in full strength, leading the remaining troops stationed in the Central Plains Garrison in a surprise attack to hem in the rebel mob.

In truth, the Central Plains Garrison hadn't much strength left to speak of. If the two sides really fought it out, neither side would easily prevail. But the bandit rabble had grown accustomed to the garrison troops' flirtatious back-and-forth style of provoca-tion. Believing themselves to be infallible fighters, uncatchable as a slippery loach, the bandits were reluctant to commit their resources to this fight in earnest. They once again employed those familiar hit-and-run tactics, retreating with the intent to lead Cai Bin's forces on a wild goose chase—only to turn and find Gu Yun, who had long been lying in wait.

Gu Yun commanded his heavy armor infantry to move their cannons into position and aim directly into the bandit mob. When the bandit leader saw that the young noble masters from the capital were once again trying to frighten them, he ordered his men to charge through the heavy armor formation. The line of heavy armor broke at the slightest touch, and light cavalrymen rode to the fore, "struggling" to repel the enemy. Seeing that these cannons were no different from papier-mâché models incapable of opening fire, the bandit leader was smugly pleased. His tactics became increasingly brazen, and he personally led the charge through the enemy's light-armored cavalry. When the bandits had completely fallen into

Gu Yun's trap, those papier-mâché cannons suddenly roared to life. Caught off guard, the bandit mob fell to pieces. They were given no opportunity to retreat; that skittish light cavalry, which had been cautiously evading their attacks, now galloped over to join General Cai's troops in surrounding the bandits on both sides—indeed sealing them up much like a potsticker.

In this way the bandit mob was soundly defeated, and the legendary "Fire Dragon" captured alive. The bandit leader's body was pitted with scars, so ugly Gu Yun's eyes hurt at the mere sight of him. He planned to toss the man to Shen Yi to play with as soon as possible, and commanded offhandedly, "Ask him the whereabouts of his accomplices, the identity of his instigators, the location of his base, and whether he has anything in it worth plundering."

Shen Yi choked on his own breath and began coughing violently. "Sir, has poverty driven you mad?!"

Gu Yun waved a hand. "I'm not saying beat him up...just...*rigorously* extort a confession. I'm gonna go catch up with Old Cai."

He was about to leave when he noticed one of his personal guards holding a peculiarly shaped shortsword. It was slightly longer than a dagger, and its tip curved back in a graceful arc, quite unlike the shortswords commonly used in the Central Plains. Gu Yun found it somewhat familiar and reached out to take it.

"Sir, we found this on the bandit leader."

Gu Yun drew the shortsword from its scabbard and ran a curious finger over the blade. He narrowed his eyes. "A barbarian weapon?" he asked in a low voice.

"It's a scimitar from the eighteen tribes," Chen Qingxu offered as she stepped over. "My lord, have the steel panels come loose?"

"No. We've troubled Miss Chen to no end following us as we ran all over the place in the middle of the night." Gu Yun shook his head, then took the shortsword by the hilt. "Huh. The hilt's so short; won't one's hand get stuck?"

"It's not that the hilt is short; it's just that it doesn't fit the marquis's hand. This blade belonged to a woman." Chen Qingxu took the scimitar and tested its weight. "The Eighteen Northern Tribes endure a life of hardship exposed to the elements, fighting ferocious beasts for every morsel. That's why their blades often have this groove on the hilt—it prevents the wielder from losing their grip should they encounter a particularly powerful foe. This blade is very finely wrought; it must have belonged to someone of high status. The hilt was likely specially commissioned, so the owner must have had very small hands—even smaller than mine—and was likely a woman. Look here, my lord."

Chen Qingxu turned the hilt over for Gu Yun to inspect. Ringing the pommel was a complex design: a totem of countless entwining flowering vines wreathing what appeared to be a burning flame in the center. "I saw this floral design on some abandoned ruins within the eighteen tribes' territory," she said softly. "According to kidnapped Chinese slaves I spoke to, this is the sign of the goddess of the eighteen tribes."

"I know." Gu Yun's face was grave. "And I also know who the symbol in the middle represents."

Shen Yi, who had joined them at some point, inhaled sharply when he saw the design. "The heart of the earth?"

"The what?" Chen Qingxu asked, puzzled.

"Huge'er... Xiu-niang," Shen Yi responded. "Didn't...didn't she die years ago? How could this be..."

Gu Yun beckoned him to follow. With the shortsword in hand, he turned and strode back into the room where the bandit leader known as Fire Dragon was confined, dismissing the soldiers standing guard with a wave of his hand. His expression as he held the shortsword was absent joy or anger. The gently curved blade appeared very old, but it was as viciously sharp as ever. Such a blade could effortlessly shear off a chunk of flesh were it to bite into a body.

Gu Yun pressed the tip of this sword to the underside of Fire Dragon's chin. "I hear you refuse to reveal your rebel army's base, and that you won't tell us who convinced you to take advantage of the chaos to harass General Cai's army either?"

"Fuck you, you useless pretty boy!" Fire Dragon spat.

Gu Yun smiled, reveling in the man's contempt. In his opinion, cursing someone by calling them a "pretty boy" was much like calling a woman a huli jing—it only meant the one being reviled had a lovely face.

"I suppose it doesn't matter whether you speak or not," Gu Yun said, the very picture of calm. He turned to Shen Yi. "The nation is in crisis, yet this man plotted conspiracy and colluded with foreign enemies, betraying his country by working with the northern barbarians. Your barbarian backers haven't even set foot in the country, yet you're already licking their boots... Interrogating you is a waste of time. I'll make the pronouncement tomorrow—you're to be publicly executed by a thousand cuts!"

Halfway through Gu Yun's speech, Fire Dragon's face took on a look of bewilderment, which slowly melted into horror. When he saw Gu Yun straighten irreverently and realized the man wasn't joking around, Fire Dragon began to struggle desperately against his bonds. "You government dogs, this is slander! My brothers all know that I, the great Fire Dragon, am an upstanding and dauntless man of courage! How dare you sully my name with these lies...!"

"Slander?" Gu Yun waved the sword that had once belonged to a woman of the eighteen tribes before Fire Dragon's face. "We of the

Central Plains refer to these things as *wolves' fangs*. This crescent arc here at the tip of the blade is typical of these barbarian-made weapons. Is this not yours?"

Fire Dragon was stunned.

"The scabbard and groove both seem to be unique. A top-grade leather scabbard, and a totem on the hilt so finely wrought it could be mistaken for a living flame—this is no doubt the work of a master blacksmith. An ordinary barbarian hasn't the means to wield a blade like this, so it stands to reason that its owner was someone of great wealth and high status." Gu Yun lifted his chin slightly and looked askance at Fire Dragon. "You ugly brute, your brothers know that you carry this trinket with you day and night, but none of them know its origin, do they? *Tsk*, a band of ignorant peasants."

"Hold on! Wait...wait a minute!" Fire Dragon cried. "That...that blade belongs to my greatest nemesis; it's not..."

Gu Yun burst into laughter. "Oh yes, that sounds totally believable. I've seen people carry lovers' tokens, but this is the first time I've seen someone so attached to their hated foe. What kind of sentimental hatred is this? Please enlighten me."

"That woman drugged over a hundred of my brothers and stabbed them to death one by one. Then she set fire to our stronghold and torched the entire mountain. Even the birds were burned to a crisp. I was the lone survivor, but I was left covered in these scars. I don't fucking know where she came from. I didn't know she was a barbarian, either. I carry this blade as a reminder of my past humiliation!" Fire Dragon bellowed furiously. "Filthy government dogs! You can slander me however you like, but if you dare say I colluded with that woman's ilk, even if I die, I'll come back as a ghost and bite you to death!"

"Those old teeth of yours must be mighty sharp then," Shen Yi said with a thin smile. "Go on, tell us the rest of this tall tale. So a barbarian woman burrows her way into a bandit nest for heaven knows what reason, then burns down a mountain full of bandits singlehandedly? Truly a novel tale. Marshal, I don't believe I've ever heard such a fascinating story even from the theater troupes when they performed at your estate."

Gu Yun sighed. "What theater troupes? I can't even afford meat anymore; I was eating porridge every day..."

Fire Dragon stared blankly. "Marshal... Which marshal?"

Gu Yun flourished the shortsword in his hand with a malicious smile.

Fire Dragon inhaled sharply. "C-could it be that you're Ma...Ma..."

"Calling for your mama? Well, she can't help you now." Shen Yi cut him off. "Speak: let's hear how you colluded with the barbarians to prey upon your fellow countrymen."

Fire Dragon's face flushed with anger. "I said she's my enemy! Heavens strike me down, I swear I'm not fucking lying! That woman was traveling with a small merchant caravan. I think she was separated from her family and had paid the merchants to bring her along. I don't know where she was going because we robbed them before they reached their destination. She was a looker, so we took her back to our mountain hideout. She had an infant with her, barely a month old. She was also pregnant with a second child..."

Shen Yi felt a prickle of unease but remained outwardly calm. "When was this?"

"Nineteen...maybe twenty years ago."

Gu Yun and Shen Yi exchanged a furtive look in the dim lamplight—that was around the time of the barbarian goddess's escape. In that case, the infant was likely Chang Geng—but what of the child in Xiu-niang's belly?

"What happened next?" Shen Yi asked.

Fire Dragon looked up and said in a hoarse voice, "Lots of people offed themselves when they were dragged back to the mountain, but that woman was different. She had a beautiful face, but her mind seemed broken. She didn't respond when spoken to and didn't cry when beaten. She never resisted, no matter what we did to her. After a few months, she went into early labor and gave birth to her child."

Gu Yun's hand tightened slightly around the hilt of the short-sword. For some reason, he was suddenly filled with apprehension. His intuition, which had for years never failed him, began to stir.

"They say women who've recently given birth are unclean, so no one touched her right away. No one paid her much attention at all, but to keep her from making a run for it, we chained her by her ankle and left her in her room. We gave her a little food every day, and she managed to scrape by... After some time, one of my stupid brothers who was obsessed with that bitch's beauty went to see her in secret. But when he got back, he was spooked. He told me the woman had only one child left—that the other babe had disappeared."

Shen Yi seemed to forget that he was trying to extort a confession. He blurted, "Which one?"

"The fuck should I know? They were half-dead whelps who looked like giant rats, all skin and bones." Fire Dragon immediately grew guarded. "Why do you ask?"

Shen Yi froze, then lashed the horsewhip in his hand violently to the side. "If you don't know anything, then why the fuck are you still talking?" he asked coldly. "What's so strange about a barbarian brat dying? We asked you to explain the presence of this blade—why are you dragging this out? What are you waiting for?"

But instead of growing angry again, Fire Dragon's expression became tense. "No...a dead child isn't strange. Kids like that have ignoble fates, and plenty of them end up dead. What was strange

was that, according to my brother, there was no body. That woman was chained in the room. There was no way for her to leave, so she couldn't have buried it—yet she didn't toss the body outside, nor did she keep it with her. The child...just...*vanished* into thin air. One of my brothers who'd been on patrol at the time claimed he saw firelight coming from the woman's room in the middle of the night. At first, I thought she must have been secretly cooking to feed herself, but later, I heard that the entire time she was chained in that room, there were crows circling the roof beams..."

Shen Yi's skin broke out in gooseflesh. He glanced instinctively at Gu Yun.

The scarred corner of Fire Dragon's eye twitched several times. "Everyone grew anxious after that incident. Some said the woman was a demonic enchantress—that she was abnormal—and wanted to kill her right then. Others were enraptured by her beauty and couldn't bear the thought. We brothers argued among ourselves for a long time, but never came to any kind of conclusion. At the time, my dage found her obedient, capable, and good in the sack, so he spared her. We kept her with us, along with that half-dead brat, for a few years..."

Fire Dragon sighed. "But that woman really was a demon. Seriously—if none of the men sought her out at night, she would come up with all sorts of ways to torture that child. You could hear the little brat yowling from a mountain away. There were a few times my brothers couldn't stand it anymore and told her to cut it out. She'd nod obediently, then turn around and start up again the next minute."

Gu Yun shot to his feet. Shen Yi's heart clenched in apprehension. He could see the veins bulging across the top of Gu Yun's hand where he gripped the shortsword behind his back.

Fortunately, Fire Dragon did not notice; he seemed immersed in his own memories. "It's said that a tiger, though cruel, will not eat its own cubs," he mumbled. "We were bandits, malicious individuals one and all with no fear of divine retribution. Even so, we'd never seen such a vicious woman... Who knows what kind of love potion she fed our dage. He insisted it was fitting that a woman with such a disgraceful background should remain on the mountain, and that we ought to consider her one of us. He was obsessed with her, and it was his obsession that ended up getting him killed!"

There was a subtle hoarseness to Gu Yun's voice when he finally spoke. "How was he killed?"

"Poisoned. That barbarian woman's body was steeped in poison. She concealed her true nature for many years. Over time, we dropped our guard; we were easily taken in by her ruse. She killed everyone in our mountain stronghold, even her fellow women, those who had been kidnapped and taken up the mountain just like her. Slaves, hostages—she didn't spare a single soul. And when she was done, she burned the mountain to the ground." Pain flashed across Fire Dragon's face, and he began to curse, letting loose a long string of obscenities.

This time, no one was of a mind to cut him off. Gu Yun's expression had become unsightly; he could barely contain himself.

"I happened to be sick to my stomach that day. I didn't dare drink anything, whether wine or water. That was the only reason I had the strength to crawl out of that sea of fire and survive. The knife... I pulled that knife out of my dage's chest. If I ever see that woman again, I swear to all the gods I'll chop her to pieces!"

"Was she carrying the child when she killed everyone and set fire to the mountain?" Gu Yun asked in a low voice.

"She was carrying that brat in a basket on her back," Fire Dragon said. "The kid always looked half-dead. When I saw them, he seemed boneless lying inside the bamboo basket, staring at the corpses all over the ground. He didn't even cry. After all these years, if he didn't end up dying by that woman's hand, then he's surely become a bloodthirsty monster."

At this point, Gu Yun turned and left without another word.

Shen Yi hurried after him. "Sir? Sir!"

"We cannot allow that man to live," Gu Yun said, his speech quick and muted. "Old Cai is still here—shut that pus-filled blister up permanently and cleanly before he notices." Gu Yun's footfalls came to a halt as another thought came to him. His face turned stormy. "I forgot—there's also that Jialai Yinghuo. Back in Yanhui Town, he and Xiu-niang were in constant communication. That barbarian certainly knows something."

"Sir..." Shen Yi was alarmed.

"He didn't tell me." Gu Yun's shoulders suddenly slumped. Even now, the steel panels affixed to his body held him upright, his posture unnaturally stiff. "He never told me anything. He didn't mention it at all... I knew that woman's head was filled with thoughts of vengeance, that she wouldn't have treated him especially well. But still, they were blood relatives..."

"You had no idea what that crazy woman Huge'er did back then," Shen Yi hurried to cut in. "Twenty years ago, you were a snot-nosed brat learning to write. Enough already, Zixi. This isn't your fault!"

"When we found him in that snowstorm, it wasn't because he was a naughty kid who had snuck off to play," Gu Yun said quietly. "It was obviously because he couldn't bear the abuse anymore, so he..."

And yet, out of the kindness of their hearts, they had sent him right back.

Shen Yi didn't know what to say. After a long silence, he finally murmured, "What if...and I'm just speaking in terms of *what if*...the surviving child wasn't the noble consort's son..."

Shen Yi couldn't help but recall how years ago, a young Chang Geng had calmly said to his face that he wasn't a prince, that his foot's small deformity had been smashed into being by Xiu-niang herself.

Gu Yun jerked his head up. "What are you trying to say?"

"It doesn't matter who his mother is, whether it's the shamaness of the eighteen tribes or her sister. The problem is...who fathered Huge'er's child?" Shen Yi licked the corner of his mouth nervously.

Back then, the noble consort's sister had been living in the imperial palace, waiting to be wedded to a member of the imperial family. Was the Yuanhe Emperor someone capable of stealing from his own coffers? If the late emperor had indeed been so shameless, then everyone could breathe a sigh of relief. But...what if he hadn't?

If the father wasn't the late emperor, then the most likely suspect was the man who had helped the sisters escape that year—someone who harbored evil intentions yet had access to the forbidden areas of the palace. Someone who had the ability to free the shamaness of the eighteen tribes and assume control of the operatives planted by that pair of sisters... All of these specifications, when put together, easily called to mind one Great Master Liao Chi and his Dongying spies.

Shen Yi's entire body turned ice-cold. "Sir, this is..."

Gu Yun glanced up at him, his eyes sharp as knives. Shen Yi shut his mouth immediately.

"We will never speak of this again." Gu Yun looked back down and ran his fingers over the shortsword in his hand. When he next spoke, his voice was like iron. "As for the northern barbarians, sooner or later I'll take care of them too. Henceforth, I don't want to hear any mention of this."

"Yes, sir," said Shen Yi.

Gu Yun left, his expression bleak as stagnant water. With the steel panels preventing him from bending a centimeter, his departing figure seemed particularly brooding as he sought out Chen Qingxu once again.

"Miss Chen, a word," Gu Yun said.

Perplexed, Chen Qingxu followed him over to the side of the room.

"Miss Chen, you are a master of medicine and have spent over half a year traveling through the barbarians' territories. I would like to seek your guidance regarding a certain matter."

Chen Qingxu curtsied hastily. "I dare not accept such praise."

Gu Yun helped her rise absently, his thoughts elsewhere. "Do the barbarians have any sort of special shamanic techniques that...make use of infants?"

Chen Qingxu was shocked.

Gu Yun didn't miss the trace of astonishment that flickered briefly across her face. "What is it?"

Chen Qingxu was silent for a long while, shifting uneasily from foot to foot. Finally, she exhaled heavily. "Marshal...have you ever heard of Wu'ergu?"

WICKED GOD

GU YUN FROWNED, sifting carefully through his memory. "It sounds familiar. I do think I've heard this name before... Some kind of god in the north?"

"Wu'ergu is the leader of the four great wicked gods worshipped by the eighteen tribes," Chen Qingxu said carefully. "According to legend, the god has four legs, four arms, two heads, and two hearts, and presides over tempests and famine. Wu'ergu is an avaricious god, and his arrival is heralded by upheaval in heaven and on earth. He is the most fearsome god of the northern barbarian territories, said to be destined to devour all living creatures."

Gu Yun hummed in response, failing to grasp her point.

"I spent half a year wandering deep in the grasslands, but even so, I have gleaned merely a smattering of knowledge when it comes to the eighteen tribes' shamanic arts. It is impossible for outsiders like us to fathom the profound nature and long history of this practice. Many shamanic techniques are inseparable from strange legends involving their wicked gods. The most ruthless among them is this Wu'ergu." Chen Qingxu paused briefly. "Four legs, four arms, two heads, and two hearts—what image does this bring to mind?"

Gu Yun hesitated. "It sounds like what you would get if you fused two people together."

"Indeed," Chen Qingxu said. "The wicked god Wu'ergu swallowed his brother the moment he was born, thereby doubling his divine powers. Within the eighteen tribes, there is an ancient shamanic technique: First, a pair of brothers linked by blood are selected and 'merged together' shortly after birth. The...peculiar individual who results from this ritual acquires the power of the wicked god. They are also referred to as a 'wu'ergu.'"

After hearing this, Gu Yun said nothing for some time. He pressed a hand to his chest—it was supported and protected by steel panels, yet for some reason, he still felt a stab of pain beneath his ribs.

"My lord, your injuries—" began Chen Qingxu.

"I'm fine." Gu Yun waved away her concern. He licked his lips, then asked slowly, "Miss Chen, I don't quite understand—what do you mean by 'merged together'?"

Chen Qingxu seemed to waver.

"It's okay," Gu Yun said. "Go ahead and speak."

"I've heard only rumors, so this may not be entirely accurate," Chen Qingxu said, lowering her voice. "The shamans place a pair of infants in a sealed off space with no light, water, or food... Inevitably, one of the two will suffocate. They remove the dead infant and re-fine its body using a secret technique."

For a moment, Gu Yun thought perhaps his medicine had worn off and his ears were failing him. "...What?" he squeezed out with difficulty.

"They refine the body," Chen Qingxu enunciated the words clearly. "Then, using the barbarian shamaness's secret potion as an excipient, they slowly feed the resulting tincture to the surviving sibling."

"Can a child survive such a thing?" Gu Yun blurted out.

"The marshal underestimates the eighteen tribes' millennia-old shamanic arts," Chen Qingxu said with a sigh. "Never mind refining the bodies of living humans, there are even records of lost shamanic techniques that can transform the dead into walking corpses. The tribes believe the infants who have undergone such refinement are the embodiment of Wu'ergu. Even in early childhood, they display either extraordinary physical strength or unusual intelligence. This is because, as they see it, these individuals are actually two people with four legs and two heads, and can draw on the wicked god's powers."

"This isn't really...my area of expertise," Gu Yun began hesitantly. "Please forgive my ignorance, Miss Chen, but this sounds like super-stitious hokum propagated by the uncultured masses."

"To put it in terms more congruous with our own frame of refer-ence, my lord can regard wu'ergu as a virulent poison that destroys the mind. After all, there are indeed some madmen who possess incredible physical prowess and are capable of seeing things from perspectives inaccessible to the average person. It's not unusual for such individuals to appear extraordinarily quick-witted when they can maintain clarity of mind."

"And what of the things that cannot be explained using our frame of reference?" Gu Yun asked.

"To be honest with you, Marshal, the reason I trespassed into the eighteen tribes' territory and inquired after the shamanic arts wasn't solely to find a cure for your eyes and ears. It was also to track down what information I could on the wu'ergu. But the barbarians have very few written records of this ritual. There is only one story passed down from ancient times that tells of a great general named Wu'ergu. This general was cruel and bloodthirsty, but emerged vic-torious from every battle and singlehandedly unified the eighteen tribes' territories into what we see today. It's said this hero lived for thirty-two years and remained unmarried their entire life, because they were 'neither dead nor alive, neither man nor woman.'"

Gu Yun broke out in gooseflesh.

"After researching this individual's life history and the circumstances of their birth, I learned that their mother originally gave birth to fraternal twins, a boy and a girl. However, there was no later mention of the girl, nor was her death documented in any records... There are two possible explanations: either the girl was lost in the course of the family's decline, or..."

The twins had been transformed into a wu'ergu, and the dead girl had been fused with her living twin. The boy and girl had grown into one being and become "neither dead nor alive, neither man nor woman."

The hand pressed against Gu Yun's chest clenched into a fist. Chen Qingxu asked nervously, "My lord, have the steel panels come loose?"

Gu Yun bent over at the waist. The moment stretched. Finally, he sucked in a deep breath and said in a low voice, "Why would anyone do such a thing?"

Chen Qingxu helped him to a seat. "In almost all cases, it's only when their nation has fallen or their family is in imminent danger that the people of the eighteen tribes can bear to do a thing so cruel as sacrifice their own kin to a wicked god for the sake of vengeance. Whensoever a wu'ergu comes into the world, their arrival portends a sea of carnage."

"Just now, you said the wu'ergu is like a poison that destroys the mind," Gu Yun said. "Please explain what you mean."

"Wu'ergu inevitably go insane," Chen Qingxu said. "Initially, they are beset by constant nightmares. Then, over time, they become increasingly susceptible to paranoia. If they do not make some attempt to regulate their mental state, they will also begin to hallucinate, until finally..."

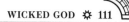

"That's why..." Gu Yun said merely two words, yet his voice was already so rough that it cracked. Only after vigorously clearing his throat could he continue. "That's why you prescribed the pacifying fragrance."

Chen Qingxu fell silent. Of course she knew whom Gu Yun was talking about. She had no way to refute it; her silence was a tacit admission.

Gu Yun closed his eyes briefly. He recalled Chang Geng mentioning offhand, on more than one occasion, that he suffered from poor sleep due to excess internal heat in the liver or some such thing. Gu Yun had never taken his words seriously. He'd assumed the boy had been consumed by his medical studies with the Chen family, rambling on and on like an old geezer about the need to maintain good health every hour of the day. But all this time, he'd been secretly bearing such great hardship.

"How far along is Chang Geng's condition?" Gu Yun asked.

For a time, Chen Qingxu didn't respond.

"Tell me," Gu Yun said, his voice faint. "No matter how bad it is, I can handle it. So long as I live, regardless of whether he's mad or witless, I'll take responsibility for him to the end."

"His Highness..." Chen Qingxu began slowly. "His Highness is incredibly strong of will and calm of mind. Even after so many years, he has rarely suffered wu'ergu attacks. He's well aware of his condition, so he shows much greater restraint than the average person. But recently... Ah—I've already treated him with acupuncture, so my lord needn't worry."

Her words were vague, but Gu Yun understood—*He had always been calm of mind and rarely suffered wu'ergu attacks, until recently.*

It was because of me, Gu Yun thought, lost. He jerked upright like a reanimated corpse and staggered several steps forward, his expression no less pained than if he had been stabbed with a knife. He shook off Chen Qingxu's attempts to lend him a steadying arm and hobbled off in a daze. With the rigid steel plates keeping his spine straight, he seemed like an iron puppet running on its last dregs of violet gold.

Chen Qingxu stood in place for a time, a grave expression on her pale face. She couldn't help but turn her eyes in the direction of the capital—the wooden bird she had sent a few days prior should have arrived by now, but...was the decision she had written of in her letter truly correct?

The sky above the capital was deeply overcast. The wooden bird was almost invisible as it cut through the air, its tiny body vanishing into the oppressive black clouds that hung overhead.

Zhang Fenghan stepped down from a horse-drawn carriage, then turned back toward the man inside with cupped hands. "Thank you, Your Highness, for going out of your way to bring an old geezer like me this far."

Chang Geng lifted the hanging screen on the carriage window. "I've spent too many days at the office of the Grand Council," Chang Geng said with a smile. "It's high time I returned to the Marquis Estate, at least for a fresh change of clothes. This was on the way for me, so Master Fenghan needn't be so courteous—although, did the Lingshu Institute not provide you with a carriage?"

Zhang Fenghan seemed unbothered. "They're all being used to run errands. I never leave the capital anyway; it's only right that I give this weary old body of mine some exercise. With fighting breaking out in every quarter of the nation, there are many demands on the national treasury. Any bit of money saved counts. Even if I can't turn the tide myself, surely I can still do my best with what little strength I have."

Chang Geng laughed. "Indeed, this junior has been enlightened."

As Zhang Fenghan hastily moved to protest—he dared not accept such praise from the prince—Chang Geng called out to him once more. "Master Fenghan, please wait a moment."

Chang Geng pulled something out and handed it over with both hands: it was Zhang Fenghan's memorial, in which he had brazenly demanded the emperor lift prohibitions on civilian trade of violet gold. "Please forgive me, Master Fenghan, for intercepting this memorial without permission instead of submitting it to His Majesty. It's just the two of us here, so I'll speak frankly. Civilian use of violet gold has always been a sore spot for His Majesty. The regulations on trade have not loosened since the reign of Emperor Wu. Consider things from His Majesty's perspective—to him, violet gold is as significant to his authority as the imperial jade seal. If you were His Majesty, could you allow commoners to carve imperial seals out of radishes and sell them for fun?"

Zhang Fenghan had known the memorial he submitted was a useless endeavor; if it hadn't been returned by the Grand Council, it would have undoubtedly angered the Longan Emperor once again. But the idealistic spirit of the literati was a strong force in him. Regardless of whether or not his advice was followed, he felt compelled to say his piece. Never had he expected Prince Yan, heedless of his own position, to personally seek him out and explain the realities of the situation—much less to speak with such candid honesty.

Zhang Fenghan's wizened face flushed slightly at Chang Geng's sincere words. "Your Highness..." He sighed. "What Your Highness says is reasonable. This old dotard has caused undue trouble for you."

"I am aware that Master Fenghan is sincerely concerned for the nation and its people. You are the backbone of the Lingshu Institute. Great Liang has seen hard times in recent years, and the responsibility of maintaining all the military's armaments has fallen to you," Chang Geng said with a wave of his hand. "Protecting you is the least we can do. How can this be considered undue trouble?"

Zhang Fenghan was at something of a loss. The look in Prince Yan's eyes was as genuine as his tone; it contained none of the nauseating sentimentality that might color such words in the mouth of another. For a moment, Master Fenghan didn't know how to respond and repeated, "My apologies, my apologies," again and again.

"Since the day my childhood friend Ge Chen entered the Lingshu Institute, he's been yakking my ear off about Master Fenghan," Chang Geng quipped amiably. "He's desperate to absorb your every scrap of wisdom, up to and including emulating your habits of drinking houkui tea and eating pickled radish. The way I see it, he's done everything but buy himself a white-haired wig to wear."

This time, Master Fenghan's face really did turn bright red. He wished dearly to drag his freshly accepted disciple Ge Chen over that instant and slap him silly. What was he doing, spilling all these trivial nothings into the ear of Prince Yan?

"Ge Chen and I grew up together in Yanhui Town. Back when we were kids, we were unlucky to be caught up in the barbarian invasion. He has no family to speak of and has spent all these years following me..." Chang Geng paused, seeming rather embarrassed as he glanced at Zhang Fenghan. "I'll stop rambling and come to the point: May I be so bold as to request a favor? Ge Chen has asked me to tell you, on his behalf, that he has always admired Master Fenghan's moral character. He would like to take you as his...ah, as his parental figure. He wants nothing else but to care for Master Fenghan with all his heart in the future. This is his most fervent wish. What do you think?"

Zhang Fenghan's breathing quickened. After returning to the capital with Shen Yi, Ge Chen had opted to remain and had formally enrolled in the Lingshu Institute. Diligent, clever, and highly gifted, he got on with Zhang Fenghan like a house on fire. In no time at all, the old man had accepted Ge Chen as his direct disciple. But a disciple was different from a godson. Zhang Fenghan had spent his life uncorrupted by politics. He was possessed of neither power nor influence, and had an irascible personality. What possible gain could there be in associating with him? What protection could he provide? Even if there was no one to care for him in his advanced age save a couple of old dogs, who would be willing to pay him any mind?

Chang Geng watched his expression carefully. "Ay, I told him ages ago that Master Fenghan prefers peace and quiet, and wouldn't like a chatterbox like him. Please don't feel awkward about this. I'll scold him later on your behalf. That idiot's always been easygoing; you can rest assured, he won't take this to heart."

"Your Highness, please wait!" Zhang Fenghan said in a rush. "Your Highness! I...this...this old geezer..." In his haste, Zhang Fenghan began to stutter, sweat beading on his forehead. Chang Geng remained silent, a picture of calm amid chaos as he watched Master Fenghan, the corners of his lips quirking up in a smile. That smile was clear and unclouded, like the brilliant grin of a young boy, touched with just the right amount of mischief.

It was rare for Zhang Fenghan to see the fourth prince acting anything but experienced and mature. When he recovered his senses, he couldn't help but laugh. "Your Highness is really..."

"In that case, I'll let him know. I'm just around the corner up ahead. Take care, Master Fenghan," Chang Geng said briskly. "I'll have Xiao-Ge select an auspicious date to come do his kowtows— ah, it looks like it's about to rain. Please take an umbrella with you just in case."

Zhang Fenghan, the prickly old thorn who had left Li Feng covered in stinging puncture wounds, bade goodbye to Chang Geng with a beatific smile, gazing after Prince Yan's carriage until it faded into the distance.

The moment Chang Geng was out of sight, the skies opened with a light pattering of rain, exactly as the prince had predicted. Zhang Fenghan opened the umbrella that Chang Geng had left him. He felt deeply moved. The past half year had seen the country devastated by war. Yet despite the turmoil, when he saw these young folks, Master Fenghan felt that the pillar standing indomitably above Great Liang's gilded palace had yet to fall, that there was still this handful of people supporting it.

There were indeed many brilliant talents in the world. Yet it was often the case that those who were too clever lacked valor and were inclined to put their own safety before matters of principle. Only a truly wise and courageous individual, one who took the lead in lifting the rafter, might gather such talents together. Those who walked at the forefront must doubtless exhaust all their strength and ingenuity, and might not meet a favorable end. Even if their sacrifice wasn't worth it, their life had already been forfeited. But without these great slabs of stone, would not those tens of thousands of grains of sand have long been washed away by the river of time?

Zhang Fenghan glanced back and saw the snowy white corner of a monk's robe flash past the end of the alleyway. Schooling his face back to seriousness, he quickly walked over.

The restaurant in the alley was nowhere near as grand or impressive as the Kite's Flight Pavilion of times past. It was nothing more than a casual little tea shop, so the shabby and finicky Master Fenghan seemed not the least bit out of place as he stepped inside. He closed the umbrella and shook off the raindrops that clung to

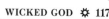

its surface. Hearing a light knock on the wooden staircase above, he lifted his head to see Great Master Liao Ran removing his own dripping-wet conical bamboo hat. The monk nodded down at him from the second floor. Master Fenghan caught on immediately and wasted no time ascending the stairs.

The two of them entered the innermost private room one after another. A middle-aged man was waiting for them within. He was forty to fifty years of age with a perfectly ordinary face. His manner of dress wasn't particularly ostentatious, and, at first glance, he had a friendly look about him. Even the corners of his eyes and the tips of his brows were rounded. Had any members of the Ministry of Revenue been present, however, they would have been deeply shocked: this individual was none other than the richest man in Jiangnan, Du Wanquan.

Du Wanquan had made his fortune in Jiangnan and had once personally organized a merchant fleet to sail west. In all the years since the establishment of maritime trade by Emperor Wu, this man was the one and only business tycoon in all of Great Liang to visit the Far West. Though the journey was treacherous, he reaped huge profits and became known to the people as the "God of Wealth" upon his return. Later, he relocated his family to the northwest, where he was elected Chairman of the Silk Road and Central Plains Chamber of Commerce.

In the early days of the war, the Marquis of Anding had for reasons unknown been punished with a salary deduction and ordered to reflect on his mistakes in the capital, failing to return to his post on time. This sharp-nosed merchant had taken the lead in rallying members of the chamber of commerce and evacuating people in groups. Consequently, the ensuing turmoil in the Western Regions resulted in few civilian casualties. It could be argued that the God of

Wealth's good instincts were to thank for an extremely timely rescue for the masses.

Precisely how much wealth Du Wanquan possessed, no one knew, but they all said he was rich enough to rival the nation. Granted, given Great Liang's current state of impoverishment, rivaling the nation was hardly an extraordinary feat. Yet at present, such a God of Wealth was currently huddled in a room with a monk from the National Temple and an old curmudgeon from the Lingshu Institute within a barebones little tea shop.

Du Wanquan politely rose to his feet at the sight of Zhang Fenghan and offered him the seat of honor. "Please come in, please come in," he said with cupped hands. "It's been over ten years since we last met, but I can see Master Fenghan hasn't changed a bit. The master is more graceful in bearing than ever."

"Hardly," Zhang Fenghan politely deflected the compliment. "I've grown old."

Du Wanquan's expression turned solemn. "Before I embarked on this trip to the capital, my wife and children made every effort to dissuade me. They feared that the situation in the capital was still unstable, and that this city would become the final resting place of this weary old body. I said to them, 'Isn't Master Fenghan both older and more capable than me? When the enemy soldiers besieged the capital, he faced them without an inch of steel, upright and fearless. I am but an insignificant businessman; I can scarcely compare to such an unparalleled patriot of the nation—but if I lack even the courage to pay a visit after the fight is over, what kind of coward would that make me?'"

The God of Wealth was a long-time veteran of the business world, the living embodiment of the expression, "amiability attracts riches." Though distinct in his approach, the impression he left was not unlike that of Prince Yan. With a handful of words, both men had the ability to bring a blush to their listener's face while simultane-ously making them feel they had gained something in the encounter. Zhang Fenghan quickly recognized that if they continued exchang-ing pleasantries like this, they would still be standing here when the sky darkened. He had little choice but to accept the seat of honor.

Liao Ran pressed his palms together in greeting. "Du-xiansheng is a very busy man with both his family and business to attend to," he signed, "while Master Fenghan must hurry back to the Lingshu Institute. Perhaps we can save the small talk for another time. Please forgive this junior for presumptuously overstepping his authority and raising the matter at hand."

As he spoke, he drew a string of Buddhist prayer beads from his lapels. The beads came loose with a light tug. Liao Ran pried open the largest spacer bead and produced an old piece of hollowed-out wood. Its outer surface was rough and unadorned, but inside, it was filled with countless tiny gears lying quietly dormant.

Master Fenghan and Du Wanquan shared a glance. Setting the pleasantries aside, they took similar pieces of hollowed wood from their own lapels. When placed together, these three pieces of wood began to slide toward each other on the table, their gears interlock-ing seamlessly in an instant to form the upper half of a wooden tablet inscribed with the character *Lin*.

"It's been over two hundred years since this tablet was last pieced together," Du Wanquan sighed. "At that time, our predecessors en-trusted this tablet to the founding ancestor of this dynasty. They chose the best person to lead the country and bartered their service for two hundred years of peace and prosperity. Now that this responsibility has passed into the hands of our generation, I hope that we, too, will make the correct decision... Since Great Master Liao Ran has gath-ered the 'Linyuan' together today, you must have a candidate in mind."

"Zhong-lao[7] and the Chen family's representative are both currently on the front lines and cannot be present at this meeting," Liao Ran signed. "Zhong-lao sent a messenger to bring his piece of the tablet alongside a letter with his recommendation several days ago. As for Miss Chen, she is in a faraway region rife with unrest, so I have yet to receive word. However, I imagine we'll hear from her within the next day or so."

Du Wanquan glanced down at the Linyuan tablet on the table and straightened in his seat. His expression solemn, he said, "Please go on, Great Master."

"Amitabha Buddha." Liao Ran pressed his palms together and bent his head. "Since the outbreak of the war, a particular individual has been using the Linyuan Pavilion's wooden birds to send dispatches. In doing so, this person has preserved some much-needed room to maneuver for our besieged capital. They have assumed leadership in a time of crisis, eradicated enemies within our own ranks, and guarded the city walls with their own body. They have also defied an imperial decree, refusing the throne—"

At this point, Zhang Fenghan expressed his approval. "I agree with the Great Master regarding this man. Most of my interactions with Prince Yan have been in the imperial court. Although he is young, he possesses both integrity and talent. I am willing to entrust my piece of the tablet to him. It shames me to admit that an old geezer like me, who spent so many years idling away, failed to be of use at the most critical juncture. When I heard the battle report from the front lines, I was completely dumbfounded. Never had I imagined that the Western army could truly lay siege to the capital, nor did it occur to me to use wooden birds for communication... What do you think, Du-xiansheng?"

---

7   老, lao, a suffix attached to the surname of venerated elders. Denotes a particularly high degree of respect.

The two who had already spoken turned to look at Du Wanquan in unison. Du Wanquan took a moment to mull things over before speaking. "Prince Yan is of extremely lofty status," he said diplomatically. "Naturally, someone like myself has never met him in person. However, I hear he studied under the venerable Zhong-xiansheng and is close with the Chen family's representative. I'm sure those two know him much better than I, so why not hear what they have to say first?"

Liao Ran produced a wooden bird from his lapels. On the belly of the bird was a finely crafted seal, still unbroken.

"This is from Zhong-lao," Liao Ran said. "This humble monk has yet to open it. Du-xiansheng, if you please."

Du Wanquan rubbed his hands together, rather embarrassed. "Don't mind if I do." He carefully broke the seal, opened the bird's belly, and removed a fourth piece of wood. With this, more than half the character for *Yuan* appeared, leaving only one corner missing. A sheet of billow paper from Zhong Chan lay beneath the fragment of tablet.

"Zhong-lao personally taught Prince Yan how to dispatch troops, organize military formations, and shoot from horseback," Zhang Fenghan said. "Such a close master-student relationship cannot be expressed in words; there's no way he'd—"

Yet as he watched Du Wanquan smooth the billow paper missive from General Zhong Chan over the table, his voice faltered.

The note read: *This child has the ability to pacify the nation. However, he suffered an extremely difficult childhood. Although he is benevolent in his youth, there is no guarantee he will remain so past middle age. He is also afflicted with the hidden danger of wu'ergu. I advise us to proceed with caution.*

POWER

ZHANG FENGHAN had spoken so effusively, only to have to immediately eat his words. He stared at that slip of paper for some time, flummoxed. "What does this mean? What... what does he mean by 'the hidden danger of wu'ergu'?"

Liao Ran furrowed his brow, uncertain where to start. Some moments passed before he began to sign. "It's a type of northern barbarian poison. As a child, Prince Yan was taken from the palace and ended up stranded in Yanhui Town, where he was abused by a shamaness of the north. The Chen family has been working on a treatment, but they have yet to find a definitive cure..."

Zhang Fenghan was incredulous. "Seriously? Is everyone in the Imperial Academy of Medicine dead? This—"

"Master Fenghan, please calm yourself," Du Wanquan interrupted. "I have traveled frequently throughout the northwest in recent years because of the Silk Road and have heard something of these barbarians' shamanic arts. The rumors I've heard suggest that wu'ergu damages the mind—I'm sure this is General Zhong's concern as well. He is worried that His Highness cannot bear so many mental burdens."

"The nation is on the verge of toppling. The Marquis of Anding has once again rushed back to the northwest despite suffering grave injury. Meanwhile, Prince Yan is a selfless individual who spares no effort in stabilizing the nation. Master Du, your words are truly dis-appointing," Zhang Fenghan said solemnly. "Besides, Great Master Liao Ran has just said that Prince Yan has been afflicted with this poison since childhood. Yet at present, I see nothing abnormal about him. In the future, he may continue to be unaffected. If old General Zhong can't trust Prince Yan, then who else can we possibly find to assume control of the Linyuan tablet?"

Ever since the capital siege, Zhang Fenghan had become Prince Yan's most loyal supporter. Even the umbrella at his side had been freshly borrowed from the man's carriage. He became feverishly excited at the mere mention of the prince, as if he wished to crow to all under heaven that His Royal Highness was the greatest in the land. Now, though the old Lingshu scholar had already spoken at length, he had yet to vent his indignation. He continued, unsatisfied, "The current situation is different from that of two hundred years ago. Back then, the imperial court was extorting taxes from its citizens and had lost the support of the people. Heroes gathered from all corners of the nation to stand against this injustice. But at present, enemies have invaded from without our borders. As for His Majesty... Although His Majesty has been rather extreme in some of his methods, he can still be considered diligent in governance and benevolent toward the common people. He is not at fault. In these troubled times, if the Linyuan tablet were to fall into the hands of another, can we guarantee their loyalty to the throne? Prince Yan is a member of the imperial family. In our moment of greatest peril, he was handed the opportunity to ascend the throne and flee to the eastern capital—but rather than escape to Luoyang, he remained on the city gate tower! If such an individual is unworthy of being entrusted with the Linyuan tablet, who else is there?"

Du Wanquan was accustomed to smoothing things over; he had no intention of picking a fight with Zhang Fenghan. After listening patiently, he merely smiled. "This, I would believe. Prince Yan's moral character and talent are beyond reproach. In the matter of the wu'ergu, however, we are all of us laymen. I think we ought to hear what Miss Chen has to say. Let's order some food and eat while we wait. We can make our decision once Miss Chen's letter arrives. What do you say?"

The tension in Zhang Fenghan's features eased. Shaking his head, he said in self-mockery, "I really am getting on in years, yet I still have this horrible temper. Please don't take my words to heart, Master Du."

Barely had he finished speaking when there came the fluttering sound of wings from beyond the window.

Du Wanquan smiled. "Speak of the devil."

The God of Wealth reached over and pushed open the window, just wide enough for a little wooden bird, vividly lifelike, to flit in. It pecked lightly at the table a few times, then settled down on its belly and fell still. This little creature was even more delicately constructed than the one sent by General Zhong; whereas the latter had been brought by a trusted messenger, Chen Qingxu's was made to fly all the way back from the northwest, where she was advancing with the army.

This wooden bird's belly had been sealed using a special mechanism: unlike the symbolic paper seal used by General Zhong, this one comprised a series of tightly fitted locks. Twenty-seven tiny holes had to be probed with a fine needle in a specific sequence. One wrong poke, and the remaining violet gold within the bird's belly would ignite and prevent those who attempted to force the lock from obtaining its contents. The construction of these special wooden birds was dreadfully complex, such that there were only a bare handful of them within the Linyuan Pavilion. Even

Chang Geng didn't know of their existence—thus, back when the Westerners had laid siege to the capital, he'd expressed doubts about the security of using wooden birds for communication.

Du Wanquan took out a silver needle, and the others watched the careful movement of his hands. For a split second, an inexplicable anxiety seized Zhang Fenghan's heart. Just as the God of Wealth cracked the wooden bird's seal, but before he could remove the letter, the old Lingshu scholar called out, "Wait."

Du Wanquan and Liao Ran looked up as one.

Though they were both members of the Linyuan Pavilion, Master Fenghan resided at the Lingshu Institute year-round. He wasn't terribly familiar with Chen Qingxu, this junior of his who spent all her days wandering the land. He had rarely met her in person and didn't know her well at all—yet for some reason, he had a sudden premonition that her decision might not be to his satisfaction.

"Right now, everything south of the Yangtze River along the East Sea has fallen to the foreigners," he said slowly, his face tense. "Old General Zhong is personally holding the front line, but he is merely holding it and dares not take rash action. With the troops and armaments at his disposal, there's no way he can cross the river. They say the foreigners are as savage as they are ruthless, that they have already burned the Jiangnan Academy to the ground. This is not irreparable—books that have been lost can be reprinted. Theories and doctrines can be re-established. But our people who perish are gone forever."

The old Lingshu scholar's voice shook. "The land of 'osmanthus in autumn and miles of lotus blossoms in summer'[8] has become a mound of scorched earth. Meanwhile, our national treasury stands

---

8   A line from the lyric poem 望海潮 · 东南形胜, "The Vantage Ground of the Southeast, to the tune of 'Gazing upon the Tide'," by Liu Yong, a Song dynasty poet.

empty and our violet gold stores are critically low... Our nation is like a drafty room, with gusts of wind blowing in from all sides. If the Linyuan Pavilion chooses to look on without lifting a finger, we may as well disband and go home now. How can we claim we pursue the Dao and serve the mandate of heaven? If we are convinced that we cannot remain silent, then the tablet must re-enter the world. We are mere commoners; we do not wish to entrust this responsibility to the wrong person—but as things stand, we have Prince Yan in the imperial court and Marshal Gu beyond the Great Wall. Regarding Marshal Gu... I mean no disrespect, but he has long had dealings with the Linyuan Pavilion yet never expressed an interest in associating with us more closely. With the Black Iron Battalion under his command, he turns his nose up at our organization; he is far too busy to concern himself with the disorderly jumble of resources we offer. My esteemed peers, if you pass Prince Yan over on account of such...such *baseless* reasons, then what is your next plan of action?"

He spoke with heartfelt sincerity, doing his utmost to win Du Wanquan to his side. Listening to Master Fenghan speak, even Liao Ran felt moved. But the God of Wealth was a sophisticate—how could he be so easily carried away? Though he wore an ardent expression, he spoke as evasively as ever, avoiding the major issues while engaging the trivial ones. "Truth be told, Prince Yan has worked closely with the Linyuan Pavilion since childhood and may already be considered one of our members. For instance, the communication network used during the capital siege...was not His Highness the one who built it using Linyuan Pavilion's resources? When disaster strikes our nation, none of our members would hesitate to help where we're needed. The ceremony of entrusting someone with the tablet is just that—a ceremony. There isn't really much difference, is there?"

"That is not the issue. Master Du has misunderstood the point," Liao Ran shook his head as he signed. "Without the tablet, should trouble arise, the Linyuan Pavilion will offer minor assistance and minimal effort. Only upon the appearance of the tablet are pavilion members required to make every effort and offer all they have in service of the nation. It's entirely different. The Linyuan Pavilion has been silent for two hundred years, held together and summoned solely by the pieces of this wooden tablet. In times of chaos, everyone looks after their own hide. Even for people like you and me, the utility we can offer may be little more than running errands and delivering letters—in that case, we may be even less useful than some of the larger sects of the jianghu."

The weight of these words was profound. Du Wanquan's features shifted subtly. The God of Wealth was not like Master Fenghan, so poor he kept only dogs for company. He was blessed with a sprawling household and tremendous wealth. The barefooted man with neither wife nor child kept his entire household fed so long as his own belly was full, but this wasn't the case for those who wore shoes. If there was anyone here most against the resurfacing of the Linyuan tablet in the world, it was undoubtedly the God of Wealth.

Liao Ran had shown him face by making his point without going into detail, and had refrained from bluntly stating his true meaning: the Linyuan tablet had the power to mobilize the mysterious Daofa Court. Any pavilion member who turned traitor by refusing to comply with the Linyuan tablet's directives would be hunted to the ends of the earth and executed by the Daofa Court. To put it more plainly, absent the authority of the tablet, the God of Wealth would likely have to scoop out no more than a handful of jingling pocket change as a courtesy. With the tablet in play, however, even if Du Wanquan lost his entire fortune, he would have no choice but to accept the price.

Liao Ran re-strung his Buddhist prayer beads one by one. "Master Du, please show us the Chen family's piece of the tablet."

There was a moment of silence. Du Wanquan opened the wooden bird's belly, and the final piece of the tablet clattered onto the table. In seconds, it had automatically joined itself to the others, completing the character *Yuan*.

A piece of billow paper marked with Chen Qingxu's messy scrawl rolled out. Liao Ran smoothed it out but found only one succinct line of words: *The Chen family will do all we can.*

It was a long while before Zhang Fenghan reacted. "That's it?"

Liao Ran's smile was exasperated. Chen Qingxu was known to be taciturn. It was just as well if she didn't offer much when speaking, but when it came to pen and paper, she had absolutely no patience for writing at length. A yes was a yes and a no was a no. In her hands, the most ponderous thing in the world would be reduced to one bare sentence inked with bold flourish.

"If Miss Chen has spoken thus, the slow-acting poison in His Highness's body shouldn't pose a problem." Liao Ran turned to Du Wanquan. "What say you, Master Du?"

The Linyuan tablet was split into five pieces, and no one person had the right to overrule the others. The score was now three to one. Du Wanquan knew it didn't matter whether he agreed or not; the result had already been settled. The God of Wealth forced out a laugh. "Great Master Liao Ran is being much too polite. I hear that Prince Yan has recently been championing the war beacon tickets. If, when the time comes, I can do anything to help, please do not hesitate to ask."

"Master Du," Zhang Fenghan tactfully moved to placate him, "no eggs remain whole when the nest overturns. A man forced to leave his home in times of turmoil is no better than a dog living in times of peace. Perhaps that is what they mean when they say vast wealth becomes nothing more than sand washed away by water."

Finding that he had been dragged into such a terrible predicament by a bunch of destitute paupers, Du Wanquan was still dejected. He half-heartedly cupped his hands and said, "It's as you say. Master Fenghan is truly a man of noble character."

The three finished their simple meal in a hurry, the mind of each man weighed down by his own concerns. They soon parted ways, the wine barely touched.

As the Linyuan Pavilion members were making their decision, Chang Geng arrived back at the Marquis Estate.

Ge Chen was waiting for him in the study. Chang Geng instructed the servants not to disturb them and stepped calmly in, closing the door behind him. The sprawling Marquis Estate was practically uninhabited. Many of the elderly servants were either deaf or had trouble moving about, and it was difficult to say whether they were there to wait on their master or were simply enjoying their retirement in their master's house. Oftentimes, Chang Geng would call for a servant to relay some instruction only for no one to show up at all, and occasionally, he was pressed to make his own tea. Yet there were also times when this was very convenient; for instance, he had no need to be wary of eavesdroppers.

Ge Chen rose to his feet when he saw Chang Geng, his naturally round baby face tight with anxiety. In contrast, Chang Geng was perfectly unperturbed. He beckoned for Ge Chen to speak. "You've intercepted it?"

Ge Chen nodded in the affirmative, digging out a sheet of billow paper from his lapels. "Just as you asked, I used the pretext of 'conducting maintenance' on the aerial exclusion field to secretly intercept the wooden bird and swapped out the message inside. I can guarantee you the seal has been seamlessly restored." Ge Chen pressed his lips together, then continued. "At the end of last year, when Xiao-Cao traveled north to find Miss Chen, he personally witnessed her releasing wooden birds. He caught one in secret and made a mold of the lock. There shouldn't be any issue—but Dage, why did we interfere with Miss Chen's wooden bird? What does her note mean?"

Chang Geng didn't respond for a long while. He smoothed that wrinkled slip of paper out to read. The handwriting was identical to that on the note Liao Ran and the others had received, but its contents were quite different.

This one read: *Pray forgive my ignorance. Despite years of searching, I have failed to find a cure for wu'ergu. I am unable to live up to the great trust placed in me. Regarding the Linyuan tablet, I advise us to proceed with caution.*

After reading the message, Chang Geng was unmoved. He burned the slip of paper to ash and thought without much surprise, *Just as expected.*

Based on the understanding of the Linyuan Pavilion he had developed over the years, final decisions were made by a group of either three or five individuals, with five being the more likely scenario. The Linyuan Pavilion had access to many unique and extremely elaborate steam-powered inventions; thus, it stood to reason that there must be a member of the Lingshu Institute among their number. Next, the Chen family who had treated Gu Yun's eyes and ears so long ago had supposedly undertaken the task in the name of the Linyuan Pavilion. There was no way Gu Yun would trust Linyuan unconditionally, so a former subordinate of the old marquis must have facilitated the connection. Thus, one member of the group must represent the military.

The monk Liao Ran acted as a liaison, connecting all corners of the nation, so it was probable that he was also a core member, representing the National Temple. Of the remaining two members, one likely controlled "wealth," while the other was a member of that same Chen family of Taiyuan Prefecture.

Of the five, Liao Ran and the representative of the Lingshu Institute were the two with whom he felt confident of his chances. The remaining three hung in the balance.

Aside from Chang Geng himself, there was no one in the world who knew more about the horror of wu'ergu than Miss Chen. She wasn't the type to make things personal, so there was no way she would support him purely out of sentiment. Those who controlled material wealth were easily weighed down by their own business. In a situation like this, their representative would certainly shrink back from action. And as for the military...if Chang Geng was correct in his guess and the representative really was old General Zhong, he wouldn't necessarily speak in Chang Geng's favor.

The latter two had their own connections and methods of communication—it would be very difficult for him to interfere. On the other hand, Chen Qingxu was currently traveling northwest with the army. When the time came to cast her vote, she would inevitably send her decision by wooden bird. She presented the sole opportunity for Chang Geng to exploit.

Faint candlelight illuminated Prince Yan's young and handsome face; he seemed a bit unreal.

"Dage..." Ge Chen called out hesitantly. The round-faced boy was faithful and true when it came to his childhood friend Prince Yan, but he wasn't stupid. He could guess that Chen Qingxu's encrypted wooden bird was connected to the Linyuan Pavilion's final decision. Although he had swapped out her message in accordance with

Chang Geng's orders, he did feel some pangs of misgivings. Chang Geng always acted with open honesty and a magnanimous sensibility. He never did anything that couldn't bear scrutiny under the light of day, but this time... Was it for the sake of power?

"It's not that I absolutely must obtain the Linyuan Pavilion." Chang Geng seemed to sense his thoughts and, with a bland expression, calmly explained. "But my time in the imperial court has been too short. I enjoy His Majesty's support, as well as that of Justice Jiang and a whole team of new attendants at my disposal, but my roots remain shallow. There are many things I cannot fully put to use. Some things may be deferred, but the front line cannot wait for either violet gold or money. At a time like this, I have no choice but to settle for seeking the strength of the Linyuan Pavilion. I would slowly address all these difficulties in a fair and aboveboard manner if we only had more time—but I'm afraid the foreigners won't afford us the luxury."

Hearing this, Ge Chen straightened up, and the doubts in his heart evaporated in an instant, leaving a feeling of mild embarrassment in their stead. "Both Xiao-Cao and I understand... Oh, Dage, you need to be sure to look after your health too. The marquis will definitely take me to task if he returns to court and finds you collapsed from exhaustion." Ge Chen shuddered as he envisioned the specifics of the marquis taking him to task, quite terrified by his own imaginings.

Chang Geng's serious expression softened. "I plan to manage things just until this crisis has passed. Who would willingly take on such a difficult and thankless task with the nation at peace? Plus, it's not like I'm working for free. When the time comes, I'll have His Majesty grant me a mountain somewhere with the most beautiful scenery. I'll plant a grove of peach trees so I can admire their blossoms in the spring and eat their fruit in the summer. There should also be a hot spring at the base of the mountain. I plan on raising a flock of chickens and ducks spanning as far as the eye can see. Then I can cook their eggs by tossing them directly in the hot spring—"

Ge Chen's stomach rumbled. Chang Geng paused, and the two of them burst into raucous laughter. Chang Geng bounded to his feet. "It's getting late. Instead of bothering Uncle Wang and the others, let's go wrap ourselves some dumplings."

Ge Chen was mortified at the thought. "Th-that's not right, Dage. How can I let a prince mix filling and make dumpling wrappers... That's way too..."

Chang Geng looked askance at him. "Do you want to eat or not?"

Ge Chen chirped without the slightest hesitation: "Yes!"

The two snuck through the pitch darkness and into the Marquis Estate's kitchen, shooed the elderly cook dozing there back to her sleeping quarters, and banged about for a good while. As they listened to the striking of the night watch, with one person lifting the lid of a cooking pot and the other wielding the strainer, the pair casually polished off over sixty dumplings right there in the kitchen, Ge Chen yelping as he burned himself on the piping hot filling. It felt like they had returned to their childhood days in the countryside.

Such happy moments could only be stolen in the middle of the night. In broad daylight, Chang Geng's every step was taken with utmost apprehension.

One month later, the matter of the war beacon tickets was still up in the air. Just as Emperor Li Feng was on the verge of being pestered beyond endurance, a silent purge began to unfold. The Department of Supervision submitted three memorials in a row accusing Prince

Yan of pulling the wool over the eyes of the court. They claimed that the Grand Council under his administration had secretly blocked memorials from reaching the emperor's desk in a bid to prevent legitimate complaints from being heard by His Majesty. As for his proposal regarding the war beacon tickets, it was a complete farce. He was trampling the dignity of the nation underfoot and bringing disaster to both the country and its people.

In response, Prince Yan ordered his attendants to bring out the written records of every memorial that had been submitted and returned, then presented them to the court. Each and every rejected memorial was clearly documented, including the date it was received and a detailed explanation of why it was rejected. All these briefings had in turn been submitted to the Warm Pavilion. There were no discrepancies whatsoever. The rest of the court was stunned speechless.

Immediately thereafter, citing that he was obviously too incompetent to reassure the masses, Prince Yan requested the Longan Emperor relieve him of his position. Li Feng refused as usual, only for Prince Yan, freshly twenty and still in the bloom of youth, to resign on the grounds of illness and shut himself away in the Marquis Estate.

The court was teeming with sly old foxes skilled at maneuvering around all sorts of situations and people, yet none had ever seen someone throw such a brazen tantrum. Li Feng didn't know whether to laugh or cry.

But the moment Prince Yan left—before the emperor could sneak out of the palace in plain clothes and coax his younger brother back to court—disaster struck.

First, there was the Grand Council. The department, now leaderless, became as disorganized and snarled as a knotted ball of hemp.

Likewise, with no one to enforce guidelines, memorials piled onto Li Feng's desk like drifts of snow. Demands for funding and violet gold came from all corners of the country, and Li Feng was soon utterly overwhelmed.

Next, there were the two Ministers of Revenue and War; these distinguished heads nearly came to blows in open court. When the furious Li Feng probed deeper into the matter, he found that, despite the nation's current predicament, there were corrupt officials exploiting the situation and embezzling military funding at every level. Li Feng grew more and more incensed as further investigation unearthed a corruption case so major it shocked every echelon of society. From high officials of the second rank all the way down to minor functionaries of the seventh, a staggering number of people were implicated. Ironically, even the prattling Department of Supervision saw half their number fall.

In the ninth month, a fall of autumn rain washed over the capital, leaving behind an air of austerity. Jiang Chong personally paid a call to the Marquis Estate to present an imperial decree requesting Prince Yan's return to court. By this time, those who were observant had come to a particular realization—now, when Prince Yan once again raised the issue of the war beacon tickets, he encountered hardly any resistance. After Prince Yan successfully pushed the program through, some still worried that the first batch of war beacon tickets wouldn't sell. But to their surprise, the moment these bonds hit the market, Du Wanquan, the richest man in Jiangnan, as well as several others like him, rallied a group of upstanding civilian merchants to vigorously support the measure. With their assistance, the first batch of war beacon tickets sold out in less than three days.

Cold, hard cash flowed into the national treasury. No one had anything more to say.

At the end of the seventh year of Longan, the two armies facing off on the Jiangnan front line remained locked in a stalemate. Elsewhere, the Marquis of Anding had joined forces with the Central Plains Garrison and mopped up the rebel mob before finally returning to Jiayu Pass. When the allied armies of the Western Regions saw the enemy on their doorstep, they retreated fifteen kilometers the very next day.

Gu Yun personally drafted fourteen letters in rapid succession, which he sent to the kings of each country in the region as a "New Year's greeting." At the same time, he readied his troops for battle, preparing to launch an attack with the arrival of the very next batch of supplies from the imperial court.

On the joyous occasion of the New Year, the flames of war threatened to flare up at any minute; no lanterns or colored streamers hung beyond Jiayu Pass. The long-awaited provisions and armaments from the imperial court arrived at last—but the official leading the convoy was a rather august personage.

Gu Yun had just returned from leading a troop of light cavalrymen on patrol and had barely dismounted when he heard that Prince Yan had come. Momentarily stunned, he didn't bother to remove his light-pelt armor; he threw down his warhorse's reins and took off.

72

TROUBLED DREAMS

G U YUN RUSHED all the way back to the encampment. The troop of personal guards behind him hadn't a clue what was going on and ran after him as though thrown into field training. With no chance to change shifts or fall into formation, the band of Black Iron light cavalrymen pelted after him in a wild and disorganized column. When they saw this, the sentries on duty assumed yet another cadre of enemy troops had appeared and thought they were about to face a fearsome foe. All of them raised their field scopes and surveyed their surroundings.

The wagons from the capital were already lined up in a neat row within the Black Iron Battalion's encampment in Jiayu Pass. Logistics officers bustled about hither and thither, but Gu Yun stopped cold without warning.

His personal guards promptly drew up as well, exchanging looks of confusion. Gu Yun glanced back at them in bemusement. "What are you all rushing around in a panic for?"

His guards didn't know what to say.

Gu Yun coughed awkwardly and flicked a nonexistent speck of dust from his black-iron light pelt armor. After making such an exhibition of himself on the way here, now that he had arrived, he assumed a calm and unhurried manner without the slightest hitch.

Hands clasped behind his back, he strolled into the commander's tent as if out for a leisurely walk.

Aside from those who were on duty and had yet to return from patrol, all the officers under Gu Yun's command were clustered inside the tent. At the center of their circle was a man clad in formal brocade court robes and draped in a snowy white fox fur cloak that revealed a span of his broad sleeves. It was none other than the newly promoted Prince Yan, straight from the imperial court. He turned his head at the commotion and unexpectedly met the gaze of Marshal Gu, who was leaning against the door frame.

Prince Yan seemed surprised—but then his eyes lit up, the dust of travel washed away in an instant. He raised his hands, as if unable to control himself, and cleared his throat, a bit off-key.

At the sound of his cough, everyone glanced toward the doorway and rose from their seats. "Marshal."

Some reunions feel instantaneous, while others seem to have taken a lifetime. Two people who had parted in anger or who had a strained relationship would feel that they had been separated for a mere blink of an eye. But for two who had parted with so many uncertain truths yet unraveled and lingering, with ambiguous feelings between them— those separations felt like they had lasted an entire lifetime.

Gu Yun felt all sorts of emotions surge in him, thoroughly blocking up that heart as wide as the mouth of the Yangtze River like tightly packed granules of sand. After a long moment, a sputtering rivulet of scalding water finally seeped out and melted through his extremities in a continuous stream. The hands Gu Yun held clasped behind his back began to sweat.

Feigning respectability, he raised a hand to wave away the courtesies and sauntered in. "The border's not safe right now—why has Your Highness come in person?"

"I wanted to get here before the end of the year. I've brought everyone some New Year's gifts."

Gu Yun made a great show of propriety and hummed in response. "Thank you for your hard work," he said blandly. "It's been rough for everyone this past half-year, so squeezing rations out of the imperial court has been especially difficult. Are there any decrees from His Majesty?"

Since he'd come out and asked directly, Chang Geng had no choice but to present the decree first. The appearance of this killjoy of an imperial edict instantly spoiled the convivial mood as officers on both sides fell to their knees in a flurry of sound. Gu Yun was about to kneel as well to receive the decree when he was stopped by an outstretched hand. Chang Geng moved to pull him to his feet. "His Majesty told me Imperial Uncle can just listen to the order. There's no need to stand on ceremony."

Whether intentional or not, Chang Geng lowered his voice slightly when he said those words: "Imperial Uncle."

Thanks to Li Feng saying *Imperial Uncle* this and *Imperial Uncle* that ad nauseam, Gu Yun had come to reflexively develop a tension headache whenever he heard the phrase "Imperial Uncle." But hearing Chang Geng suddenly refer to him this way now, the title felt like a little hook tugging at his heart even as the words *the rules of etiquette must be upheld* formed a disorderly line on his tongue.

It was the twelfth month, late winter in the bitterly cold northwest, yet Gu Yun was covered in hot sweat beneath his chilly armor... He listened to the decree with only half his attention. Fortunately, any serious business raised by Li Feng would ordinarily be noted in the official reply to his regular military report; his imperial decrees were primarily composed of flowery nonsense about rewarding the troops for their service. It mattered little whether he listened or not.

Gu Yun failed to return to his senses even when the surrounding officers thanked their sovereign for his grace and rose once again to their feet. It was usual in these sorts of circumstances for the most highly ranked officer to step forward and offer some heroic words about rendering their service to the nation to repay the emperor's kindness; at that point, the decree was considered to have been properly passed on. But with Gu Yun so eerily silent, everyone else followed suit. The top brass of the Black Iron Battalion exchanged glances—what issue had the Marquis of Anding taken with this rather inconsequential decree?

Only when the hush fell around him did Gu Yun realize he'd made a bit of a fool of himself. He raised his head nonchalantly. With an air of unfathomable profundity and without the slightest change in expression, he said, "Oh. His Majesty exaggerates. These are all things we ought to do. Old He, have someone organize a welcome dinner for His Highness Prince Yan... No need for anything fancy, we're all friends here. Let's pick up the pace and finish cataloging all the provisions we've received before sundown—what are you all staring at me for? Get going; don't you have jobs to do?"

Overcome by a renewed sense of veneration for the unflappable Marshal Gu, the officers marched out in single file.

Members of the Black Iron Battalion were highly efficient as a rule. Everyone left in the blink of an eye, and the commander's tent, which had until now been bursting with noise, immediately quieted. Gu Yun sighed softly in relief. Chang Geng's eyes had been glued to his body all this time, so sticky that it took every ounce of Gu Yun's strength to turn his head away.

Perhaps it was due to the voluminous fox fur cloak draped over his body, but Chang Geng looked thinner than before.

The things Gu Yun had heard from Fire Dragon and Miss Chen on the road to the northwest flashed through his mind one after another. For the first time in Gu Yun's life, he had no idea where to start. A thousand varied emotions filled his heart, but he had no clue what kind of expression he ought to adopt, which caused his face to appear calm and aloof. He beckoned Chang Geng closer, as if he'd left home just the day before. "Come here, let me get a look at you."

For a moment, Chang Geng couldn't figure out what Gu Yun was after. He retracted his shameless stare, suddenly feeling apprehensive.

In the past half year, he'd raised quite a stir in the capital. He had no idea what of his exploits had made their way to the border, let alone what Gu Yun would think if he knew. When Gu Yun had last left the capital, their relationship had been so uncertain, and so much time had passed since then—the situation between them was like a jar of wine hastily buried before all the ingredients had been added...

Chang Geng took a halting handful of steps to stand before Gu Yun, his heart spinning like a carousel lantern, his feelings beyond description. It was at this moment that Gu Yun reached out and pulled him into his arms.

With black iron covering him seamlessly from his shoulders to the second knuckle, Gu Yun's embrace was harsh and unyielding. The unprotected tips of his fingers, so recently exposed to the bitter winds of Jiayu Pass, were as cold as his armor, their chill penetrating Prince Yan's fox fur cloak in an instant. Chang Geng shuddered violently, bewildered by this unexpected show of favor.

Gu Yun closed his eyes and slowly tightened his embrace. The fluffy fur collar of Chang Geng's cloak swept past the marshal's face, closely followed by the scent of pacifying fragrance. Perhaps it was his imagination that the smell seemed even stronger than before. Wu'ergu was like a steel file; after twenty years, it had worn away at flesh and bone, carving out a person like this. Gu Yun's heart ached unbearably, but he dared not say a word.

An uncompromising stubbornness lay deep within Chang Geng's bones. He had been this way since childhood—he'd much rather spend his every night lying awake, waiting for the sunrise, than reveal any weakness to Gu Yun. When a person hid their wounds so none could see, no one had the right to pry open their hands. To do such a thing wasn't caring for them, but rather stabbing them once more.

"Zixi." Chang Geng didn't know what had induced Gu Yun's sudden bout of madness. He said in a low voice, somewhat awkward, "If you keep holding me like this, I'll…"

Gu Yun barely managed to master his emotions. Swallowing down the acrid taste in his mouth, he raised an eyebrow and looked at Chang Geng, his face unreadable. "Hm?"

Chang Geng didn't dare say more.

The silver-tongued Prince Yan rarely found himself at such a loss. Gu Yun looked at him and smiled, then reached out and gathered Chang Geng's fox fur cloak tighter around his thin body. "Let's go, I'll give you a tour."

The two walked out of the commander's tent side by side. The wind beyond the pass was harsh as the blade of a halberd. The billowing flags were like a flock of great peng⁹ spreading their wings overhead, and cloudless skies stretched to the horizon. The military convoy that had escorted the supply train was so long and winding, it was impossible to see its end. Ever since war had broken out on the four borders, the nation had struggled to make ends meet in all respects. How long had it been since anyone saw such a flourishing scene?

Gu Yun stopped and watched for a while, sighing. *Such an awful mess—how much backbreaking work will it take to clean it up?*

---

9   A giant mythological bird that transforms from a kun, a giant mythological fish.

"This is all I could bring for now, but I'll keep thinking of other ways to get you more," Chang Geng said. "Since the Token of Mastery Law has been repealed, the Lingshu Institute will be founding several ancillary armor-making institutes this month. They're already working to recruit talented artificers from around the country. Those who make notable contributions toward the construction of new armor and engines will be offered a chance at admission to the Lingshu Institute, regardless of their family background. Master Fenghan has said in unequivocal terms that we have nothing to fear from the western navy's sea monster, and that given enough time, he can make one to match."

"Master Fenghan has spent his whole life struggling to put food on the table. Is he now so well-provided he can eat one bowl and toss a second out?" Gu Yun laughed. "Aside from being a scary-looking money pit, does that sea monster have any practical use? It's okay if we're poor. Even if I have nothing but light cavalry, sooner or later, I'll take those mannerless trespassers and kick them back where they came from. As for you..."

He wanted to say, *Don't push yourself too hard*, but when he turned, his armor-covered hand happened to bump into Chang Geng's palm. Chang Geng instinctively grabbed his painfully frozen fingers, the movement hidden by the wide sleeves of his court robes, warm with the heat of his body.

It wasn't that Chang Geng was incapable of keeping his cool—but Gu Yun's unexpected embrace just now was like an open flame, setting all the inconceivable expectations in his heart on fire in an instant. He looked squarely at Gu Yun and asked ambiguously, "What is it?"

For the second time that day, Gu Yun's words scattered, unsaid.

To an outsider, the two of them would have looked like they had lost their minds with how they silently stared at each other.

The moment stretched. Seeing Gu Yun frozen in place, Chang Geng's eyes gradually dimmed. *I really am deluding myself,* he thought in self-mockery.

Just as he was about to step away, under the cover of those broad sleeves, Gu Yun suddenly grasped his hand in return. His cold, chapped fingers were strong as steel armor and not hesitant in the least. Chang Geng's pupils abruptly contracted into tiny dots.

Gu Yun sighed softly. He knew in his heart that after taking such a step—a decision that was half impulse and half an inability to bear seeing Chang Geng hurt further—there would be no turning back. After being tortured by wu'ergu for so many years, there was no way Chang Geng could withstand it if he did. Besides, he really was being the worst kind of a bastard, vacillating as he had been. It wasn't that Gu Yun had never played along and whispered sweet nothings before—when he got drunk, he'd certainly been known to get carried away and make all sorts of reckless promises—but for all his years on this earth, he only now realized that a solemn pledge of undying love was far too heavy a thing to utter. In the end, when he spoke, all that remained was: "I want you to take good care of yourself. So long as the green hills remain, one needn't worry about firewood. So there's no need to exhaust yourself, racking your brain like this. You still have me."

Chang Geng was dumbstruck. Gu Yun's speech went in one ear and out the other, perfectly intact. He didn't register a single word.

He stared for so long that Gu Yun began to feel a little embarrassed. "Let's go. Those yokels are all waiting to revere Prince Yan's regal presence. What are you doing, standing around in a daze sipping the northwest wind?"

In the camps of the Black Iron Battalion, one would never find any fine grape wine, beautiful songstresses, or dancing girls. Drinking was strictly prohibited in wartime, and those who dared steal a sip were punished under martial law without exception. As for beauties, the sole individual who vaguely qualified was Miss Chen. But after disassembling Gu Yun's steel panels, she had accepted a post as a combat medic at a field hospital deeper within Jiayu Pass. She was up to her eyeballs in work, and no one had seen her for nearly half a month. As things stood, all they had left was the self-titled Flower of the Northwest. He didn't know how to dance, but at least they could look at him as much as they liked, free of charge.

Prince Yan's welcome dinner amounted to little more than the addition of a few extra dishes to the table and the company of all the officers who weren't presently in charge of laying out the defense—and even these last couldn't stay too late. The soldiers worked in shifts, and every second of rest was precious. No one dared relax even for the briefest moment, so the party dispersed before nightfall.

Only Gu Yun was left to settle Prince Yan, who was still rather dazed, down for the night.

"It's boring here, isn't it? There's nothing good to eat, nothing good to drink. Day in and day out, the greatest entertainment we have is watching a bunch of guys arm-wrestle or spar. The winner doesn't even get a prize." Gu Yun shook his head. "Back when you were a kid, weren't you angry with me because I refused to bring you here? Don't you feel silly now?"

Chang Geng hadn't drunk a drop of wine, yet he felt unsteady in his gait, like he was walking in a dream. "Why would I be bored?" he asked, sleep talking.

Gu Yun thought for a second, then pulled out the small, white jade flute from his lapels. "Why don't I play you a new song I learned from beyond the Great Wall?"

Chang Geng stared at the flute, his eyes unusually dark and serene. He felt as if he'd never awaken from this vision.

It was then that Shen Yi, who had just finished securing their perimeter, returned to the camp. He was still quite a distance away when he got the news that Prince Yan had personally come bearing supplies. Although Shen Yi still carried a heart full of complicated feelings, he was hurrying over to catch up with the young prince when his eagle eyes spotted Gu Yun pulling out his precious flute from a hundred meters away. As if he'd seen a terrifying enemy, Shen Yi promptly did an about-face and took off at a run.

Gu Yun had upgraded his instrument from a bamboo flute to a jade one and spent half a year practicing on the boring and bitterly cold border. Yet amazingly, his technique hadn't improved at all. On the other hand, his capacity to make people wet themselves was greater than ever before. The borderland folk song he played was so frightfully bad it could rupture one's liver and gallbladder. A short distance away, a warhorse waiting to be saddled grew so panicked it began to whinny in abject distress, as though surrounded by a pack of wolves. The Black Hawk scouts descending from the sky staggered a few steps but failed to stick their landing, falling to their knees in a heap as if begging for New Year's money.

Chang Geng finally found evidence to prove that he wasn't dreaming—this racket far exceeded the narrow limits of his imagination.

As the song came to a close, Gu Yun, who thought he had slyly made a great romantic gesture, asked, expectant, "Do you like it?"

After hesitating at length, Chang Geng said with utmost sincerity, "It certainly clears the mind and has the ability to, uhh...repel enemies."

Gu Yun raised his hand and knocked Chang Geng on the head with the flute, not the least embarrassed by his ghastly lack of skill.

"It's to wake you up. These next few days, are you sleeping with me, or shall I have someone set up an imperial prince's tent?"

Prince Yan had just managed to clear his head only to be smacked silly by this sudden flirtation. He froze in place, momentarily stunned.

Gu Yun watched as, right before his eyes, the red flush at the base of Chang Geng's ears spread up and across his face. He couldn't help but recall Chang Geng's awkwardness as he'd helped Gu Yun change his clothes back when he suffered a high fever. Then, Gu Yun had been exasperated, but now, he suddenly felt an itch in his heart. He thought to himself, *You took advantage of me back when I broke all my bones and it was all I could do to lie as motionless as a corpse. Did you really think this day wouldn't come?*

"Why aren't you answering me again?" Gu Yun asked.

"There's no need to trouble anyone..." Chang Geng struggled for half an age, then finally gritted his teeth and steeled his resolve. "It... it just so happens that I want to check your injury."

"Just my injury?" Gu Yun couldn't help teasing him.

Chang Geng could make no response.

73

OPENING BATTLE

G U YUN HAD ISSUES with both his lumbar and cervical vertebrae. Chang Geng didn't have to conduct a careful examination—after Gu Yun removed his armor and clothes, he could tell by touch alone.

He dispelled his fanciful thoughts and frowned. "Zixi, how long has it been since you took off your light pelt?"

"I've been wearing it since I got out of those steel panels..." Gu Yun paused, feeling that something was off about his words, then hastily added, "Ah, of course, I take it off when I bathe. I don't have any nasty hobbies like that bald donkey, Liao Ran."

Chang Geng shoved him flat on his stomach. "Don't move. I can't believe you still have the gall to mock others right now."

In their youth, these military men were terrifyingly impressive, busying themselves with the occupation of war. Those who were lucky enough to live to an advanced age, however, inevitably wound up with a body full of old injuries. Lumbar and cervical displacement were far from rare in such veterans.

Light pelts were convenient, but unlike heavy armor, which had internal support, these suits rested directly on the body. When Gu Yun was at full combat readiness, he wore it even when he slept. His muscles and bones would, over time, thus become deprived of adequate rest. Chang Geng needed only press down slightly to hear Gu Yun's abused body crack in protest.

"You don't feel it now because the muscles in your back can still support the weight, but what about when you get older?" With steady pressure, Chang Geng stroked along his scapulae with both hands and began to knead his stiff shoulders.

Gu Yun had been known to shoot Shen Yi nasty looks of displeasure whenever the man nagged like this, but as he listened to Chang Geng speak with lazy, half-closed eyes, he wasn't displeased at all. Everything in the army was kept as simple as possible; even the Marquis of Anding didn't have many special privileges. Inside the tent were only a cot and a lonely gas lamp, which hung by the head of the bed. The light it cast was dim, leaving the two submerged in shadow.

"Does it hurt?" Chang Geng asked.

Gu Yun shook his head. "Word of your supply delivery will most certainly have spread by now," he said slowly, his voice muted. "The allied armies of the Western Regions are a disorderly mob. They all have their own agendas and are running their own calculations on their little abacuses. The Far Westerners no longer have the means to provide them with steam-powered engines and steel armor unconditionally. In a few days' time, there will undoubtedly be those who betray their cause and secretly crawl over to surrender to us... *pfft*, wait, hold on—"

Gu Yun hadn't reacted at all when Chang Geng kneaded his shoulders, but the moment he slid his fingers down along his spine toward his ribs, Gu Yun tensed and began to laugh. "That tickles."

Chang Geng pressed down hard, digging his fingers into Gu Yun's flesh. "It tickles when I use this much force?" he asked, exasperated. "Are you sure you know the difference between pain and ticklishness?"

"Clearly your technique leaves much to be desired," Gu Yun groused. "Anyway, even if they surrender, we'd be fools to take it at face value. These bastards are too accustomed to backstabbing and double-dealing. If we don't beat them into submission, they'll rise up again and set fire to our backyard. I plan on sending out troops on New Year's Eve. Let's serve them a proper beating for New Year's Eve dinner first."

Chang Geng stilled Gu Yun with a hand against his shoulder, then pressed his other elbow along Gu Yun's spine, methodically working his way downward. "Are there enough Black Iron Battalion troops stationed in Jiayu Pass?"

"Even if there aren't..." Gu Yun's back arched. "Ha ha ha, don't, stop it, stop it—"

Chang Geng ignored him, pinning him down with his elbows and stroking along both sides of his spine twice over before pausing his ministrations.

Gu Yun laughed so hard he nearly cried and his stomach ached. When he finally caught his breath, he picked up where he left off: "Our...our strength should be sufficient. The first thing we'll do is respond to the nations who attempt to surrender and schedule peace talks. We'll say we'll hold our fire as long as they fuck off and stay far away from our border. When the time comes, we'll mount a raid and follow up with heavy armor in the second wave of attack. Raise a great big commotion to intimidate them, mainly. Every one we scare off is one we won't have to deal with. Then, we'll take care of the rest as they come."

Chang Geng flexed his fingers. "Aren't you worried people will say you're not a man of your word if you betray their trust?" he asked with a smile.

"They're a bunch of tributary vassal states rising in revolt," Gu Yun said carelessly. "Those petty rulers are like a son beating his father; I don't see them doing the honorable thing and expressing gratitude or loyalty—ah! You...you barefooted quack!"

Chang Geng bore down on an acupoint at his waist, and Gu Yun yelped, jolting up like a fish on a hook before crashing back onto the bed board with a *bang*.

Chang Geng had no choice but to ease off. "Try to bear with it. Have none of the medics in the camp given you a massage before?"

"Hm, let me think..."

"Stop thinking, we both know no one here has the ability to pin you down." Chang Geng, rising, set his knee next to Gu Yun on the bed and switched from using his fingers to his palms. "I'll try to be gentle."

This time, he used the heels of his hands, gradually increasing the pressure as he approached Gu Yun's acupoints. Gu Yun didn't cooperate at all. The harder Chang Geng pushed, the tighter the muscles along Gu Yun's lower back became, as if trying to match his assailant in strength. Beneath his inner robe, the clean lines of his waist were clearly visible. Chang Geng found himself briefly distracted by the thought that he could easily encircle Gu Yun's waist with his two hands. He hadn't had any impure thoughts before, but now, his heart quivered and began to race. His hands unconsciously lightened their pressure, tickling Gu Yun in a different way than before.

This time, Gu Yun didn't bolt up from the bed. Instead, some inexplicable feeling seemed to slide upward in the wake of Chang Geng's touch. Gu Yun reached back awkwardly and caught Chang Geng's hand. "That's enough."

Chang Geng started in surprise. All the blood in his body rushed toward his face, and his neck turned completely red.

Gu Yun coughed dryly. "What about you? When are you returning to the capital?"

Chang Geng looked at him steadily. "I want to leave after the sixteenth."

Gu Yun didn't know what to say; these words were way too sweet. After a moment spent lost in thought, Gu Yun said quietly, "It'd be better if you didn't stay so long."

Chang Geng looked away, rather abashed. "Mm, I was just saying. The war beacon tickets have provided the national treasury with some relief, but many things are still up in the air back in court. I still—"

"Your presence here is bad for morale," Gu Yun interrupted him with a serious expression. "For my morale."

Chang Geng stared back.

Gu Yun reached up and pulled him down. Balanced with one knee on the bed, Chang Geng was caught off guard and nearly fell onto Gu Yun's chest.

Gu Yun ran his fingers through Chang Geng's hair and gripped him by the back of the head. "I heard about your war beacon tickets," he said.

Chang Geng's pupils contracted slightly, but after a moment of silence, Gu Yun didn't say another word about how he had laid out a major case of corruption to eliminate his adversaries. Instead, he merely said, "When you get back home, check over the doorjambs and under the beds; see if you can scrounge up a few taels of silver to buy some of these tickets. There's no need for your imperial brother to return the money in the future so long as he rewards me with a farmstead to live on in my retirement."

Chang Geng's emotions rose and fell in rapid succession. He couldn't help but ask, "What do you want a farmstead for?"

"After we kick out the foreigners and the world is at peace, I'm going to give up this business of fighting," Gu Yun said in a low voice as he wound the ends of Chang Geng's hair lightly around his fingers. "It's something I decided a while back. When the time comes, I'll split the Black Iron Battalion into its three divisions. The Hawks, Carapaces, and Steeds will each hold one-third of the seal of command. That way, they can work together while providing checks on each other's power in the future... As for the Black Iron Tiger Tally, I'll return it to the Ministry of War. After the dust settles, not only Great Liang, but all the vassal states beyond our borders will have suffered heavy losses and welcomed a new generation of leaders. We can expect several decades of peace. Your imperial brother finds me an eyesore, so I won't serve him anymore either. Future generations can worry about the future; I'll find myself a beautiful spot with verdant hills and crystal water to...oh, to serve as a betrothal gift."

Chang Geng listened for a while without saying a word. Under the light of the gas lamp, his eyes seemed to shimmer with tears. "That's not what you said last time."

"Hm?"

"Last time, you told me not to be scared; that if I stayed with you, you'd treat me well... Is that promise still good?" Chang Geng asked.

Gu Yun denied it outright. "When have I ever said anything so shameful?"

Chang Geng gave no quarter as he turned over these old accounts: "Last year during the first month at the Marquis Estate. That's what you said when you were trying to peel off my clothes in your room."

Gu Yun was mortified. "That was... I..."

Chang Geng couldn't bear it any longer. He lowered his head and sealed Gu Yun's mouth with his own.

My dear marshal, he thought with a mix of sweetness and sorrow. *How many famous generals in all of history have been able to safely lay down their armor and retire? Your words are like a blade to my heart.*

Chang Geng had indeed gotten too excited. Unable to find release, he seemed both reserved and impatient, and in no time at all, the reins were stolen from him by Gu Yun, who had recovered his senses.

Gu Yun flipped over and pinned Chang Geng beneath himself. He suddenly thought—no wonder the ancients said a lover's embrace was where heroes go to die. What need had he for the Marquis Estate or a countryside imperial residence; an ordinary house with a small courtyard and a tiny bedroom would do, with just enough underfloor heating to warm some wine. Holding someone so thoughtful and caring in his arms, though in the depths of winter, he felt like his bones were melting. Never mind fighting a war; he didn't even want to attend court.

This time was different from the farewell kiss they shared at the capital ramparts; it lacked the intensity of desperation. Gu Yun felt as though a corner of his heart had collapsed, offering up the softest spot in his chest. *From now on, this person is mine.*

A long time later, when both their breaths were a bit unsteady, Gu Yun reached up and turned down the gas lamp. He caressed Chang Geng's face. "You must be exhausted from traveling all this way. Stop provoking me and get a good night's sleep, okay?"

Chang Geng caught his hand. Gu Yun pecked him on the cheek and said teasingly, "I'll have plenty of opportunities in the future to deal with you. So go on, sleep."

This wasn't quite what Chang Geng had expected—but he really was bone-tired. The wild fluctuations of his emotions had drained much of his energy, and he soon fell into a muddled sleep. Gu Yun, however, only closed his eyes in a brief nap. Shortly after the fourth night watch, he draped a robe over himself and made to rise. If not for Chang Geng's visit, he would have spent this time working around the clock.

Checking on the inventory status of the provisions sent from the capital, distributing soldiers' pay, checking the status of their violet gold stores, determining how to organize their forces and devising combat strategies...all of it had to be reviewed and approved by the commander in chief. His proposal to drive a wedge between their enemies was succinct enough, but the devil was in the details. The greater their preparation before battle, the greater their odds of victory. While it was true that Marshal Gu's flute was a lethal weapon capable of besieging an army of thousands, it wouldn't do to rely solely on the fear inspired by the Flower of the Northwest's face and the piercing strains of his unholy demon music.

Gu Yun lowered his head to study Chang Geng, who was still fast asleep. Just as Miss Chen said, his sleep wasn't peaceful at all. Other people dreamed of the things they thought about during the day, but in Chang Geng's case, no matter how happy he was before falling asleep, when he closed his eyes, all that awaited him were nightmares. His brow was twisted into a tight knot, his complexion deathly pale in the light of the moon glancing off the snow beyond the pass. He clenched his fingers unconsciously as he clung to the corner of Gu Yun's robe like it was his last hope.

Wu'ergu was a poison that exhausted the mind. It was possible to suppress it somewhat through sheer willpower while awake, but the poison's influence intensified during sleep. As someone who was always sleep-deprived, just thinking about it made Gu Yun's hair stand on end. He tried to tug the corner of his robe free, but it didn't budge. Instead, seemingly startled by the movement, Chang Geng tightened his grip further, and an indescribable viciousness flickered across his face.

They were in the middle of a military encampment; it wouldn't do for Gu Yun to go out to discuss military affairs with his subordinates with a cut sleeve. He sighed and reached for the sachet attached to Chang Geng's outer robe. Fetching a nearby cup, he poured some pacifying fragrance into the bottom, packed the powder down, and set it alight.

The rich scent filled the tent almost immediately. Gu Yun set the cup beside Chang Geng's pillow, then leaned down to press a gentle kiss to his forehead. Chang Geng stirred but didn't wake completely. In his groggy, half-asleep state, he seemed to recognize the man beside him. His brow smoothed as he loosened his grip at last.

Gu Yun cast one last worried glance back before leaving, cloaked in night.

The end of the year was a terribly bleak one. On New Year's Eve, only a few lonely pops of firecrackers could be heard from within the pass. Cold winds whipped across the sand and swept bits of red paper into the air like dancing butterflies, yet there were no mischievous children waving sparklers in the streets. In the capital, half of Kite's Flight Pavilion remained collapsed. The red-headed kites that high officials and noble personages once battled for with exorbitant sums of money had likewise disappeared.

A large number of refugees had crossed the Yangtze River north into the Jiangbei region. Some had frozen to death; others had starved. The bartering of children in exchange for food was rampant, and even instances of cannibalism were not unknown.

Local governments had initially been unwilling to open the public granaries. Chang Geng had personally taken up the post of imperial envoy in the latter part of the year and traveled the country visiting the nation's regional chambers of commerce to promote war beacon tickets. He brought with him a contingent of soldiers borrowed from old General Zhong and dealt with every crooked merchant and corrupt official who refused to distribute foodstuffs he encountered along the way. Thus he killed the chicken to warn the monkey with ruthless efficiency, making examples out of petty wrongdoers in a bid to deter their more powerful fellows. At last the refugees who flooded the streets finally were able to fill their bellies with some watered-down congee.

Within a year's time, whether it was well-to-do families or poverty-stricken peasants, assets that had been painstakingly accrued over the course of centuries, hoarded by generations of individuals who couldn't bear to spend on food nor clothing, were wiped out overnight. The vicissitudes of life were like violent gales and torrential rains. Just as people are born without worldly possessions, material gains cannot be kept in death. Even if one exhausted all their strength and ingenuity, in the end, they could only trust in that unfounded adage, "man proposes, heaven disposes."

The Black Iron Battalion encamped in Jiayu Pass prepared three cartloads of fireworks as usual, hoping to imbue the incoming eighth year of Longan with good fortune. On New Year's Eve, they hung lanterns from the gate towers. Even the sentries standing guard seemed uncharacteristically absent-minded.

A scout from the Western Regions dressed in a suit of dry and withered grass stole furtively up to Jiayu Pass. Through the barrel of his field scope, he spied on the fortress from dawn to dusk. All the Black Iron Battalion sentries standing guard at the gate seemed uncommonly lax. The number of guards who usually stood like javelins had been halved, and among those who were on duty, some tweaked their ears and scratched their cheeks while others peered this way and that. There were even some who kept glancing behind them, as if in anticipation... Soon, an explanation for their distraction arrived—as it turned out, a batch of letters from home was due to arrive from the nearest relay station that day. The Western Regions scout blinked behind the lens as messengers climbed up to the fortress gate. Many of the soldiers who received letters opened them on the spot.

The light cavalry units that ran the regular patrols appeared only once that day, perfunctorily circling the area before heading back to camp. Members of the Black Iron Battalion were still human, after all. They were not immune to the pull of those handful of special days in the year.

The allied armies of the Western Regions had been on tenterhooks since the arrival of the envoy and supplies from the capital of Great Liang. From the minute they got word, they had sent scouts to keep an eye on the soldiers encamped in Jiayu Pass at all hours. The scout on duty that day waited until fireworks exploded over the gate towers of Jiayu Pass and the Central Plains folks' firecrackers popped faintly in the distance. It seemed that the New Year would pass in peace; he finally, cautiously, determined that the Black Iron Battalion wouldn't be making any sudden moves and withdrew with his subordinates.

The moment they retreated, on a small hill a short distance away, a giant boulder began to shift, splitting down the middle and folding back on the sides—it was, in fact, a Black Hawk.

The Black Hawk's wings and back had been painted the same gray as the surrounding stone, and naturalistic patterns had even been carefully traced in fine brushstrokes. At a glance, he could easily pass for the real deal. The Black Hawk waited until the Western Regions scout was a considerable distance away before launching straight up into the air on soundless wings. A thin wisp of white steam sliced through the night sky like a blade, evaporating in an instant.

That evening, under the glow of the brilliant fireworks, the Black Iron Battalion troops stationed at Jiayu Pass split into three different groups and melted into the darkness.

The lanterns hanging above the fortress swung in the night. They seemed to brim with vibrant prosperity—yet the long shadows they cast on the ancient fortress walls bespoke an indescribable haughtiness and desolation.

With a mountain of work awaiting him in the capital, Chang Geng had time for only a brief reunion with Gu Yun. He had no choice but to start his journey back before the end of the year, and by the time New Year's Eve rolled around, he had just reached the field hospital within the pass. Chen Qingxu, who had long received news of his plans, was waiting for him at the entrance of the hospital, a wooden bird in hand.

It had been half a year since last they met, but the two weren't at all awkward with each other. It was as if Chen Qingxu had never objected to Chang Geng's entrustment with the Linyuan tablet, and Chang Geng had never secretly swapped out her letter. The tablet had already been bestowed. Whatever reservations she might have about her fellow members' decision, as things stood, she was bound to obey all orders given through the tablet.

"Please don't go in any further, Your Highness," said one of his personal guards quietly. "There aren't many here who still have all their limbs. The sight may be upsetting."

"If just looking at them is upsetting to you, how do you think those who are missing arms and legs feel?" Chang Geng shot the guard a look, and the man flushed in embarrassment. "I'm here to wish my brothers a happy New Year." Chang Geng turned back to Chen Qingxu. "I'm distributing rewards and compensation from the imperial court, too, as a New Year's gift...just while I wait."

"What are you waiting for?" Chen Qingxu asked.

"A report of victory," Chang Geng said firmly. "The first report of victory. I'll bring it back to the capital and discuss with the Grand Council our next steps in dividing and conquering the nations of the Western Regions."

74

FIRST VICTORY

CHEN QINGXU EXAMINED Chang Geng's face. "I've heard Your Highness has been traveling nonstop. First, you went down south to the Jiangbei region to clean up the crooked merchants working along the banks of the inland canal. Then, you returned to the capital to manage the Ministry of Revenue and the Lingshu Institute, before wasting no time rushing to the northwest days before the end of the year. You've been constantly on the move without a moment's rest, but from your complexion, you seem to be quite well."

It was odd. When Chen Qingxu had left the capital, the wu'ergu in Chang Geng's body had progressed nearly to the point of no return. She'd assumed that after another half year of toil, it would be impossible to guess how far he'd deteriorated. When she received his Linyuan Pavilion wooden bird, Chen Qingxu had felt somewhat apprehensive, fearing that, when they met, she would find that ominous flicker of red in his eyes.

But to her surprise, Chang Geng looked much better than expected. It appeared Prince Yan had been restored to his usual state, at peace even if the sky should fall. He seemed much the same as he was during the years he roamed far and wide with old General Zhong—virtuous and upright. At the same time, there was something different about him. He didn't seem as markedly disinterested as before, nor did he seem quite so otherworldly.

"It was nothing so serious; a handful of errands," Chang Geng said, unconcerned. "People always say getting started is the hardest part, but actually, I think that's not necessarily the case. The hardest part is accepting one's circumstances. Just look at the imperial court: we've reached such dire straits; no matter how badly I do my job, the most we'll suffer is a second siege at the hands of the foreigners. It can't get any worse than that. The prospect of becoming a vanquished nation is difficult to accept at first, but it gets easier the second time around. The officials in court have grown accustomed to the idea, so they won't blame me overmuch."

"I can see from Your Highness's way of thinking that the apple doesn't fall far from the tree; you've inherited some of the marquis's central teachings." Chen Qingxu aimed a veiled jab at the ever-irreverent Gu Yun; yet after careful consideration, she felt that Chang Geng's words weren't entirely without merit. "Indeed, there are times when accepting that one's country has passed its peak and begun to decline is more difficult than the work of rebuilding the nation."

"Well, that will have nothing to do with me," Chang Geng responded with a rather laissez-faire attitude. "Zixi's had a weak constitution since childhood and needs to recuperate as soon as possible. If not for the war, he'd only be able to lead the Black Iron Battalion for a few more years anyway. If he leaves, I go with him."

Chen Qingxu was speechless. It took her quite a while to realize whom this "Zixi" was that Chang Geng was referring to. When she did, her entire being descended into chaos. It turned out the emotion overlaying the dust of long travel on Prince Yan's face wasn't the glow of good health, but the springtime flush of romance!

For a moment, Miss Chen had no idea what to say. If such unimaginable feelings could grow to maturity and blossom, then why was it that no one dared pursue a grown woman like herself when she was decently good-looking and constantly surrounded by men? Was it because her naturally cold demeanor was too strong a deterrent? Or was it because, although the upper beam that was Marshal Gu was bent, the lower beams that were his subordinates remained as straight as ever—an awe-inspiring consequence of the strict discipline with which he governed his troops?

But though Chang Geng's offhand remark induced an unspeakable wave of sour feeling in Miss Chen, it also set her mind at ease.

The northwest was far beyond the control of the emperor; even so, she had heard some news of Prince Yan's political maneuvers in the imperial court. Chen Qingxu greatly appreciated his abilities, yet at the same time, she couldn't help but worry that this man would one day become ensnared by the pursuit of power. It wasn't that she mistrusted Chang Geng's moral character...but the wu'ergu remained a lingering black cloud that couldn't be dispelled. For three or five years, he might be able to stick to his principles, but what about eight, or ten? Would power mixed with poison hasten the erosion of his mind? And if it did, with the Linyuan tablet in hand and immeasurable power at his disposal, who could stop him? So it wasn't until she heard these words that she relaxed—no matter what, so long as the Marquis of Anding was safe and sound, there would always be one person who could stop Chang Geng and pull him back.

Chen Qingxu felt a surge of relief. Thank goodness her vote hadn't affected the passing of the Linyuan tablet into Chang Geng's hands. If not for that, the nation of Great Liang likely wouldn't have been able to catch its breath in a mere half-year's time.

That slow breath had gathered momentum, and now, on New Year's Eve, it had finally amassed strength enough to topple mountains and swallow rivers.

That night, the Black Iron Battalion split its forces in three and launched a surprise attack on the encampment of the allied armies of the Western Regions.

The allied forces had been in a stalemate with the troops in Jiayu Pass for a long time. It had also been ages since they last received supplies from the Far Westerners. They lacked technical expertise, so when their armor and war chariots broke down, they had no idea how to fix them. Their allies were, to a one, profoundly incompetent idiots. None of them could be relied upon at all, and many individual nations had already begun to harbor thoughts of surrender.

That day, after receiving a scout's report stating that there was no movement on the part of the Black Iron Battalion, the allied armies of the sixteen nations sighed in collective relief. Patrol guards wandered idly to and fro, while the ill-prepared commanding officers of each nation focused their attention on squabbling with each other. The entire encampment was covered in a thick blanket of darkness.

When the black crows came, it was like a bolt out of a clear sky. Many soldiers barely had time to pull on their pants before they met the attack in a chaotic flurry. They were blown away by the menacing Black Iron Battalion like a pile of fallen leaves.

One of the smaller kingdoms, encamped further away, saw that the situation was unsalvageable. After quickly weighing their nation's meager power against that of the Black Iron Battalion, the king and commander in chief made a prompt decision and were the first to beat a hasty retreat with their troops in tow.

Their escape acted as a signal, and pandemonium erupted among the allied forces. Just as things were about to get truly out of hand, the Black Iron Battalion dropped a stack of copied letters from the sky to scatter across the field like paper money. In the past weeks, several Western Regions heads of state had reached out to Gu Yun in secret, penning personal missives full of indistinct hemming and hawing. Now, the Marquis of Anding did an about-face and turned his back on these associates by sending copies raining down from the heavens. Paired with the first group of deserters who had hightailed it out of there, the whole made for quite the showstopping spectacle.

But before any of the tiny, double-crossing nations of the Western Regions could turn to each other in flustered embarrassment and re-swear their loyalties, the booming sound of a Great Liang copper squall reverberated across the sky.

In a resounding voice, an eloquent Black Hawk called out—first in the standard language of Great Liang's officials and then once again in the common tongue of the Western Regions—the names of each little nation that had turned traitor. He then brazenly declared: "Since you have already acknowledged your allegiance to Great Liang, please lay down your weapons and step aside. Blades have no eyes; the Black Iron Battalion can't be faulted if we inadvertently wound our allies!"

The allied armies of the Western Regions promptly burst into an uproar. Who could stop and carefully verify the authenticity of those letters at a time like this? Most would have time for merely a brief skim from start to finish, and, upon taking in the nauseatingly cordial appellations and humble posturing splashed across the page, would take the correspondence as definitive proof of their allies' betrayal. Facing iniquitous turncoats within and powerful enemies without, every nation's military force fell into disarray. No matter where they turned, everyone looked like a villain. They clashed in a disorderly battle, unable to distinguish friend from foe.

It was the first day of the eighth year of Longan. The clock had struck midnight, and the people of Great Liang said goodbye to the old and ushered in the new.

With the return of its commander in chief, the hibernating Black Iron Battalion, having previously retreated in defense, finally bared the fangs it had concealed for over half a year. It pointed its iron sword west, and with a roar, cut through the allied armies of the Western Regions like a kitchen knife through vegetables.

The allied forces suffered a massive defeat and fled in all directions. In a single night, they witnessed the true strength of that Black Iron Battalion that had once decimated the eighteen tribes with a mere thirty armored cavalry.

On the second day of the new year, the scattered remnants of the Western Regions' forces fought and retreated in turn, and the Black Hawks captured the leader of the head of the sixteen-nation coalition, the king of Qiuci.

At the same time, the reports of victory reached the field hospital within the pass. This was the first meaningful victory Great Liang had claimed since losing half the country to enemy hands. The entire field hospital erupted with excitement. The wounded soldiers with amputated limbs, Prince Yan's stoic personal guard—all of them sobbed disconsolately into each other's shoulders as if they were close confidantes.

Chang Geng heaved a long sigh of relief. He began to instruct his servants to prepare immediately for their return to the capital, but despite calling several times, no one paid him any mind. He shook his head helplessly and fished out a handkerchief, which he handed to the silently weeping Chen Qingxu.

They had all waited too long for this day. The country was like a great mansion on the verge of collapse, buffeted by winds and rain. Yet as long as the stone pillar that was the might of the Black Iron Battalion remained intact, there would inevitably come a day when the ruins of the nation would be put back to rights.

On the fourth day of the new year, the allied forces of the Western Regions retreated to the entrance of the Silk Road. Their whereabouts were leaked by captive Chinese slaves among them, which allowed Loulan to set an ambush. When the allied armies of the Western Regions had invaded Great Liang months ago, enemy forces had occupied Loulan, executed the nation's king, and forced the young drunkard of a crown prince into exile. Now that the people of Loulan were finally presented the opportunity to exact vengeance, they killed till their eyes turned scarlet with bloodlust.

The allied forces once again suffered heavy casualties and were soundly defeated.

On the Festival of Breaking Fifths,[10] the Black Iron Battalion sliced through their opposition to recover twenty-seven frontier passes along the Silk Road, then dispatched troops to occupy the allied nations' former encampment, where they took prisoner every Far Western foreigner who had yet to evacuate.

Shen Yi burst into the commander's tent. "Sir, those bastards from the Western Regions have shrunk back into their shells. We've got a letter requesting that we open peace talks. They're scared they won't be able to explain themselves to their foreign backers and are

---

10 The fifth day of the Lunar New Year, after which the New Year taboos may be broken.

offering a prisoner exchange: their foreigners for the Great Liang citizens they've captured. What do you think—"

"Do it!" Gu Yun didn't hesitate for a second.

His decision raised an immediate storm of protest inside the commander's tent. The words "Marshal, please reconsider" rose and fell in rapid succession.

Shen Yi, too, was taken aback. "Sir, we've yet to submit our battle-field report to court. The prisoners we captured include important foreign dignitaries. Sending them back without court approval... would it not be inappropriate?"

"If not for the Black Iron Battalion's retreat back then," Gu Yun shot back, "these citizens would still be within the borders of their nation. Even if they'd been displaced by the war, they would have still been able to line up somewhere in their homeland and receive a bowl of congee. They wouldn't have been taken captive for no good reason, to be humiliated and treated like animals... I'm not blaming any of you. After all, at the time, it was Prince...it was I who gave the order. It is solely thanks to the contributions of our own citizens, who were subjected to such degradation, that the Black Iron Battalion was preserved long enough to achieve the victories of today. We would be remiss in our duty if we mistreated these heroes of the nation."

At these words, silence descended within the tent. No one raised any more objections. However, everyone soon discovered that Gu Yun hadn't had any intention of sending these prisoners of war back without court approval to begin with.

The two sides met to exchange their respective captives at the agreed upon time and place. But as the allied armies of the Western Regions turned to leave in disgrace, a light-pelt-armored Black Steed stealthily whipped out a headless wooden arrow and lightly poked at the chest of the man next to him. A hidden bag of chicken blood—prepared well in advance—burst at the impact. From a distance, the torrent of crimson was quite convincing.

The "struck" man was highly dedicated to his role. He swayed dramatically back and forth, then, satisfied with the quality of his performance, entered the final act: playing dead.

Gu Yun turned to the gobsmacked enemy troops. "These bastards are worse than dogs and pigs, addicted to treachery. They dare use this prisoner's exchange as a pretext to mount a sneak attack on our troops." He ordered ruthlessly, "Seize them at once!"

The light cavalry at the vanguard promptly scattered, and the several dozen heavy armor units hidden behind them stepped forward. Gu Yun had barely finished speaking when their cannons opened fire.

During the Western Regions' rebellion in his youth, Gu Yun had yet been unfledged; he wasn't nearly so shameless. Later on, when the Silk Road opened and all parties were on friendly terms, the Marquis of Order displayed the elegant bearing befitting a representative of a great sovereign power; he'd kept his subordinates in check and gracefully adhered to the five Confucian values of benevolence, righteousness, propriety, wisdom, and sincerity in his treatment of the foreigners.

No one would have suspected that he was capable of lying through his teeth and setting right and wrong on their heads before their very eyes.

The allied armies of the Western Regions who had come for the prisoner exchange as well as the foreign captives still in the hands of the Black Iron Battalion were flabbergasted. But before they could so much as raise their own weapons, Black Hawks screeched down from the heavens and cut off their retreat. An arrow sliced across the sky and brought down the enemy signal flare that had yet to reach the apex of its flight, and the Black Iron Battalion had the whole place cleaned up in short order.

Only then did Gu Yun turn to Shen Yi and say, "I used these prisoners of war as bait to catch a big fish—this can't be considered acting without court approval, right?"

Shen Yi thought it wise to remain silent.

Most of the Central Plains captives taken by the allied armies of the Western Regions were merchants who had traveled thousands of kilometers to do what business they could here. They had misjudged the situation and remained rather than leave with the God of Wealth, Du Wanquan, and had thus fallen into their present predicament. Among them were small businessmen as well as others who followed the merchant caravans scraping out a living. Men and women, young and old—all together there were no more than thirty of them left. The rest had died at the hands of the Western Regions soldiers.

That night, escorted by the Black Iron Battalion and leaning against each other for support, these Central Plains captives who had suffered all manner of degradation stepped back into the safety of their own nation's borders. It was impossible to say who started it, but about thirty meters from the entrance to the Silk Road, just before crossing the boundary, the whole party fell to their knees and knocked their heads against the ground, weeping bitterly. The wails that echoed through the air were so mournful even the solitary swan goose passing overhead couldn't bear the sound.

Rather than hustling them along, Gu Yun waved his hand, ordering the military escort to stop and wait silently to the side.

Among these captives, there was one whose eyes were dry. He was a man about thirty years of age with a scholar's air of gentle refinement. A young man of sixteen or seventeen years followed at his heels as he made his way over to Gu Yun, stopping deferentially just beyond the circle of Gu Yun's personal guards.

One of the guards turned to whisper in Gu Yun's ear. "Sir, on our way here, I heard it was this scholar who organized the captives and devised a plan to leak the whereabouts of those Western Regions thugs, enabling the prince of Loulan to mount his sneak attack."

Gu Yun nodded minutely and watched as the scholar and his young companion knelt down. Though Gu Yun had behaved like an unscrupulous hooligan mere hours ago, he didn't dare treat these people with anything less than respect. He hastily ordered his men to help them up. "Xiansheng, there's no need for this. Please get up—what's your name?"

The scholar refused to rise. "Marshal, this lowly citizen's name is Bai Chu," he said in a low voice. "I am but a poor scholar who failed the imperial examination on multiple occasions. My parents died early, and my family fell into poverty. Thus, I gave up my dream of entering civil service and came to the Silk Road last year with my younger brother, hoping to eke out a living writing and doing calculations. I never imagined we would encounter such a catastrophe. Though I lack for talent, I am nevertheless a student of the ancient sages. I understand that 'one must not dishonor one's forebears, must not allow others to insult one's person, and must not bring disgrace upon one's dignity and ideals'—these are the principles of a man of integrity.[11] Nevertheless, a slave to my circumstances, I fell into enemy hands. For the sake of survival, I allowed myself to be roundly humiliated and castrated by those foul foreigners..."

For a moment, Gu Yun didn't know what to say. Stepping forward, he approached the pair of brothers and said softly, "It was our fault for arriving too late."

---

11 Excerpt from 报任安书, "Letter to Ren'an," by Sima Qian.

"The only reason I've dragged out my feeble existence this long is to witness the recovery of our nation's lands with my own eyes," Bai Chu continued.

Gu Yun cupped his hands solemnly. "You have rendered outstanding service—I will most certainly be reporting this back to the imperial court."

Bai Chu chuckled softly. "I daren't claim credit with this broken body of mine. But this lowly citizen does have one presumptuous favor to ask."

"Please speak," Gu Yun said.

"I have a younger brother named Bai Zheng. He's just sixteen years old, yet to come of age. Though he is untaught in most of the six arts,[12] he is not unskilled in horseback riding and archery. This lowly citizen of course knows that the Black Iron Battalion is a lethal weapon of the nation, and that every one of its members is an elite soldier of the highest caliber. Under ordinary circumstances, it would be unimaginable for someone of my brother's aptitude to join their ranks. However, I beg the marshal to please let him, at the least, run errands and attend to your needs as a servant. Please allow him to be at your beck and call and train for a few years so that in the future, our parents looking down from the heavens can see him grow into an upstanding and dauntless young man."

Gu Yun glanced at the youth, taking in his stocky build. The boy didn't interrupt but merely wiped at the tears spilling from his red-rimmed eyes. Gu Yun sighed to himself. "Xiansheng," he said, "please rise. These are all trivial matters..."

Bai Chu pressed down on his brother's head as he stepped forward and forced the boy to kneel before Gu Yun. "Kowtow to the marshal."

---

12 The basis of education in ancient China, the six arts comprised the disciplines of rites, music, archery, chariotry, calligraphy, and mathematics.

This youth seemed to be a rather honest child. His elder brother told him to kowtow, so he threw himself wholeheartedly into the endeavor, his motions not at all perfunctory. The stone bricks beneath his feet rattled with the impact of his forehead knocking against the ground. What could Gu Yun do but lean down and help him up?

The instant his hand brushed the young boy's shoulders, he jerked back in surprise. The child's shoulders were shaking uncontrollably—not out of excitement, but fear.

Several thoughts flashed through Gu Yun's mind at once—

The Western Regions nations had suffered an attack and heavy casualties because their location on the Silk Road had been leaked by the captives. How could they not be furious?

And when it came down to who would bear the brunt of their anger, surely the allied forces would turn their blades on the most suspicious Central Plains captives first. Perhaps they would pass over the others, but regardless of whether the leader of the captives had incited this act of rebellion or not, he would be implicated. The enemy wouldn't care if the man was innocent, and they certainly wouldn't need any concrete evidence. So long as they had the faintest of doubts, he would not be spared.

For this prisoners' exchange with Great Liang, these nations needed only hand over some of their old, weak, and infirm captives. How could they possibly release someone like Bai Chu?

It was true that just now, he'd vaguely sensed something was off; but when Bai Chu gave his speech over the sorrowful wailing of so many dozens, Gu Yun was distracted by a surge of guilt. He didn't have the time to consider the matter in full!

Gu Yun immediately took a step back and raised his guard. "Bai Chu" unleashed a furious roar. His entire body swelled, and his hollowed cheeks turned round as cracks spread through every centimeter of his skin. A tattered human skin mask slid from his face.

"Marshal!"

A Black Carapace infantryman lunged forward without hesitation, grabbing Gu Yun and turning to shield him with the three layers of steel plating covering his back.

With a thunderous *boom*, Bai Chu exploded. Towering waves of fire swept out in all directions, and the body of the youth lying prostrate on the ground was blasted to smithereens. Ears ringing, Gu Yun's last sensation was a sharp stab of pain as his back collided with the ground. Darkness swallowed him.

75

LOVE LETTER

S HEN YI WAS BRINGING UP the rear as ordered when he heard the explosion; he looked back and nearly spat out his lungs in terror. His knee-jerk response was to charge over at once.

But General Shen had experienced the ebb and flow of life on the border for too long. He was no longer that impulsive young Lingshu scholar of years past. With the first sway of his majestic steed's head, Shen Yi snapped back to his senses. Tightening his grip on the reins, he pursed his lips and issued a lengthy whistle. "Black Steeds, hold your positions. Black Hawks, observe the enemy's movements and relay my orders..."

But before he could finish, another Black Hawk scout alighted before him. "Report for the marshal!"

"Hold it, the marshal is occupied right now." Shen Yi stopped the soldier. "What's happened? You can report to me first."

The Black Hawk scout responded immediately: "General Shen, after retreating back to their respective borders, the sixteen kingdoms of the Western Regions have reorganized their troops and gathered their last eighteen war chariots. They are advancing toward our encampment as we speak. I fear they intend to launch a counterattack..."

"What is their strength?" Shen Yi asked, voice low.

"Based on what I could see from the sky, excluding the war chariots, they march with a minimum thirty to forty thousand armored infantry and cavalry..."

"General Shen!" A member of Gu Yun's personal guard scrambled over. Shen Yi whipped around so fast he nearly pulled a muscle. His scalp prickled with fear—he couldn't imagine how they would defend the twenty-seven passes at the entrance of the Silk Road should something terrible have happened to Gu Yun.

Would they be forced to retreat yet again?

The guard sucked in a deep breath. "The marshal orders you to immediately execute the king of Qiuci in the stretch of no-man's-land between the two armies and mount his head on a flagpole. The Black Iron Battalion is to turn out in full force and face the enemy head-on. Leave nothing in reserve—this will be a fight to the death!"

Halfway through the speech, Shen Yi's heart, which had been caught in his throat, crashed back into his chest. He barely heard the rest of it and, for the first time in his career, had to ask the overwrought personal guard to repeat the message. Only then did he raise his voice for the rest of the troops: "The rebel...*cough*, the rebel army is an arrow at the end of its flight. Like an autumn cricket facing the frost, this is their dying struggle. Heed my orders and prepare for battle!"

In the instant Bai Chu blew himself up, the heavy-armor infantryman had protected Gu Yun with his own body. The Black Carapace warrior had been blasted to pieces on the spot. Gu Yun's consciousness flickered; caught in the force of the explosion, he coughed up a mouthful of blood and promptly went deaf in one ear.

When he awoke moments later, his first thought was that the enemy would use this opportunity to strike back—there was no time to worry about aught else. After launching two unsuccessful rebellions, the hatred the kingdoms of the Western Regions felt toward Great Liang would surely burn for several more generations. Now, after witnessing the Black Iron Battalion's ability to rapidly make up ground, they at last knew fear. This would very likely be their last stand.

When a terrified He Ronghui dragged Gu Yun from the wreckage, half his body was covered in blood—some his own, some belonging to the Black Carapace. In the blink of an eye, every hidden reserve of strength lying dormant in his body seemed to erupt, and countless thoughts swirled through his mind. Gu Yun grabbed He Ronghui by the elbow and relayed his orders: kill their prisoner and meet the enemy with everything they had. Then, as if having burnt through the last of his vital energy, he murmured haltingly, "Shen...Jiping is acting commander in chief on all military matters until further notice... Do not disclose what happened here..."

He Ronghui nearly burst into tears.

Gu Yun's ears were ringing; he could barely hear. "Suppress the news..." he mumbled. "Anyone who dares breathe a...a single word of what happened here today will be court-martialed... Summon Miss Chen from the field hospital..."

Gu Yun's chest seized with a sharp spasm of pain. He'd barely recovered from his previous injuries and now there was a fresh splash of color on top of the tapestry of old hurts. Darkness flickered at the edges of his vision, yet he continued to fret. "W-wait! Tell the messenger to make sure Prince Yan's carriage has left for the capital before sending for Miss Chen. Don't tell her what happened straight off, have her come in secret. We must..."

His voice failed, and the hand clutching at He Ronghui fell limply to the ground. Scared half to death, He Ronghui reached out with trembling fingers to check for breath; though feeble, it was still there. Only after this assurance did General He suck in several shallow gasps of air and bend to lift the unconscious Gu Yun.

Shen Yi exchanged a glance with the red-eyed He Ronghui across the distance, then whistled once again. "Execute the king of Qiuci!" he shouted furiously. "Follow me, brothers, to crush the rebels!"

The allied armies of the Western Regions knew they couldn't defeat the Black Iron Battalion, so they had cooked up this malicious scheme amid their frantic retreat, arranging for a Western Regions suicide bomber skilled in disguise to assassinate Gu Yun. When they saw the explosion, they thought their plot had succeeded. Morale soared. Yet somehow, just as they were anticipating seizing the entrance to the Silk Road in one fell swoop, before they had even reached any of the major strategic passes, they ran headlong into the full strength of the Black Iron Battalion.

That explosion seemed to have thoroughly enraged this dense army of ironclad war gods. The commander in chief of the Qiuci army had believed that, once he repelled the Black Iron Battalion, he would soon welcome back his royal liege. When he looked up, however, he was greeted by the sight of his king's head suspended on a flagpole, fluttering gently alongside a battle flag like some ugly knotted tassel. The Qiuci commander tumbled from his horse with a horrified cry.

The Black Iron general riding at the head of the army wore an iron visor. Hidden beneath the heavy black-iron armor, it was impossible to discern his identity. As if concerned that the enemy wouldn't see what was hanging from the flagpole, the general waved his hand amid the gale, prompting a light cavalryman to whip out his windslasher and slice through one of the ropes around the flagpole with a terrifying flourish. The severed head of the king of

Qiuci plummeted to the ground and rolled all the way to the bare stretch of dirt between the two armies. The Qiuci commander in chief stumbled over and clutched his king to his chest. After staring down at that severed head for a long while, he lifted his face to the sky and wailed, howling in mourning before both armies.

His voice was like the call of a bugle to the Black Iron Battalion; in the next moment, the lines of heavy armor began moving as one. Clad in light pelt and sitting astride his horse, the commander in chief of the Black Iron Battalion held his windslasher aloft, then swung it down in a swift arc. Twenty thousand mounted black crows, previously silent as the grave, advanced as one, the cries of battle muffled beneath the deafening rumble of footsteps and hoofbeats.

The Western Regions troops were stunned. Aside from Gu Yun, who else would dare take unilateral action and execute the king of Qiuci? Could it be that Gu Yun still lived? It seemed that, not only had they failed to kill their quarry, they had also managed to enrage the Black Iron Battalion.

By nightfall, the sea of sand was soaked in blood. Black-iron heavy armor faced off against the Western Regions' war chariots, driving their enemy ten kilometers beyond the Silk Road. The counterattack had failed; the allied armies of the Western Regions scattered once more. The fiendish Black Iron Battalion hounded the fleeing troops all the way back to their own borders, beheading nearly ten thousand enemy soldiers and slaughtering every member of the Qiuci nobility they could run down.

In the northwestern field hospital, Chen Qingxu had just finished seeing off Prince Yan's convoy, which was returning to the capital with a report of victory in hand. She had barely wiped the tears of joy from her cheeks when a pair of Black Hawks burst in. "Miss Chen, the marshal requests your presence on the front lines."

The next time Gu Yun woke, it was to someone trying to pry open his mouth and feed him medicine. He couldn't hear a thing. Gu Yun gasped shallowly and felt an intense wave of pain, as if his heart were on fire. It hurt so much tears nearly sprang to his eyes. In his foggy, half-awake state, he wondered, *Am I about to die?*

As soon as this thought popped into his head, Gu Yun gritted his teeth. *That won't do,* he thought. *Jialai Yinghuo yet lives, and Jiangnan remains in enemy hands. I would never be able to rest in peace.*

The strength of this conviction was like a shot of adrenaline to the heart, and Gu Yun came fully awake with a shudder. Shen Yi was struggling to wrench open his jaw to feed him medicine. The man was so worried, he had broken out in a cold sweat. When he suddenly felt Gu Yun unclench his teeth and swallow on his own, he was overjoyed. He called out to him at once, "Zixi! Zixi, open your eyes and look at me."

"He'll be fine so long as he's regained consciousness and can get down his medicine," Chen Qingxu hastily interjected. "Your hand is shaking, General Shen; you're choking him—give it here!"

Gu Yun had managed to survive the suicide bomber's attack only to suffer a near-death experience from this Shen bastard attempting to shove a bowl of medicinal soup down his throat. Heaven knew whence Gu Yun managed to muster the strength as he struggled to shove this walking, talking calamity off himself. The instant he moved, the entire commander's tent boiled over in a frenzy of activity. A whole gang of big, burly men promptly burst into howling tears and scrambled forward to offer their help.

Chen Qingxu couldn't stand it anymore. "That's enough!" she barked. "Get out! All of you!"

Gu Yun's sensitive nose detected a woman's sweet perfume—he knew Chen Qingxu had come. He turned his head slightly to avoid the bowl of medicine pressed against his mouth and opened his eyes with difficulty.

Chen Qingxu knew what worried him and hurriedly wrote into his palm, *Prince Yan has already returned to the capital. He doesn't know.*

Gu Yun's sickly pale mouth quirked slightly in what might've been read as a smile. He forced himself to down the medicine, and his mind grew slack once more.

In addition to reopening his old injuries, Gu Yun's lungs had been damaged in the explosion, and he ran a high fever that came and went for the entire night. Those words, *I would never be able to rest in peace*, propped him up like a giant boulder, and the next morning, to the amazement of all, he pushed himself up and tossed back his medicine like water. Then, he summoned all the commanding officers under his purview and listened, one by one, to their battlefield reports.

When the meeting concluded, Chen Qingxu brought over another bowl of medicine. Gu Yun accepted it and knocked back its contents in a single gulp. It was difficult to say whether it was because he had hit his head or because the deafening explosion had damaged his hearing further, but his ears, already reliant on medication, were still ringing after all this time.

After setting down the empty bowl, the first words out of Gu Yun's mouth were: "When did Prince Yan leave?"

Chen Qingxu was as succinct as ever. "The morning of the third."

Gu Yun breathed a sigh of relief. He was confident that he had the front lines in the Western Regions entirely under his control.

So long as Chang Geng was already gone, there was no way a word of what had transpired here would find its way back to the capital. With this, Gu Yun could finally lay both his public and private concerns to rest. He automatically categorized this incident as a false alarm and turned toward Chen Qingxu with a smile. "I've gotten a bit carried away recently," he said ruefully. "I committed a momentary oversight and made a spectacle of myself. I'm terribly sorry you've had to witness such an embarrassing scene."

Chen Qingxu didn't return his smile. She pulled a chair over and sat, assuming a position that indicated she intended to speak at length. "My lord, there's something I must tell you."

There were some doctors who were easily angered and frustrated: if a patient refused to cooperate, they would fly off the handle in rage. Then there were those doctors who regarded their patients like sheep let out to pasture: if you sought them out, they would treat you; if you refused to accept it, then they'd leave it at that. They wouldn't force you into anything. Whether you underwent this or that treatment, whether you lived or died, the choice was yours.

Chen Qingxu clearly belonged to the latter category. Whether Gu Yun marched to the front lines with his body held together with steel panels or whether he obstinately and repeatedly increased the dosage of his medication, she never said a word. She rarely regarded him with such solemnity.

"Please go ahead, Miss Chen," Gu Yun said.

After a moment's deliberation, Chen Qingxu finally began. "There is not a part of the human body that works in isolation. Our eyes and ears are both connected to our internal organs. The long-term effects of the marquis's encounter with poison as a child have lingered to this day. Furthermore, you have repeatedly suffered serious injury over the course of the current campaign, resulting in trauma to your five viscera. Now that the rebellion in the Western Regions has been quelled, it is my professional opinion that it would be best if the marshal took this opportunity to escort the war prisoners back to the capital and convalesce for some time. Otherwise..."

Gu Yun grasped her meaning at once. "Otherwise there will come a day when I will be beyond the help of any miracle cure, is that it?"

Chen Qingxu's expression remained unchanged as she nodded. "I'm sure the marquis is well aware of the state of his own body."

Gu Yun hummed in response, then lapsed into a long silence.

When a person was still in their twenties or thirties, it was difficult to feel things like "old age" and "illness" brought on by the passage of time. Young people rarely took their occasional bouts of indisposition seriously. Absent direct personal experience, others' well wishes for good health and similar exhortations became nothing more than unheeded advice, in one ear and out the other. After all, there were far too many concerns that took precedence over concern for their mortal flesh—fame and fortune, loyalty and righteousness, home and country, duty and responsibility...even love, hatred, sentiment, and regret.

Gu Yun was no exception.

He'd always imagined that he was destined to be buried in the borderlands, that he would become a sacrifice of the nation. He regarded himself as a bundle of fireworks—by the time he fizzled out, he would have successfully upheld the Gu family's reputation for devotion and sacrifice. But when it had truly come down to it, Chang Geng had appeared out of thin air and, with a slap of his hand, sent Gu Yun's plans spinning away from their original trajectory. Gu Yun couldn't help but indulge in wild fantasies and yearn for more—after wearing himself down for the sake of the nation, he wanted to give what remained of his hale and hearty years to Chang Geng.

If Gu Yun died early, Chang Geng would have to bear that northern barbarian woman's vicious curse alone. What would happen to him in the future? If there came a day when the wu'ergu flared up, and he really... Who would come look after him? Who would care for him?

Chen Qingxu wasn't skilled with words, so she had been worried her clumsy tongue wouldn't sway Gu Yun. She hadn't expected that, before she could even finish outlining her main points, Gu Yun would respond, "I understand. Thank you very much. I'll thank you for your trouble in the future as well, Miss Chen. An extended convalescence might not be possible for me right now, but so long as I don't have to enter the palace to meet with His Majesty and there are no more urgent crises on the border, I'll do all I can to refrain from using that medicine. How does that sound?"

Chen Qingxu was startled. Quite suddenly, she found that Gu Yun seemed to have changed.

In Gu Yun's hands, the third generation of the Black Iron Battalion had become a monolithic whole. When he gave an order, he demanded strict compliance, and his every word was regarded as law. Thus, because Gu Yun had commanded that the news of what transpired on the Silk Road be suppressed, the report the capital received was of the great victory on the northwestern border and nothing more.

Master Fenghan wept on the floor of the imperial court as he listened to the military dispatch. The country erupted in excitement. Even when Gu Yun later submitted a memorial begging forgiveness and describing his unauthorized execution of the king of Qiuci, it seemed a trifling matter. Besides, who didn't know of Gu Yun's beastliness; his vicious strong-arming on the battlefield was hardly news.

Li Feng himself felt that this indeed seemed entirely in line with his character.

Only Chang Geng frowned when the apology memorial arrived at the Grand Council. Though he couldn't explain why, he felt that there was something hidden between the lines. But before he could ponder it further, the Black Hawk special envoy who delivered the memorial pulled out a second envelope. "Your Highness, I have a personal letter to you from the marquis."

The last time Gu Yun wrote him a personal letter was back in the early years of his deployment to the Silk Road. He'd penned a grand total of two letters, one of which had been ghostwritten by Shen Yi.

Chang Geng's self-restraint was second to none; he calmly accepted the letter and expressed his thanks. The instant the special envoy was out the door, however, Chang Geng dismissed the pair of young eunuchs attending to him and opened the letter with desperate impatience. His hands were nimble to begin with, and he handled the letter with such care that, even after he unsealed it, the envelope remained so pristinely intact it could have been reused.

The first thing that fell out was a tiny sprig of pressed apricot blossoms.

It was as though Gu Yun had been possessed by the spirit of Shen Yi. He wrote extensively about every sort of thing, regardless of importance. His barbed tongue held nothing back as he maligned the allied armies of the Western Regions, describing the way the enemy troops pissed their pants in terror so vividly Chang Geng could practically see it. Had there been anyone else in the office of the Grand Council just then, they would have been terribly alarmed—when had anyone ever seen the mild-mannered Prince Yan sit down at his desk piled high with official documents and laugh with such abandon?

At the end of his letter, Gu Yun wrote:

A stand of apricot trees was growing at the entrance of the pass. Alas, over half of it was burned by the flames of war with no hope of recovery. I'd originally thought they were all dead, but one day on my way back, I saw that these withered trees had gained a new lease on life: tender flower buds had sprouted from the ashes, pitiful and lovely. There's no shortage of killjoys in the army; waxing poetic to soldiers about blooming flowers is to cast pearls before swine. Thus, I thought it would be better to seize the opportunity before me and picked this for you to enjoy...

Here, the Marquis of Anding's famous semi-cursive script, so masterful as to be worthy of being handed down as an heirloom, was interrupted by a blotted-out line. Chang Geng vaguely made out the words, *I hope that in early spring next year, I'll be able to pick some plum blossoms from the Marquis Estate*—but perhaps he felt it would be inauspicious to speak of the future. Thus, he had crossed it out and signed off with a self-assured flourish. Whether it was intentional or a coincidence, who could say, but next to his signature, there was the faint impression of a flowering branch cutting gracefully across the character *Gu*. Just looking at that flower-embossed character, Chang Geng could feel a subtle fragrance assaulting his senses. It was elegant beyond compare.

Chang Geng was overwhelmed by the ardor simmering beneath Gu Yun's restrained exterior.

However crude and thoughtless these aristocratic noble sons appeared ordinarily, they were all practiced in the art of sentimental verse and similar tricks; which of them didn't have a handful of precious wooing techniques up their sleeve? Chang Geng couldn't help but recall the roguish elegance Gu Yun had displayed that night he got dead drunk. But he wasn't the type to get jealous over unproven love affairs; rather, he found this side of Gu Yun rather cute.

Chang Geng sipped a cup of herbal tea and slowly read Gu Yun's personal letter from top to bottom three or four times, wishing to etch every word into his mind such that, even with his eyes closed, he could produce an exact replica with ink and paper. Only when he was satisfied did he place the letter and pressed flowers into that leather sachet he kept on his person at all times.

Then, picking up a brush, he wrote the word *Nobility* on a sheet of paper and briefly closed his eyes.

When invoked, the name "Prince Yan" represented the imperial family. With the nation in crisis, the interests of the nobles and the throne were in an unprecedented state of unanimity. So long as Chang Geng did not overstep the bounds of propriety, no blind fool would jump out to make life difficult for him. Already, many wealthy noble families had gone so far as to express wholehearted support for the war beacon tickets and even invest in the endeavor themselves...

But what came next?

The moment the nation began its recovery efforts on the borders, it would mean huge sums of military spending. Meanwhile, refugees continued to cross the Yangtze River in a steady stream. The entire populace within Great Liang's borders was in a state of heightened anxiety, and many were idle, without work or purpose. The small cushion of emergency funding raised by the war beacon tickets would be exhausted all too soon, and the imperial court couldn't subsist indefinitely on borrowed money. Bold reform—agricultural, tax, civil, commercial—was of critical importance, but to tamper with any of these spheres now would cause irreparable damage.

When the time came to act, every single noble official of the court would become his enemy.

Chang Geng's warm smile cooled as he struck out the word *Nobility* with a light flick of his weasel-hair brush. In the glow of the lamplight, the young prince's profile was terribly handsome, but also terribly ruthless.

Whether it was Master Fenghan, Ge Pangxiao, Miss Chen—even Gu Yun— all of them seemed to imagine that the person who lifted the rafters of the nation could gently lay down his burden and walk away with a sweep of his sleeves once construction was complete.

But how could that be?

In times of great peril, the pursuit of power had always been a life-or-death struggle on a road of no return.

76

AT ODDS

SOME DAYS LATER, news that the kingdoms of the Western Regions were suing for peace reached the capital. After submitting a memorial to the Longan Emperor, the Grand Council spent a full day urgently discussing the matter. In the end, they drafted a formal response to the Marquis of Anding in which they imparted two instructions: First, ensure that the rebels couldn't rise up again for three to five years. They couldn't afford to worry about their backyard catching fire while dealing with the Far Westerners out front. Second, they required violet gold, the more the better. Though the emergency within the national treasury was at least temporarily resolved, Great Liang's difficulties with respect to violet gold were ongoing. One of the reasons the northwest had been chosen as the starting point to break the siege on their borders was because it was the site of the Black Iron Battalion's current encampment. The other was to ameliorate their violet gold shortage as quickly as possible.

As for the rest of the details, big or small, they were all left to the discretion of the Marquis of Order.

Soon thereafter, Prince Yan entered the palace to give a brief report to Li Feng on the latest developments on the battlefield as well as the impact of the war beacon tickets.

Li Feng, counting on his fingers, was stunned by the effectiveness of these bonds. He couldn't help but ask, "How could there be so much money?"

"It's not surprising. The concerns of the court officials align with those of Your Majesty. Many of them are willing to offer up their own wealth to save the nation. At a crucial time like this, what sense is there in worrying about their own skin? Most of them spared no expense in supporting the war beacon tickets." Chang Geng began with a round of unhurried flattery before continuing. "Among the common people, there is a saying: the merchant stores leather in the summer, collects linen in the winter, hoards boats in a drought, and purchases carriages in a flood in preparation for times of scarcity.[13] Those who become wealthy merchants generally have more vision than peddlers who only chase after the petty profits right in front of their noses."

Li Feng considered a moment. "So then, in your opinion, what are these merchants looking to gain from us?"

"The merchant may be extremely wealthy," Chang Geng responded without hesitation, "but he still must brave the elements and endure hardship over the course of his life. In some ways, he's hardly better off than the farmer who eats by the grace of the heavens. One decree from the imperial court may cause the merchant to lose a vast family fortune. Or he might encounter violent marauders while traveling and lose both his property and his life. In this time of national crisis, a group of wealthy merchants from various chambers of commerce headed by the richest man in Jiangnan, Du Wanquan, have bravely stepped forward. On the one hand, they wish to serve their country; on the other, it may be that they hope to find a patron in Imperial Brother."

---

13   Lines from 国语, Discourses of the States, a collection of speeches attributed to rulers and ministers from the Spring and Autumn period.

Li Feng was long accustomed to the sounds of flattery and not so easily moved. He gazed impassively at Prince Yan, waiting for the meaning hidden in his words to reveal itself.

Chang Geng didn't keep him in suspense. He continued, striking while the iron was hot: "Now is when our need for money is greatest. The imperial court intends to circulate a second batch of war beacon tickets. In Brother's opinion, would it not be fitting to sweeten the deal for the leaders of these chambers of commerce, and thus encourage more people to support the nation by turning out their pockets?"

Li Feng made not a sound. He regarded Chang Geng with an odd look in his eyes.

"Sincerity" was a time-sensitive quality that came with an expiration date. Here was a prime example: during the capital siege, wracked with grief, indignation, and guilt, the Longan Emperor had wished dearly to knock his head against the late emperor's mausoleum and die. At the time, he had sincerely intended to pass the throne to Chang Geng.

Likewise, now that the situation had stabilized, the way Li Feng viewed Chang Geng had slowly shifted. This change in perspective was also wholly sincere.

Prince Yan—Li Min—was yet in his early twenties. In an ordinary household, he would still be considered a young lad just beginning to learn how to support the family. Yet in a short half-year, he had singlehandedly defused the crisis in Great Liang. Now, as Li Feng looked upon this young man with splendid future prospects, standing steady and self-possessed in the Warm Pavilion, he felt unspeakably...envious.

Consider the current occupant of the throne: in the few years since his ascension, he'd already had his hands full dealing with two successive rebellions. Then there was the absurdity of the "Northern

Camp Mutiny," and finally, even the foreigners had tried to get in on the action, invading the country and forcing countless citizens from their homes... The nation had hit rock bottom; yet the tide had begun to turn the moment Prince Yan took control of the Grand Council.

How was Li Feng to feel?

And how would historians view this period a hundred years hence? Li Feng had absolutely no desire to know.

Most importantly, Li Min—his fourth imperial brother—was still so very young.

A heavy gloom settled over Li Feng's heart, and his manner turned cold. "All lands under heaven are the territory of the sovereign," he said evenly. "As citizens of Great Liang, is it not their duty to sacrifice their family fortune for the sake of the country and its people? They want us to promise them certain benefits—if we do so, are we not condoning the buying and selling of official posts? Whatever next!"

Chang Geng was a skilled reader of body language. A brief meeting of eyes was enough for him to divine the reason for the emperor's sudden antipathy. Though he sneered inwardly, outwardly he adopted a heartfelt expression of astonishment and confusion. "Your Majesty—"

"Enough!" Li Feng interrupted impatiently. "Let the Ministries of Revenue and Rites determine an appropriate reward for these socially conscious civilian merchants. Anything is fine so long as they do not overstep the bounds of reason in honoring their service."

Chang Geng affected a sulky expression. After a long silence, and seemingly with great reluctance, he finally responded in the affirmative.

Li Feng glanced at him. Then, with pointed nonchalance, he said, "Wei Shu, the Minister of Personnel, is getting on in years. It rained last night, and when he rose early this morning to hurry to court, he took a fall in his home and broke his leg. We sent an imperial physician to assess him, and his condition does seem serious. The Wei family has already submitted his letter of retirement... With this, we fear the post for the Minister of Personnel will be left vacant. A-Min, as the head of the Grand Council, can you recommend any potential candidates to fill the position?"

This wasn't a particularly clever way of sounding him out—but just because it wasn't clever didn't mean it wasn't effective. Li Feng was a paranoid man. Whether Chang Geng exploited the situation to recommend his own people or answered the question flawlessly without missing a beat, neither scenario would please him. The former would prove Chang Geng too ambitious, while the latter would prove him too calculating.

Taken aback, Chang Geng blurted, "What? Minister Wei broke his leg?"

It seemed he really had no idea.

Only after uttering these words did Chang Geng seem to "regather his wits" and realize his response had nothing to do with Li Feng's question. He furrowed his brow in thought for several long seconds before sighing, seemingly overwhelmed with exhaustion. "This is... Please forgive me, Your Majesty. In recent days, this subject has been spending all his time fretting about money. I really haven't had time to consider anything else. Perhaps I haven't seen the memorial submitted by the Ministry of Personnel just yet. As for the minister, it's an extremely important position, and I can't seem to think of a good candidate off the top of my head..."

Li Feng suspected he was trying to dodge the question. "No matter, just speak your mind."

Chang Geng pressed a hand to his tightly knitted brow. After a pause, he said, "How about this: why not publicly evaluate the candidates in court? Perhaps there is someone capable among our number."

Li Feng was speechless.

This answer truly exceeded his expectations. Surprised at Prince Yan's bold and imaginative way of handling things, Li Feng was nearly taken in. "How would we evaluate them?" he asked without thinking.

"For example, you could inquire into their work history as an official—their achievements, their meritorious service over the years, so on and so forth. Everything's on record." Chang Geng paused shortly, and his tone shifted. "You could also add criteria such as whether this person has a sense of responsibility and righteousness... For instance, whether they've purchased any war beacon tickets... Speaking of which, I've just had a thought—in order to facilitate the smooth implementation of war beacon tickets, perhaps we could incorporate the number of war beacon tickets bought as an evaluation criterion for the imperial examination going forward. That wouldn't count as buying and selling official posts, would it?"

After all that talk, the little brat had managed to steer them back around to his original topic. Li Feng felt that if he were to crack Prince Yan's pretty little head open, he would find that the man's brain had transformed into a pile of silver ingots.

The Longan Emperor was torn between laughter and tears. "You... what nonsense!"

This time, Chang Geng didn't bother wheedling. Instead, he quietly begged forgiveness, an expression of undisguised worry on his face.

This brief yet odd exchange dispelled most of the gloomy misgivings in Li Feng's heart. It was quite evident that Prince Yan's mind wasn't on the Ministry of Personnel at all. *In any case,* Li Feng thought to himself, *he's certainly devoted to his work.*

The stormy clouds of Li Feng's mood dispersed. He waved a hand at Chang Geng. "Forget it. You can head back for now. Let us put further thought into the matter."

Chang Geng made a murmur of assent and said his farewells, sensing he'd passed this test. But as he was about to withdraw from the Warm Pavilion, Li Feng suddenly called him to a halt.

"A moment, A-Min. There's one more thing," Li Feng said pleasantly, as if having an amiable chat about everyday trifles. "You are no longer a child. It's not proper for you to be always alone like this; it's time you started a family."

Chang Geng's heart stumbled in his chest.

"Grand Secretary Fang's granddaughter is seventeen this year and is yet unbetrothed. From what I hear, the girl has a fine reputation and comes from a line of scholars, so she's certain to be well-educated. Her family background wouldn't bring disgrace upon you either. This young lady would make for an ideal match. When your sister-in-law heard about it, she was awfully eager to arrange things for you herself, so I thought I'd ask. If the girl is to your liking, then I'll go ahead and say yes on your behalf. What do you think?"

To say it was a good match was an understatement. Though Grand Secretary Fang Hong had been retired from service for many years, he had been the examination mentor for more than half the important officials in court. He had three sons, all of whom were highly accomplished. On top of that, his second son, Fang Qin, had just stepped up as the Minister of Revenue. The Fang family had been the unofficial leader of the richest and most powerful noble families since the Yuanhe era.

Yet Chang Geng's expression turned ugly in an instant.

Li Feng raised a slender brow. "What's wrong?"

Turning back to Li Feng, Chang Geng lifted the hem of his robes and knelt. His face was tightly drawn, yet he made not a sound.

Mystified, Li Feng asked again, "What are you doing?"

Chang Geng continued kneeling in silence.

However intimately Li Feng treated this brother of his, he was still the emperor. Seeing Chang Geng like this, his expression grew overcast once more. "If you don't like the girl, you can just say so. You're an imperial prince. Who could possibly force you into a marriage? Why act out like this?"

"This subject...is unwilling." Chang Geng kowtowed solemnly; even the tone of his voice sounded off. "The wife of one's elder brother must be respected like one's mother. I have betrayed Her Majesty's loving care. Please punish me for this transgression, Brother."

Li Feng frowned. "Why? Have you heard something bad about the girl? Or is there someone else in your heart? There are no outsiders here; there's no need to censor yourself. Go on, speak."

Chang Geng's eyes darted around the Warm Pavilion, but he refused to utter a sound. The rims of his eyes turned faintly red.

Of course Li Feng wasn't asking for the sake of finding Prince Yan a good match. In truth, he had absolutely no wish to see the Fang family form a marriage alliance with the fourth prince. The reason he'd so innocently raised this topic was because he wasn't done testing Chang Geng's loyalty. Still, he hadn't expected such an extreme reaction. His curiosity was piqued. He dismissed his attendants with a wave of his hand, instructing them to wait for his summons outside.

Once the two brothers were the only remaining souls in the Warm Pavilion, Li Feng asked, "Now, can you talk?"

Chang Geng bowed deeply once again. But in lieu of speaking, he began to slowly loosen the collar of his court robes.

Startled, Li Feng rose to his feet. "This..."

Prince Yan's young chest was covered with old scars. The most shocking was a burn scar beside his throat. It was very thin, like a lash mark left by a fiery stick.

"Please forgive my breach of etiquette before the throne, Brother," Chang Geng said quietly. There was a barely discernible tremor in his voice.

Once his initial alarm passed, Li Feng understood immediately. After a long minute of dumbstruck silence, he softened his tone and asked quietly, "Is this...that barbarian woman's doing?"

Chang Geng's face was pale. He reached up and gathered his loose robes back together. The fingers with which he had drawn his bow atop the capital ramparts and later shot the leader of the Dongying scoundrels dead were trembling violently. He lowered his lashes. "It is the coward's way to view the entire world with distrust on account of the actions of a single individual, but..."

He gritted his teeth, his voice faltering. When he continued, it was with difficulty: "Miss Fang is pure of heart and elegant in nature. She deserves to marry someone who can support her over the course of a lifetime. I possess a strange temperament and cannot abide close physical proximity with another. As for marriage...it would be best if Brother never brought this matter up again."

Li Feng was stunned. "This is preposterous. You're a prince of the first rank. How can you possibly remain unmarried?"

"Then perhaps it would be better if Your Majesty revoked my title of nobility and allowed me to wander the world in the company of mountain monks."

Li Feng was struck dumb. This Prince Yan seemed like a magnanimous, erudite, and sensible man, but in reality, he was given to tantrums. When he lost his temper, he wasn't violent like a howling storm, throwing cups and bowls. Rather, he uttered just one sentence: *Find someone else, I quit.*

This infuriated Li Feng to no end, but what could he do? After venting his imperial temper, he told Prince Yan to get the hell out. Prince Yan raised no objections and, indeed, got the hell out.

A palace attendant with discerning eyes trotted eagerly up to Chang Geng. "Your Highness, are you returning to the Grand Council?"

Prince Yan barely went home twice a month; he practically lived in the office of the Grand Council. Today, however, Chang Geng paused briefly and stared, blank-eyed, into the distance, seemingly lost in thought. The attendant dared not disturb him. He hovered on the sidelines, trying not to breathe too loudly.

"No," Chang Geng said in a low voice. "I'm going home."

No one—not even Gu Yun—had ever seen the scars on his body before. He'd always considered them evidence of an untouchable period of time in his life. Never had he expected that they would one day become instrumental in putting off dealing with Li Feng.

The horse-drawn carriage trundled over the wide flagstone roads that crisscrossed the capital. Chang Geng, who had been resting his eyes in meditation, blinked them back open.

One day, things would truly get out of hand.

One day, he would become even more ruthless than he was right now.

Yet he didn't feel upset at the prospect. This was the road he had chosen to walk, one step at a time. He had made his decision long ago; there was nothing to regret.

He made his way back to the cold and cheerless Marquis Estate. Without disturbing or consulting anyone, Chang Geng slipped into Gu Yun's clean and simple bedroom and lay down on the bed. When he closed his eyes, it seemed to him that the blankets still carried the subtle fragrance of medicine.

Over half a month later, after interminable rounds of wrangling and debate, the Longan Emperor finally rejected Prince Yan's absurd proposal to confer titles of nobility upon buyers of the first batch of war beacon tickets based on the size of their monetary investment. Instead, he promised the various chambers of commerce that, once the situation had stabilized, the national government would establish trade routes guarded by the military against bandits and thieves. When the time came, those who had purchased war beacon tickets could use them to directly qualify for membership with the participating chambers of commerce without any additional fees.

A month after that, another shocking development came in the form of a new decree. Implemented with a top-down approach, it declared war beacon tickets a significant component of civil servant examinations.

A heretofore unseen blade slowly bared itself.

The instant this decree was revealed, a shock wave reverberated throughout the nation.

Great Liang's imperial court did not treat its officials poorly, nor were officials' salaries particularly low. However, the exchange of favors on which the world of officialdom relied was extraordinarily costly. This had particularly been so during the reign of the late

Yuanhe Emperor. The nation's strength had reached an unprecedented zenith for several years thanks to the iron-blooded exploits of Emperor Wu, and extravagance had long become the rule rather than the exception. Now, by encouraging officials to buy war beacon tickets to pad their future prospects, was the court not flagrantly encouraging corruption and fraud?

The borderlands caught wind of the situation within a matter of days.

"Zixi!" Shen Yi tossed his reins to a nearby guard and barged directly into the commander's tent. He had opened his mouth to say more when he spotted the platinum-rimmed glass monocle perched on Gu Yun's nose. With this, he knew that Gu Yun had once again skipped his medicine. He swallowed his words back down. Who knew what had gotten into him, but recently, so long as Gu Yun wasn't in the presence of outsiders, he was reluctant to take his medicine. Perhaps he indeed intended to make peace with life as a blind and deaf man.

Shen Yi raised his hands.

"No need," Gu Yun said. "Go on and speak. It'll give me a chance to practice lip-reading."

Shen Yi sighed. "Did you hear about the latest government reforms?"

Gu Yun had been quite a proficient lip-reader when he was younger. But in recent years, between his reliance on medication and the consideration of those around him in using sign language, he had grown somewhat rusty. There was nothing for it but to slowly grow accustomed again. It took Gu Yun a while to figure out what Shen Yi was talking about. When he did, he slowly wrinkled his brow and nodded his head.

"What in the world is going on with Prince Yan? If things continue like this, won't people say he's creating corrupt officials and sycophantic ministers? Even if this solves our most urgent need, what will we do in the future? This may be fine and dandy for influential noble families, but won't the scholars from humble backgrounds tear him to pieces? Plus, as the sole head of the Grand Council, he's already like a tall tree battered by the wind, a magnet for criticism and envy. Seriously..." Shen Yi's anxiety overflowed into his speech. When he was like this, his lips moved as quickly as a chick pecking rice, flapping up and down. Gu Yun felt himself grow dizzy looking at him. He understood barely half of what Shen Yi said, but managed to catch the last bit about the tree.

Finally, Shen Yi said, "How will he clean up this mess in the future?"

Gu Yun was silent.

"Zixi, say something."

"We can't continue fighting like this," Gu Yun said out of nowhere.

Shen Yi heaved a sigh. He suspected that for all his rambling just now, Gu Yun hadn't "heard" a thing. *Practice lip-reading, my ass,* he thought. *More like I'm the one giving my lips a workout.*

He was about to switch back to signing when Gu Yun continued undeterred: "I've been a bit too impulsive. It served me right to have something blow up in my face. Thankfully, I survived the ordeal without any serious injuries. But lately, I've been doing a lot of thinking... Jialai Yinghuo is no spineless coward like these creatures of the Western Regions. It's very likely that we'll have to fight a few tough battles on that end. I'm afraid we don't have the strength or resources to defeat him in a decisive battle right now, so we must think in the long term."

Shen Yi started in surprise. "You plan to..."

"I've kept the imperial court hopping with all my requests," Gu Yun said softly. "It's high time I took a break."

77

NIGHTMARE

I N EARLY SUMMER of the eighth year of Longan, the kingdoms of the Western Regions gathered what remained of their troops, opened the gates of their capital cities, and submitted a joint letter of surrender to their suzerain begging forgiveness. For the second time in two decades, the countries of the Western Regions sat down with representatives of Great Liang at the entrance of the Silk Road and were forced to negotiate a peace.

Gu Yun had no interest in meeting with his defeated foes and sent Shen Yi to speak on his behalf.

Thus, Shen Yi came bearing Great Liang's harsh demands in hand. The conditions for surrender began with relieving the Western Regions nations of a huge sum of gold and silver. Then, so that they might more closely monitor their vassal states, the imperial court wished to establish military bases within each of the defeated nations. Henceforth, aside from their ally Loulan, Great Liang's vassal states were forbidden from stockpiling engines and armor—including light-pelt armor—and any military armaments they currently possessed were to be melted down and destroyed. Finally, Great Liang demanded these nations hand over, at minimum, seventy percent of the violet gold they excavated each year in tribute.

Even Shen Yi felt his teeth begin to ache as he read through these clauses; Great Liang was set on scraping the marrow out of the defeated three times over. As expected, the representatives of the allied nations promptly began wailing in despair.

The first round of peace talks broke down. The next day, Gu Yun led three hundred suits of heavy armor on a night raid against what remained of the Western Regions' encampment, which had already declared surrender. The ensuing artillery fire painted heaven and earth crimson. Thus did the Marquis of Order fulfill, through personal intervention, the most salient points of the second term demanded by Great Liang. The attack was an open declaration: it was fine if the Western Regions nations refused the remaining two terms; in that case, the Marquis of Anding would immediately lead his army to raze the captured cities.

Razing a city was antithetical to the natural order; under ordinary circumstances, it was something only barbarians would do. Such brutal acts were rarely perpetrated by Great Liang's military, and so initially, the people of the Western Regions were determined to resist. Once Gu Yun ordered the city gates blasted open, however, the representatives the allied armies had sent to the negotiation table finally lost their nerve.

Three days later, after several unsuccessful attempts to bargain, the Treaty of Loulan was signed into effect. Under the watchful eye of Gu Yun's heavy-armor infantry, each nation began by disposing of their armaments with as much speed as possible. Then, despite an endless stream of complaints, they scraped together the first batch of violet gold tribute extorted from them by Great Liang.

At the end of the fifth month, Gu Yun and Shen Yi secretly escorted this violet gold from the Western Regions back to the capital.

A heavy fall of rain had scrubbed clean the streets and alleys of the capital, and the scattered petals of pagoda tree blossoms littered the long thoroughfares. The winds stirred up by the new government reforms were howling, but the raindrops that fell were small. Miraculously, the storm everyone expected did not come.

First of all, the rich and powerful noble families weren't stupid. Even if they were dismayed by Prince Yan's increasingly creative methods of digging money out of their pockets, they knew that the ones who most abhorred the new policies were the poor Hanlin scholars who had risen through the imperial examination and had barely two silver coins to rub together. They saw no need to stick their necks out on behalf of others, so initially, they hunkered down in their homes, prepared to watch the drama unfold.

To their surprise, things took a strange turn. Aside from a handful of stubborn old Confucian scholars who stepped forward with long spiels about impropriety, the new policies barely made a ripple in court.

Chang Geng first submitted a memorial to win over the emperor. In it, he presented to Li Feng his long-term plans for the war beacon tickets and clearly delineated the entire process in fine detail, skillfully downplaying some aspects while exaggerating others. Finally, he painted a rosy picture for the emperor: over time, use of the war beacon tickets, which had been implemented first among the upper echelons of society, would trickle steadily downward. All the gold and silver in the nation would be eventually collected back into the national treasury. Private transactions among the common people would be conducted using tickets, with the value of each ticket determined by the imperial court. Never again would the leaders of the nation find themselves in a situation where private stockpiles of gold and silver gathered dust while the national treasury stood empty at a time of great crisis.

Li Feng had previously considered some of Prince Yan's ideas rather unorthodox and inappropriate. Now he realized that it wasn't so much that this person was inappropriate as that he was doing his level best to trample the word "propriety" completely into the ground. Just as there was once a founding emperor who cast colossi out of gold by gathering all the weapons in the land, here now was a Prince Yan who sought to collect all the riches of the nation.

Still, the idea was too tempting. Once Li Feng grasped the base concept of using a few paper notes to conduct business in place of gold and silver, despite some vague feelings of uneasiness, he couldn't resist the allure. After holding onto Chang Geng's memorial and mulling its contents over for three days, in the end, he swallowed this rosy picture without a backward glance. He ordered Chang Geng to oversee its execution, though he repeatedly warned him against taking drastic measures. When it came to the up-and-coming talents of the imperial court who hailed from humble backgrounds, the prince was to take particular care bringing them around to this new scheme.

Emperor Li Feng had no idea that, long before Prince Yan had submitted his memorial requesting government reform, the richest man in Jiangnan had led thirteen wealthy merchants from all over the country to the capital and treated those very talents to dinner at the tiny restaurant where the Linyuan tablet selection committee had gathered to make their decision.

This restaurant had once been obscure and woefully rundown. Years ago, it had been hidden like the glow of a firefly beneath the moon by the splendor of Kite's Flight Pavilion, to the point that those without acute eyesight were almost guaranteed to miss it. Yet in a lucky turn of events, it had escaped the devastation that befell the capital and remained standing to this day. At the start of the year, it had undergone renovations and staged a grand reopening to welcome new customers. Two additional stories were added above what was originally the second floor, and the damaged bricks and broken roof tiles were tidied up and neatly put in order. The establishment was rechristened Southward Tower—a timely name that evoked in all who heard it the grief of losing half the country to enemy hands. Few knew that this formerly struggling restaurant was one of Du Wanquan's properties.

The first time the two parties met, they found no common ground. Scholarly intellectuals held themselves as morally beyond reproach. After experiencing the ebb and flow of bureaucracy for so many years, they were reluctant to rub elbows with these merchants who stank of copper. Most who came did so simply to half-heartedly fulfill a social obligation.

Yet after speaking with Du Wanquan at length, these members of the literati realized that the man was no simple merchant.

Du Wanquan once sailed west and saw the wider world with his very own eyes. His personal conduct, manner of speech, patterns of thought—everything about him was vastly different from the average trader. Between his silver tongue that could practically call back the dead and Jiang Chong's calm mediation, many attendees soon began to reconsider their stance.

Later, when the new reforms began to silently permeate all levels of society, Du Wanquan's party reserved the largest private room at Southward Tower and again sent invitations to eight important ministers of the imperial court, headed by Jiang Chong. Every one of them was an official who lacked financial backers, who had risen to their position through the imperial examination and had built up their career from nothing.

This time, their clandestine meeting lasted over eight hours. Only when the moon climbed high over the branching trees did Jiang Chong raise his cup in a final toast from his position in the seat of honor.

Rising solemnly to his feet, Jiang Chong looked around the room and found that, after so many rounds of toasts, a number of the meeting's attendees had become drunk.

"Today," he said, "we ate and drank to our heart's content. Everyone must be tired, so I won't spoil the mood—I'll just offer a few words. Please feel free to drink what remains in your cups; we'll disperse after this. If we intend to continue fighting this war, then the success of the war beacon tickets is imperative. Every one of you is wholly devoted to our nation..."

Jiang Chong stopped in the middle of his speech and threw back his cup of wine, leaving the rest unspoken. *Every one of you is wholly devoted to our nation, but please take some time to consider your own future prospects.*

After so many years without an avenue to voice their political concerns within the imperial court, the wealthy merchants who desperately wished for someone to speak on their behalf met with these powerless yet uncorrupted civic officials and formed an official alliance.

After seeing the ministers and merchants out, Du Wanquan returned to Southward Tower alone and stepped into the room next door. No servants waited inside, and save for the dim gas lamp hung overhead, the lights were dark. A small cup of yellow wine, a bowl of plain congee, and a plate of side dishes sat on the table. There was still a fair bit of wine left, the congee was half-eaten, and the side dishes were practically untouched, yet the person sitting at the table had already set down his chopsticks.

Dropping his suave demeanor, Du Wanquan respectfully stepped forward to make his greeting. "Your Highness."

Chang Geng nodded politely. "Master Du."

Du Wanquan glanced at the congee and side dishes on the table.

"It's very admirable, the way Your Highness is ever so frugal, but Southward Tower is one of my own establishments. Why not order something better suited to your tastes? Summer is fast approaching—I'll have the kitchen prepare some nourishing dishes with cooling properties..."

"There's really no need. These dishes suit my taste perfectly," Chang Geng said with a wave of his hand. "The success of today's event depended entirely on Master Du. I'm sorry to have troubled you so much."

Du Wanquan hastily assured Chang Geng that it was hardly any trouble at all. Seeing him rise to his feet, Du Wanquan courteously picked up an umbrella. "The carriage is waiting in the rear courtyard. Please follow me, Your Highness."

When the monk Liao Ran had first called for the assembly of the Linyuan tablet, the most reluctant member of the party had been Du Wanquan. It was true that he had relied on the power the Linyuan Pavilion wielded within civilian society to make his fortune in his early years. However, after fighting tooth and nail to build his family business, Du Wanquan would never admit how much help he'd received. Now, this organization wanted him to throw away the fruits of a lifetime of painstaking labor for the sake of some man he'd never even met—no human being would be willing to do such a thing. Yet after knowing Chang Geng for just over half a year, Du Wanquan was now the one most eager to follow at Prince Yan's heels and remain at his beck and call.

The God of Wealth had traveled the world for many years; his knowledge and experience far exceeded that of ordinary people. He had the vague sense that although Chang Geng was indeed working to save the country from its current crisis, he was at the same time laying the groundwork for something else.

Du Wanquan felt an indescribable excitement. The nation of Great Liang walked a precarious path, flourishing under the rule of Emperor Wu, peaking and declining during the reign of the Yuanhe Emperor, and reaching an impasse under the Longan Emperor. It was indeed about time for the dawn of a new era. Somehow, thanks to a wooden tablet, he had managed to board this boat. Perhaps it would prove to be a great opportunity.

Chang Geng strode toward the door. Suddenly, he touched a hand to his waist, and his footsteps froze.

Du Wanquan's sharp eyes noticed at once. "What are you looking for, Your Highness?"

"It's nothing." At length, Chang Geng said somewhat absentmindedly, "I've run out of incense." What with everything that needed his attention recently, he'd depleted his pacifying fragrance too quickly and hadn't had time to mix a new batch. Chang Geng sighed. He smiled at Du Wanquan. "It's no matter. Please, there's no need to see me out, Master Du. Send word to Master Fenghan. Tell him that the issue he is so greatly concerned about will someday be solved."

Chang Geng usually abstained from drinking, but sitting in a corner and eavesdropping for over eight hours had left him utterly exhausted. He had ordered a cup of wine hoping to stimulate his senses, but not only did his slight tipsiness fail to help him sleep, when he went home for the night, he didn't feel drowsy at all.

Chang Geng tossed and turned for hours. It was long past midnight when he finally sank into a fitful slumber.

In his half-asleep state, he seemed to hear someone enter the room. He started awake, flipping over to switch on the tiny gas lamp hung at the head of the bed. Perhaps it was because of the damp from the recent heavy rains or because it had been ages since someone last slept in this room—the gas lamp flickered erratically before sputtering out.

The intruder took a seat on the little couch at the side of the room with familiar ease and laughed. "What are you doing in my bed?"

Chang Geng was stunned. As his eyes acclimated to the darkness, he saw in what little light there was that it was Gu Yun, who had returned. "Didn't you say it would be another two days before you reached the capital? How are you back so soon?" he blurted.

Gu Yun stretched languidly, then leaned against the arm of the couch. "I missed you, so I rushed back on my own."

They had last said goodbye on New Year's Eve. In the blink of an eye, winter had melted into spring. Now it was summer. It had been half a year since they had seen each other. Gu Yun's battle reports often included hidden messages to Chang Geng, and every now and again, he would send a personal letter. But how could splotches of ink on white paper compare to the man himself appearing before his eyes? Chang Geng had missed Gu Yun terribly. He rushed forward to embrace him.

But Gu Yun leaned back, easily evading his grasp. His body seemed flimsy as a slip of paper as he floated over to the window in the twinkling of an eye. The rain had stopped. Moonlight reflected quietly off the puddles outside and spilled into the room in twining streams. Gu Yun turned, backlit, and Chang Geng noticed he was wearing his ever-present light pelt armor.

"What are you doing, pawing at me the minute you see me?" Gu Yun asked with a soft chuckle. "I just came by to see you."

Chang Geng didn't know whether to laugh or cry when he heard Gu Yun's initial question. What a hypocrite—as if he wasn't the more handsy of the pair. When he heard the rest, however, his smile faded. He faintly sensed something was off. "Zixi, what's wrong?"

Gu Yun didn't respond. The two of them—one sitting and one standing—faced each other in solemn silence, as if bidding their final farewells. Inexplicably, Chang Geng's heart began to pound, thundering in his chest with such force he felt it could hold nothing else. He could scarcely breathe. Unable to bear it a moment longer, he got to his feet and walked over to Gu Yun. The distance from the bed to the tiny window was no more than four or five steps, but somehow, he couldn't seem to reach his destination.

Every time he moved forward, Gu Yun took a step back.

Chang Geng turned and picked up the gas lamp affixed to the head of the bed, furiously twisting the knob at its base. The lamp emitted several sputtering gasps before coming alight, flooding the room with brightness. Despite the harsh glare, Chang Geng turned frantically toward Gu Yun. The man standing by the window was pale as paper. His complexion had a grayish cast unseen on the face of the living, and two lines of blood dripped from the corner of his mouth and along the cinnabar mole at his eye.

The gas lamp crackled before going out once more.

Gu Yun sighed softly. "I can't bear the light. Why would you turn on the lamp... Chang Geng, I'm leaving."

What did that mean, *can't bear the light*? Chang Geng nearly went mad on the spot. He lunged forward, grabbing desperately at Gu Yun, but all he managed to touch was icy black armor. "Stop!" His voice was hoarse. "Where are you going? Gu Zixi!"

"I'm going where I ought to go." Gu Yun's voice carried a slight chill. "You're fully fledged now. Skillfully taking control of the Linyuan Pavilion, heroically seizing the Li family's nation—what unstable situation, what favorable stroke of luck...everything lies in the palm of your hand. What extraordinary methods you employ. Hasn't Li Feng died by your hand as well? It won't do for me to linger, so I've come specially to say goodbye."

Chang Geng panicked. "No, wait, I didn't..."

He wanted to protest that he'd done no such thing. But even as the words lined up on the tip of his tongue, he found himself unable to speak them aloud. Confusion seized his heart; for a moment, he felt that he really had done everything Gu Yun accused him of.

"The late emperor entrusted me with bringing you back from Yanhui Town and caring for you till adulthood," Gu Yun said, voice low. "I'd always hoped that, even if you weren't an exceptional talent capable of supporting the nation, at the very least you would become an upstanding individual of noble and benevolent character. But what did you do?"

It was an early summer night, yet Chang Geng had never felt so cold.

"I cared for you as the late emperor wished. I never expected to raise a wolf that bites the hand that feeds it." Gu Yun exhaled softly. "It's been two hundred years since the founding ancestor established the nation of Great Liang. I thought our nation would persist forever. Who would have thought the imperial jade seal would be destroyed by my own generation..."

Chang Geng wanted to grab him, or maybe raise hell, screaming and shouting, but he was frozen in place. He could only watch, glassy-eyed, as Gu Yun turned away from him, his movements featherlight, and left him with these final words: "I'm going to plead forgiveness beneath the Nine Springs now. We won't meet again."

He passed through the wall and vanished, leaving behind a deserted, open window. Rent with grief, Chang Geng jerked awake with a panicked cry, his heart pounding like a drum. Only after several heaving breaths did he finally return to his senses. He slowly exhaled the stagnant air in his chest and belatedly realized—it was all just a too-vivid nightmare.

Perhaps it was because of the wine he drank that his head was throbbing and his whole body was sore. Despite a night's sleep, he felt as tired as if he hadn't slept at all. Chang Geng spent several minutes attempting to ground himself. He decided he'd get a drink of water, then close his eyes in meditation for a while.

But just as he pushed himself up, he noticed a dark shadow inhabiting the wooden chair by the window. The intruder's breaths were soft yet deep—clearly this was a martial expert. Chang Geng had been so startled by the crashing of his own heartbeat that it had taken him some time to notice their presence.

"Who's there?" he called sharply.

The intruder responded with a soft chuckle. "What are you doing in my bed?"

There could be no greater shock than this. Chang Geng hadn't completely shaken off his nightmare to begin with; his elbows went weak, and he collapsed back onto the bed. Gu Yun's lousy bed was hard everywhere, from the bed boards to the pillow, so this was no laughing matter. The meticulous and cool-headed Prince Yan nearly blacked out when he knocked his head against a pillow.

Startled, Gu Yun hurried over to the bed and helped him up. He had left Shen Yi and the rest of his personal guard behind and hurtled back two days ahead of schedule. He'd originally planned on resting for the night before sneaking over to give Chang Geng a fright the next morning, but when he entered his room, he found his bed occupied by a certain someone. Gu Yun knew from his talk with Miss Chen that Chang Geng slept poorly. He struggled to fall asleep, and even when he managed it, he was easily startled awake. Finding him at rest, Gu Yun couldn't bear to rouse him.

"Where did you hit your head? Ay, let me see," Gu Yun said, flummoxed. "Usurping my bed certainly is contemptible behavior, but I didn't even say anything—why do you look like you've seen a ghost? Speak, have you done some terrible deed behind my back?"

Chang Geng caught his wrist with a trembling hand. This time, he touched warm flesh, and exhaled in relief.

Gu Yun could see Chang Geng wasn't quite himself. Thinking some idle chat might calm him, Gu Yun began, "Why haven't you asked me why I came back two days early?"

Chang Geng's face changed immediately.

Gu Yun continued with his crow's beak: "I missed you, so I rushed back on my own..."

"Stop talking!" Chang Geng snapped.

Gu Yun faltered at the miserable desperation in his voice. "Chang Geng, what's wrong?" he asked cautiously. He reached for the bed-side lamp. With a slight twist, the gas lamp flickered violently once, twice, then died with a popping sound, broken.

By some miraculous coincidence, in that split second, nightmare overlapped reality. Chang Geng let out a hoarse cry as the dull ache in his limbs poured into his heart like a tide, transforming into a hundred thousand terrifying apparitions that unhinged their bloody maws and swallowed him whole.

78

FEAR

G

U YUN had witnessed a wu'ergu attack before, but back then, he hadn't known what he was seeing. Chang Geng's symptoms had also been less severe then, and he'd mistaken it for a qi deviation. This time, he watched as Chang Geng curled into a ball, all the muscles in his body tense as a solid wall of steel. He was seized with violent tremors, as if enduring some extreme agony. Gu Yun was surprised to find that he couldn't pin him down; Chang Geng was shockingly strong.

Jerking out of Gu Yun's hold, Chang Geng clawed at himself, his fingers hooked like the talons of a hawk. Gu Yun couldn't sit by and watch as he mutilated himself. He grabbed his arms. "Chang Geng!"

His voice seemed to restore to Chang Geng a sliver of clarity, just enough that he froze momentarily. That worthless bedside lamp that kept failing at the most critical juncture emitted a series of wheezes before finally coming to life with a sputtering gasp, casting its dim, wavering light upon Chang Geng's bloodred eyes.

Gu Yun was stunned. Chang Geng's lips and face were deathly pale. It was as if all the warm vitality in his body had gathered in that bloody stare, and what had previously been a set of perfectly ordinary eyes now contained a pair of twinned pupils.

He looked exactly like that wicked god of legend.

When Gu Yun had first learned about wu'ergu from Miss Chen, he'd merely felt a deep ache in his heart; he hadn't truly believed some of the more outrageous effects she described. It was only now that a chill slowly crawled up his spine. Faced with Chang Geng's unfeeling, bloodthirsty eyes, this veteran general's body turned cold with fear.

The two stared at each other. Gu Yun felt as if he'd encountered a feral beast in the wilderness, and for a moment, he dared not look away. Slowly, he unclenched his fist and stretched his empty hand out to Chang Geng. Chang Geng didn't try to evade; on the contrary, as that warm hand pressed against his cheek, he lowered his head and nuzzled into Gu Yun's palm with a blank expression.

"Do you know who I am?" Gu Yun asked quietly, his heart in his throat.

Chang Geng lowered his uncommonly thick lashes and breathed, "Zixi."

Thank goodness; Chang Geng could still recognize him. Gu Yun sighed in relief, failing to notice the strangeness of his tone—but he'd relaxed too soon. Before the breath could fully escape him, Chang Geng made a grab for his throat. "I won't let you leave!"

The throat was the most vulnerable part of the body; Gu Yun instinctively flinched back and parried that ice-cold hand. Pressing his advantage, Chang Geng caught Gu Yun's wrist, yanking it violently down. Gu Yun curled his fingers and jabbed at the sensitive knot of nerves in Chang Geng's elbow. In that small space there on the bed, the two exchanged several blows in rapid succession. This lunatic was an exemplary martial artist to begin with, but now, possessed by the spirit of a wicked god, his strength became still more extraordinary as he struck out wildly. By contrast, Gu Yun was afraid of accidentally hurting him. On the verge of breaking a sweat, he cursed furiously, "I just fucking got back—where the hell would I go?"

Suddenly, Chang Geng stilled. Gu Yun withdrew the hand he had pressed against Chang Geng's neck and rapped him lightly on the chin with his knuckles. "Wake up!"

Perhaps this strike was too weak—not only did it fail to rouse Chang Geng, it made him narrow his bloody eyes. Like an enraged leopard, he turned his head and bit down on Gu Yun's arm.

Gu Yun had no words. Had he known this would happen, he would have slapped him with his full strength!

Gu Yun let out a soft hiss, the corner of his eye twitching violently. Over the course of his life, he had been hacked at with swords and blasted with bombs, but this was the first time anyone had taken a bite out of him like they were trying to eat him alive. He was sorely tempted to fling his arm out and knock loose this madman's front teeth. He stopped dead, his arm held stiff for half an age, but in the end, he couldn't bear to do it. At length, Gu Yun relaxed the muscles in his arm and squeezed intermittently at the back of Chang Geng's neck. Drawing in a sharp breath, he said, voice low, "Flaying skin, stripping tendon, eating flesh—how deep does our enmity run? Do you really hate me so much?"

These words seemed to strike a nerve. Chang Geng blinked, and twin lines of tears rolled down without warning.

Chang Geng made not a sound as he held the flesh of Gu Yun's arm between his teeth and wept. The tears seemed to wash away the terrifying bloodlust in his eyes, and by intervals, Chang Geng's jaw slowly relaxed. Gu Yun carefully extracted his bleeding arm, gave the wound a cursory glance, and cursed softly under his breath. "Son of a bitch."

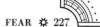

Despite the imprecation, he nevertheless took Chang Geng into his arms. He wiped the tears from the corners of Chang Geng's eyes and patted him soothingly on the back. Chang Geng slumped against his chest for nearly an hour before slowly salvaging his mind from the maelstrom of chaos. It was like waking from a dream; he sat dazed and absent as his scattered memories gradually returned to him. When he recalled what he had just done, Chang Geng promptly broke into gooseflesh. His entire body, which had previously been slack as wet mud, suddenly tensed, alerting Gu Yun that he had resurfaced.

"You're awake?" Feigning calm, Gu Yun pushed Chang Geng away and flexed his stiff shoulders. He raised a hand and asked, "How many fingers am I holding up?"

Chang Geng's mind was a tangled mess. He didn't dare meet Gu Yun's eyes, but when he glanced down and saw the bite mark already scabbing over on Gu Yun's arm, his expression turned even more unsightly. Cradling Gu Yun's arm in his hands, his lips trembled, but he couldn't speak.

"Oh, I got bitten by a dog." Gu Yun glanced at the wound indifferently, then teased, "That dog had very straight teeth."

Chang Geng staggered to his feet to fetch clean water and a silk handkerchief, then bowed his head and carefully cleaned Gu Yun's wound. He looked as if he had just been violated, with not a single one of his three immortal souls or seven mortal forms at home in his head—the picture of indescribable misery.

Gu Yun had been born with an overprotective nature. If he were to take personal attachments out of the equation and operate on pure feeling, perhaps the quality that moved him most powerfully was vulnerability. To this, even beauty came second. His eyes softened as he took in this scene. Lifting his hands, he began gently combing through Chang Geng's mussed hair with his fingers.

"Last autumn, when Jiping and I traveled through the Central Plains, we encountered a group of insurrectionist bandits seeking to profit from the nation's misfortune." Gu Yun's voice was slow, his tone even gentler than the motions of his fingers. "With the help of Old Cai, we took care of those miscreants and captured their leader. That bandit called himself Fire Dragon; he was covered in scars and had a burn across his face. In the course of his interrogation, we found a barbarian woman's sword... It had once belonged to Huge'er."

Chang Geng's hands trembled violently; the silk handkerchief slipped out of his grip and fluttered to the ground. He bent to retrieve it with a stricken expression, but Gu Yun caught his hand. "Can you really remember what happened at such a young age?" Gu Yun asked softly.

Chang Geng's hand was as cold as that of a corpse.

Gu Yun sighed. "Miss Chen's told me everything already. As for that—"

"Don't." Chang Geng cut him off.

Gu Yun obediently shut his mouth and said no more, watching him in silence.

Chang Geng sat stiffly, but his hands became suddenly nimble as he quickly dressed Gu Yun's bite wound. As he finished, he rose to his feet and turned away from Gu Yun. "It's been years since the Prince Yan Estate was built, but there's been no one looking after things there all this time. It's not very appropriate, so I...I'll return to the Grand Council first thing in the morning. Once I take care of business there, I'll move my things over to the Prince Yan Estate..."

Gu Yun's expression abruptly clouded over.

Chang Geng's incoherent speech stuttered to a halt. He couldn't help but recall how overwhelmed he'd felt at Gu Yun's sudden change of heart when he'd come to the northwest at year's end

to deliver rewards to the troops. Had that only been because he'd learned the truth about wu'ergu? Because he pitied him?

It was illogical: Chang Geng had no qualms about baring his old scars to Li Feng; yet when it came to Gu Yun, he kept himself tightly covered, afraid to let him glimpse even the smallest of clues. He thought he'd done a good job keeping things under wraps, yet the truth had still leaked out through the gaps between his fingers. Chang Geng clenched his jaw; he could still taste the blood in his mouth from when he had lost himself just minutes ago, coppery and sweet.

Ever since he'd received word that Gu Yun would return to the capital to report on his duties, Chang Geng had spent every waking moment looking forward to his return. Every second had felt like torture as it ticked by—yet when the long-awaited Gu Yun finally arrived, Chang Geng wished to disappear from this man's sight. His mind was a tumultuous mess, and his instincts screamed at him to flee. He turned toward the door to leave at once.

"Stop right there—where are you going?" Gu Yun asked.

Chang Geng, in his muddle-headed daze, ignored him.

"Li Min!" Gu Yun snapped.

In all Chang Geng's life, Gu Yun had rarely spoken to him harshly, much less in anger. But he was unused to being questioned—in the army, no one dared to do so due to his high rank. Such a stern reprimand carried a hint of fury and the deadly sound of metal striking stone. Chang Geng shivered as he instinctively came to a stop.

Gu Yun's expression was grim as an overcast sky as he sat by the bed. "Get the hell over here."

Chang Geng was lost. "I..."

"Walk through that door today and I'll break your legs," Gu Yun said, an audible chill in his voice. "Even His Majesty won't be able to save you. Get back here—don't make me say it a third time!"

Chang Geng didn't know what to say. Here was the first person to openly threaten to break Prince Yan's legs since he began chairing the Grand Council. Confounded by Gu Yun's sudden fit of temper, Chang Geng really didn't dare take another step. He screwed up his courage and glanced back over his shoulder at Gu Yun. All sorts of unspeakable grievances and agonies welled up in his chest... His face was still stained with tears, but he was already too clear-headed to cry anymore.

Gu Yun seriously couldn't stand the way Chang Geng was looking at him. He stood and stepped forward to meet Chang Geng, as if in compromise, and embraced him from behind. Then, he all but dragged him back and tossed him onto the bed, tugging the now-cool sheets over him. "All these years, why didn't you tell me?"

Chang Geng took a deep breath. "I was scared," he said quietly.

Scared of what? Startled, Gu Yun lifted Chang Geng's face with his hand. "Scared of whom? Scared of me?"

Chang Geng gazed at him deeply. With that single look, Gu Yun suddenly understood the meaning of the words "love begets fear." At first, Gu Yun wanted to ask, *Why would you be scared of me? Did you think I'd scorn you? That I'd doubt you?* but even as the words reached the tip of his tongue, he swallowed them back down. For a moment, he didn't know what to say—so he acted instead. He grabbed Chang Geng by the collar and kissed him firmly on the mouth. Chang Geng's breathing immediately grew heavy.

Bracing himself with a hand beside Chang Geng's ear, Gu Yun raised an eyebrow. "Are you still scared of me now?"

Chang Geng stared.

Gu Yun gazed imperiously down at him, and a wave of heat surged in his heart. Licking his lips, he decided he might as well go all in with the indecent behavior and reached for the front of Chang Geng's disheveled robes.

There came a sudden knock at the door, shattering the mood. An unfortunate and undiscerning soul by the name of Huo called out, "Your Highness, it's almost time for morning court. Do you require assistance changing your robes?"

Gu Yun was speechless. They'd tussled the whole night through, and before they knew it, day was about to dawn.

Huo Dan's first round of knocks were met with silence. Thinking Chang Geng must be so exhausted he'd failed to hear, he was about to knock again when the door suddenly swung open. Captain Huo nearly jumped out of his skin when he saw who it was. "M-my lord!" he stuttered in astonishment.

When did their Marshal Gu come home? And how did he get in without alerting any of the estate guards? Did he jump over the wall?!

Inside the room, Chang Geng felt rather awkward. Straightening his sorry appearance, he called, "I'll be right there..."

Gu Yun cut him off with a voice that brooked no protest. "Go beg sick leave on behalf of His Highness. He won't be attending court today."

Huo Dan was shocked. "Then...shall I send for an imperial physician?" he asked.

"An imperial physician? Imperial physicians are all a waste of space." Gu Yun peevishly cast down this casual piece of slander before turning back into the room. "Don't bother us unless it's urgent. Now go."

Huo Dan was flabbergasted.

Chang Geng, now arbitrarily detained, looked at the aggressive and bossy Gu Yun in mild exasperation. "I'm not sick."

"If you're not sick, does that make me the sick one in this equation?" Gu Yun dug out a packet of pacifying fragrance and dumped a handful into the incense burner standing nearby. There was no need to dance around it anymore. "Miss Chen asked me to bring this back for you."

A subtle and refreshing scent filled the room. Chang Geng sniffed the air. "Miss Chen changed her formula?"

Gu Yun rubbed at the teeth marks on his arm. "Bitey little lunatic."

The pacifying fragrance quickly took effect, filling Chang Geng's lungs and relaxing his body until he couldn't muster the slightest bit of strength or hostility. He leaned weakly against the head of the bed and stared up at Gu Yun with vacant, glassy eyes. His hair was loose and disheveled, and he seemed utterly spent, yet his disoriented gaze chased after Gu Yun. All in all, he looked rather sickly—nothing like a man who possessed a silver tongue but iron teeth.

"Zixi, can I hold you?" Chang Geng murmured.

What a sap, Gu Yun thought. Nevertheless, he came over and sat on the bed, allowing Chang Geng to lean over and relentlessly wrap his arms around Gu Yun's waist however he pleased.

"Beg sickness." Gu Yun broke the extended silence. "Isn't there the Grand Council? Jiang Hanshi is fairly capable; he merely lacked opportunity before. Now that he's been promoted, I'm sure he'll flex his skills. The tribute of violet gold from the Western Regions will arrive in the capital in a matter of days. We can take a proper rest for a few years. The barbarians have no skill in industry and manufacturing; we can afford to drag this out, but Jialai Yinghuo can't. As time goes on, the situation on the northern front will undoubtedly undergo a shift. All that remains is Jiangnan... The foreigners have traveled thousands of kilometers across the sea at enormous expense to get here. But even a strong dragon cannot defeat a snake in its own nest—no matter what happens, we hold the advantage, right?"

Chang Geng lay in his arms and opened his eyes a crack. He could feel Gu Yun's calloused fingers absentmindedly stroking the top of his head, making his scalp tingle.

"The reforms have just begun," Gu Yun said in a low voice. "You were the one who initiated them, but they haven't raised too many waves with the other officials. In fact, most of them seem to tacitly agree with you. If you retreat now, regardless of whether the reforms succeed or fail, the rewards and consequences will fall on someone else. Don't fight for credit and you won't necessarily take the blame either... So let's forget all this, go home, and rest for a couple of years, okay?"

Of the thousands of words Shen Yi spewed, the only ones Gu Yun had taken to heart were, *How will he clean up this mess in the future?* The Gu family had borne the title of marquis for generations, and they were members of the imperial household to boot. The rise and fall of influential officials, the ebb and flow of bureaucracy—Gu Yun had seen it all. He was eminently aware of the end that awaited prominent ministers and valiant generals. Even in times of great prosperity, how many imperial kinsmen managed to escape the vengeance meted out by their powerful enemies and their critics' clever pens?

After a long silence, Chang Geng finally responded. "I can't retreat," he said quietly. "The first incision has already been made. We're scraping poison from the bone, and the patient's flesh has already been cut open... If I turn back now, ought I leave them with their skin sliced open or sew them back together again?"

Government reforms were merely the first step. If they were regarded as merely a means to implement the war beacon tickets, they would go no further than this. He was certain that in the future, after the end of the war—or perhaps even before—there would come a time when the whole court fought over the war beacon tickets. When that day came, not only would corruption become widespread, the war beacon tickets themselves would become completely worthless. And if that should happen, Great Liang would fall yet more rapidly into decline.

Gu Yun tightened his arms around him. When Chang Geng opened his eyes once more, the bloodlust and twin pupils had faded away. He flipped over, clumsily pressing Gu Yun—this man who occupied his thoughts day and night—into the soft brocade blankets. "Zixi, do you know what wu'ergu is?"

Gu Yun blinked in surprise.

"Wu'ergu is the name of a wicked god. It's also the oldest curse the barbarians know. When their tribe is on the verge of annihilation, they take a pair of children and refine them into a wu'ergu. The resulting individuals possess unparalleled strength. They will call down a reign of carnage and destroy any enemy, no matter how powerful."

Chang Geng lay on top of Gu Yun, and his chest thrummed as he spoke. Though slightly hoarse, his voice was as gentle as ever. "Before she died, Huge'er told me that by the end of my life, my heart would be filled with only hatred, brutality, and suspicion; that I would become a violent lover of bloodshed with carnage following in my footsteps; that I'd be doomed to drag everyone to a miserable death; that no one would love me or treat me with sincerity."

Gu Yun sucked in a sharp breath. He'd always felt that, as a child, Chang Geng had had far too many concerns weighing on him. His mind was labyrinthine, filled with countless twists and turns, impossible to fathom. He never expected that at the end of those twists and turns lay such a noxious sequence of words.

"But there *is* someone who loves me and treats me with sincerity...

right? Just now, it was you who brought me back to myself," Chang Geng said quietly. "There wasn't a day she treated me with warmth. I refuse to live according to her wishes. Do you trust me? Zixi, as long as you say the word, I will climb any mountain of swords and wade through any sea of flames."

79

A HEART-TO-HEART

HE WAS THE ILLUSTRIOUS PRINCE YAN, the leader of the Grand Council. Yet every time he jolted awake from the nightmares Xiu-niang had branded into his bones, the only person he could think of, yearn for, anticipate, and believe in was Gu Yun.

The weight of this one person was so heavy in his heart that there were times he struggled to carry the burden.

Great Master Liao Ran had once told him: "The suffering of mankind lies not in letting go but in holding on. The more things you hold, the fuller your hands, and the more they will weigh you down with every step forward." These words resonated deeply with Chang Geng, and he had to admit that Liao Ran was right. To him, Gu Yun alone weighed over a thousand kilograms—yet he was incapable of letting him go. The moment he did, he would have nothing left.

If a person didn't have anything worth treasuring in their life, wouldn't they just be a ship without a rudder, drifting wherever the currents carried them?

Gu Yun wrapped an arm around Chang Geng's shoulders and tapped lightly at the curve where his shoulder met his neck. Chang Geng winced in pain, but his gaze, fixed on Gu Yun, never wavered. "Why on earth would I want you to climb over a mountain of swords and wade through a sea of flames?" Gu Yun asked.

"I want there to come a day when the nation is thriving, and the common people have worthwhile work. When the whole country is at peace, and my general need not defend our borders to the death. I want to take a stand like Master Fenghan and unravel the tangled relationship between imperial authority and violet gold. I want all the land-bound steam engines to be ones that work the fields, and for the giant kites soaring overhead to be filled with ordinary folks traveling to visit their ancestral homes with their entire families in tow... I want every person to be able to live with dignity." Chang Geng tightened his hand around Gu Yun's, interlacing their fingers until they were intimately entangled.

Gu Yun was taken aback. This was the first time Chang Geng had bared his heart to him like this. Listening to him speak, Gu Yun felt his blood begin to race. But when he stopped to think about it carefully, every single one of these things seemed unfortunately unattainable.

"I can do it, Zixi. Let me try," Chang Geng said in a low voice. He had the strength of a wicked god—why shouldn't he try to pull apart this bloody world and establish an unprecedented new path for the common folk?

Back in Yanhui Town, a fourteen-year-old boy had once told a young general who'd barely come of age his vision of what constituted a life worth living. At the time, Gu Yun, who had yet to shed the recklessness of youth, had dumped a proverbial bucket of ice water over his head, coldly informing him that heroes don't get happy endings. Now, after several tours of duty in the yellow sands of the desert and a visit to the imperial dungeons, Marshal Gu had personally lived those words of warning. Yet for some reason, he found himself unable to utter them a second time before Chang Geng.

If Gu Yun were in Chang Geng's shoes, and someone pointed at him and said, *Gu Yun, you ought to hurry and fuck off back to the Marquis Estate to enjoy your life in retirement. You're lucky you've managed to survive till now. If you don't retreat today, sooner or later, you'll die an ignominious death*—how would he feel?

Life in this world was like trudging through icy sludge; it was inevitable that one would struggle to make progress. Over time, one naturally froze through and through. How difficult it was to maintain a heart that shed hot blood, that pressed ahead despite knowing one faced the impossible. If, on top of all of that, someone should place more obstacles in their way—if even their closest friends and family did so—wouldn't that be far too sorrowful?

Gu Yun was silent for a long time. Just as Chang Geng began to show subtle signs of nervousness, he opened his mouth. "I've kissed you and hugged you—what more do you want me to say? Men who talk too much don't have time for other things. Understand?"

Astonished, Chang Geng watched as, with a flip of Gu Yun's fingers, the half-dead gas lamp beside the bed went out. Dawn had yet to break, and the room was plunged into darkness. The bed curtains that were ordinarily tied back drifted gently in the cool early-morning breeze that spilled through the gap in the window and fluttered down, obscuring everything. Before Chang Geng could react, he felt the fabric loosen at his waist—at some point, his belt had disappeared. Chang Geng was still caught up in his oath about the mountain of swords and sea of flames and had yet to regather his wits. With a *fwoom*, his face went bright red.

"Z-Zixi..."

Gu Yun hummed absentmindedly in response as he impatiently flung off the silk cloth covering his wounded arm. Leaning back lazily into the pile of soft brocade blankets, he trailed the tip of his finger over Chang Geng's lapel. "Back at the hot spring villa, you said you dreamed of me... What did you dream about, exactly?"

Chang Geng could make no response.

"Aren't you quite the skilled speaker?" Gu Yun chuckled softly. "Let's hear it."

Chang Geng had never before experienced such provocative flirtation. His tongue promptly tied itself into a knot. "I... I..."

"When it comes to this sort of thing, it isn't enough just to think about it." Gu Yun caressed Chang Geng's waist through his clothes, then slid his hand down to where thigh melted into pelvis. Chang Geng nearly leapt right out of the bed as he forgot how to breathe. Overwhelmed, he seized Gu Yun's mischievous hands. A line of fire scorched its way from his belly to his throat; he felt as though he were about to be burned to ash. Meanwhile, Gu Yun had already loosened his lapels.

As cool air touched Chang Geng's chest, he seemed to come to a realization. He tried to pin down Gu Yun's questing hand, but it was too late—the scars of all sizes that covered his chest beneath the collar were exposed. As those lightly calloused fingers skimmed over them, the sensation was indescribable. On the one hand, Chang Geng couldn't help but flinch away; on the other, his mouth was dry, his ears faintly ringing. He didn't know whether to advance or retreat.

Gu Yun had been traveling for days, then spent a whole night waiting beside his own bed. As luck would have it, the bit of medicine he'd taken chose this precise moment to wear off. His vision began to blur, but the mood was perfect. It wouldn't do to dig out his glass monocle now and spoil the ambience—wearing it made him feel like an artificer preparing to dismantle a suit of armor.

Thus, he relied entirely on his sense of touch. He slid his hands over the uneven surface of Chang Geng's scars, the feeling even more shocking than seeing the marks with his eyes.

"Do they hurt?" Gu Yun asked quietly.

Chang Geng lowered his gaze to stare at him intently, then side-stepped the question. "They healed ages ago."

A hundred different emotions welled up in Gu Yun's heart. For a moment, even his surging lust subsided. He narrowed his increasingly unfocused eyes and carefully stroked his fingers over those scars. Chang Geng couldn't bear it anymore; with a soft whimper, he grabbed Gu Yun's wrist.

"Don't be scared," Gu Yun coaxed him. "I'll take good care of you."

If the half-blind man could've seen Chang Geng's face just then, he probably wouldn't have said anything like *don't be scared.*

Chang Geng leaned down and kissed him, and Gu Yun grew impatient once more. Yet just as he was about to press Chang Geng onto his back and get down to business, for some unfathomable reason, Chang Geng suddenly blurted out, "Yifu..."

Gu Yun froze.

With this single utterance from Chang Geng, Gu Yun went soft. His blazing carnal desire, so intense a moment ago, was instantly extinguished, stamped out, and shoved into an iron cage. Gu Yun sucked in several heaving breaths. He had half a mind to shout, *What the hell are you saying at a time like this?!* But after thinking on it, he realized—the guy wasn't entirely off the mark.

Apparently, there were some men who privately enjoyed the thrill of such moral taboos and were eager for their lovers to call them all sorts of nonsense in bed. Unfortunately, Gu Yun had absolutely zero interest in such things; he couldn't understand the appeal at all. In the past half year, he had finally, with great effort, grown accustomed to Chang Geng addressing him with his courtesy name. He had also slowly stopped viewing him as his godson. Yet he had never expected to crash head-first into the word *Yifu* at such a critical moment. The force of the impact left him dizzy with shock.

Chang Geng didn't seem to notice his discomfort. He called out to Gu Yun with that moniker several more times, as if unable to help himself, and kissed him haphazardly again and again. Folded within this intimacy was a piousness that made the old pervert feel as though he were sitting on pins and needles. Coupled with the "Yifu" appellation, the resulting effect was rather remarkable. Gu Yun felt as if his entire body were crawling with ants. In the end, he couldn't bear it any longer and turned his face away. "Stop calling me that."

Chang Geng paused and gazed at him for a few beats in silence. Then he leaned in and murmured into Gu Yun's ear, "Yifu, if you can't see clearly, then close your eyes, okay?"

No matter how hard of hearing Gu Yun might be—and he wasn't even all that deaf yet—he could tell Chang Geng was doing this on purpose. "...You're into this, aren't you?"

Chang Geng's eyes gleamed breathtakingly bright within the darkness of the bed curtains. He lowered his voice and softened his tone, relentless as he pouted into Gu Yun's ear, "Yifu, back then, you told me you would protect me even once we reached the capital—do you remember?"

Gu Yun's face contorted through several different expressions. He was completely defenseless against Chang Geng's new style of mischief and could only plan a strategic retreat. He pushed Chang Geng away. "That's enough, stop being shameless. Don't you have work to do...*sss!*"

"And what work am I supposed to do?" Taking advantage of his position, Chang Geng pressed Gu Yun back down into the bed. His hand had already found its way to the arch of Gu Yun's lower back. Back in Jiayu Pass, when he had realigned a certain man's bones, he had become intimately familiar with his body. Now, with a doctor's firm hand and ruthless accuracy, he struck. Gu Yun shuddered violently and felt himself go weak at the waist. He instinctively tried to curl in on himself, but Chang Geng tapped a handful of acupoints, and half of Gu Yun's body went numb. Chang Geng calmly picked up where he'd left off. "Didn't Yifu just help me beg sick leave? Aren't you going to take good care of me?"

"Bastard!" Gu Yun swore.

Chang Geng turned a deaf ear. He seized his opportunity and closed in on Gu Yun. In a manner that left no room for dissent, he pressed his knee between Gu Yun's legs, shoving them apart. Gu Yun broke out into gooseflesh. He pushed at Chang Geng's shoulder, caught that disrespectful hand, and twisted it behind Chang Geng's back. Chang Geng didn't resist, his body yielding as he allowed Gu Yun to manhandle him as he pleased. Tilting his head back to reveal the vulnerable line of his neck, he murmured coyly, "Do you want me, Yifu?"

Gu Yun hesitated; he couldn't get over this hurdle in his heart. The instant his grip loosened, Chang Geng slipped free like a loach and once again pressed in. He embraced him, running his hands along Gu Yun's spine as he breathed into his ear, "In that case, why not allow this dutiful son to attend to Yifu's needs?"

Gu Yun didn't know what to say. He was starting to realize that perhaps it was his unlucky year. Perhaps he had incurred the wrath of Tai Sui; that must be why he was suffering one setback after another.[14]

The sun climbed high overhead and the sky turned bright in the blink of an eye. The dazzling light of early summer streamed through the bed curtains in thin bars, yet their brightness paled in

---

14 Tai Sui, also known as the Grand Duke and the God of the Year, is a powerful deity who governs humans' fates and fortunes. In Chinese astrology, Tai Sui corresponds to the planet Jupiter, which has a twelve-year cycle. Each year of this cycle corresponds to a year in the Chinese zodiac. Over the course of Jupiter's twelve-year cycle, those whose zodiac sign corresponds to the stars that stand directly opposite Jupiter are considered to have offended Tai Sui and will experience bad luck or disturbances over the course of the year.

comparison to the brilliance of Chang Geng's eyes. He finally understood the meaning of "after years of wishful thinking, it takes but a
moment to fall fully into delirium." His nightmares were far more
terrifying than reality, but reality was far more maddening than his
erotic dreams.

After the madness passed, he didn't feel hollowed out at all. His
mind was at ease—more at ease than it had ever been in his entire
life—as his hands wandered over Gu Yun's body without pause. He
said Gu Yun's name again and again, his lips tucked against Gu Yun's
ear, such that even he found himself a bit annoying; but he couldn't
control himself, couldn't stop.

He called Gu Yun all sorts of appellations at random—sometimes it was *Yifu* while other times it was *Zixi*. The syllables pressed
against Gu Yun's ears and burrowed down, forcing the deaf man to
hear them though his medicine had long worn off. Gu Yun could
feel a steady stream of heated breath brushing against the side of his
neck. Earlier, thanks to a momentary slip on his part, Gu Yun had
missed his opportunity to take control of the situation and been
thoroughly ravished by the little brat. Now, he was sleepy and tired,
yet still, Chang Geng wouldn't let him be. Unable to reason with
him, Gu Yun grumpily pushed him away. "Be quiet."

When he saw the exhaustion on Gu Yun's face, Chang Geng
obediently shut his mouth. Instead, he began to lightly knead at
Gu Yun's lower back. He used just the right amount of pressure,
relieving Gu Yun's fatigued muscles without triggering his extraordinary ticklishness.

Gu Yun chewed over this revelation in silence. So last time, he
had been tickling him on purpose! Chen Qingxu, that quack—was
she teaching Chang Geng to cure disease and save lives or was she
imparting crooked sorcery?! He was about to give Chang Geng a

piece of his mind when Chang Geng suddenly frowned. Laying his palm over Gu Yun's chest, he pressed lightly against his ribs a few times before grabbing Gu Yun's wrist and settling his fingers against his pulse.

Gu Yun snapped, "What are y—"

"When did you get injured again?" Chang Geng interrupted.

Gu Yun turned mute.

Shit. It seemed, aside from crooked sorcery, that charlatan Chen really did teach Chang Geng some actual medicine if he could detect it with just a touch. In this moment of crisis, Gu Yun whipped out his tried-and-true weapon—*I'm deaf, I can't hear anything at all.* Affecting an expression of perfect innocence, he rolled over with his back to Chang Geng and fell still, indicating that he had fallen asleep: all irrelevant parties ought to take their leave.

Chang Geng examined him from head to toe, but it had already been quite some time since Gu Yun had acquired those terrifying blast injuries. Chang Geng's medical expertise wasn't quite as remarkable as that of Chen Qingxu, and by this point, Gu Yun's wounds had more or less healed. Chang Geng was unable to find anything of note, and thus the two of them had each successfully managed to pull one over on the other.

His Highness Prince Yan claimed illness and did not show his face in court for an entire day. Important ministers of the palace and Grand Council all sent representatives to ask after his health, but each and every one was rebuffed by Huo Dan. Huo Dan had come up through the military; he would never disobey a direct order from his commanding officer. If Gu Yun said they were not to be disturbed, then Huo Dan would stand by the front gate in silence like a door god and forbid anyone from doing so. Meanwhile, despite pondering it at length, Huo Dan still couldn't figure out how

Gu Yun had managed to sneak in. With little better to do, he spent his time tightening up the lax security of the Marquis Estate.

Gu Yun had raced back to the capital like a bat out of hell and returned two days earlier than anticipated, then went an entire night without sleep. Sure, he'd finally managed to eat his fill, but he'd ended up in the wrong position and nearly choked to death. Physically and mentally spent, he slept late into the afternoon.

When he awoke, his body and mind still felt extremely strange; who knew whose sick leave it was at this point. He wanted to chew Chang Geng out, but at the same time, he felt that verbally eviscerating him over such trifles would make him appear petty. In the end, he sullenly thought to himself, *Next time, I'll have to make sure to sew his mouth shut.*

Gu Yun groped around for his glass monocle, but the small object had disappeared. He fumbled around fruitlessly for half an age until a warm hand took hold of his own.

Leaning in next to his ear, Chang Geng said, "General Shen and the others haven't yet arrived. You don't have to go out today, so can you not take your medicine? I'll take care of you."

Gu Yun didn't use his medicine all that often these days anyway, so he nodded, unconcerned. "You don't have to take care of me, I'm used to it. I can't find my monocle—go fetch me a spare."

Chang Geng hugged him tightly, refusing to let go. "I took your monocle. I'm not giving it back."

Their relationship had undergone a subtle shift that was difficult to describe. Truth be told, even when they had still been godfather and godson, their relationship had always been incredibly close. When Chang Geng had brazenly unleashed his amorous feelings in the heat of battle, Gu Yun had initially tried to deflect him using gentle persuasion and compromise until eventually, he'd found himself ensnared as well. Personal letters and battle reports had come and gone in an unbroken stream, and the depth of affection expressed therein could certainly be considered profound...yet none of it could compare to the ardent passion they felt now. Even were the enemy to besiege the capital a second time, they would dismiss it from their minds. Their entire world had shrunk down to a tiny patch of earth containing only two—nothing else mattered.

"Why did you take my monocle?" Gu Yun asked.

Chang Geng smiled. "I like it."

He carefully helped Gu Yun into his clothes, then bent to help him slip into his shoes, his every motion painstakingly attentive.

Prince Yan, with his plain clothes and ascetic habits, always seemed much like a monk. Those who didn't know him well would assume him a paragon of virtue. But after this latest encounter, Gu Yun finally realized that this man's dignified skin hid a mountain of unspeakable *interests* far beyond ordinary human understanding.

He liked what? The fact that Gu Yun was blind?

Chang Geng wasn't a particularly loud speaker, so to make sure Gu Yun could hear him, he whispered his words directly into Gu Yun's ear. Even phrases like "mind the doorsill" made Gu Yun feel as though they were intimately entwined. When he reached the door, Gu the Blind instinctively reached out to feel for the door frame but found his hand gently yet implacably intercepted by Chang Geng. "Don't touch anything," Chang Geng said, unyielding. "Just hold on to me."

Chang Geng had nearly taken leave of his senses, mesmerized by this unprecedented measure of control. He refused to release Gu Yun for even a second. Every now and again, he would say a few words before leaning in to request a kiss. He was thoroughly enjoying himself and didn't seem at all tired of this enterprise. Gu Yun, on the other hand, soon grew agitated by the sticky sweetness of it all. Heaven help him, Gu Yun just didn't get it. Previously, Chang Geng had been so distant and restrained that he found it inappropriate to even look at Gu Yun while helping him dress. How on earth did a man like that become so unhinged after having sex once?

Gu Yun tactfully rejected his proposal. "I can't see; that doesn't mean I can't walk. You don't have to keep clinging to me—aren't you fantastically busy?"

Chang Geng kissed his earlobe. "Then come with me to the study."

After Gu Yun had left for the northwest, his study had basically become Chang Geng's domain. Gu Yun was on the borders year-round; when he walked in, the room seemed foreign for a moment. Chang Geng helped him to a chair.

As they sat with sunlight streaming over them from that familiar angle, Gu Yun suddenly remembered something. He stretched out his leg, and his foot bumped a little wooden stool, just as expected. "This old thing is actually still here."

Chang Geng leaned down to pick it up. Drawn in vibrant detail on the stool's wooden surface was a group of tiny tortoises biting each other's tails to form a circle. Next to the doodle, etched in a childish script, were the words, *Though long lives the sacred tortoise,*[15] *surround him ten to one.*[16]

...These lines were utterly mismatched.

Chang Geng laughed until he ran out of breath. He tugged Gu Yun's hand over and pressed it to the inscription. "Your doing?"

"Don't laugh. I didn't do much serious studying as a child." Gu Yun's eyes curved in a smile. "And what little studying I did was at the palace with His Majesty and Prince Wei. The old marquis

---

15 Line from the *yuefu* poem 龟虽寿, "Though Long Lives the Sacred Tortoise," by Three King-doms-era warlord Cao Cao.

16 Line from *The Art of War* by Sun Tzu.

wasn't exactly a lettered man himself; he mostly read books on military strategy. He hired a pedantic old Confucian scholar to come recite the classics at me, but I'd fall asleep listening to him drone on after less than an hour. I had to find other ways to amuse myself—oh, you can go ahead and do whatever you need to. It's been ages since I've been home; I'll just walk around a bit by myself."

"No, wait," Chang Geng said hastily. "I like listening to you talk. What happened next?"

Gu Yun looked embarrassed. It really wasn't anything to be proud of, but it was rare to see Chang Geng so light-hearted. After a moment of hesitation, Gu Yun decided to view this as a means to make him happy and continued, "Back then, I was the worst troublemaker you can imagine. Even my xiansheng grew to fear my antics. But he didn't dare lecture me to my face. Instead, he would go lodge his complaints with the old marquis behind my back. If my old man didn't beat me, he'd punish me by making me hold a horse stance while standing on a bench; I'd fall at the slightest wobble. That bastard was seriously nothing like a real dad... I felt that old goat was a despicable person, forever tattling on me. So I hatched a plan with Shen Jiping: we swiped some laxatives and secretly dumped all of them into Xiansheng's tea.

"Honestly, a single dose of laxatives might not have been so bad. But we were both young and reckless, and Xiansheng was old and in poor health. He nearly died from our prank. Never in the two hundred years of the Gu family's history had there ever been such a wicked little miscreant. The old marquis was apoplectic and wanted to whip me to death. Thankfully the princess stopped him... Oh, but my mom later told me—it wasn't that she didn't want to see me beaten, but that her own body was weak, so it was difficult for her to conceive. She feared if I were flogged to death, it would spell the end of the Gu line."

Chang Geng took a moment to imagine the scene. If he had such a hellion for a child, he probably would've tried to whip him to death too. But when he remembered the nightmare child in question was Gu Yun, he felt that if he were the old marquis, even if someone really *had* died, his only option would be to pay for that life with his own. He would never have the heart to harm a hair on Gu Yun's head.

After trying and failing to restrain his laughter, he asked, "And then what happened?"

Gu Yun hesitated; he really couldn't maintain the smile on his face any longer. His mirthful expression faded, and after a lengthy silence he finally said, "And then, my parents decided I would become absolutely lawless if things went on this way. They took me with them to the Black Iron Battalion's encampment on the northern border."

And thus, his rowdy childhood had come to a swift end.

SECRET CONCERN

THOSE DAYS WERE PROBABLY the most indelibly painful time of his life. Gu Yun paused. He hadn't planned on continuing this story. But perhaps these words had been stored in his heart for too many years; he found himself unable to stop.

"Life on the northern border...was truly bitter. The war had just ended, and there were wounded soldiers everywhere you looked. The sun set over yellow sand every day, and not even in the princess's tent could you drink a mouthful of hot tea. How could it possibly be as agreeable as the life of a noble young master in the capital? I threw a furious tantrum at first—I wanted to go back—but the old marquis refused. When he was fed up with my tantrums, he dragged me to the drill grounds as punishment. Every day, when the officers of the Black Iron Battalion drilled their troops, I had to follow along and train alongside them. If I slacked off even a little, he would beat me right there in full view of those iron giants."

The old marquis had a good read on his son's lousy personality. The boy was finicky and unruly, but though the little brat barely cleared the height of a grown man's thighs, he would never humiliate himself by crying before an audience.

Chang Geng had plastered himself to Gu Yun's back, resting his chin on Gu Yun's shoulder. Now he ghosted his lips over the base of Gu Yun's ear. "Had I been born twenty years earlier," he said quietly,

"I would have picked you up and stolen you away. I would have raised you properly in the lap of luxury."

Gu Yun considered the picture painted by Chang Geng's words. It was so sappy he didn't know how to respond, torn as he was between laughter and tears.

To be honest, when he thought about it objectively, many of the families that lived so extravagantly didn't survive past three generations. Gu Yun came from just such an affluent background, and he was also an only son. If he really had been allowed to grow up in the capital, wild as he pleased, who knew how ungovernable he would have become. Only with a hard-hearted father like the old marquis, who had no qualms about using such vicious methods of discipline, would the Black Iron Battalion gain a worthy successor.

But who could have imagined the enormous price paid to see Gu Yun make something of himself?

"Uncle Wang said your temperament changed after you returned from the northern border. You didn't want to see anyone and ignored everyone you met." Chang Geng paused, then tugged Gu Yun's hand closer, writing into his palm, *Do you hate the late emperor?*

Gu Yun unconsciously groped for the wine jar at his waist. Only after he'd reached out did he remember he'd decided to stop drinking. The jar of wine had long been removed.

Gu Yun pressed his lips into a thin line. "I don't... Go pour me a cup of tea."

For a moment, Chang Geng thought he'd heard wrong. In the days after the capital siege, Gu Yun had been so grievously wounded he could barely sit up, yet every time he opened his mouth it was to recklessly demand wine. How was it that after fighting a few battles in the Western Regions, he suddenly understood the importance of preserving his health? Chang Geng had always been quietly critical of this alcoholic's drinking habits, but this unexpected change in disposition caused his heart to stumble in his chest with a *thud*, more shocked than happy. Rising to his feet, he brewed a cup of spring tea for Gu Yun and surreptitiously pressed his fingers to Gu Yun's wrist, a frisson of suspicious concern once again unfurling in his heart. He hated that his inferior skills couldn't seem to detect a thing.

Even without the use of his eyes and ears, Gu Yun could sense Chang Geng's tension. He realized he'd accidentally given himself away. Chang Geng was much too perceptive. As a famously flawed individual, it would have been better to keep up his terrible habits; the people who cleaned up after him were already accustomed to it. On the contrary, a sudden change of course would serve only to alarm.

Gu Yun casually gulped down the tea, then licked his lips and said, "I don't know where I left my wine jar. Do we have any of Old Mister Shen's home brew left?"

To Chang Geng, this sounded much more like Gu Yun's usual style. After all that worrying, it turned out he was merely thirsty from talking so much. Relaxing slightly, Chang Geng readily shot him down. "It's all gone. You'll have to settle for tea."

Gu Yun clicked his tongue without much sincerity. In the next moment, something was pressed to his mouth, and the sticky-sweet fragrance of glutinous rice assaulted his nose. Gu Yun reared back. "What's this? I don't want—mmph—"

Chang Geng had leaned forward and fed him the item in question from between his own lips.

Gu Yun's brow twisted into a knot. He disliked eating sweets and could barely stand the nauseatingly sweet combination of Chang Geng and that lump of tea pastry. But he didn't spit it back out.

As with that eggshell-studded bowl of soup noodles all those years ago, he wolfed the whole thing down. Chewing through the cloying bean-paste filling, the taste so oversweet it was almost bitter, he suddenly felt a flicker of unease.

Chang Geng's soppy displays of affection were abnormal. Likewise, his rapid shift to anxious suspicion when he heard Gu Yun ask for tea was also abnormal. Such emotional extremes were exhausting and typically couldn't be sustained for long. In most, they lasted for a short while, after which they would devolve into either apathy or confusion. Or the person in question would shift their attention, allowing those feelings to dissipate out of an instinctive sense of self-preservation.

Chang Geng...

Gu Yun's expression turned solemn. "Chang Geng, give me my monocle."

"No." Chang Geng encircled Gu Yun with his arms from the side, as if to keep him captive. He persisted with his interrogation: "Why don't you hate him?"

His voice was eager yet detached. An eagerness stemming from a desire to get to the bottom of this matter and determine whether or not Gu Yun felt animosity toward the late emperor. As if the instant Gu Yun admitted that yes, he did hate him, Chang Geng would promptly take some particular action. A detachment that manifested in his apparent disregard for the fact that the "late emperor" of whom he spoke was his father. He mentioned the man with the indifference one reserved for a stray cat or dog on the side of the road.

Gu Yun's heart sank. After a beat of silence, he responded to Chang Geng's query with one of his own, "What about you? Do you still hate Huge'er?"

Chang Geng didn't expect Gu Yun to toss the question back at him. He blinked in mild surprise—if Gu Yun had been able to see, he would've found that though they were no longer red, the shadow of a second pupil yet lurked within Chang Geng's eyes.

"If she were to stand before me now," Chang Geng replied in lofty tones, "I would tear out her tendons and skin her alive—but she died a tragic death without a proper burial. Even if I wished to dig her back up and whip her corpse, it would be a futile effort. However much I loathe her, I have no way to vent my hatred. And if I had, isn't that exactly what she would want, since it would speed the work of the poison in my body?"

That was absolutely not how Chang Geng truly felt. No matter how careless or deaf Gu Yun might be, he could still tell this much.

Gu Yun was about to respond when he felt the person plastered to his side flinch. It was the panicked startle of one who had poured their full concentration into an endeavor and been suddenly interrupted. A slight breeze drifted in at their backs; someone had opened the door to the study.

Gu Yun turned. "Is that Uncle Wang or Old Huo?"

Standing at the door, the old housekeeper raised his voice and called out, "My lord, it's me. The Lingshu Institute has sent someone over to see His Highness Prince Yan!"

The twinned pupils in Chang Geng's eyes dwindled to one, as if stimulated by a bright light. He reflexively released Gu Yun, showing his usual "touch not that which runs contrary to propriety"[17] brand of restraint. Yet halfway through his transformation he seemed to recall something, a lost expression flickering across his face.

Gu Yun acted as if he didn't notice. "Go ahead and take care of what business you need to. It's been days since I've had a proper meal,

---

17   A line adapted from The Analects of Confucius.

so I'm off to find one. And that thing you made me eat...I choked it down, but it's giving me heartburn."

Chang Geng started in surprise, then clapped a hand to his forehead and rubbed his brow in dismay. "I... That... I really..." He jumped to his feet. "I'll go tell the kitchens to make you something easy to digest," he said, agitated.

Uncle Wang was quick to obey. "Understood; this old servant will go at once."

Chang Geng bolted toward the door of the study, then stopped short as he remembered something. He patted himself down and pulled Gu Yun's glass monocle from his lapels. He turned to hand it to Gu Yun; the metal frame and connected chain were warm with his body heat. Chang Geng carefully wiped the lens clean and set it on the bridge of Gu Yun's nose, his eyes lingering on Gu Yun's face for a long interval. Suddenly, he said in a low voice, "Zixi, just now, I...I honestly thought I was dreaming."

That's the only reason I dared to act so presumptuously.

After being flustered by Chang Geng's bizarre behavior for an entire afternoon, at these words, Gu Yun nearly blew a gasket. He was sorely tempted to retort, *Why don't I slap you so you can see if it hurts?* But before he could put thought to action, Chang Geng paused, then straightened back up. "In all my life, I've never had such a wonderful dream," he said with a hint of self-mockery. His mouth crooked up in a stiff smile. "If only I never woke up."

Gu Yun was silent.

The moment Chang Geng returned to normal, Gu Yun could no longer find it in his heart to castigate him. He felt that, if such a thing were to happen a few more times, Gu Yun would have no choice but to descend into madness right alongside him. He summoned an inscrutably steady expression and bade him leave with a wave of his hand.

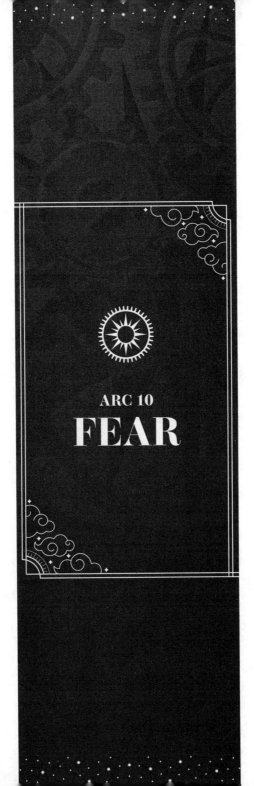

ARC 10

FEAR

81

MARRIAGE

THE EIGHTH YEAR OF LONGAN, early summer. Although the unfortunate Marshal Gu had incurred the wrath of Tai Sui, the fate of the nation of Great Liang, after hitting rock bottom, seemed to slowly show signs of recovery like tender shoots breaking through an endless field of white snow after a long winter.

After decisively quashing the rebellion of the western vassal states, the Marquis of Anding signed the New Silk Road Accords. The Black Iron Battalion escorted the tribute of violet gold from the Western Regions to the capital. With battle cries resounding throughout the nation, Great Liang finally carved a path forward.

Shen Yi and company had just ridden into the capital with their consignment of violet gold when the Lingshu Institute came out with another piece of good news: there had been a breakthrough in the development of Gu Yun's great iron bow, which had never seen widespread use in the army. Despite his humble origins as the son of a butcher, Ge Chen was indeed a brilliant young talent blessed with natural genius. He had invented a new type of gold tank that was exceedingly light and easy to use. It could be attached to an archer's bow and be perfectly controlled by human strength alone.

The draw weight of the prototype iron bow, which could only be fully drawn by a master archer, had been reduced by over fifty percent, allowing parhelion iron arrows to fly effortlessly from human hands. What's more, these shots were extremely accurate, since the weight of the iron arrows made them more resistant to being blown off-course by powerful winds. Once these bows saw large-scale production, the use of the old parhelion bows within the Great Liang military would be discontinued. Individual iron arrows could also be specially fitted with engine systems that would allow them to accelerate a second time in midair after being released or even explode after touching down in enemy territory to devastating effect.

By the end of the sixth month, between the Black Iron Battalion's fierce vigilance and the steady worsening of domestic disputes within the Far Westerners' home nation, the situation on both the northern and southern fronts simultaneously fell quiet. For a short spell, the nation of Great Liang had an opportunity to catch its breath. Every member of the imperial court, from top to bottom, knew that the most urgent matter at hand was reassuring the hearts of the people. In this regard, the most pressing matter was the resettlement of the refugees who had been driven from their homes by the flames of war.

But how should they go about aiding and resettling these displaced citizens? There was no way they could provide these refugees with land or property. Even the most incorruptible official in the world would be hard-pressed to find the noble character and steadfast integrity required to give up their own home to another.

The Grand Council organized several grand assemblies to discuss the issue with the officials of the court, but still, they generated no feasible solutions. All they managed to drum up was a pile of rotten ideas like sending the refugees into the wilderness to cultivate virgin land. The Longan Emperor flew into a rage. He berated the court ministers as useless loafers, howling, "Why not suggest that we pack the refugees off to the East Sea and task them with filling it with pebbles?!"

Prince Yan of the Grand Council took the lead in remaining silent and abstained from expressing his stance. Meanwhile, the Six Ministries and various other officials submitted memorials, passing the buck to and fro, arguing themselves into a stalemate in the middle of court.

It was then that Du Wanquan, leading a group of thirteen prominent merchants hailing from every corner of the country, stepped forward and submitted a memorial in which he declared that they were willing to emulate the Far Westerners in establishing privately operated factories, and would bring in refugees from all over the land to operate them. This way, not much land would be needed. Chang Geng had confiscated a number of properties when he had traveled the banks of the inland canal punishing corrupt officials who profited from the plight of the refugees—these lands alone should be sufficient for the endeavor. They also planned on recruiting civilian artificers and tasking them with the development of a series of civilian-use engines based on schematics from the farming puppets that had been implemented in Jiangnan years ago.

Following the issuance of the second batch of war beacon tickets, a hidden undercurrent of power in the imperial court gradually reared its head. While they had lain dormant, these individuals seemed to have nothing to do with each other. But now, though they maintained a low profile, they began to push their agenda forward.

A petition came before the Longan Emperor requesting the court grant special concessions to the civilian merchants who had been first to step up in support of the war beacon tickets. For instance, they asked that these merchants be allowed to directly submit memorials for the emperor's personal approval via the Grand Council.

They also asked that, under the condition that the military was well-supplied, the emperor allow them to buy a fixed amount of violet gold on an annual basis.

This memorial was initially submitted by the Ministry of Works. Meng Jue, the Minister of Works himself, was a Hanlin scholar of humble origins. In the memorial, he wrote: *This plan would kill three birds with one stone. Not only would this resolve the refugee crisis afflicting our nation, it would also demonstrate the imperial court's commitment to treating those who have made contributions to our country with fairness. Furthermore, the profits from selling violet gold at a premium to these wealthy merchants may be used toward additional military supplies.*

A single stone raised a thousand waves. As it dropped, some of the sharp-nosed, high-ranking noble officials finally returned to their senses.

After being absent from court for so long, Gu Yun had the pleasure of listening in on the grand assembly, bearing personal witness to its magnificent devolution into belligerent saber-rattling. Stupefied by what he heard, he suddenly felt that this place was vastly more treacherous than any head-on attack or covert action he witnessed on the front lines.

The thirteen merchants' memorial stoked conflicts that had accumulated between the powerful noble elite and the brilliant but poor young scholars for generations. By this point, those with brains began to suspect that a backroom deal had been struck between the government officials and the merchants. Meanwhile, those with particularly sensitive noses had already caught a whiff of the inexorable future toward which this emergent force was pushing them: one in which the very foundations of the land-owning upper crust would be shaken. Faced with the threat of imminent decline, a sense of crisis quietly took root among the court's elite.

In court, the pro-commerce faction accused the nobles alternately of forming cliques for private gain to bring disaster upon country and people and commentating from the sidelines when they held no stake in the matter. Some among them furiously jabbed their fingers at the other party and shouted, "If you're so smart, why don't you invite the refugees to stay in your fancy villa?!" In response, representatives of several key noble families returned fire, their faces flushed with fury as they shouted things like, "How can mere merchants be allowed into the dignified venue of the imperial court?!" and "Violet gold is a treasure of our nation, how can we allow it to fall into the hands of private businessmen?" In the end, they did away with all subtlety and straight-up accused the opposing faction: "I wonder how many bribes my respected colleagues have taken to throw in their lot with these money-grubbing peddlers."

The military generals attending the assembly took in the Marquis of Anding's silence, glanced at each other in bemusement, and continued watching from the sidelines, allowing members of the Grand Council to step forward in turns to smooth things over.

Lifting his head, Gu Yun glanced at the Longan Emperor. Li Feng really had aged. The man had yet to turn thirty, but his hair was already streaked with gray, and a cloud of exhausted gloom hung over his brow. Gu Yun was struck by a thought: *Would it have been a mercy for him to have been hit by a stray arrow and perish aboard the red-headed kite back when the capital had nearly fallen?*

As if sensing his gaze, Li Feng looked up and met Gu Yun's eyes.

When the court session concluded that day, Gu Yun was kept behind in the palace. After falling out with Li Feng before the war, Gu Yun had been fighting nonstop all over the country; the two had barely any opportunity to meet in private. It felt like a lifetime had passed since the last time they chatted idly about current events in the halls where they had grown to adulthood. Li Feng had been seized by a momentary impulse when he asked Gu Yun to stay, but now that they were rambling through the imperial gardens, he suddenly felt painfully awkward; he realized he had nothing to say.

It was then that the crown prince, fresh out of his lessons and passing the gardens, came over to say hello.

Li Feng had little interest in the imperial harem and wasn't blessed with many children. The crown prince, who had just turned eight, had yet to hit his growth spurt and was still very much a child. He was reserved when he saw Li Feng and politely stepped forward to make his greeting. "Father."

He cautiously glanced up at Gu Yun, as if he wanted to strike up a conversation but was uncertain as to his identity. Gu Yun smiled down at him. "Your subject Gu Yun pays his respects to Your Highness."

The crown prince was stunned. The little boy loved listening to stories about great big heroes. Seeing Gu Yun in the flesh, he was torn between uncontrollable excitement and the need to maintain the dignified bearing expected of a crown prince before his father. His tiny face turned bright red as he stammered, "M-Marshal Gu! No wait...uhh... Granduncle, th-there's no need for such courtesy. This solitary one—I... I've studied Granduncle's writings before."

Gu Yun's expression turned a bit queer. "Your Highness is far too kind." The word "Granduncle" was like a fatal strike to the heart. He suddenly felt as though he had sprouted a meter-long beard.

That day, Li Feng dismissed his attendants, leaving the crown prince alone to accompany them on their stroll. What he discussed with Gu Yun was a mystery. The palace attendants knew merely that the young crown prince seemed to get on splendidly with the

Marquis of Anding, and that the young lad clung to him and refused to leave. In the end, he clambered onto Gu Yun's back and fell asleep, and it was the Marquis of Anding who personally delivered him to his residence in the Eastern Palace.

Before he left, the Longan Emperor specifically bade Gu Yun come to the palace and guide the crown prince more often if he had the time. Sovereign and subject had the most amiable chat, as if the quarrel between the emperor and the Marquis of Order, and the previous impasse between political and military power, were nothing more than a ripple in a pond, deliberately forgotten.

Elsewhere, Jiang Chong hurried into a private room in Southward Tower. He pulled a secret missive from his sleeve and handed it to Chang Geng. "Your Highness, please take a look. We've yet to establish a stable foundation in the imperial court, and now, it seems we may have acted with undue haste."

It was a copy of a memorial. Jiang Chong lowered his voice. "This was leaked from the palace. After today's court session, a number of influential noble families banded together and submitted this memorial to His Majesty through Imperial Uncle Wang. I'm afraid they've been planning this for quite some time."

Chang Geng calmly accepted the document. "Imperial Uncle Wang? Has he even finished wiping his own ass? The nation has been in a state of chaos due to the war. Does he think that, since General Tan died defending our walls, there is no one else who will investigate him?"

Jiang Chong dropped his voice lower still. "Your Highness, Imperial Uncle Wang is the empress dowager's kin. Short of conspiring against the state, nothing will compel His Majesty to touch him... Besides, who would dare raise that old case? Even if we really did leverage it to bring down Imperial Uncle Wang, wouldn't that also prove that the late emperor was duped by a wicked enchantress into wounding his loyal subject? It would garner him the reputation of an incapable ruler. The son speaks not of the faults of the father—His Majesty would never oust Wang Guo over something like that."

Chang Geng skimmed the copied document, his face devoid of emotion. Suddenly, he hummed in surprise.

"What is it?"

"This doesn't look like something that wine-guzzling waste of space Wang Guo came up with. Who wrote this?" Chang Geng asked.

"Ah. Speaking of, this person does seem to have quite an affinity with Your Highness," Jiang Chong said. "Didn't the Fang family once hope to make a marriage match with the prince? The person wielding the knife behind this memorial is Miss Fang's uncle—the current Minister of Revenue, Fang Qin. The late emperor personally named him Zhuangyuan[18] in the eighteenth year of his rule. He was the sole individual to rank first in all three levels of the imperial examination during the Yuanhe era. The man's been an extraordinary talent since childhood."

Ever since Fang Qin took over the Ministry of Revenue, it had been operating in an organized and highly efficient manner. He worked well in tandem with the Grand Council, never hampered their work, and could be considered a highly capable official. Unfortunately, his views were shaped by his circumstances. He was born into the Fang family, so as their representative, he was destined to become an outstandingly talented stumbling block for Chang Geng's plans.

---

18 Title bestowed on the scholar who achieves first place in the imperial examination.

"The examination mentor to half the court and a celebrated figure." Chang Geng rapped his knuckles lightly on his writing desk. "It's high time the swallows that nested in the noble halls flew into the homes of ordinary folk."[19]

Jiang Chong's heart thudded in his chest at the killing intent within those words. Before he could think on it further, however, Chang Geng continued in a nonchalant tone, "Minister Fang is indeed talented—truly a competent minister capable of governing the nation."

Prince Yan spoke briskly, and his praise sounded genuine. It was as if the trace of inexplicable malice an instant ago had been wholly a product of Justice Jiang's imagination. Yet still, there seemed to be a subtle undercurrent to that phrase, *governing the nation.*

Fang Qin's memorial took direct aim at the Longan Emperor's weakness. He made no comment as to whether recruiting refugees to work in factories was wise or not. Rather, he clamped down on the administrative security issues of violet gold and refused to let go, going so far as to invoke Gu Yun's name—*This violet gold was paid for in blood, spilt by the tens of thousands of Black Iron Battalion soldiers fighting on the front lines. Would it not chill the hearts of loyal subjects and generals if it was put to frivolous use?*

Gu Yun wasn't the type to worry about such things, but Li Feng's sore spot had been well and thoroughly poked. Chang Geng himself had once advised Master Fenghan to back down on the issue of violet gold. Since the reign of the wise and fearsome Emperor Wu, the precious fuel had become like a second jade imperial seal in the eyes of the imperial family. On top of that, after his private violet gold stores, accumulated over generations in the Sunlight Palace, went up in flames, Li Feng had become all the more insecure when it came to this subject.

---

19 A reference to the poem 乌衣巷, "Wuyi Lane" by Liu Yuxi.

Fang Qin went on to provide a thorough analysis of a long list of possible consequences that might result from the sale of violet gold to civilian merchants. For instance, after making this allowance, how would the court determine whether a merchant's violet gold was purchased through official channels or obtained through smuggling? If the price of smuggled violet gold was cheaper, wouldn't profit-seeking merchants naturally acquire it through illicit means and excuse possession of it with their special permits? Private stockpiles, illegal sales, and smuggling of violet gold had continued unabated despite repeated prohibitions—would not these activities become even more difficult to police moving forward?

Another example: Assuming no unexpected disasters, these proposed factories would likely outlive their founders. Even if the imperial court granted no more than thirteen civilian merchants these special permits, what of their children and grandchildren? Facilities that burned violet gold would burn more and more of it over time. Otherwise, they would be unsustainable. Would the imperial court extend the special permits to these merchants' posterity as well? What if future generations branched off from the family? What if the factory was sold to an outside party? If these permits could be bought and sold, would it not be frightfully easy for villainous characters to hoard armor and engines—to plot rebellion in the future?

On the contrary, if these special permits were a one-off grant attached to an individual and not to the factory, then in the future, when these thirteen permit-holders passed and the factories necessarily shut down, would the nation not face a second wave of out-of-work refugees? The current generation knew their displacement was the fault of foreign adversaries—and that it was the imperial court that provided them with a bite to eat and a roof over their head—but could the same be said of those who would be displaced again several decades from now? They would blame the government for revoking the special permits and destroying their livelihood. Would these measures not simply sow the seeds of countless future disasters in the interest of solving a temporary crisis?

These and countless other concerns were laid out within the memorial. Finally, Fang Qin elegantly signed off: *In conclusion, those who advocate for the sale of violet gold to civilian merchants must be either simple-minded fools with their heads up their asses, giving no consideration to how this mess will be cleaned up in the future, or shit-stirrers seeking to fish in muddy waters—in which case, who can say where their true intentions lie?*

Every word of the lengthy memorial penned by the talented Minister Fang was a knife stabbing into the Longan Emperor's heart.

"If this had been submitted to the Grand Council first, as it ought to have been, we might've been able to block it." Jiang Chong sighed. "But alas, Your Highness, the Fang family's influence within the court runs deep."

Chang Geng suddenly shook with silent laughter. Jiang Chong looked at him, baffled. After a moment, Prince Yan picked up a cup of tea from his desk and took a sip, unruffled. "Minister Fang discusses an urgent matter of utmost importance. He's not just blowing smoke either—everything he's said is perfectly within the realm of reason and propriety. Even if this memorial were submitted to the Grand Council, what justification would we have for blocking it? Hanshi, aren't these words rather improper? What do you take the Grand Council for? A venue to abuse power and engage in fraud, deceiving those above and deluding those below?"

His tone was gentle, yet the contents of his speech were serious in the extreme. "Your Highness," Jiang Chong began, stricken.

Chang Geng's severe expression eased as he cut him off blandly: "These words that flew from your mouth to my ears today will not reach another. I'll overlook this for now, but I do not wish to hear such talk in the Grand Council again in the future."

"Yes, Your Highness." Jiang Chong's face was solemn as he hastily responded, "This lower official has spoken in error."

Chang Geng's countenance warmed as he proceeded to lie through his teeth. "My experience is limited, and I often lack insight and self-control when I come up against unexpected complications. I take you for one of my own, so my mouth runs away from me. I spoke impulsively. Please don't take my words to heart, Hanshi-xiong."

Jiang Chong repeatedly assured him that he dared not. He had been personally promoted to his position by Prince Yan, so most took him for Prince Yan's trusted confidante. Yet Jiang Chong found himself increasingly mystified by this superior to whom he owed so much. The noble elite, led by the Fang family, would not sit idle while the young upstarts of the imperial court capitalized on this opportunity to climb to positions of greater power. They would without a doubt spare no effort to suppress them. Others may not have realized it, but Jiang Chong knew well that the rise of these so-called "young upstarts" had been singlehandedly orchestrated by Prince Yan. Moreover, the situation currently under debate had been in the works since the enactment of government reforms—if not earlier, since the initial implementation of the war beacon tickets.

This protracted deployment of opening moves seemed intended to trigger a certain set of circumstances—but to what end?

Was His Highness Prince Yan merely doing this to save the nation from an unexpected crisis out of duty and selflessness? Was he really as he seemed—so absent personal wants and desires that, the very second their enemies fell back, he would immediately resign his position and go home to live as an idle prince sponging off the imperial coffers? If that was truly the case, why go to such lengths and lay out such a grand scheme?

But if Prince Yan had some other aim and was merely weaving this enormous web of lies to deceive the nation…what could he possibly be pursuing? He was the sole remaining blood-related brother of the reigning emperor, Great Liang's sole prince of the first rank. If he wished to rise higher, there was only one position left.

But that didn't make sense either. If Prince Yan had his heart set on the throne, why would he defy the Longan Emperor's verbal decree to abdicate in his favor? Even if Jiang Chong were to surmise that Prince Yan began to covet the throne after that day, why would he, as a prince of the first rank, go out of his way to offend so many important ministers of the court? Shouldn't he be trying to win them to his side instead?

Jiang Chong was deeply perplexed. "Your Highness," he began cautiously, "never mind His Majesty, even this lower official has misgivings about the proposal to build privately-owned factories after reading this memorial. But if that plan fails, how will the court compensate Master Du and the other merchants who have made great contributions to the state, much less resettle so many refugees?"

"Now, this is where you've got things wrong," Chang Geng said with an enigmatic smile. "When His Majesty reads this memorial, he will be filled with doubts about the sale of violet gold to civilian merchants. Seeing as Minister Fang has already outlined the situation so clearly, the merchants' proposal is no longer feasible. We would be better off thinking about how to solve the problem at hand—that way, wouldn't everyone be satisfied?"

Jiang Chong stared at him in astonishment.

Chang Geng waved a hand. "Go home and get some rest. Ask everyone to come to the office a little early tomorrow—the Grand Council will discuss this matter prior to the court assembly. We mustn't let my imperial brother down."

Jiang Chong murmured his assent and rose to take his leave. Prince Yan's serene speech exuded an inexplicable confidence—it was as if the prince had long foreseen the appearance of Fang Qin's memorial and had planned his response in advance. However...if he had the solution in hand, why did he not mention it earlier but insist on beating around the bush? Aside from exacerbating the friction between the war-beacon-ticket-buying upstarts and the old-money nobility, what did this accomplish?

"Wait—Hanshi." Chang Geng called out.

His mind laden with worry, Jiang Chong snapped back to attention. He hastily schooled his expression into one of rapt interest, thinking Prince Yan had another urgent matter to discuss.

"Since you're heading out, please put in an order for me with the kitchen: two catties of fried yellow croaker to go. I'll take it home with me in a bit—many thanks!"

Justice Jiang slipped on a step and nearly tumbled down the rest of the stairs.

Gu Yun, detained by the Longan Emperor, managed to take his leave just before the palace locked its gates.

The allocation of military supplies throughout the nation had to be reviewed by the Marquis of Anding before it could be reported to the Grand Council and forwarded to the emperor for approval. Gu Yun had been expecting to receive the latest proposal for violet gold allocation after the grand assembly. He hadn't anticipated that the emperor would keep him until this late hour. Shen Yi was left to wait for him until the curtain of night began to draw closed. Just as he was yawning from the excruciating boredom, he spied Gu Yun slowly making his way out.

"What took you so long?" Shen Yi walked up to join him. "For a moment there, I thought you'd gotten into another spat with His Majesty."

Gu Yun accepted the prepared memorial from Shen Yi and flipped through it casually. "I'll look this over when I get back—anyway, what's there to argue about in our old age?"

Shen Yi stared at Gu Yun, thunderstruck. "In...in our *old age?*" he forced out around his knotted tongue. "Sir, are you all right? What exactly did His Majesty say?" He'd actually managed to tag the so-called Flower of the Northwest, who spent all his time peacocking about, with the label "old"!

Gu Yun glanced woefully at his shoulder; the patch of drool left by the little crown prince when he fell asleep on Gu Yun's back had yet to dry. It was easy for a person to feel they were still young when they were single too long—but somehow, in the blink of an eye, he'd become a "granduncle." He suddenly realized that, at his current age, if he wasn't particularly blessed with longevity, more than half of his life might be over.

"It's nothing," Gu Yun said absentmindedly as he walked. "Perhaps he was feeling disheartened from all the fighting in the grand assembly. He shared a few depressing words with me... His Majesty has always been competitive. No matter what he does, he wants to beat everyone else. He thought about climbing Mount Tai to complete the Feng Shan sacrifices[20] when he first ascended the throne, but now, with the nation in its current state, he... Ay, he hasn't had it easy either."

---

20 An official rite performed by the emperor to pay homage to heaven and earth. Completion of the Feng Shan sacrifices allowed the emperor to receive the Mandate of Heaven, thus legitimizing his rule.

274 ☀ STARS OF CHAOS

Shen Yi listened in silence with his hands clasped behind his back. He was exhausted by these sordid affairs of the imperial family. Starting with the Yuanhe Emperor presently lying in the imperial mausoleum, their members became increasingly erratic. When happy, they would honor you with unparalleled favor and grant you power enough to upend the world, only to turn around in a towering fury a few days later and clap you in irons. In the worst-case scenario, you wouldn't even know by whose hand you might lose your life.

Just look at the Yuanhe Emperor—had he taken decisive action earlier, Gu Yun would have long reincarnated and would by now be reaching the age to take a wife in the next life. He wished to eliminate the Gu family, yet time and again, he couldn't bear to commit. In this, he was like a cruel hunter who had wiped out a tiger's den: he'd already done the deed, yet couldn't follow through and kill the cub shivering in fright. Instead, he insisted on bringing the creature home and raising it like a housecat. He was utterly sincere when he killed and utterly sincere when he cared, and in the end, he had managed to raise the bane of his existence in the deeply devoted Gu Yun. It was honestly difficult to say whether he had succeeded or failed.

Shen Yi sighed. "We spend all our days fighting out there on the borders, so we don't learn of the difficulties in court until we return. Prince Yan has really had it rough this past year. You know, my dad was just harping on about this the other day. He said I'm like the old frontiersman losing his horse—I've received a blessing in disguise.[21] My family has never been a famous noble clan, but we're still a household that has lived off the imperial coffers, producing talents through the imperial examination down the generations. When I

---

21   A famous parable from the Huainanzi that tells of an old man who loses a horse only to see bad luck transform into good fortune in a repeating cycle, starting with the lost horse returning with another horse in tow from the nomadic tribes of the northern steppes.

willfully joined the Lingshu Institute, my old man took it in stride, but all my gossipy aunts lost their minds. Later on, I left the Lingshu Institute and ran off with you to join the army and scandalized them even more...but anyhow. Either way, in the eyes of my aunts and uncles, I'm a failure beyond redemption."

"You have legitimate military achievements to your name," Gu Yun objected. "How does that make you a failure?"

"Right? But my old man is actually pretty pleased with how things turned out," Shen Yi said. "According to him, there are all sorts of interests lurking beneath the surface of the imperial court now. The situation is becoming hopelessly complicated, so I'm better off following you out onto the battlefield. At the very least, we soldiers can rest assured that the muzzles of our cannons and the tips of our swords are pointed at the enemy."

But Gu Yun didn't find this assuring at all. Instead, his heart felt all the heavier. He had no idea what sort of role Chang Geng played in the chaotic imperial court. Thus far, the Grand Council appeared to be a temporary body specially created to help organize the nation's resources and coordinate the officials of various departments. Though it was at the center of state affairs and had the power to lead the Six Ministries and submit memorials directly to the emperor, its members retained their original posts. It seemed the Grand Council could be dissolved at any moment once the war was over.

With Prince Yan at its head, the Grand Council's work had revolved around the needs of the emperor and the nation's five major military regions, yet its members' true allegiances remained obscured behind a dense and indecipherable cloud.

"But enough of these vexations," Shen Yi interrupted his thoughts. "Right, is His Highness Prince Yan still living at the Marquis Estate? What exactly is going on between you two?"

Gu Yun was silent.

Shen Yi failed to notice the words *Where do I begin* writ clear on Gu Yun's face and began prattling on his own: "I've heard Prince Yan used to stay at the office of the Grand Council for weeks at a time; it's only recently that he's started to come and go at dawn and dusk. Is it just me or does this change coincide with your return to the capital…? Hey, speaking of which, he probably wouldn't play around with you like this if he weren't serious." He went on a long and earnest ramble full of pointless heartfelt nonsense. It was difficult to tell whether he was earnestly sighing over the plight of Prince Yan and urging Gu Yun to accept him at once, or whether he was earnestly warning Gu Yun that such a relationship was universally abhorrent to all levels of society and he ought to decisively reject Chang Geng without delay.

Whichever it was, Gu Yun failed to comprehend a word of it. Frowning, he said, "I don't understand, what do you mean?"

"What I mean is, I don't know what you should do either," Shen Yi said, scratching his head, restless. "I'm worried for you."

Gu Yun felt that Shen Yi wasn't so much worried for him as adding to his worries. He'd already slept with the man, so Shen Yi's sincere speech and all his heartfelt emotions were eight lifetimes too late. But even if Marshal Gu's skin was a meter thick, it would be inappropriate to declare this kind of truth to the world. He glanced back at Shen Yi, who was blindly dogging his heels with seemingly no intention of returning to his own home, and arched an eyebrow. "What are you following me for?" he asked grumpily. "Are you planning to come back to the Marquis Estate and observe how I worry myself sick?"

Shen Yi scoffed in disdain. Then, he mumbled under his breath, "Zixi, we go way back—won't you let me come over and bum a meal?"

"Is your family really that broke?" Gu Yun asked, perplexed.

Shen Yi went uncharacteristically quiet. After hemming and hawing, he said, "My dad...has been trying to arrange a marriage for me lately. He's a bit, uhh...overzealous. I can't afford to make the old man angry, so all I can do is take cover—are you done? Careful you don't pull a muscle laughing so hard. What an ingrate you are—here I am, worrying on your behalf, and there you are, delighting in my misfortune..."

Gu Yun was laughing so hard he could scarcely breathe. "I...have truly been enlightened. This is the first time I've ever seen a general begging for his supper to avoid being forced into marriage."

"Gu Zixi, is there any friendship left between us? If so, then shut your damn mouth. Treat me to a nice meal and I might forgive you." Shen Yi deeply regretted not taking advantage of the days when Gu Yun was bedridden to exact his vengeance. As expected, it was the fate of the honest man to be bullied.

Only after exhausting himself laughing did Gu Yun half-assedly console him, "Consider yourself lucky. Your dad is still alive and well to try to marry you off. Even if I wanted to get forced into marriage, there's no one to do the honors."

Shen Yi looked downcast. "My dad's probably anxious to continue the Shen family line; he's afraid I'll die on the battlefield. It's true that I've made him worry to no end all these years, but I...I know what kind of person I am. I'm a long-winded worrywart by nature. If I had a wife and kids, I fear it would be difficult for me to remain on the borders. And you—you're such a lonely and helpless wretch. If I left..."

Gu Yun's smile slid from his face as he looked back at Shen Yi from a few steps ahead.

"But lately, I've noticed you've started thinking about retiring after fulfilling your duties. If we really do manage to beat back the foreigners, the emperor will have no excuse to hassle you again. Plus, Prince Yan is still in the imperial court. His Highness has always been meticulous, kindhearted, and just. And when it comes to you...I'm sure he'd take good care of you. After frivolously doing as I please for so many years, it's high time I settled down and started a family."

"Jiping," Gu Yun began slowly, "could it be that..."

Shen Yi waited expectantly.

"...you're secretly in love with me too?"

Shen Yi tripped over a raised slab of stone on the ground.

Gu Yun shook his head with a sigh. "Those endowed with beauty can never live in obscurity.[22] Ay, being this handsome is such a burden."

Unable to bear it any longer, Shen Yi howled, "Have you no shame?!"

General Shen's multitudinous worries melted into fury. The two bickered all the way to the front gate of the Marquis Estate, where they ran into Prince Yan, who had just returned from Southward Tower.

Before General Shen, Chang Geng politely made his greetings, then handed a packet of fried yellow croaker to Gu Yun. "Fresh from the frying pan. Yifu mentioned these were really good last time so I bought some on my way home."

Shen Yi laughed stiffly.

Gu Yun coughed stiffly.

The way Chang Geng looked at Gu Yun, with that expression— Shen Yi suddenly felt that coming to the Marquis Estate to cadge a meal was a mistake for which he'd paid with his eyes. Meanwhile, Gu Yun heard the word *Yifu* and immediately felt his lower back begin to ache; he likewise turned mute.

---

22 A line from the poem 长恨歌, "Song of Everlasting Regret," by Bai Juyi.

Thus, His Highness Prince Yan conquered two hale and hearty generals the moment he appeared. Beaming from ear to ear, he ushered them through the door.

82

IDLE WORRIES

SHEN YI WAS, after all, the commanding general of a region. Gu Yun was the only one so casual in his interactions with him; others had to treat him as a respected guest. Gu Yun didn't care to manage the home, so Chang Geng went personally to give the servants instructions.

Shen Yi had been wound tight as a bowstring since he stepped through the gates of the Marquis Estate. He fidgeted in his seat for a while, then snuck a glance at Prince Yan's upright back and scooted over to Gu Yun. "You *did it*?"

Gu Yun once again had no idea where to begin. After a moment of hesitation, he offered a vague hum of agreement.

Shen Yi was appalled. Now he understood why Gu Yun had been so evasive on the way here. Caught between incredulity and helplessness, all he managed was a long, stuttering string of "you-you-you." Gu Yun offered no further explanation. He plopped down nearby like a dead pig unafraid of boiling water, opened the oil-paper packet, and plucked out a crispy fried yellow croaker.

Shen Yi knew Gu Yun could be at times flippant and careless, but he didn't expect him to take it this far. His meddling inner-courtyard auntie's heart roiled in his chest as he admonished, "You... How could you just... You've had your momentary satisfaction, but what're you going to do from here on out, hm? Go the rest of your lives like this? It's absurd! You have great power and prestige, no one's in charge of you—but what about Prince Yan? Did His Majesty agree? If something happens and you two go your separate ways, are you just going to throw away a years-long relationship? You... What can I even say about you, Gu Zixi? You're practically a beast!"

Gu Yun licked some salt and pepper crumbs from the corner of his mouth. Between him and Chang Geng, exactly who had been the "beast"? Gu Yun had truly been wronged to hell and back by this accusation. But he could only affect an inscrutable aloofness. Gu Yun sat where he was and refused to explain himself.

Every consideration Shen Yi raised was self-evident nonsense— Gu Yun had of course thought of all of them himself. If it was merely that he found it hard to resist, he would just have to control himself. The world was a complicated place to be sure, but even if he couldn't control others, he could at least control himself. If, instead, it was a love etched down to his bones, impossible to forget, he could simply smash a brick over his own head and thunk those oceans of sentiment right out of his brain. Parents, grandparents, ancestors—even his own name could be thunked clean, to say nothing of affections.

However...

Chang Geng had been afflicted with wu'ergu since childhood, which made him incapable of ever letting go. Still, Gu Yun felt he had perhaps sabotaged himself in his attempts to be clever. Even now he didn't know whether taking that final step had been right or wrong. But these dangerous entanglements and worries were impossible to discuss with anyone else.

Gu Yun maintained his unperturbed expression. "Once we recover Jiangnan, I'll take him away. Who cares what others say? Every day I'm alive is a day I'll keep him safe."

He said this as if it were the easiest thing in the world. Shen Yi spent several minutes trying to catch his breath in his rage and rolled his eyes at Gu Yun. Gu Yun took another yellow croaker between his teeth, paused, then broke off half and offered it to Shen Yi. "Hurry up and eat, then get out. Haven't you seen how busy he is, working in the Grand Council from dawn to dusk? Have a little tact."

Shen Yi nearly choked to death on that fish, about to collapse from fury. "I came all this way because I was worried for you, and here you are acting like a man who's lost his head to lust. Gu Zixi, I finally understand what people mean when they say it takes time to get the measure of a man."

"What part of a man are you trying to measure? Why are you so indecent?"

The army was filled with red-blooded men. Some hailed from scholarly families and could've passed the examinations to enter the Son of Heaven's court, while others were common military men who couldn't read a single character before they joined up. Their tastes ranged from the highbrow to the vulgar, and nothing was off-limits in their banter. Making up dirty jokes in private was a common pastime—many perfectly ordinary phrases could be twisted to have countless profane associations.

Shen Yi started and thought back over the last few words he had carelessly said. By the time he figured it out, he was certain Gu Yun was a lost cause. "*You're* the indecent one!" he roared.

Chang Geng had been speaking to Uncle Wang at the gate. When he heard this shout from inside, he shot a confused look toward General Shen, who had begun hollering again. He turned back to Uncle Wang. "Do we still have any of that loquat syrup sent from the palace last time? Bring General Shen a bowl; I'm afraid he's going to hurt his throat."

Gu Yun lackadaisically swung one leg over the other as he sat and watched the show. Once Shen Yi's anger fizzled, he finally said, "All right, Jiping, you can stop throwing a tantrum in my house. I know you're in a bad mood. As for the matter of marriage—though they say it comes down to the wishes of one's parents and the arrangements of the matchmakers, you don't have to marry anyone you don't like, no matter whose daughter she is. However complicated the Shen clan might be, what authority do they have over members of my Black Iron Battalion?"

Shen Yi stilled for a moment, a gloom settling over his face. "I'm not afraid, I just..."

Gu Yun nodded. They were noble young masters who had grown up from boyhood together; they didn't need to explain their troubles to one another. Both understood perfectly.

"I've listened to how my aunts and grandmother speak of my father since I was young. All they talk about is how much of a disappointment he is, a man with neither civil nor martial achievements who spends his days holding an idle post in the Imperial Astronomical Bureau, loafing around with a bunch of Daoists and monks." Shen Yi sighed. "There were three children in my father's generation. My eldest uncle had a malformed foot and couldn't pursue an official career, and my father had an apathetic temperament. All those years, my third uncle held up the entire Shen family singlehandedly...while I ended up quitting the Hanlin Academy to join the Lingshu Institute. My grandfather nearly fainted when he found out. He wanted to disown me, but my father and third uncle violated filial piety to protect me. The family's discipline whip was brought out and everything. My grandfather's hand slipped, and my third uncle took a hit to protect me. He was already working himself to the bone, deficient in both blood and qi, and he spat blood after my grandfather's strike.

Afterward, his condition rapidly deteriorated. He was gone before he turned thirty-five... That was part of the reason I insisted on leaving the capital and joining the army with you."

Out of guilt, to get away from home...and to garner some accomplishments of his own to silence those haughty relatives. When outsiders looked at a noble family of means, how could they not feel some measure of envy for that lifestyle marked by fine food and brocade clothing. Only those who actually lived it would know it also came with countless restrictions.

"Sometimes, I'd wonder if there's any point to it all," Shen Yi said softly. "There really isn't any. You fight on the border of life and death time and again, all to make a decent name for yourself. But when you go home and throw open the doors, it's the same as when you left. Unless you sever ties with your whole family and get yourself expelled from the clan, you'll be a puppet on a string, led around by that complex tangle of relationships forever... I'm talking just to talk; don't take it to heart. My problems aren't anything major. Compared to your family affairs, mine really aren't worth a whistle."

Gu Yun laughed. "They're all idle worries."

"Right?" Shen Yi laughed in self-derision. "Did you see the memorial old General Zhong submitted? Aside from military affairs, he also reported in detail on the dire conditions of the refugees in Jiangbei. And it's still summer. If we can't get them settled by early autumn, who knows if they'll make it through the year... They wake up every morning not knowing where they'll put their heads at night. It's only those with sinecures like us who have idle hours to stew in worry over the trivial matters in our own backyards."

He sighed, and both men sank into silence. Gu Yun suddenly said, "Bring General Zhong's memorial to me tomorrow. If the timing is right, I'll present it in morning court. I've had enough of listening to them bicker."

Shen Yi blinked in surprise. Any attitude expressed by the Marquis of Anding was backed by the full authority of the army. In all these years, he had never taken a stance on domestic affairs. Now was he going to stand with the Grand Council...with Prince Yan?

Chang Geng, who had at some point wandered over, cut in. "There's no need. Yifu, why would you personally speak up about such small matters?"

Upon noticing Chang Geng, Shen Yi unconsciously corrected his lazy posture and sat up straight. "Your Highness works yourself to the bone for the common people and the good of society. We money-wasting soldiers who know how to spend and not how to earn wish to donate our meager abilities to the cause as well."

Chang Geng smiled. "Nonsense, General Shen. It's thanks to the soldiers who have bathed themselves in blood that we have this space to breathe now. There are numerous considerations at play in the proposal to build factories along the banks of the canal; your involvement would likely only complicate things. I can handle it; you don't have to worry. I guarantee I'll have everything arranged before winter sets in."

The Prince Yan of today was no longer that naïve child from Yanhui Town. When danger encroached upon the nation, there were always those who stepped forward to take up the burden. This prince may have been young, but his command of the Grand Council lent him a steady aura of power that was obvious in all he did. He spoke as if in casual conversation, but when the words left his mouth, they struck the ground with force.

Shen Yi realized quite suddenly that ever since Prince Yan had assumed control of the Grand Council, the military had received all the money and rations they asked for. Batch after batch of engines and armor had been delivered to the front lines without the slightest hesitation. If Shen Yi hadn't himself come from the capital and wasn't intimately aware of the ragged condition of the court, he would have wondered why it seemed, when it came to provisioning, that the nation was better off now than before the war.

Assuming a serious expression, Shen Yi cupped his hands in a bow. "Regardless, this lower general thanks Your Highness on behalf of the thousands of soldiers on the border."

"What is General Shen saying?" Chang Geng said with a smile. "I merely perform my duties. Besides, Yifu has thanked me already, hasn't he?"

Gu Yun was speechless. *This little bastard!*

Chang Geng tugged that oilpaper packet from Gu Yun's hands. "A few snacks to dull your hunger is fine," he said in gentle tones, "but don't eat too much. We're having dinner later."

Old bachelor that he was, Shen Yi was almost too embarrassed to sit there a moment longer. This time Gu Yun didn't need to chase him off; he felt the urge to turn tail and flee of his own accord. Meals at the Marquis of Anding's estate truly made one's teeth ache.

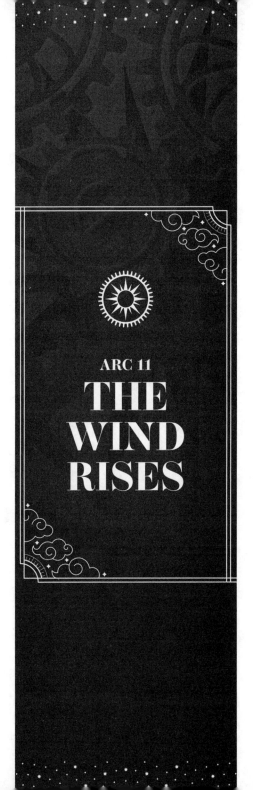

ARC 11

THE WIND RISES

83

COUNTERATTACK

LATER THAT EVENING, after seeing off a mentally and physically traumatized General Shen, Chang Geng snatched away the cup of wine that Gu Yun was still refusing to put down.

Gu Yun chuckled lazily. "There's no wine left, just some dregs at the bottom. I'm appreciating the scent."

Chang Geng tossed him a packet of pacifying fragrance. "If you want something to appreciate, appreciate this."

Gu Yun shook his head in fond exasperation. His lifestyle may have been somewhat self-indulgent, but he never failed to control himself when he intended to. It had been ages since he had last touched a drop of drink. He'd had a few cups tonight because Shen Yi was there; just enough to moisten his lips. And he only refused to put the cup down because he knew Chang Geng wanted to nanny him. Chang Geng loved governing him far too much—he wanted to see to every little thing, and he was never willing to delegate tasks to others. It was as if only personally attending to Gu Yun in this way would allow Chang Geng some peace of mind. These were all minor affairs, so Gu Yun was happy to humor him.

The two washed up and returned to their room, though not to engage in any intimate activities. Gu Yun patted the bed and said to Chang Geng, "Bring your acupuncture needles here."

Just days ago, Chang Geng had first suffered a horrible shock and fallen into despair, nearly losing himself in hallucinations. Then, his long-cherished wish had come true overnight, and he had been overcome with joy, on the verge of insanity. Gu Yun had kept his concerns to himself at the time. But when Shen Yi and the others reached the capital a few days later, he paid a visit to Miss Chen.

The minute Miss Chen stepped through the door, she pricked Prince Yan, whose eyes were still splitting into twinned pupils here and there, into a veritable porcupine. "Since ancient times, extreme joy has led to sorrow," she said pointedly. "Exhilaration evolving into mania is not unheard of. This is true even for ordinary people. Your Highness, given your condition, I advise restraint."

Afterward, she leveled Gu Yun with a meaningful look. The words *you beast* flashed beneath her speech to strike the Marquis of Anding from across the room. She rattled off a list of prohibitions for Chang Geng—wine was forbidden, along with spicy foods, loud noises, and carnal pleasures—then instructed Chang Geng to pacify his spirit and settle his heart with acupuncture before bed every night. As for the acupoints Chang Geng couldn't reach himself, Gu Yun would have to assist.

Thus had Gu Yun spent several days under Miss Chen's tutelage. Fortunately he had studied martial arts since youth, so locating all the acupoints was no trouble.

Now, Chang Geng laid himself calmly at the head of the bed. He loosened Gu Yun's hair from its knot and played with a scattered strand as he gave his back over to Gu Yun's amateur hands, utterly unconcerned that he might be poked in the wrong spot. No matter how great the stress he was under, this was always the most peaceful part of his day. Chang Geng wished he could remain like this until the end of time.

Gu Yun understood absolutely nothing about the art of acupuncture; he worked purely off rote memory of what Miss Chen had taught him. He'd heard plenty of alarmist rumors of how a misplaced needle could leave one paralyzed forever, and so was afraid to approach the task with anything other than the utmost focus. He didn't dare place a needle a millimeter too shallow or too deep, a considerable challenge for his ailing eyes.

Only when the last needle was placed did Gu Yun breathe a sigh of relief. He had worked up a light sweat and picked up a handkerchief to wipe his hands. When he looked back, he saw that Chang Geng had turned his head to the side and was staring at him, unblinking. The bloody tint and double pupils had disappeared from his eyes. Under the hazy glow of the gas lamp, his distant gaze seemed to hold a peaceful little world, illuminated by the gentle gleam of the lamp's flame and sheltered beneath the shadow of an ancient stone Buddha.

"What are you looking at?"

The corner of Chang Geng's mouth quirked up stiffly. With the needles applied, his face was once again paralyzed; he couldn't quite manage the smile.

Gu Yun's gaze slid across the smooth lines of Chang Geng's back. He very much wanted to have his revenge, but he didn't dare disobey doctor's orders and touch Chang Geng at a time like this. He coughed dryly. "Okay, stop laughing at me and get some rest. Don't you have to be up early tomorrow?"

"Zixi," Chang Geng had very few facial muscles at his disposal and could only speak at a low volume. The softness of his voice added to the impression that he was imploring Gu Yun for comfort. "Can I have a kiss?"

Gu Yun gave him a warning look. "Don't you ever learn? You've been pricked into a hedgehog and you're still trying to seduce me."

But Chang Geng had seen through this man long ago. A single *Yifu* could make him submit without a fight. This sort of honorable gentleman beneath a roguish mask would never touch a hair on his head while he was covered in needles. Thus, Chang Geng looked fearlessly at Gu Yun and smiled—even if he couldn't move his mouth, the smile was clear in his eyes.

I'm letting him walk all over me, Gu Yun thought to himself.

Gu Yun wasn't some wrinkly old monk. It was impossible for him to remain unmoved at the sight of the young man's bare, wide shoulders and narrow waist, his skin like jade and hair like satin, dark and pale in vivid contrast. Gu Yun was compelled to go sit off to the side and rest his eyes.

After a moment, he heard a faint rustling sound. Gu Yun opened his eyes to find that Chang Geng had pushed himself up to a seated position, stiff as a reanimated corpse, and scooched over to him. Chang Geng pressed a light kiss to his mouth, then gently tugged at Gu Yun's lip, working it between his own as his dark lashes fluttered at variance with the artificial stiffness of his face.

Gu Yun thought to push him away, but with all the needles in Chang Geng's body, he had nowhere to put his hands. Before he could extend his arms, Chang Geng had pressed him down onto the bed. To have his lover throw himself at him in his half-naked state—Gu Yun's throat visibly bobbed. He was exercising so much restraint, he felt he was on the verge of forging himself into steel. He slapped His Highness Prince Yan's venerable buttocks in frustration. "The needles are still in your body, have you gone mad again?!"

Chang Geng lay on top of Gu Yun, chin tucked into the crook of his neck, and muttered, "I'm all right. It's just that on that day, whenever I thought how you were actually in my arms, I felt I was trapped in a dream, unable to wake. All these years, my good dreams have been few and far between. I feared it was simply a happy beginning before some demon or ghost leapt out to run me through. I was just frightening myself and got stuck in my own head."

Gu Yun looked up at the bed curtains and thought a moment. "What are your nightmares about?"

Whether Chang Geng heard him or not, who could say. He looked at Gu Yun and spoke not a word as he pressed a trail of kisses over his cheek. Gu Yun reached up to cover his mouth. "Don't start. It's not like you'll take responsibility for putting out the fires you set."

Chang Geng sighed. For the first time in his life, he didn't want to follow his doctor's orders at all. He reluctantly fell still. "You look really good in court attire," he said quietly.

Gu Yun had finally found a spot with no needles. He lazily wrapped his arms around Chang Geng. "What *don't* I look good in?"

He was getting drowsy—Chang Geng didn't sleep well, so he always kept some pacifying fragrance lit in the room. Perhaps it was effective at pacifying Chang Geng's spirit; it was certainly effective on Gu Yun, who, caught in the crossfire, had begun to get tired earlier and earlier. Ever since he had suffered the sneak attack in the Western Regions, his old injuries had been acting up. Half a year had passed, and his condition was improving bit by bit. But it was noticeable to him how his energy was much lower than before. When Gu Yun was on the front lines, he never fully lowered his guard. Now that he had returned to court and didn't need to sleep with a knife under his pillow, he had relaxed the tiniest bit, and often found himself overcome with an enduring fatigue. Within the space of their brief exchange, his eyelids had already slid closed.

Chang Geng loved Gu Yun's self-righteous shamelessness. He quietly laughed at his response. "If only you wore it for my eyes alone. Court attire for my eyes alone, armor for my eyes alone, casual clothing for my eyes alone as well. No one else would be allowed to cast their greedy eyes on you..."

There was a core of truth to his words, but Gu Yun, with his eyes closed, thought he was merely joking and making pillow talk. He chuckled mischievously and replied, "The rest may not be possible, but wearing nothing at all can be for your eyes alone."

A change rippled across Chang Geng's eyes. The needles in the back of his hand and his wrist didn't stop his hand from wandering upward. In no time he'd managed to grope Gu Yun awake. Gu Yun held Chang Geng's hand down, avoiding the forest of needles. Hazy with sleep, he said, "Stop messing around. Do you want to be poked full of holes again?"

Something lightly knocked on the window from outside.

The fogginess cleared from Gu Yun's eyes. "Hm? I'll get it." He carefully disentangled himself from Chang Geng and went to open the window. At once, a dirty wooden bird flew inside and crashed headfirst into his hands. The bird was quite worn and infused with the fresh scent of sandalwood incense. The light fragrance invaded Gu Yun's doglike nose.

He handed the wooden bird to Chang Geng. "Is it that bald donkey Liao Ran? Where's he run off to this time?"

After Li Feng had purged the National Temple, he had intended to pass the position of abbot to Liao Ran, who had performed a meritorious deed in saving the life of the emperor. Contrary to his expectations, Liao Ran stubbornly refused the promotion and carried on even now as a temple member in name while he traveled the world as a wandering ascetic.

"He's helping settle the refugees in Jiangbei." Chang Geng climbed stiffly to his feet. "Among the civilians, a monk's word often carries more weight than any local official's." As he spoke, he pried open the wooden bird and read over Liao Ran's letter. The lingering smile on his face gradually disappeared. After a time, he breathed a faint sigh and set the letter aside.

Gu Yun took it and skimmed the contents. "A plague in Jiangbei? How come I haven't heard about this?"

"The climate there is hot and humid. If too many people die and their bodies are not buried in time, plague is almost inevitable... We just performed repairs on the canal basin last year. I assigned the local officials the task of making arrangements for the refugees, which they were all pleased to count among their political achievements. And yet these bastards—they've learned to lie in their reports," Chang Geng sank back down on the bed. He looked especially stiff and tired, as if his mind and soul were fixed to his body by that handful of silver needles. His gaze fell upon a corner of the bed, and the light of the gas lamp spilled across the bridge of his nose to cast half his face, gaunt with recent worries, into shadow. "I thought we could clean house once and that would be that for a few years, and we could make further plans down the line. Who would've thought..."

If the nation hadn't rotted to its roots, perhaps it wouldn't have spawned such brazen local officials, as stubborn as cheap jerky in their crooked ways.

Noting his lack of surprise, Gu Yun asked, "You already knew?"

Chang Geng was silent for some seconds. "Zixi, help me remove the needles. It's about time."

Countless people were running themselves into the ground with exhaustion, countless people were losing their lives, yet the court still argued. Gu Yun removed the needles from Chang Geng's body with great efficiency, then picked up a thin robe and draped it over Chang Geng's shoulders. He slid his arms around Chang Geng's waist. "Stop

298 ☼ STARS OF CHAOS

thinking about it and get a good night's sleep. If anything is troubling you, tell me; you don't have to bear everything alone."

This seemed to strike a nerve in Chang Geng. He turned to look at Gu Yun. "You'll help me no matter what?"

Gu Yun considered for a moment. "The natural order and the laws of ethics come first, but those aside, if you asked for the stars, I wouldn't fetch you the moon. Rain or shine, I'd climb a ladder to pluck them from the sky. How's that for you?" By the end, he had slipped back into a jocular tone. But this time Chang Geng didn't laugh. Perhaps it was because the needles' seal on his body still lingered, or perhaps it was because he understood the unspoken meaning behind Gu Yun's words.

Gu Yun brushed his lips against the shell of Chang Geng's ear. "Come here, lie down."

Chang Geng suddenly turned and grabbed Gu Yun's chin. A typhoon rose in those eyes which had been calm as a sea of stars. With his usual elegant and gentle mien tossed aside, his face was pale, and his eyes were terribly dark; veins stood out on the back of his hand as the power of the ancient evil god thrummed beneath his skin. Yet the instant a crease appeared between Gu Yun's brows, Chang Geng let go. He stared at Gu Yun, an indescribable expression on his face. "Zixi, don't take back the things you've given me."

Gu Yun assented, unperturbed. "Okay—I'll hand all the Marquis Estate's earnings over to you; just give me a couple pieces of silver a month as spending money, all right?" he said, deliberately missing the point.

Chang Geng's face went dark. Gu Yun grabbed him and tumbled them both into bed with a laugh. "I won't abandon you, I swear it to heaven—why are you so paranoid? Sleep, I'm so tired I can barely keep my eyes open."

Chang Geng refused to drop it. "Even if I actually..."

"I won't abandon you even if you actually go mad." Gu Yun pillowed his head in the crook of his elbow, blithely stroking Chang Geng's side with the hand he had draped over his body. Eyes closed, he said, "If you dare go out and hurt people, I'll break your legs, tie you up in a room, and keep watch over you all day. Satisfied? Must you come looking for a scolding in the middle of the night..."

He hadn't said a single pleasant word, yet Chang Geng's breath came faster, and light flared in his eyes. He wished to devour the man in front of him...but recalling his doctor's orders, he didn't cross the line. He was afraid to take risks with the wu'ergu. He satisfied himself with staring at Gu Yun for a while, then reluctantly lay back down. Chang Geng closed his eyes and imagined the scene Gu Yun had painted. His whole body went stiff. He almost wished Gu Yun *would* break his legs and lock him in a room—even a dark little attic would be okay, he wouldn't breathe a word of complaint.

He tossed and turned. In the end, he failed to resist temptation and grabbed Gu Yun's wrist. "It's a promise. If I really do go mad, lock me away. Or if one day you go before me, give me a bottle of arsenic, and I'll end myself after seeing you off—" He stopped with a sharp wince of pain.

Gu Yun had slapped him on the rear. It wasn't a teasing little tap this time; it had real force behind it, and it stung like fire.

"End yourself, my ass," Gu Yun furiously hissed at him. "Shut up. If you're not going to sleep, then scram."

Prince Yan, who had started to rave almost the instant the needles were removed, was finally cowed into submission by this smack and shut his mouth. Yet as Gu Yun's consciousness sank into sleep, still he worried. When Chang Geng said he would "end himself," he was probably serious. Perhaps Chang Geng naturally possessed such a temperament, or perhaps the wu'ergu was subtly acting on him over time. Although Chang Geng hid it as best he could, Gu Yun understood better by the day the volatility of his moods and the extremity of the paranoia buried deep within his marrow.

How long could things go on like this?

The Longan Emperor had formerly held grand assemblies once every ten days. But circumstances being what they were, countless issues stood unresolved, and grand assemblies were now held daily. Every civil and military official in court had to galvanize themselves to rise at four in the morning and crawl into bed at midnight, and the Grand Council arrived over an hour earlier than the rest. When Huo Dan woke Gu Yun the next day, Chang Geng had already gone. Gu Yun hadn't so much as stirred at the noise of his departure—he didn't know if it was because Chang Geng's movements were too quiet, or that he had slept too deeply.

"Snuff that thing out," Massaging his temples, Gu Yun pointed at the incense burner. "It nearly sent me to an eternal rest."

Huo Dan obediently snuffed the incense burner but didn't hesitate to get a word in edgewise. "Sir, this is just ordinary pacifying incense to aid sleep. Why is it that it has little effect on others, but acts like the strongest sleeping draft on you? You can't blame the incense burner. If you're so fatigued all the time, it's because you're lacking qi and blood. You're still so young, sir; you can't go on like this."

"Shush." Gu Yun shot him a look, then lowered his voice. "I'll go ask Miss Chen for a few prescriptions tomorrow. Don't run your mouth around other people, you hear me?"

Captain Huo was a staunch believer in the saying, "Military orders carry the weight of a mountain." He immediately gave a well-practiced response: "Yes, sir!"

The day's grand assembly began with teeth bared and fur flying. Several major noble families locked arms and threw down the memorial Jiang Chong had copied for Chang Geng before the entire court. Lü Chang, the Assistant Minister of Revenue, was first to step forward and present an impassioned critique of the "wild avarice" baldly evident in the Ministry of Works's plan to allow thirteen prominent merchants to trade in violet gold. The two groups nearly tore into each other there in the middle of the assembly hall before the Longan Emperor in a towering rage shouted for them to cease.

Fang Qin, unperturbed, watched from the sidelines. He glanced at the emperor's expression of displeasure, then gave the members of his own party a meaningful look. He knew he had hit one of the emperor's sore spots. Just as expected, Li Feng heaved a long sigh, rubbed at his temples, and said at length, "Let us consider the matter more fully before making a decision. We also believe it rather improper to allow civilian trade in violet gold. What is the Grand Council's stance?"

Jiang Chong stepped forward at this summons. "Your Majesty, the members of the Grand Council arrived early today to discuss this very issue. We share Assistant Minister Lü's worries—we, too, believe it would be improper to allow civilian merchants to trade in violet gold."

Everyone was startled by this pronouncement. Fang Qin glanced at Prince Yan, suddenly confused. Whose team was this mysterious prince on?

Li Feng had a good impression of Jiang Chong; he was a pure official, loyal and honest, whom Li Feng had personally promoted. He found this statement quite to his taste, so he signaled for him to continue.

"However," Jiang Chong went on, "the refugee situation is pressing. Many bandits roam the area between the Central Plains and Central Shu. The Marquis of Anding defeated a fire dragon—who's to say there isn't a water dragon, wind dragon, or heaven knows what other beast lying in wait out there, looking for an opportunity to strike. As long as these miscreants stand to gain some benefit, their numbers will be endless. The refugees are upstanding citizens today, but if they find themselves in desperate straits with no honest means to make a living, they may take to the woods and become outlaws tomorrow. The war on our borders is ongoing. If our own backyard catches fire, how are we to rebuild our strength? Our foreign enemies would laugh till their teeth fell out. What's more, this subject has heard news of plague in Jiangbei. If these reports are true, it would be frost atop snow..."

He had hardly finished speaking when the court exploded.

Li Feng's vision went dark. "A plague? What plague?"

Fang Qin started, no longer so unperturbed. He quickly came to some realization and looked up at Assistant Minister Lü, who had been so aggressive moments ago, in disbelief. Prince Yan had ousted a large batch of officials from regions along the canal last year, and every noble family had been eagerly stuffing their own relatives into the empty positions. The Governor of Liangjiang, the region that encompassed Jiangbei and Jiangnan, was Assistant Minister Lü's brother-in-law, the husband of Minister Lü's full sister from his father's primary wife. The Lü patriarch of this generation was rather lackluster himself, but he had in-laws everywhere in the court. Noble Consort Lü was the mother of the eldest prince. This family's roots ran deep...but Fang Qin never thought they would be *this* bold!

In Great Liang, when it came to remote regions far from the emperor's eyes, it was not uncommon for local crises to either go unreported or be greatly exaggerated. In the case of the former, this was to protect the officials' reputations and records of service, while in the latter case they would hope to embezzle excess relief funds supplied by the nation. Now that Great Liang was weak and poor, these corrupt officials must have figured it would be too hard to skim anything off the top, yet feared they would be censured if the plague was severe. Furthermore, the Lü family must have thought themselves especially clever—afraid the emperor's concern for his people might override his concern for violet gold and thus lead him to side with the merchants, they had deliberately prevented news of this plague from spreading.

Fang Qin thought his way through the whole mess in the blink of an eye. He sent a fierce glare in the direction of that Lü bastard, clenching his jaw so hard his gums nearly bled. He thought viciously, *Don't they know you can't keep fire wrapped in paper? Prince Yan performed a surprise inspection of the canal region just last year. How many months has it been? The severed heads of the last batch of criminals haven't yet rotted into skulls!*

The Longan Emperor was an assiduous and frugal man who hated nothing so much as he hated embezzlement and corruption. Meanwhile, Prince Yan was an eccentric who never joined factions nor sought personal gain. He had a reputation for being a smooth-talking charmer yet could turn on anyone in a heartbeat. The Lü family was practically begging one of these two to strike them dead. If Fang Qin's plans failed here at the eleventh hour, it would all be because these oh-so-clever idiots had dragged him down!

At the head of the hall, Li Feng's temper flared. "My dear Minister Jiang, explain yourself clearly!"

Chang Geng took a calm step forward. "Your Majesty, this subject often copies sutras and pays respects to the Buddha in his free time, and maintains a close personal friendship with Great Master Liao Ran. After Great Master Liao Ran refused the title of Abbot of the National Temple, he went south to Jiangbei to provide aid to the refugees in the area. As a civilian, he couldn't trouble the local officials. So he simply traveled, begging alms and preaching sermons, and collected donations from the wealthy merchants in the region to help solve the most pressing emergencies. Some days ago, the great master sent this subject a personal letter by messenger. He expressed that the crisis was severe and begged assistance without delay. The severity of the plague in Jiangbei as he described it was far beyond anything I had heard. However, I had just received the letter, and have not yet had time to confirm the truth of the matter. Justice Jiang has spoken too rashly in his urgency; please do not blame him."

Prince Yan cast Assistant Minister Lü a placid glance before his eyes swept, seemingly by chance, over Minister Fang, whose face was now ashen.

Li Feng sucked in a deep breath, a note of danger creeping into his voice. "The Six Ministries, Nine Ministers, and Grand Court hadn't an inkling of this disaster, yet it was revealed by an...an ascetic *monk* who travels with nothing but a worn alms bowl and the rough-spun clothes on his back. If his account is true..." After a long silence, he ground out, "We can no longer say who is the true power in this court."

Every official in the hall fell to their knees.

84

UNDERCURRENT

COLD SWEAT TRICKLED DOWN Assistant Minister Lü's back. By this point, he had frozen entirely. Fang Qin heaved a rueful sigh. *Can't accomplish anything even with backing. Useless thing.*

He stepped forward to speak, his words slow and measured. "Peace, Your Majesty. This subject believes the situation may be less severe than Great Master Liao Ran claims. The climate of Jiangbei is hot and humid. The region's summers are punishing, and the refugees are weak of constitution and prone to illness. That a number of them have been laid low by heat sickness is nothing strange; it may not be a true plague. Consider, Your Majesty: if anyone had such masterful control of the situation, how is it that they could prevent all of Jiangbei from spreading the news, yet fail to prevent Great Master Liao Ran from sending one letter to the capital?"

Chang Geng didn't look up as he listened to Fang Qin's response. He chuckled lightly. "Minister Fang, I'm not sure I understand. Do you mean to suggest that Great Master Liao Ran cannot tell the difference between a plague and heat sickness, or do you mean to suggest that the monk is so brazen as to frame the highest authorities of the region? Or, perhaps, do you mean to suggest that I am cutting stories out of whole cloth, falsifying evidence at random to eliminate my opposition?"

306 ☼ STARS OF CHAOS

Fang Qin stepped back at once. "Your Majesty, please judge the situation with clear eyes. This subject would never dare."

Li Feng had just begun to frown when Chang Geng smoothly cupped his hands and spoke again. "I am young and inexperienced, too prone to bluntly speaking my mind. Minister Fang, please do not take it to heart."

Once more addressing the full assembly, Chang Geng continued. "On the first and fifteenth of each month, it is Great Master Liao Ran's custom to burn incense and pray. He personally draws a protective talisman, seals it within an embroidered pouch, and has it delivered to me via relay station. These missives carry well-wishes—prosperity for the nation, good health for Imperial Brother, and other things of this nature. Brother, you should be aware that after a protective talisman is sealed, it is not meant to be opened. But the last few protective talismans I received had signs of being opened and resealed. I can't imagine who it is that wouldn't allow this subject so small a personal indulgence..."

Fang Qin choked.

Chang Geng retrieved an item from his lapels. It wasn't the letter Gu Yun had seen the previous night, but a handful of yellowed paper strips the width of a finger—how long he had spent collecting them was anyone's guess. They had been pieced together into one whole and secured with glue. On each individual strip was inscribed a string of indecipherable ink symbols, but with all of them lined up, side by side, a complete passage was discernable beneath the complex pattern. It read: *The plague in Jiangbei is severe, and bodies lay scattered across the wilderness. The roads between relay stations have been blockaded. The court must prepare to address the situation.*

"The message was hidden beneath a pattern of Sanskrit script and other symbols, split across four pieces of paper, and mailed in random order," said Chang Geng.

The Longan Emperor recognized Liao Ran's handwriting on sight. Fang Qin opened his mouth, but Chang Geng cut off whatever speech he had prepared. His voice rose. "As Minister Fang has pointed out, this testimony was not acquired through legitimate channels. There is still doubt as to its veracity. Thus, this subject did not report the contents immediately. I had intended to submit a memorial to Your Majesty this very day requesting permission to travel south to Jiangbei and investigate the refugee situation myself, with the twin purposes of aiding the relief efforts and verifying the truth of this report. Yet as you see, Justice Jiang got carried away and spoke too soon, revealing this matter prematurely."

Jiang Chong tactfully kowtowed. "Please forgive me, Your Majesty."

The unspoken implications of Prince Yan's announcement caused all present to break out in gooseflesh. Fang Qin's head began to throb—Prince Yan was traveling south again!

Concepts like "the law ought not punish the majority" were meaningless to Prince Yan. His heroic path of slaughter from south to north was still vivid in everyone's minds. Prince Yan showed not the slightest concern for the court, which at this rate might run out of officials to do its work, nor for making himself thousands of enemies. He struck without a word of warning, neither integrated himself with the majority nor formed factions of his own, and showed respect for no one's reputation. Nevertheless, he was the emperor's own brother. So as long as he didn't commit treason, no one could touch him.

The Fang family had tried many times to make a show of goodwill toward Prince Yan, yet he parried every attempt with an impenetrable neutrality. When they attempted to send the prince gifts, the Fang family would deliver the goods one day, and war beacon tickets stamped with the Lingshu Institute's special anti-forgery seal would arrive on their doorstep the next. He was uninterested in wealth and indifferent to beauty. When others tried to gift him lovely young ladies, he sent them back the very next day. If they really couldn't be taken back, he tossed them in the Prince Yan Estate to tidy the courtyards. But the Prince Yan Estate was an empty shell. Prince Yan had never spent a night there since its construction.

The Fang family's principal wife's daughter, whose suitors were so numerous their footsteps could flatten the thresholds of the Fangs' home, was nothing to him. Eager to claim the as-yet-vacant position of Prince Yan's primary consort, some fool went as far as involving the harem in an attempt to worm their way in. Who knew what the emperor was thinking—not even the empress escaped a scolding over this incident. His exact words were: "Ignorant women should not meddle in court affairs"—as if he would enable his brother to stay single for the rest of his life. No one dared broach the topic again.

Quick as he was, Fang Qin immediately changed his tune. "Your Majesty, this subject has heard that many malfeasants have hidden themselves among the refugees in Jiangbei where they cause no end of trouble. The region is close to the front lines, and the Westerners watch it with their covetous eyes. His Highness is of noble status and the Grand Council cannot spare him. Sending a dragon disguised as a fish into such murky waters poses too much of a risk."

Li Feng frowned and turned to Chang Geng. "Send someone else to investigate; that will suffice. It's not appropriate for you to do everything yourself."

On one hand, Li Feng quite liked Chang Geng's impetuous nature. Once the fourth prince had an objective, he would see it through to the end no matter what rich or powerful figure stood in his way. Li Feng found this person useful, though perhaps not politically shrewd. Moreover, Chang Geng was his only brother. Though they hadn't grown up together and weren't close, now that the Li family was on the verge of losing nation and clan to foreign enemies, Li Feng had little choice but to grudgingly aim his targetless familial affection in Chang Geng's direction.

Yet while the Longan Emperor didn't find his brother a threat, he was still something of a headache. Prince Yan was ordinarily gentle, considerate, and humble—but when he was at work, it was a completely different story. This was the young man who had dared toss Li Feng's Shangfang Sword back at him as an army bore down on the city walls. And now, in the Grand Council, this same young man was indiscriminately ruthless with anyone unfortunate enough to cross him.

With a wave of his hand, Li Feng said, "The matter is settled."

Chang Geng would not relent. "Brother, there are great numbers of refugees scattered all across Jiangbei. We do not know the situation; for all our grand debate in court over how to settle these people, we have taken not a single look ourselves. Is this not the same as discussing military strategy on paper alone? Since every lord has their own rationale but not a one can present a tidy solution, this subject may as well make the trip himself and report to Brother upon my return."

The corner of Li Feng's eye jumped.

Gu Yun, who had stayed a wallflower this whole time, suddenly strolled forward. "Since Prince Yan has his heart set on it, Your Majesty may as well grant his request. If corrupt officials are running rampant in Jiangbei, who else possesses the authority to take control of the situation? If it's his safety that concerns you, this subject will escort him on his way. There will be no need to worry yourself over refugees and roaming bandits."

Chang Geng started in surprise. He hadn't expected Gu Yun to insert himself like this; it wasn't a part of his plan.

Shen Yi snuck a glance at Gu Yun, who, with his head lowered, shot him a look in return—a look that was improper from any angle. Shen Yi averted his eyes, teeth aching. He felt all the adulterous men of legend must have worn this same look on their faces.

Such words would have sounded like pompous bluster coming from another, but they left Gu Yun's mouth with steely resolution. Gu Yun thought for a moment, then threw in another convenient excuse: "We will need to recover Jiangnan sooner or later. This excursion presents the perfect opportunity to examine the situation on the front lines. In fact, I had been planning to submit a memorial with this exact request—what a coincidence. I can also escort His Highness Prince Yan on the way. I'll return him to you in one piece, I promise."

Once the Marquis of Anding was involved, how could anyone else argue?

Li Feng delivered the edict the following day: Prince Yan would serve as official imperial envoy while Xu Ling, the Right Assistant Supervisory Commissioner of the Department of Supervision, would act as his assistant. Together they would investigate the deliberate cover-up of a plague in Jiangbei. The Marquis of Anding would escort them, and a member of the Lingshu Institute, Ge Chen, would accompany them to scout the armaments of the Western army in Jiangnan.

Fang Qin left the court assembly furious. Too astute to show any sign of rage before others, he waited until he was in the privacy of his own carriage to let his face go dark. Here was a man with stunning literary talents, once lavishly praised by the late emperor. He had countless tricks up his sleeve and the fortitude to support the heavy weight of a reputable clan like the Fang family even as a second son. He had breezed his way up the ladder in court, and his record of service had been nothing short of stellar since the day he was appointed to the Ministry of Revenue. Even that thorny Prince Yan of the Grand Council was cordial to him, and often spoke in praise of him both in and out of his presence...yet he had to spend his days aligning himself with vermin like Lü Chang.

It was often said that gentlemen form no factions. Yet people also spoke of "power and influence" as an inseparable unit. Without power, there was no influence—so, without influence, whence came power?

Those who climbed from the schools of the sages to the Son of Heaven's great hall were naturally in a different class from the useless leeches who scraped by on their family's prestige or purchased titles. The former desired, as a matter of course, to accomplish great things and leave behind a legend for posterity. Were his surname not Fang, he would surely have found a place for himself beneath Prince Yan's banner, toiling to put this rotten, ailing court in good order. Sadly, no one could choose the circumstances of their birth. The first thirty years of Fang Qin's life had been spent well-fed and richly attired, wanting for nothing under the protection of his clan. Thus, the next thirty years of his life must be spent working himself to the bone for this selfsame clan, a trap that would ensnare him until death.

His carriage came to an abrupt halt. A servant's voice came quietly from outside: "Old Master, Assistant Minister Lü has stopped the carriage. He says he needs to speak to you."

Fang Qin's eyes went cold—he wished this Lü bastard would hurry up and die. After sitting for a moment, stiff and expressionless, Minister Fang rearranged his face into amicability, lifted the curtain, and scolded the coachman half-sincerely. "Negligent servant, have you no sense of propriety? Invite him up already; why report to me first?"

His servants were accustomed to taking blame for their master. The man mounted a laudable performance of reverent terror, then invited the agitated Lü Chang into the carriage before setting off toward Assistant Minister Lü's estate.

Lü Chang was covered in a sheen of cold sweat. He threw himself to the floor of the carriage in a bow the instant he stepped through the door. "Minister Fang, please save me!"

Fang Qin, sneering to himself, affected a look of shock as he helped the man up. He decided to play dumb. "Yannian-xiong, what's all this?"

Of course Lü Chang knew the distinguished Minister Fang was pretending to be daft. But he was in crisis; he clung to any savior he could grab hold of, regardless of their attitude. He breathlessly confessed everything his brother-in-law—the current Governor of Liangjiang, Yang Ronggui—had done in gory detail.

Yang Ronggui was bold indeed: he had concealed a plague in Jiangbei from the court, performed a purge of all local factions, and imprisoned every dissident who dared rebel against his control. He had sent people to occupy the relay stations and assassinated eighteen county-level scholars who had set out for the capital to bring suits before the emperor, making the killings look like attacks by greedy refugees and bandits. There were listed various other crimes of the sort, too numerous to record.

Fang Qin's heart pounded in his chest. His horizons had truly been broadened this day.

"Minister Fang," Lü Chang sobbed, "I concealed the truth not to protect my own family, but for the sake of our grand plan. Don't you see—in his extremity, His Majesty has even agreed to something so injurious to the pride of our ancestors as those war beacon tickets. If he were to learn Jiangbei was in such a state, and if the Grand Council were to fan the flames, he might really give in to those despicable merchants and this factory nonsense!"

Fang Qin found himself disgusted by Assistant Minister Lü's snot- and tear-covered countenance. *What a load of horseshit.*

But on the surface, he heaved a mournful sigh. "Yannian, you're mistaken. Don't you remember? When Zhang Fenghan of the Lingshu Institute lost his head and requested His Majesty rescind the ban on civilian use of violet gold, Prince Yan rejected his memorial. Have you forgotten Prince Yan's surname just because he's always in the company of those pedantic, penny-pinching scholars? His name is Li! No matter the circumstance, would the Li family ever allow a bunch of civilian merchants to peddle violet gold? Prince Yan wasn't planning to support those merchants at all. He clearly caught wind of your brother-in-law's deeds and used this issue as a spark to the fuse, a feint before launching his real attack against us."

Assistant Minister Lü had no more words; he could only wail. His looks were less than impressive in the first place, and with this, his visage became utterly repulsive. Heedless of Fang Qin's attempts to forestall him, he knelt again and kowtowed like he was pounding garlic with his forehead. "Minister, save me," he repeated again and again.

Fang Qin didn't want to save him; he rather wanted him to go to hell. "Prince Yan has that Marquis Gu at his side. One word from the Marquis of Anding could pull even General Zhong's garrison from the front line at Jiangbei. You think he can't handle a few prefectural offices? Yannian, it's not that I'm refusing to help. There's nothing I can do!" As if overcome with sorrow, Fang Qin covered his face with his sleeve and began sobbing bitterly. "Master Yang and I passed the imperial examination in the same year; we were once classmates who went on spring outings and frolicked together in lakes. Now we two hold official positions in far-flung regions, and calamity has befallen him. Do you not think I wish to save him?"

Lü Chang was speechless. He had come to plead with this man for his brother-in-law's life and ended up watching him cry instead. What an absurd sequence of events. Fang Qin certainly lived up to his reputation as first among the ruthless Fang clan.

Inwardly, Lü Chang gritted his teeth, but outwardly, he maintained his woeful mien. "Minister Fang, if too much is unearthed over the course of this investigation, it will be a serious offense punishable by the execution of the entire family to the ninth degree. Our clans have been joined for generations. Even if the bone breaks, tendons connect the split halves. You can't sit by and do nothing."

Fang Qin's face spasmed. Lü Chang had aimed right for his weakness with these words. Fang Qin had a younger half sister on his father's side who had been born to a concubine brought into the household as a maid. She wasn't a favored child and reached her teens without having held more than a handful of conversations with her elder brothers. However, this young and naïve Miss Fang had caused quite the scandal when she made a failed attempt to elope.

In truth, ever since the nation had opened to maritime trade, social mores had steadily declined. If such an incident had occurred along the East Sea coast, where minds were more open, it wouldn't have been a very shocking thing at all. Some bored old matrons and foolish men might have gossiped about it for a while, but that would have been the end of it. A few might have even praised the girl for her courage at such a young age. After all, plenty of Far Western women went out on the streets with their backs bared, and their families didn't raise any fuss.

Unfortunately, this had happened in the Fang family.

Since the first years of the Yuanhe era, a particular trend had emerged within the court: the more open-minded the common people became, the more the noble families clung to their traditional values, as if any concession would be seen as a failure to demonstrate decorum and dignity. This incident was a slap to the Fang family's face.

They had intended to shut the girl away for a few years, then send her off to a temple to become a nun. But fortuitously, the Lü family had been seeking connections at just the right time. The Fang family was quietly overjoyed and leapt at the opportunity like flies toward a pile of shit. In the end, Miss Fang was married to Lü Chang's paternal cousin, who held a purchased official position.

There were only so many notable clans within the capital, and they married back and forth among themselves. Everyone was related in some way or another, and thus, glory and defeat were shared between the lot of them. Lü Chang's words were both reminder and threat.

Fang Qin stopped his crying. He slowly straightened, then examined Lü Chang. *A mere assistant minister dares to threaten me... I can't keep this person around any longer.*

"Master Lü, please rise." Fang Qin considered for a time, then said deliberately, "My response is unchanged. There's no one you can plead to for help. If you want an opportunity to turn things around, you must start with His Highness Prince Yan himself."

When Lü Chang heard him return to this subject, his face stretched as long as a bitter melon. "But that..."

Fang Qin raised a hand to silence him. He poured himself tea from the pot on the small table, then lowered his voice. "Who is

Prince Yan? The entirety of the national treasury passes through his hands. How could he be impressed by your paltry little gestures? And some men are fastidious by nature and unwilling to allow miscellaneous persons close; it's no wonder if they don't enjoy feminine charms. Besides, the tawdry powdered wenches you threw at him were no unparalleled beauties. I wouldn't take them, much less Prince Yan."

Lü Chang blinked. "Then..."

Fang Qin dipped his finger in the tea, then slowly wrote four words on the table: *Don the yellow robes.* He gave the dumbstruck Lü Chang a meaningful look, then wiped the words clean.

Lü Chang stared, tongue-tied, as the moment stretched. He sat down heavily beside the table, his lips trembling as he said, "Minister Fang, this is...this is..."

Fang Qin sneered. "This is what? What were you planning to do? Ambush and murder Prince Yan on his way south the same way you murdered those poor scholars who hadn't the strength to subdue a chicken? Do you think the Marquis of Order stands there all day in court, saying not a word, as decoration? Or do you really believe your brother-in-law has such absolute control over the Jiangbei region that the imperial envoy will return empty-handed? If that were true, how would that wicked monk's letter have reached the Grand Council in the first place? Our sitting emperor does not tolerate disloyalty or betrayal. Don't you remember: back when they fell out, he threw even the Marquis of Anding into the imperial dungeons without a second thought. Are you under the impression that he harbors nostalgic sentiments for the Lü family—for any of us?"

In the time it took to burn a stick of incense, Lü Chang stumbled out of Fang Qin's carriage, terrified out of his wits. He drifted through the gates of the Lü Estate like a wandering ghost.

"Return to the estate," Fang Qin ordered his driver. He silently lit a stick of incense to drive away Lü Chang's stench. It was time certain people learned that common interest didn't grant them free license to use others as they pleased.

Pale smoke wound through the carriage as Fang Qin sat and rested his eyes. *If I can drag Prince Yan into the muck while I'm at it, I can kill two birds with one stone.*

If that Prince Yan truly was selfless and impartial, so pure as to have no regard for imperial power, Fang Qin would fail to defeat him with this maneuver. He had, however, one more killing blow up his sleeve. Prince Yan was merciless and immovable; he gave no indication of any deeper ambition, as if he were merely an exceedingly loyal official. Yet, upon careful reflection, his influence showed in every step Great Liang had taken to reach its present position. If this sort of individual wasn't with you, they were sure to be a formidable foe against you. And even if he was a revered prince of the first rank, some things were beyond his control...

85

GREAT CONDOR

A FTER BRIEFING JIANG CHONG and the rest of the Grand
Council on their responsibilities while he was down south,
Chang Geng finally managed to return to the Marquis
Estate shortly before sunset. Gu Yun had occupied himself directing
the servants to pack their luggage. The man had taken a leisurely seat
on a railing in the courtyard and was now fiddling with the white
jade flute Chang Geng had gifted him, occasionally raising it to his
lips to produce an invigorating tune.

If Chang Geng had one regret, it was that he'd given Gu Yun a
flute with holes. If he'd only known earlier, he would have given him
a solid stick of jade to play with.

Catching sight of Chang Geng in the distance, Gu Yun waved
him over. "Chang Geng, come here, I'll play a little something
for you."

An earnest attempt to play was exactly what Chang Geng most
feared. He strode over and wrapped his arms around Gu Yun, pulling him off his perch atop the railing. He leaned close to his ear and
murmured, "Save your mouth for other things."

Gu Yun had no rejoinder. He increasingly found that the saying
"those who come near ink are stained dark" was entirely true: Chang
Geng seemed to be acquiring more and more of Gu Yun's own elegant demeanor by the day.

The two strolled toward the inner courtyard. "Why did you suddenly say in court today that you wanted to go to the front lines in Jiangbei?" Chang Geng asked. "You gave me a scare."

Gu Yun clasped his hands behind his back, rubbing his fingers over the surface of the white jade flute. A faint smile hovered at the corner of his mouth as he said, "I've wanted to quit the capital for a while now. Rather than marinating in this foul atmosphere, I find it's much more refreshing being on the front lines."

Chang Geng laughed. "So, you're going for a vacation?"

"Mm, a vacation," Gu Yun said. "And because I'm worried about you."

The smile froze on Chang Geng's face. He knew what Gu Yun meant when he said *I'm worried about you*—he was worried for Chang Geng's safety as he plunged into the crowds of Jiangnan refugees with an entourage of a few scholars. Yet a curious thought sprouted in the depths of his heart, a voice that said to Chang Geng, *Why is he worried about me? Is he worried I'll pull some unsavory trick, or that I'll ally with Zhong-lao's Jiangbei Garrison and force a certain someone to abdicate?*

Sensing him stop in his tracks, Gu Yun looked back in confusion. "What is it?"

Chang Geng met his open gaze and sucked in a deep breath. He rubbed his forehead. *What am I thinking? Am I going mad?*

Gu Yun had always been his source of solace...but on reflection, that stopped being so the moment Chang Geng's sentiments had overflowed their banks. Since the day Gu Yun turned and looked him in the eye, it was no longer true.

Without these returned affections, Gu Yun was a comfort; with them, he was temptation and turmoil.

Affection, desire, sight, scent, sound, and taste, never-ending greed, day after day, terror and anxiety, jealousy and pining, worry over every

loss and gain... The seven emotions, spirit and soul, turning over themselves, the six sensory faculties choked by mortal dust.

Chang Geng closed the distance between them and grabbed Gu Yun's hand with a note of panicked urgency—as if only when he had this man in his hands would his heart settle back into his chest. Gu Yun raised an eyebrow but seemed not to mind. He spread his fingers and let Chang Geng stuff his hand into his own. Even on a scorching summer day, the general's hands weren't terribly warm. The small bit of heat in the center of his palm was all saved for Chang Geng.

Just then, Uncle Wang strode in on rapid steps. Seeing these two getting handsy with each other in the courtyard, he dropped his gaze to the floor with a peculiar expression on his face. *Out of sight, out of mind.* "My lord, His Highness the Crown Prince is here," he reported.

"Ah?" Gu Yun was surprised. "Quick, invite him in."

Moments later, the eight-year-old crown prince pelted over to Gu Yun on his short little legs. The Marquis Estate was sprawling, but in consideration of his image, the little highness refused to let anyone carry him. By the time he reached Gu Yun, sweat was beading on the tip of his nose. Once he entered the courtyard and saw Chang Geng there, however, he stopped running at once and slowed to a stately, measured gait. He opened his mouth to greet his "imperial granduncle," then remembered that Gu Yun didn't seem to like being referred to this way. Instead, he placed his hands together in a bow like a little adult and said, "Marshal Gu, Fourth Uncle."

Gu Yun crouched down to his eye level. "Your Highness, what are you doing out of the palace so late at night?"

"Father said Marshal Gu is accompanying Fourth Uncle south," the little crown prince recited carefully. "I came to bid Uncle and

Marshal Gu a formal farewell..." He forgot his lines halfway through. The child looked around and thought for a while, his ears going pink, but maintained an even expression. Finally, he continued, "I hope my subject will have a safe journey to Jiangbei and return soon!"

Gu Yun found this endlessly amusing, and he chuckled as he listened. The young crown prince snuck him a look, but though he was being laughed at, he didn't get angry. He clumsily produced two protective talismans and handed one each to Gu Yun and Chang Geng.

"Your Highness, after bidding us farewell, do you have any other instructions?" Gu Yun teased.

The young crown prince was embarrassed. He held his tongue for some time, but in the end he couldn't resist and tugged tentatively at Gu Yun's sleeve. "I wanted to ask for one of Marshal Gu's ink treasures. Father said he also received Grand...Marshal Gu's calligraphy in the past."

Gu Yun was quite taken with the child, and immediately leaned down to scoop the little crown prince up in his arms. Off he strode to the study and wrote something for the boy right then and there. The young crown prince ordered his servants to pack up the piece in a brocade box, then rushed back to the palace, jubilant.

After escorting the crown prince from the estate with all due formality, Chang Geng finally said, "All those years ago, the late emperor used me as a chess piece to tie you down. Is Li Feng not playing the same old trick, using the crown prince to mend his relationship with you?"

Gu Yun didn't know whether to laugh or cry. "What's this? Now you're jealous of a child?"

Chang Geng looked at him, a fake smile pinned to his face, and suddenly said, "Yifu plays favorites. You never held *my* hand and taught me how to write, stroke by stroke."

Gu Yun was speechless. Who was it exactly who had once mimicked his handwriting so flawlessly that even He Ronghui of the Black Iron Battalion was fooled?

In fond exasperation, he said, "And are you also eight years old?"

Chang Geng's face was placid as he proceeded to stab into Gu Yun's heart. "No one taught me when I was eight years old either. Huge'er would simply take burning sticks fresh out of the stove and…"

"Okay, okay," Gu Yun said hastily. "I'll make it up to you, all right?" Gu Yun picked up the brush he had just used and handed it to Chang Geng, then wrapped an arm around his shoulders to take Chang Geng's hand in his own. He placed his other hand on the table, looked down in thought for a moment, then guided Chang Geng's hand to write the character of his given name in regular script: *Min.*

Chang Geng was instantly enveloped in the faint medicinal scent that clung to Gu Yun's body. He subtly took a deep breath. "One character isn't enough. I spent all my time at the National Temple copying sutras."

Gu Yun released Chang Geng's hand. "Get out of here. Are you trying to tire me to death?"

Chang Geng said nothing, but stared at him, motionless. After a beat, Gu Yun capitulated and let his chin drop onto Chang Geng's shoulder in defeat. He looped his left arm around his waist, draped himself over his shoulders, and began copying those thrice-damned long-winded sutras, stroke by stroke. He felt this young man was becoming more and more spoiled lately. He was getting completely out of hand.

Three days later, the official imperial envoy and his assistant—Prince Yan and Xu Ling, the Right Assistant Supervisory

Commissioner of the Department of Supervision—left the capital accompanied by Ge Chen of the Lingshu Institute and escorted by twenty guards led by Gu Yun.

Li Feng had personally named Xu Ling Tanhua for taking third place in the imperial examinations in the first year of the Longan era. It was a title associated with dashing young men, in this case borne out: Xu Ling was handsome, with finely chiseled features and a face so pale it seemed he was wearing powder. Absent such a fearsome escort as the Marquis of Anding and his men, who stood about spoiling the atmosphere, this assistant supervisory commissioner and Prince Yan together would have looked like a pair of young masters heading out on holiday.

After passing through the city gates, Gu Yun led their party straight to the Northern Camp. Although a mere scholar, Xu Ling didn't much fear Gu Yun, that black-iron murder weapon of legend. He asked plainly, "My lord, why have we come to the Northern Camp?"

Gu Yun smiled. "We're changing horses."

That they would encounter trouble on this journey was a foregone conclusion. Supervisory Commissioner Xu was prepared to find utter devastation awaiting him, ready to wear himself out countering greedy local officials. Even the presence of the Marquis of Order didn't increase his sense of safety—especially as he found that the man himself was in high spirits, as if taking a pleasurable jaunt to the suburbs and not preparing to enter the den of a vicious beast.

As Xu Ling looked around in confusion, Ge Chen strolled into the Northern Camp with the easy air of familiarity. Since taking Master Fenghan as his teacher, Ge Chen had gradually assumed Master Fenghan's responsibilities with regard to the handling of military equipment, and he came often to the Northern Camp on errands.

Here, he was a familiar face. He led their party straight toward the warehouse where the Northern Camp's engines and armor were stored. "Your Highness, Commissioner Xu. This way, please."

Xu Ling was shocked by the sight before him.

On a stretch of level ground stood a kite the same size as the earlier model red-headed kites, but with a much more understated exterior. It had none of the carved railings or jade pillars meant to evoke a resemblance to pleasure boats; its outer shell was of simple black iron. This kite stood, quiet and imposing, in place without a single fire pinion to be seen. Instead, rows of exhaust pipes the size of cannon barrels were arranged along all four of its support beams. The lines of its frame were fluid and elegant, like a set of hawk armor magnified countless times.

Xu Ling was awestruck. "What is this?"

Ge Chen, in a tone that made clear how immensely pleased he was with himself, introduced the creation. "It doesn't have an official name yet. This kite is the only one of its kind in all Great Liang. The idea was to install a hawk's propulsion system into a small kite, but we went through many failures before this success. It can carry multiple passengers much faster than those lumbering giant kites. But it's not a mature technology—the court has just the one. It burns a large amount of violet gold and can't carry much, and this will be the first time it's used outside test flights...but once we solve the efficiency problem, this aerial war chariot will bomb those hairy foreigners right back to where they came from. My shifu said if it's adopted by the military, we could call it a 'great condor.'"

Xu Ling shot a look of disbelief at Chang Geng, who didn't seem surprised in the least. How long had Prince Yan been planning to clean up the pests in Jiangbei? He had a ship that could traverse a thousand kilometers in a day all prepared!

"We'll head straight for the front lines in Jiangbei," Chang Geng said. "The Marquis has sent word to Zhong-lao already. We'll leave this ship with the front-line garrison, then make our way north in disguise. The relay stations along the roads running north and south are no doubt on guard against us. Why should we step into their trap? How about it, Commissioner Xu? Are you brave enough to ride this untested aerial war chariot?"

Xu Ling had made his way up from a humble background, and he had his pride. He felt it beneath his dignity to bow to power and nobility or align himself with merchant wealth. He had been renowned as a prodigy since childhood and clearly possessed spectacular talents. And yet—how many times in his life had he been made to give way to those who traded in money and power? Even as a great talent whose reputation resounded throughout the capital, how could he harbor no resentment or worry after wasting countless years and months in the court?

There had been rumors before this that when Prince Yan had purged the regions along the canal, he had made a great show of severity, but was in truth merely giving noble families of the court an opportunity to insert their own people. Xu Ling had joined Prince Yan on this mission in full awareness of how deep the roots of the officials in Jiangbei ran, as well as the complexity of the local power dynamics. This wasn't what worried him—on the contrary, his greatest concern was that by the end of the investigation, he would find he had been tricked into doing someone else's dirty work.

Only now did he see that Prince Yan meant serious business. Heart surging with emotion, he raised his voice and said boldly, "As one who lives off the country's coffers, how can I shrink back at such a critical moment? After you, Your Highness!"

When Gu Yun had flown from the northwest to Jiangnan in hawk armor, he had made the journey in just a few days. This aerial war chariot was larger than a Black Hawk, and slower as well—but not by much. It would take no more than two and a half days to fly from the capital to the front lines in Jiangbei. If all went to plan, they would arrive in Jiangbei before news that Prince Yan had left the capital could reach those with an interest in hearing it.

Chang Geng and his party had no sooner left than certain interests within the capital began to stir.

The Longan Emperor was a frugal man. Since the initial state of emergency had been declared, the capital city had been gripped by a tense atmosphere, leaving its streets even quieter than at times of national mourning. No one wanted to peeve the Longan Emperor at a time like this: song, dance, and entertainment were all put to a halt, and a dozen or so legally operating brothels closed up shop. Places where one could sit idly and pass the time were in short supply.

With Gu Yun's departure, Shen Yi lost yet another spot to drink and chat. He found himself with nowhere left to go, and dearly wished he could put down roots in the military garrison long-term. Yet he'd hidden away there for a mere handful of days when the Shen family sent their people to drag him back.

What choice did Shen Yi have but to follow his family's servant home as if heading to the gallows. Before he had set a foot through the gate, the crested myna Old Mister Shen kept in a cage hanging by the door began to prattle at him in daring fashion: "The little two-legged beast is back, the little two-legged beast is back!"

Shen Yi picked up a seed husk and flicked it at the bird's head. "Shut your beak, you old feather duster."

The bird screeched back in protest at the abuse, "The little beast has no fur, the ill omen of a little beast has no fur!"

Shen Yi started and handed his reins to his escort—it had been a long time since he'd heard the words "ill omen." He turned to the servant. "Who's come to call?"

"General, Third Madam has come with Young Master Hui. They're speaking with the old master inside."

Shen Yi was struck by an unexpected sense of foreboding. This third madam was his third uncle's widow. His third uncle had passed before his time because of him, leaving behind his wife and young son. Shen Yi's cousin Shen Hui had been frail and sickly since he was a child, and had acquired an addiction to brothel-going as an adult. He'd never done a day of work in his life and spent all his time patronizing houses of ill repute; the signs of ill-health on his face now were undeniably compounded by excessive carnal indulgence.

Old Mister Shen had always felt guilt toward his sister-in-law, and she had always blamed Shen Yi for her husband's death. Their families hadn't spoken for many years. Shen Yi could still vividly picture this woman in mourning robes, jabbing her finger in his face as she cursed him for an ill omen. "What brings Aunt here?"

"This…" the servant began. "I'm not entirely sure, but Third Madam brought many gifts and was awfully polite when she came in. A visit from relatives can't be a bad thing."

Shen Yi hummed in acknowledgment and strode inside with a heavy heart. Sure enough, his third aunt and cousin were both there. The once-beautiful widow's loveliness had faded with age. The Third Madam before him now had protruding cheekbones and a chin sharp enough to stab a man. Shen Hui was in even worse condition: the dark bags under his eyes hung so low they nearly smacked his toes, and the whole of the man was little but a pinched-faced empty shell. He offered Shen Yi an obsequious smile the moment he saw him.

Shen Yi suddenly felt terribly uncomfortable.

Before he could make his greeting, his aunt had already risen. Wadding the handkerchief she held into a ball, she said with a smile, "After so many years, Jiping has made his way up in the world. As the commander in chief of the Southwest Army, you're the commanding general of a whole region; your prospects are unlimited. Ay, as a mother, I don't have your father's resoluteness. Had I more foresight, I would have kicked your good-for-nothing cousin out of the house and let him wander the world for a while. Perhaps then he wouldn't have found himself in this sorry state."

Unsure of her intentions, Shen Yi remained silent aside from some rote words of courtesy. His third aunt seemed rather afraid of him. She persevered through her enthusiastic greetings, then sat to the side and averted her eyes. Nonetheless, within a few exchanges, Shen Yi came to understand the reason for his third aunt's visit—it seemed this cousin of his, Shen Hui, had gotten himself into trouble.

Shen Hui had neither literary nor military accomplishments. His family had purchased a minor and worthless official position for him, but he spent near as much time slacking off as he did doing any work. Recently, the Longan Emperor had formally banned officials from visiting brothels, but certain fools hadn't taken the decree seriously. Since the legal red-light districts were off-limits, they and their fellow mongrels had gathered to visit illegal establishments. Sneaking a taste was one thing, but after a few bowls of wine, they'd gotten into a jealous brawl and were subsequently dragged before the capital magistrate.

The entire nation was steeped in gloom, yet this band of idiots still had the spirit for such antics. The capital magistrate sent every one of these wastrels to prison without a second thought. They were descendants of notable families all and ought to have been freed with a little string-pulling; unfortunately, they'd managed to make their mess just as the Longan Emperor had turned his attention to rectifying societal values and run right into the cannon muzzle.

After hearing the full tale, Shen Yi's mouth began to twitch. *If this bastard Shen Hui were my son, I'd have beaten him to death ages ago. Yet you still let him out to embarrass himself like this?*

Third Madam dabbed at her tears. "I pleaded with everyone I could think of for this wretched creature; I called on every connection I have. Finally, one of my dearest friends, who married Minister Lu from the Ministry of Justice, spoke up on his behalf and managed to bail him out."

Sitting on the sidelines, Shen Hui quietly chewed his way through a handful of sunflower seeds, as if he wasn't the one who'd caused all this trouble in the first place.

Shen Yi took a moment to respond. Although he had been born to one of the capital's noble families, he rarely interacted with this set. He could scarcely follow this web of in-law relationships.

Old Mister Shen took the opportunity to weigh in. "If that's so, we ought to make a visit and give our thanks as well."

"Isn't that right." Third Madam perked up. "We paid a call to Minister Lu the following day with generous gifts to express our thanks. But not only did he reject the gifts, he said, ever so politely, that it was a small favor—that he did it to make a favorable impression on our Shen family since we may end up as relatives in the future. That was when I realized how we'd benefited from relation to our General Shen."

Shen Yi looked to her, then to his father, finding it difficult to keep the smile on his face. He asked stiffly, "Aunt, what do you mean by this?"

No matter how scholarly he might be, Shen Yi had acquired a harsh edge to his aura after his time on the battlefield. When Third Madam spotted his chilly expression, her face twitched, and she awkwardly averted her eyes as if she couldn't bear to meet his gaze. "Hasn't Erge been matchmaking for the general recently?" She continued slyly, "You may not be aware, but that friend of mine has a sister who is Assistant Minister of Revenue Lü's second wife. Assistant Minister Lü's daughter is yet in her boudoir awaiting betrothal. She is both beautiful and talented, and has a good reputation in the capital to boot. The girl was very much smitten with the general after he came to the capital's rescue in our hour of need—after all, who doesn't love a hero? But our general is so occupied with affairs of state and rarely interacts with the civil officials. Assistant Minister Lü's daughter is a shy girl and didn't wish to brashly inquire after the matter herself. Hence, she asked me to test the waters."

86

NO ONE

ONE HOUR LATER, Shen Yi claimed he had business to attend to that evening in the Northern Camp and made his excuses; sadly, he wouldn't be dining at home. With Old Mister Shen alone left to host, an old idler who did nothing but recite sutras and walk his bird and knew not a thing about the affairs of the court or harem, it really wouldn't do for his brother's widow and child to stay for dinner. Third Madam and her son said their goodbyes and left as well.

As mother and son reached the gate, the myna bird perched there like the Shen Estate's door guardian opened its beak once again. This immortal feather duster watched Third Madam's sedan chair depart and ferociously flapped its wings. "The whore is walking her dog, her mangy dog."

Shen Hui's expression went dark. Shen Yi, who had dipped into the last reserves of his patience to politely see these guests out, ducked his head and rubbed his nose to hide the smile curling at the corner of his mouth. He'd always found this bird foul-mouthed and annoying, and dreamed fondly of someday plucking its feathers and tossing it in the stewpot. Only now did he learn it could charge the enemy lines with the best of them. He was much appeased and decided he ought to procure some good rice and brew a fine wine for this venerated elder to accompany its meal. But for appearances' sake Shen Yi offered a likely explanation: "The beast is hung at the gate every day and gets teased by everyone who passes by; the creature's learned a bunch of street curses. Cousin, don't stoop to the level of a bird."

Shen Hui was a wastrel who had been emptied out by drink and sex. He didn't dare voice his displeasure, so he merely turned to Shen Yi with a smile that was more a pained grimace and fled. Shen Yi watched until mother and son had disappeared into the distance. His expression became stormy. He stood at the gate for a moment, then stroked the myna bird's tail and muttered to himself, "I've heard of poor families who couldn't afford food selling their children, but has anyone ever witnessed a family coming to a general's estate to sell the general?"

The myna had no sense of loyalty. It pecked at his hand, then squawked, "Pah, stupid beast! Sue your pants right off!"

Shen Yi stared at the creature. Maybe he should toss it in a stew after all.

After a private chuckle at his own expense, he walked back and was greeted by the sight of Old Mister Shen, cane in hand, beckoning him over in his flowing, immortal-like getup. "Jiping, come here. I have something to speak to you about."

Shen Yi hadn't wanted to make a fuss in front of outsiders, but now he stepped over in a huff and said, "The Lü family produces noble consorts; I can't afford to marry one of them. If you're so set on it, marry her yourself—and don't say I owe them a favor because of Third Uncle. Even those who hold onto favors to blackmail people with don't insist on repayment with one's own body."

Old Mister Shen fell quiet for a beat, then said slowly, "Since childhood, no one's wanted you. I never thought I'd see the day you'd be waiting to sell yourself to the highest bidder; frankly, I'm proud of you."

Shen Yi choked. "You, sir, understand nothing at all," he spat. "Cut it out and go walk your bird; stay out of my business!"

"I may have just a few breaths left in me, but I know something of the situation outside," Old Mister Shen said placidly. "Since the time of Emperor Wu, our dynasty has been especially wary of private dealings between civil and military officials. Senior officers of the military have married princesses, but it's rare for them to marry the daughters of these prestigious families. Never mind yourself, even Marshal Gu back then...didn't he lose his bride shortly after their engagement, before she could even cross the threshold?"

The old man stretched his vowels like he was singing opera. Shen Yi's eyelid jumped. He sensed a wealth of meaning hidden beneath those melodic tones. Old Mister Shen ignored him. He shook his head dramatically and sighed. "When the capital was besieged, His Majesty was forced to return the Black Iron Tiger Tally to Marshal Gu. Now, there are certain people who show increasing disregard for the Son of Heaven."

This involved Gu Yun too?

Shen Yi was confounded. He pondered for a long time before finally picking out some of the threads—when the Westerners besieged the city, Li Feng was first forced to return military power to Gu Yun. He then saw the private violet gold stores in the Sunlight Palace, accumulated by generations of emperors, burned because of those same Westerners... Now, the pressure on their borders was unabated, and the Longan Emperor's powerlessness over the state of his own nation was more apparent each day. Li Feng himself was not unaware of this. Otherwise, with that nasty temper of his, how could he have taken the initiative to repair his awkward relationship with Gu Yun?

"Yesterday, as I observed the stars," Old Mister Shen rambled on portentously, "I saw the greedy wolf star Tan Lang overtake the emperor Zi Wei[23] in brightness. All other stars in the sky were dim. The people's hearts are restless as wild grass, and the deer has already gone to the central plains,[24] ripe for the hunter's arrow. I fear chaos is imminent..."

Shen Yi interrupted him. "Dad, wasn't it cloudy last night?"

"Ignorant child," Old Mister Shen didn't spare him a glance. "Let me ask you this: What is the name of the current captain of the Imperial Guard?"

Shen Yi stared in confusion—the Imperial Guard had no dearth of young master soldiers seeking to gain experience and trading on their families' status to jockey for position. But by custom, their highest commanding officer was a soldier with real military accomplishments transferred from the Northern Camp.

When the city had been besieged, over half the elite soldiers of the Imperial Guard, their captain Han Qi included, died for their nation in the western outskirts. Their maiden family, the Northern Camp, was also nearly wiped out. The capital's defenses had suffered serious losses, and now had a serious lack of talent. Most of the Imperial Guard's remaining members were the young master soldiers whom Han Qi had turned up his nose at and left behind at the city walls to fill out the numbers. After the siege, all of these young masters had added one military accomplishment to their name, and their positions had risen accordingly. For the first time, the Imperial Guard's highest commanding officer had never undergone training in the Northern Camp. The position was held by one of Han Qi's assistant

---

23 *Tan Lang, also known as Dubhe or Alpha Ursae Majoris, is a primary star in Zi Wei Dou Shu astrology. Tan Lang is the star of desire, talent, intelligence, and ambition. Zi Wei, also known as Polaris, the North Star, is another primary star that represents the emperor or leadership. For more on these stars, see the glossary entry for Sha Po Lang.*

24 *"Hunting deer in the central plains" is an idiom for fighting to seize the throne.*

captains, a man named Liu Chongshan. He was the younger brother of Lü Chang's eldest brother's wife.

Shen Yi thought it over for a long time before he untangled this complex network of relationships. Shocked, he strode forward and lowered his voice. "Dad, it's true what they say—old ginger is the spiciest. Give me a hint here. Marshal Gu and Prince Yan just left, and the Lü family is already pulling this stunt. What are they thinking?"

Old Mister Shen tapped the ground with his rosewood cane and muttered, "I only walk my bird, what do I know? Can't you fly by yourself now that your wings are fledged? Still begging for hints!"

Shen Yi was accustomed to being bullied by Gu Yun on a daily basis and had cultivated a great man's flexible nature. He ignored the barbed words and continued to press. "Could it be that a mere assistant minister dares to..."

"A mere assistant minister?" Old Mister Shen looked up at him and snorted. "Great General, the Fang family has taught half the court, and the Lü family has in-laws everywhere. Believe you me, they can squash a country bumpkin soldier like you leading troops in some backwater as easily as a flip of the hand. Do you really think your position as commander in chief of the Southwest Army means a thing here?"

Shen Yi shook his head. "This is preposterous. Since ancient times, there have been plenty of useless A-Dou emperors[25] who accomplished nothing, yet people didn't go around plotting treason—it runs against the most basic ethics..."

"If Prince Yan is going to Jiangbei, the Lü family must be in a precarious position. If they were to cling to ethics now, they'd be twiddling their thumbs as they wait for the family to be exterminated!

---

25 A-Dou was the childhood nickname of Liu Shan, the second and last emperor of Shu Han. He was commonly perceived as an incapable ruler.

Is His Majesty an A-Dou? Is he willing to be subordinate to anyone else?" Old Mister Shen whipped out his cane and struck at Shen Yi's left leg. "If they take that path and wait, all they'll find is death!"

Shen Yi instinctively dodged to the right. Old Mister Shen raised his cane again and aimed at his right leg from his other side. "And if they choose *this* path and act, so long as they dare to think it and dare to do it, if they can grasp that lifeline, they can rule above all the rest. Which would you choose?"

Shen Yi frowned deeply. "They plan to use Prince Yan..." The thought sent a shiver of fright through him. The Imperial Guard had always been the emperor's trusted protectors. If these protectors committed treason and the capital was caught unawares, the Northern Camp, which was forbidden from entering the city without summons, would never arrive in time to stop it. And if Prince Yan acquiesced and actually allowed himself to be pushed onto the throne by these people, where should Gu Yun stand?

Would he tolerate these usurpers on account of his personal feelings? According to Shen Yi's understanding of him, Gu Yun would never.

But foreign enemies were lurking at the borders, and half their nation had fallen into enemy hands, as yet unrecovered. If Li Feng perished tomorrow, would Gu Yun raise an army to oppose Prince Yan and return the nation to the hands of the eight-year-old crown prince? Shen Yi couldn't be sure...but no matter what Gu Yun chose, with this in the way, all paternal and filial ties, bonds of friendship, or unmentionable private affections would likely come to an end.

Possibilities whirled through Shen Yi's head: no, if *he* could see this, how could Prince Yan miss it? If he truly valued Gu Yun so much, Prince Yan would never...

"How about this?" Old Mister Shen offered. "Write a letter.

Come up with a solid, plausible reason to delay the engagement. Deliver it to the Lü family in person."

Shen Yi was taken aback. "No means no—why delay? Besides, it's not as if I'm calling off an existing engagement; why should I visit them in person?"

Old Mister Shen eyed him meaningfully, then harrumphed and turned away. A moment later, the look of surprise faded from Shen Yi's face and was replaced with one of amazement—his dad wanted him to play both sides and avoid offending the Lü family at this delicate juncture!

Shen Yi couldn't help the way his voice rose. "Dad, I may use such underhanded tricks when facing enemies on the battlefields along our borders, but I've never used them elsewhere. If I want to marry someone's daughter, I'll find a matchmaker and offer betrothal gifts, and if I don't, I'll refuse the offer. How could I play games with something like this—what kind of man would that make me? Do you seriously think that motley crew can strong-arm Prince Yan into doing as they wish?"

Old Mister Shen fell still, his back toward Shen Yi. "When Prince Yan joined the court and took over the Grand Council, he first solved the problem of the empty national treasury, then escorted military supplies to the border and helped push the Black Iron Battalion back to its old lair in the Western Regions. He's brought peace to the land and repelled the barbarian tribes. How grand these accomplishments are—but have you any idea what he's thinking?"

Shen Yi was angry now. "Since when has Prince Yan ever formed factions or sought personal gain? He only wants to recover peace for the nation and then take...take...go into seclusion and quit the court. Think how young he is—has it been easy for him to work himself to exhaustion like this? And on top of all that, a passel of old fools like yourself follow him around making delusional guesses about his intentions. I've...I've had it up to here with you!"

"Have I stepped on your tail?" Old Mister Shen scoffed. "Look at Prince Yan's current accomplishments—does he need to form a faction? Plenty of people are willing to follow him! Haven't you heard the saying 'three men make a tiger'? The first man is those upstarts in court who were promoted during the implementation of the war beacon tickets and new government reforms. The second man is those who wish to stabilize the nation and serve the country and its people. And then there's the third man. The third man is those whom Prince Yan has offended. The former two want him to don the emperor's yellow robes, while the latter want to roast him over an open fire—at the end of the day, these 'three men' are the same. The former two are willing to support his ascension, while the latter is willing to fan the flames and watch as his plots are revealed and he's sentenced for treason. Use your brain. Without the grand crime of treason, who could lay a hand on Prince Yan?"

Shen Yi's lips moved, but he couldn't get a word out.

Old Mister Shen continued, "Do you know what it means to be 'driven up Mount Liang'?[26] Do you know what it means when people say 'the tree that stands above the forest is ravaged by wind'? People's hearts are not like water; waves can rise without a breeze. With these three men and their alleged tiger, do you really imagine His Majesty will allow Prince Yan to take his accolades and retire in the future? Which of us is the ignorant one here?!"

Shen Yi felt as if he had been dropped into a pit of ice. After standing frozen a moment, he finally turned on his heel and left without a word, his face ashen.

---

26 A reference to the classic novel Water Margin, in which the protagonists of the story are forced by circumstance to gather on Mount Liang to launch a rebellion against the government.

Old Mister Shen roared after him, "What are you going to do?!"

Shen Yi didn't even turn his head. "What I ought to! Go walk your bird!"

In the capital, few found peaceful sleep that night.

Elsewhere, Gu Yun and the others secretly neared the front lines in Jiangbei. Their journey had been swift as the wind and perfectly smooth thus far, but as they approached their landing, disaster struck—they had arrived at a bad time and ran smack into a great, earthshaking thunderstorm. To achieve both speed and fuel efficiency, this aerial war chariot couldn't be too heavy. It could travel a thousand kilometers in a day through clear skies, magnificent as anything, but it promptly failed in the face of wind and rain. In minutes, this great condor became a plucked quail.

Buffeted by the rushing winds at high altitude, the ship heaved left and right. While the others braved the tossing deck, Ge Chen, their precious Lingshu scholar, was the first to go down, so dizzy he couldn't even claw his way to standing. Prince Yan attempted to alleviate his symptoms with acupuncture, but had only placed the first needle when the great condor lurched to the side. If Gu Yun hadn't grabbed Ge Chen's collar with his quick reflexes, the scholar would have been sent crashing against the foot of the bed—and that freshly inserted needle would have embedded itself deep into his tender flesh.

The group followed the instructions of the barely breathing Ge Chen to adjust the preset bearing in an attempt to detour around the storm, but ended up spinning in place until the whole crew was utterly lost. With the world hidden behind a uniform gray curtain of pouring rain, Gu Yun's field scope was useless. He had no choice but to direct them based on pure instinct. "Go lower, lower!"

Another bolt of lightning cracked down, nearly brushing the side of the great condor. The ship shuddered in the gale winds, and with a dying shriek, heeled entirely to one side. Caught off guard, Gu Yun stumbled and crashed into Chang Geng. Chang Geng wrapped one arm tightly around his waist and gripped the railing with the other, his face dripping with the Jiangnan rain.

Beside them, Xu Ling clung to another length of railing. He hoped to never fly again for the rest of his life. Trembling, he asked, "My lord, at this rate will we survive to investigate the corruption case?"

"This is nothing," Gu Yun laughed, unconcerned. "Don't worry, Commissioner Xu. Who hasn't crashed a Black Hawk a time or two? No need to panic. I'm here; I promise no one's going to die."

Xu Ling looked at him, stricken.

A guard shouted through the piercing wind and bitter rain, "Keep going, keep going! Sir, I can see land!"

Xu Ling sucked in a deep breath. Before he could begin reciting *Amitabha Buddha*, another guard yelled, "Sir, Scholar Ge said there's something wrong with our right wing. The angle of heel is too large!"

"Wha…" Before Gu Yun could complete the word, he felt a warmth beneath his ear. While everyone was screaming themselves hoarse fighting with the great condor, Chang Geng had stealthily licked Gu Yun's neck.

Beneath the din, Chang Geng breathed into his ear, "Dying for love right here wouldn't be so bad, would it?"

Gu Yun was speechless.

Prince Yan could stand unmoved before a toppling mountain. He was actually in the mood to fool around in these circumstances. Gu Yun readily admitted defeat. He suddenly felt that Master Fenghan had a point—was His Highness born without a sense of crisis?

The guard yelled again, "We're landing, hold on…careful!"

Gu Yun's vision went dark. Pitching to one side, the great condor tilted its neck and slammed into the ground. Everyone on board was nearly thrown from the ship. Without loosening his hold on Gu Yun, Chang Geng tumbled several times before colliding with the mast and coming to a halt. There was a great *crack*—Gu Yun grabbed Chang Geng's collar and hauled him to the side. The mast toppled, missing the pair by centimeters.

The scattered guards all jumped in fright and yelled. Only then did Gu Yun realize he and Chang Geng were tangled up in a rather compromising position. Mindful of the others present, he coughed uncomfortably—which merely served to draw more attention to them—then crawled to his feet to survey their surroundings.

It was deep in the night, and the great condor had landed in a fallow field so large its edges couldn't be seen. It was strangely quiet, without a single village, building, clucking chicken, or barking dog. Only the soft, intermittent call of summer insects broke the stillness.

Gu Yun was struck by an ominous premonition. "Where are we?"

One of the guards staggered forward. The man hadn't fully caught his breath, and he gasped out, "Sir, in the confusion, we seem to have crossed the river."

Commissioner Xu was still trying to get back on his feet. When he heard this, he stumbled and sat heavily back down. They had nosedived right into enemy territory!

Chang Geng turned to smile at Gu Yun. "Marshal, we've flown too far."

Gu Yun awkwardly rubbed his nose. "All this racket. Let's not attract the Western soldiers too. Go ask Xiao-Ge—what should we do with his undependable little condor?"

Two of the guards dug Ge Chen, who had nearly gone to see

the late emperor, out of the debris. He batted their hands away in a flurry of limbs and leaned over to retch.

"Don't puke yet." Gu Yun hoisted Ge Chen by the collar and forced him to raise his head, compelling the poor young man beyond his limits. "First, tell me if we can take this thing apart."

Ge Chen didn't know what to say. He'd once heard that General Shen spent over three hundred days of the year wanting to throttle the Marquis of Anding. At this moment, Ge Chen felt a powerful sympathy.

Before half an incense stick's worth of time had passed, the Marquis of Anding's guards had followed Scholar Ge's directions and efficiently removed the great condor's propulsion system with a cacophony of clangs and crashes. They split it into four pieces, each carried by one man, and left behind a pile of useless scrap. Gu Yun poured a little violet gold into the great condor's cannon muzzle and pulled out his firestarter. "I'll count to three. Run."

Xu Ling only had time to see Prince Yan gesture before two guards each took hold of one of his arms; they picked the confused man up and everyone ran against the direction of the wind. There was a *boom*, and an enormous explosion shattered the gloomy sky. Thunder rumbled through the heavens in answer, and the very ground trembled beneath their feet.

Gu Yun had blown the remains to bits.

Xu Ling paled in fright. "My lord, what if we attract the enemy troops?"

"Nonsense, how will we get back if we don't attract the enemy troops?" Gu Yun said brashly. "We can't exactly swim across the river, can we? Commissioner Xu, you'll be fine as long as you stick with me."

Commissioner Xu found that he didn't dare trust a word out of this man's mouth.

87

SCHOLAR

BEFORE JOINING THIS MISSION, Commissioner Xu had been much like the rest of Great Liang—he held an absolute, irrational faith in the Marquis of Order and the Black Iron Battalion he represented. As if, were one in the company of Gu Yun, they could walk unscathed into a dragon's nest or tiger's den; even if the sky collapsed, he would be there to hold it up. By this point, Xu Ling's faith had crumbled utterly.

Assistant Supervisory Commissioner Xu's pretty face was ashen. Clinging to his last wisp of hope, he asked, "Marshal...was crossing the river also part of your plan?"

"Of course not." Gu Yun looked at him in bewilderment and sighed. "I told Master Fenghan we wouldn't be able to rely on this thing. Black Hawks fly so quickly because they rely on manual operation in the air. This giant hunk of metal does well enough in mild weather but gives up as soon as it encounters a little wind and rain. Taking it onto the battlefield would be the same as delivering our heads to the enemy on a silver platter—and see, it broke down, just as I thought."

Ge Chen turned from puking his guts out, face blotchy with tears, and said, "This lower official...will...will definitely give Master Fenghan a full accounting once we return."

Xu Ling's stomach was twisting itself into knots in fright. He couldn't be as optimistic as Scholar Ge—he feared he might *never* return.

At least there was one individual who could talk like a reasonable person here. Chang Geng turned and gave his assistant envoy a smile. "Don't listen to him; he's just trying to scare you. This is an open plain without a single tent in sight, which means we're nowhere near the enemy vanguard. It's also a stormy night, and the sound of the explosion will have blended into the thunder. The marshal has a plan. We won't attract a large number of enemy troops; at most, an alert patrol might come investigate."

Gu Yun smirked.

Xu Ling looked at Prince Yan with tears in his eyes. Despite the treacherous situation they were in, at least he could prostrate himself before Prince Yan in admiration of his bravery and composure in the face of danger. "Your Highness, your wisdom is profound," he said in full sincerity.

"What wisdom?" Chang Geng waved him off. "He's tricked me every which way since my youth; I've had plenty of experience."

Somehow, Xu Ling felt there was an unusual intimacy in the way Prince Yan spoke of Gu Yun.

Lying in wait in the middle of nowhere on a blustery night wasn't exactly the height of comfort, but fortunately, the Western patrol arrived with alacrity. Before long, a group of soldiers appeared, cursing in their foreign language. The ground shivered with hoofbeats, and Gu Yun's mischievous smile slipped into a frown. "Odd," he said quietly.

Xu Ling had learned to startle at Gu Yun's every move. "Marshal Gu, what's odd?"

"The newcomers have...three, four, five...why are they so few?" Prince Yan lowered his voice. "Are the Westerners playing children's games with their patrols?"

"I don't know." Gu Yun shook his head. "Let's take them down first. Does anyone speak their foreign gibberish?"

The group turned as one to Prince Yan. Chang Geng stared at the two dozen guards gazing at him like baby birds waiting to be fed and said, "Why is everyone looking at me?"

Ge Chen was shocked. "Your Highness, you don't speak their language either?"

Chang Geng was mystified. "I do know some Suzhou vernacular, but since when have I ever known any foreign languages?"

Perhaps it was because they found his conduct mysterious, his considerations thorough, or because they found him in general a capable person. But after the past year or so, everyone seemed to think that no matter the occasion, Prince Yan would know something of everything and always have a ready solution.

Assistant Envoy Xu suddenly spoke up. "This lower official actually understands a bit."

Everyone who had been staring at Prince Yan swiveled their heads to look at him—Prince Yan among them. Xu Ling coughed self-consciously but met their gazes. "When His Highness and Marshal Gu defended the city gates and the officials followed His Majesty to stand beneath the ramparts, I was there too. The uselessness of scholars was impressed upon me then, but without knowledge of all the six arts, I haven't the ability to ride or shoot, or slay enemies on the battlefield. Thus, I resolved to learn some foreign languages. I thought, if we have to fight again, I can at least aid our generals by running errands and repeating messages. Then I won't have lived as a man in vain."

His last words rang with determination. But for Assistant Envoy Xu, their party was composed entirely of jianghu veterans and black crows, crafty and cunning. They moved like the wind on foot and were well accustomed to both taking lives and risking their own. Their journey had been peril after peril. Any normal person would probably have collapsed into a gibbering mess long ago. Weak scholar though he was, it was thanks to Commissioner Xu's dedication to service that he'd managed to grit his teeth and endure the journey thus far.

Battered by wind and rain, this solitary scholar stood between heaven and earth.

Gu Yun rubbed his chin, too embarrassed to tease him further. "In that case, we'll call on Commissioner Xu's services in a moment." The jovial light faded from Gu Yun's eyes, replaced by a cold, steely gleam. "Here they come!"

As he spoke, a Western patrol clad in light armor appeared before them. One man broke away from the group, did a few laps around the debris and the conflagration the rain had yet to extinguish, and garbled out some words. Xu Ling quietly translated. "He said, 'With all this rain, a fire shouldn't start out of nowhere. But there are no outsiders in this area. What on earth happened?'"

What did he mean, *there are no outsiders in this area*?

Gu Yun looked away as another Western soldier picked up a burnt piece of debris and turned it over in his hands. He suddenly sprang into the air and yowled something at his comrades.

"He said, 'This bears the mark of Great Liang's military factories; Great Liang's spies have snuck in,'" Xu Ling explained hastily. "Marshal Gu, they're getting nervous. Have we been discovered?"

Wood could be burned, but stone and iron could not. They must have recognized the mark of the Lingshu Institute.

"Marshal Gu, these foreigners are likely going to sound the alarm and summon..."

Gu Yun put a hand on the windslasher hanging at his waist. He cast a glance at Chang Geng, who had nonchalantly pulled out a small field scope and affixed it to the bridge of his nose. He wiped away the raindrops on the lens, then plucked experimentally at the string of his bow, tilting his head as if to discern whether it was waterlogged. Then, under Xu Ling's astonished gaze, he slowly drew back the string.

With a swift wave of Gu Yun's hand, twenty-some guards of the Black Iron Battalion darted through the grass.

A Western soldier unhooked a horn-shaped bugle from his waist and raised it to his lips to sound the alarm. He drew in a deep breath. An iron arrow sliced through the air—it buried itself unerringly in the man's left ear, and his head burst into a mess of red and white like a smashed watermelon, brain matter splattering his companions.

In the next moment, several black silhouettes sprang into view and launched themselves at the blindsided Western soldiers, quick as lightning. Windslashers shrieked through the air in rapid succession, and several heads hit the ground in the blink of an eye, as quick as a chef's knife chopping through melons. Just one soldier was spared, a man who had yet to dismount his horse. The man raised a pair of trembling hands as he gaped in terror at the assassins who had materialized from the brush.

Xu Ling sighed in relief and stiffly finished his previous sentence. "...summon their companions."

Gu Yun patted his shoulder. "They can't summon them anymore," he said earnestly. "Strip him down, tie him up, and bring him along; we shouldn't stay here much longer. Retreat!"

Two Black Iron guards seized the Western soldier like a pair of thugs, stripped him of his armor, and searched him like they were peeling a clove of garlic, leaving the man naked as the day he was born. The man, who by this point resembled a half-cooked white cut chicken, was bound and gagged into a trussed-up pig awaiting slaughter, then carried away.

"I can see a village over there; let's borrow a house for interrogation." Chang Geng said as he walked. "When war comes to these coastal regions, everyone capable of fleeing will flee. Only the elderly or frail invalids would have stayed behind. Nine out of every ten homes should be empty. This is a good chance to probe the locals about the situation in the occupied regions. Commissioner Xu, you'll have to take the lead. My brothers in the Black Iron Battalion aren't good with words and walk around oozing bloodlust; let's not have them scare our citizens."

"Yes, Your Highness," Xu Ling hurried to assent. He snuck a glance at Chang Geng. Prince Yan had been thoroughly soaked by the rain. A lock of hair hung loose at his temple, dripping wet. He was clearly picking his way through a desolate mire in the middle of nowhere, yet judging by his expression, he wasn't perturbed in the least. The bow that had made its debut in such spectacular fashion was once again in its place on his back.

Chang Geng happened to look up and catch Xu Ling's gaze. "Commissioner Xu, is anything the matter?" he asked good-naturedly.

Several different expressions passed over Xu Ling's face; in the end, he swallowed the words that had risen to his lips and responded with no more than a polite shake of the head.

They walked into a small village and found the place quiet as a ghost town. There were no sounds save the howling wind and rain and the crunch of their own footsteps. Thin, battered wooden doors hung ajar, and weeds grew half as high as the walls in every courtyard. Broken tiles and crumbling stone completed the tableau. In one doorway a child's pea-green dudou hung, dripping with mud; the garment had long decayed into a tattered rag.

The largest building in the village was the ancestral temple. Its courtyard was visible from a distance—a good place for outsiders to stay.

Ge Chen produced a small stick the size of a firestarter. Twisting open the top revealed a faint light that shone on their surroundings. Tiles had come loose from the ceiling of the ancestral temple so that it poured outside and sprinkled within. What furnishings they saw were either toppled or broken, and only a few ratty bolts of cloth heaped in one corner, printed with characteristic Jiangnan patterns in simple and elegant hues, retained some hint of the place's former glory.

Xu Ling scanned the interior and exterior of the ancestral temple, then said, "Looks like no one's here. Marshal Gu, could it be that all the locals have fled?"

Gu Yun frowned. He ordered a few guards to search the area, then bent to retrieve a piece of patterned cloth from the corner.

"When I was last in Jiangnan, it was a warm spring with flowers in full bloom," Gu Yun said. "Surrounded by bouquets of flowers and piles of silks, caressed by the warm spring breeze, even the rebels weren't in a hurry. They used merchant ships packed with condensed fragrance to smuggle violet gold..."

Before he could finish reminiscing, a guard charged inside. "Marshal, quick, behind the ancestral temple... In the rear courtyard, there's..."

Gu Yun raised an eyebrow. "What?"

The guard forced out with difficulty, "...the villagers."

The little villages in Jiangnan were known to meander gracefully in their layout. A small river wound through this one, and the villagers' houses stood along its banks, the burbling stream caring naught for any limitation imposed by cardinal directions. But now, everything in sight was broken down, and half of the four stone tablets at the ancestral temple's gate reading LOYALTY, FILIAL PIETY, INTEGRITY, and JUSTICE had shattered. Crushed stone had scattered into the surrounding thickets of weeds. As he walked,

Xu Ling's foot collided with something. He looked down and nearly jumped into the air—it was a human bone.

"This...this..."

Prince Yan had taken the lead as the group stepped cautiously toward the rear courtyard. The ancestral tablets were strewn across the ground, and the toppled relics of gods and buddhas were covered in a layer of dust. Atop the jet-black stone tiles of the courtyard lay countless decapitated corpses arrayed in orderly rows. Among them were men and women, old and young, the void-like eye sockets in their bleached bone faces shrouded with cobwebs.

Xu Ling sucked in an icy breath. His hand clenched around the doorframe.

"This is a well-connected location," Chang Geng said quietly after a long pause. "The open ocean and the inland canal are accessible from the north and south, while the official roads to the east and west stretch to the far ends of the nation. Travelers flow through in an endless stream, and most of the land here is flat plain. Any foreign power that occupies such a place will find it difficult to maintain tight control for long; it's too easy for people to sneak in. Their best option must have been a thorough cleansing."

Xu Ling asked numbly, "What do you mean by...a 'thorough cleansing'?"

"Send heavy armor infantry to raze the villages," Chang Geng said. "Draw a circle on the map, herd everyone within it into one spot, clean them all up. Then, dispatch troops to seize control of the entrances to the major official roads to see that no other living person enters. Something like thousands of Black Iron Battalion soldiers disguising themselves as itinerant merchants to sneak into the southwest will never happen here. Now I understand why there were so few soldiers on patrol... This place is a no-man's-land."

As Chang Geng spoke, he lashed out and kicked the Western captive in the stomach. The captive's guts were nearly ejected from his throat with the force of this furious blow. Unable to scream around his gag, he rolled on the ground whimpering like a pig being slaughtered.

Gu Yun took the little lamp from Ge Chen and shone it on a rain-soaked piece of wood, on which a line of words was carved with a fingernail.

"Sir, what does it say?"

Gu Yun's throat bobbed. "'The tears of those left behind run dry amidst the dust kicked up by foreign hooves'[27]...'hooves' is only half-written."

A body lay at the foot of the wooden post. It was mostly rotted, with white bone showing through in patches—a terrible sight. One index finger, picked clean by insects, stubbornly pointed toward the line of the poem. As if this person was continuing their silent interrogation: *Ghost fires dance through the land of fish and rice; where is the imperial army with its generals? Where is the iron cavalry?*

Only now, after an entire night in the rain, did the chill finally sink to the marrow of Gu Yun's bones. *Jiangnan has fallen to enemy hands* at last bled from words on paper into a stark and horrifying reality. For several long minutes, the ancestral temple was silent as a tomb.

Who knows how long they stood before Chang Geng lightly nudged Gu Yun. "Zixi, enough. The longer we tarry, the more can go wrong. We need to leave this place for now; rendezvousing with Zhong-lao is our top priority."

---

27 A line from the poem 秋夜将晓出篱门迎凉有感二首, "Sentiments upon Walking Out into the Cold of an Autumn Night before the Dawn" by Song dynasty poet Lu You. The following line is "Yet another year spent looking south, awaiting the imperial army."

Gu Yun's fingertips were white with tension. When he rose, his vision flickered, and he stumbled before he found his footing. Startled, Chang Geng grabbed his elbow. "What's wrong?"

Gu Yun's chest felt like it was being squeezed. A deep sense of fatigue he hadn't felt in years suddenly overwhelmed him, and for a helpless moment, he felt feeble in a way he couldn't describe. After his injuries in that northwestern pass, no matter if he abstained from drink or reduced his dosage of medicine, he had been unable to forestall his body's decline. It was as if all the unseen debts he owed had come due at once.

Today, he had no ready words to answer the interrogation of a corpse, and an uneasy weakness rose in his heart. *When will I be able to recover Jiangnan? Will I...be too late?*

These doubts and worries lingered but an instant before Gu Yun squashed them back down. He returned to normal—at least as far as outsiders could tell.

"It's nothing." Gu Yun turned to look at Chang Geng, then extricated his elbow from his grasp. As if nothing had happened, he said to Xu Ling, "Commissioner Xu, ask that white-haired monkey where their lair is, how many soldiers and sets of armor they've got, and where their armor is hidden. If he doesn't talk the first time, cut off one of his fingers, roast it, and feed him a tasty morsel."

Supposedly, many of the Western soldiers were paid mercenaries and didn't hold to any such principle as courage in the face of death. Gu Yun had numerous tricks to bamboozle and terrify the man, but he didn't have a chance to trot them out; the soldier confessed everything the instant one of the guards flashed his windslasher. It was as Chang Geng had surmised: the Westerners had cleared large swaths of the plains along the riverbank of all inhabitants, leaving one sentry post to guard each area within the no-man's-land. Each sentry post housed a dozen or so soldiers, most of whom were cavalrymen.

"A portion of the main forces serve as the vanguard to face off against General Zhong and the rest of our forces, and another portion..." Xu Ling pursed his lips, looking pained, and continued, "...went around looting and plundering, and forced captives to labor in the mines and work as slaves so they could ship their stolen goods back to their country and stop up the mouths of those who demand the pope step down."

By now, the rain had ceased, and thick clouds parted to reveal a thin stream of moonlight. Around them was desolate wasteland as far as the eye could see. The scenes of prosperity, in which farming puppets busied themselves in the fields and farmers drank tea as they discussed matters of state, had long become things of the past.

"This lower official once thought that the refugees in Jiangbei were suffering unbelievable adversity," Xu Ling said quietly. "But there they at least have straw huts to shelter from the rain and two bowls of thin porridge to claim per day..."

"Talk won't change anything," Chang Geng cut in. "Let's go. Have that Western dog lead the way to their sentry post."

Two Black Iron Battalion guards grabbed the Western soldier on each side.

"Your Highness Prince Yan!" Xu Ling took a few quick strides, calling after Chang Geng. "When will we be able to face these Western dogs in battle?"

Chang Geng didn't pause in his steps nor turn his head. "If we can successfully settle the refugees in Jiangbei, and if the heavens are merciful and do not strike us with disaster, we may spend a year or two recovering our strength. If we can hold out until the eighteen tribes exhaust their resources, we can restore our access to violet gold at the northern border. When that time comes, I refuse to believe we'll be powerless against these Western curs."

But the court was presently shrouded in the miasma of corruption, and every step forward required arduous effort. Thousands of refugees remained homeless and destitute; like this, how could the nation recover its strength and present a united front to its enemies?

Xu Ling inhaled sharply, and the rims of his eyes grew red. He caught up to Prince Yan and said in an urgent undertone, "Your Highness, are you aware—the reforms you pushed for in court caused too great a stir, and many consider you a thorn in their sides... If nothing else, just take this investigation in the south. That Yang Ronggui... If he's truly been lying in his reports, he must also have an ear to the ground; he'll have heard news of your intentions these last few days. If he gets desperate, he might exchange all the silver, gold, and treasures in his estate for war beacon tickets and claim you went to extremes to push your pet policies and forced local officials to meet all sorts of unachievable quotas. They could claim they had no choice but to shirk the law, and once the winds of change begin to blow, the Department of Supervision and Imperial Censorate will surely rise up and oppose you. What will you do then?"

A faint smile appeared on Chang Geng's face. "If it leads to someone taking responsibility for this mess of a situation, recovering Jiangnan, and bringing peace to the land, so what if I have to pack my bags? Commissioner Xu, none of what I've done is for myself, nor do I hope to gain a single accolade from those people—if someone wants to impeach me, they may do so; my conscience is clear. Whether I'm sleeping in the Grand Council or the imperial dungeons, none of my ancestors will be appearing to slap me across the face in the middle of the night. As for the rest..."

He did not continue. A sneer seemed to flash across his young and handsome face. Catching a glimpse of the lonely fury and help-lessness that hung heavy over Prince Yan, Xu Ling's heart thumped, and his face stung like fire. The prince had slapped the Imperial Censorate's face in full view of the court on more than one occasion, and the department's members all itched to dig up some dirt on the prince and beat his faction down until every one of them sported giant bumps on their heads.

Meanwhile, the Department of Supervision was the gathering place of the "purists" within the court—those who, like Xu Ling, were willing neither to cling to powerful nobles nor roll around in the muck with copper-stinking merchants. They took pride in their loyalty to sovereign alone, and viewed Prince Yan's exploits as akin to quenching a short-term thirst with long-term poison. Add in the insidious effects of the rumors flying about the court, and it was little surprise they found Prince Yan a shrewd and treacherous official who had the emperor in the palm of his hand.

When Xu Ling agreed to come south with the prince, he had indeed intended to investigate and censure the corrupt officials of Jiangbei. But he had another, more important, matter on his mind as well. While the established noble families and new upstarts were busy fighting like cats and dogs, the members of the Imperial Censorate and the Department of Supervision, who fancied them-selves above corruption, had planned to join hands to impeach Prince Yan. Xu Ling's aims in joining this venture were not entirely pure. He was here both because the Longan Emperor wanted him to keep an eye on Prince Yan, and because these two departments sought evidence of Prince Yan's disloyal intent.

And yet—even if his methods were a bit extreme, here was a man fretting and toiling over the ravaged state of Jiangnan and Jiangbei, while they in the court waited to pounce on the first mistake he made. Who, precisely, was bringing calamity upon the nation and its people?

Xu Ling's voice choked on a sob. "Your Highness..."

Chang Geng raised an eyebrow in confusion. "What is it, Commissioner Xu?"

For a moment, Xu Ling couldn't seem to speak.

Gu Yun walked wordlessly ahead of them, leading the way. That scholar Xu Ling thought he was so stealthily whispering into Chang Geng's ear, but Marshal Gu's hearing was sharp when he wasn't deaf; he had heard every word from his position downwind of them. He cast a sidelong glance at his guards, who were furious listening to this conversation, then at Ge Chen's evasive expression. He was beginning to get a sense of how this "accident" that landed them behind enemy lines had occurred.

88

WREAKING HAVOC

G U YUN LOWERED HIS HEAD. After brief consideration, he understood for whose benefit Chang Geng was making this trip south.

On some level, Gu Yun, who had grown up deep within the imperial palace, understood Li Feng better than Chang Geng did. Any leader who had high aspirations but lacked in vision could easily end up in Li Feng's position. The Longan Emperor understood how to wield power well enough, but the most capable sheepdog could only herd sheep. Even if its teeth were sharp enough to slay a wolf in one-on-one battle, it could never become the wolf king. This was the same idea.

Gu Yun didn't need to know the detailed lines of division within the court nor what political opinions they held. Regardless of what Xu Ling's goals were in accompanying them, regardless of which sect or clan he belonged to, he was Li Feng's man to the last. Li Feng loved simple-minded people like this; those who didn't curry favor, didn't form factions, and had no social standing or background. He spent his entire life searching for such "pure officials."

The question of what made an official pure aside, to the Longan Emperor, this designation held two layers of meaning: First, they were promoted by the emperor himself, had no noble families or powerful officials behind them, and had a sufficiently clean background. Second, they made the emperor feel safe and in control.

This was in fact the path Prince Yan had initially taken. At the time, he had no foundation to speak of in the court, no support, no power, and no influence. All he had to his name were a few drops of imperial blood—and even then, it was an adulterated blood that gave others pause. When he shouldered the heavy responsibility of the Grand Council, seemingly fearless in his ignorance of the dangers that lay ahead, he was precisely what Li Feng would call a "pure official."

But later, Li Feng discovered that Prince Yan was no ignoramus. He was more than capable of stirring up waves. Alarmed by his manipulations, the emperor no longer believed in his purity. Thus, he had sent someone even purer to keep Prince Yan in check.

An emperor was looking out through Commissioner Xu's bright, inquisitive eyes. Unfortunately, this long-distance field scope had a sincere nature. Prince Yan had yet to exhaust his tricks, but Xu Ling had already taken the bait hook, line, and sinker.

There was no place for anyone truly upright and above flattery in the Great Liang of today. Gu Yun had tactfully avoided domestic affairs for years, but he knew too well what these people were like. Even far away at the borders of the nation, he had heard stories of Chang Geng's deeds after entering the court. But hearing stories was one thing and seeing it himself was another. Truth be told, up until this moment, Chang Geng had still, in Gu Yun's eyes, been that innocent and kind-hearted youth of years past: talented but never arrogant, someone who had a bit of a temper but didn't take it out on others without cause. And even when he did, he would stay well within the bounds of reason, and only act out to communicate to whomever had offended him that he was angry. The one on the receiving end of his ire would feel that they had been lightly scratched by the outstretched paw of some familiar little creature, leaving behind a white mark that failed to even break skin.

Yet it could still hurt someone down to the marrow.

That youth had been warm and sincere...so sincere that, although Gu Yun was logically aware that they were one and the same, on an emotional level, he'd been unable to connect that boy to the ruthless and resolute Prince Yan, Li Min.

Today, under the battery of Jiangnan's wind and rain, these two unrelated individuals finally converged into one. Suddenly, both seemed unfamiliar. Gu Yun had never quite caught his breath after his earlier spell, and his chest began to ache with a fury. But they were behind enemy lines; the commander in chief couldn't afford to wallow in sentiment. He had no choice but to maintain a reckless look of ease on his face and silently weather this emotional blow.

Their party followed the Western captive to the closest sentry post with all speed. According to their captive, soldiers manning the sentry post split their patrols into two shifts. Patrolling the no-man's-land was easy, so as time went on, these Western cavalry-men had begun to slack off. They were caught completely unawares when enemies snuck right up to them.

"The hairy guy said the sentry post has just two suits of heavy armor," Xu Ling said quietly. "There's nothing else of use. Marshal, can heavy armor help us cross the river?"

"Of course," Gu Yun said. "It'll sink the instant it touches the water, faster than an adulterer's cage, perfect for all sorts of two-timing men and lewd women."

Xu Ling was speechless. To think, for a moment there, he'd expected the Marquis of Anding to be serious. Looking back now, that was indeed a misapprehension.

Gu Yun wiped the fatigue off his face, feigning exuberance. "Don't get ahead of yourself. We'll use the foreign skins from this sentry post to sneak in among the front-line troops along the riverbank, then seize our chance and steal one of those speedy dragonets. Commissioner Xu, don't worry. I've already notified old General Zhong. We'll have someone waiting for us on the other side once we reach the river."

Xu Ling's eyes nearly popped out of his head. "Marshal Gu has already communicated with General Zhong? When?"

"I'm psychic," said Gu Yun in all seriousness.

...There he went again.

Assistant Supervisory Commissioner Xu, who had walked into his traps time and again, finally learned to shut his mouth around Gu Yun. He had an inkling now of how Prince Yan had achieved that steady nature of his that allowed him to remain pleasantly relaxed even when the sky was falling.

Chang Geng, however, twitched. He *had* already notified old General Zhong—but he had used the Linyuan Pavilion's methods to do so. Xu Ling couldn't know of this, so he had prepared another show for the assistant envoy's benefit. Yet Gu Yun had silently diverted suspicion from him with a few short words. The Black Iron Tiger Tally Gu Yun held could deploy any military forces in the land during wartime. It wouldn't be strange if he had some unknown method of contacting the border garrisons. And no matter how dim one's wits, once Gu Yun brushed off their inquiries, they ought to know not to probe further. With this, Xu Ling wouldn't find it suspicious when they encountered reinforcements.

The rainwater dripping from Chang Geng's palms was replaced with a layer of cold sweat.

He knows. Chang Geng's heart lurched, then sank, ice-cold.

A person could plot, but success was up to the heavens. No matter how well-laid the plan, deviations and mishaps were inevitable. As far as Chang Geng was concerned, the first mishap was when, just as he was about to give the impassioned speech he had prepared to justify personally making the journey down south, Gu Yun unexpectedly stepped forward and settled the whole affair with a word.

An arrow nocked to the string had to be shot; it couldn't be aborted halfway. Chang Geng had no choice but to steel himself and continue down this path, making his arrangements all the more secretive.

When it came to Gu Yun, the ever-prepared Prince Yan always found himself blundering. It wasn't because Chang Geng didn't have the brains to plan around him, but because he couldn't quite figure out what his plans were in the first place. On the one hand, Chang Geng wanted to conceal his plots from Gu Yun just as he did from Xu Ling. Such underhanded maneuvers were dishonest, after all. Even if he had lowered himself to this level, he didn't want Gu Yun to see the way he had engineered every last detail of their adventure. He didn't dare imagine what Gu Yun would think of this. But on the other hand, he had a faint, self-destructive wish to see all his subterfuge fall apart before Gu Yun. It was an urge much like throwing a meaningless tantrum with one's closest person—he wanted Gu Yun to know exactly what kind of trash he was at his worst.

Thus was the contradictory nature of his desires. He was afraid to touch Gu Yun's hard bottom line, yet couldn't resist the urge to test him. The most mystifying thing in the world wasn't an enemy's treachery but a lover's intentions. These, no matter how sincere, would always seem ever-changing in their target's eyes.

Gu Yun turned to look at him, seemingly by chance. Chang Geng's lashes flickered involuntarily, as if he wanted to hide. Nevertheless, he met Gu Yun's eyes and stared straight back, trying to dig up a single hint with the hooks in his gaze.

Ge Chen chose that moment to tactlessly scoot over and say into Gu Yun's ear, "Marshal, I suspect the hairy foreigners' heavy armor utilizes special tricks of engineering to burn less violet gold than ours. Why don't you go handle the soldiers while I take this heavy armor apart and steal some insights!"

His popping up diverted Gu Yun's gaze at exactly the right time. Chang Geng couldn't read a thing from so brief a glimpse, and with all these obtrusive outsiders about, he couldn't just ask him and clear the air. Chang Geng was left to fret in private.

Gu Yun selected a guard to accompany Ge Chen, and that was that. "If you don't manage to glean anything useful, I'll have to assume you're being lazy and serve you a court martial when we get back. Let's go."

On his command, two dozen black crows silently surrounded the tiny Western sentry post. They swiftly dealt with the few Western soldiers inside who were still dreaming grand dreams in their beds, then dug up a map of the garrison's defenses and a few sets of light-pelt armor. Everyone donned a suit. As long as they kept their visors down, no one would be able to tell the people inside weren't the original owners.

Gu Yun pointed at their trembling Western captive. "Put him in light armor and install a fuse in his gold tank. If he causes any trouble, blow him into dumpling filling—oh right, where's Xiao-Ge?"

Ge Chen jogged up to him. "Ay, Marshal, here I am!"

In this brief period of time, Ge Chen had not only disassembled the foreigners' heavy armor, he'd taken the opportunity to pilfer their entire central propulsion system. Like a servant assigned to guard a household's treasury, he tied his spoils around his waist and refused to let them out of his hands, eyes gleaming like a rat that had fallen into the rice vat. He bounced over and said, "Marshal Gu, am I going to play a Western soldier too? I'm bringing this with me. Are there any sets of light armor that are a little larger around the stomach?"

Gu Yun looked him over with an unreadable expression, then directed his guards to truss Scholar Ge up like a chicken. He barked out a laugh. "What 'light' armor—it's dozens of kilograms' worth of weight. I have a much more suitable role for you where you won't need a costume at all. What do you think of playing the spy who crossed enemy lines to sniff around and got himself caught? If anyone interrogates us, we'll have a proper excuse. And look, with that thing, it'll seem like you got caught red-handed with stolen goods. Tie him up!"

Thus Ge Chen replaced their Western captive, a look of shock passing across his face. Two steely-faced guards grabbed him and bound him with rope, then hung him from a pole by the wrists and ankles and carried him off, swaying along with their gait. Ge Chen wasn't an idiot. He guessed he must have offended the general somehow, and Gu Yun was bullying him on purpose. He sent a plaintive look in the direction of Chang Geng. "Your..."

"Your what?" Gu Yun lowered his visor. His voice sounded from beneath the icy-cold steel as if it were covered in a layer of frost. "Gag him; captives aren't allowed to squeal and shout."

Still on tenterhooks himself, Prince Yan was too afraid to speak up. So it was with his tacit permission that Scholar Ge became a veritable human ball of injustice and was toted away on his pole.

Their party marched toward the Westerners' garrison with their "captive" in tow. They finished crossing the wide stretch of no-man's-land and reached the enemy lines as dawn approached.

By now, they could see through their field scopes that frightening Western sea monster sprawled out across the surface of the river, as well as the Western dragons boldly surging through the water, swift as tiger sharks cutting through the waves. For some in their party, this was their first time seeing these whirlwind-fast Western dragons. Xu Ling got rather dizzy trying to track them with his eyes. The Westerners' defenses were too tight. His palms were covered in cold sweat; he couldn't fathom how Prince Yan and Gu Yun had the guts to swagger about behind enemy lines.

They were still some ways out from the garrison when the dark, cavernous mouths of several short cannons swiveled in their direction. Xu Ling swallowed with difficulty. He felt a hand on his shoulder and heard Prince Yan's voice in his ear. "When you're afraid, don't think about how we'll be dead meat if someone discovers us. Think about how these are all people we're going to exact vengeance on in the future. Even if we don't take care of them today, we'll settle our accounts one by one tomorrow. We're here to kill, not to be killed."

Xu Ling heard a hunter's bloodlust beneath Prince Yan's placid tones. A shiver ran down his body. Then, as if that bloodlust had been transferred to him with the shiver, Xu Ling sucked in a deep breath and recalled the piles of white bones in the ancestral temple. He squeezed his eyes shut, finding that his fear had indeed faded.

"Keep a tight hold on our guide's fuse," Prince Yan continued. "None of us understand their foreign language, so we'll have to rely on Commissioner Xu. If he makes any suspicious moves... Commissioner Xu, are you willing to take a life?"

Assistant Supervisory Commissioner Xu had been a scholar since youth; he'd never slaughtered so much as a chicken. His hand holding the fuse shook. This was nothing to Xu Ling, but sensing his life hanging by a thread, the Western captive began to tremble as well.

The hand on Xu Ling's shoulder pressed down like an iron clamp even through the steel armor, and its influence settled Xu Ling's nerves. He gritted his teeth. "I am. Don't worry, Your Highness, I won't let you down."

Chang Geng slowly released him. Sensing Gu Yun's gaze, he hid behind his visor, afraid to return it. He discretely wiped a layer of sweat from his palms.

He could tell every person what they ought to do, but there was no one for him to look to for advice.

The Western sentries shouted something through a copper squall, likely an inquiry about their presence. Xu Ling cleared his throat and yelled back, "We caught a spy from the Central Plains while on patrol. We brought him here to ask what to do with him."

The garrison guard poked out his head and gave them a suspicious look. Gu Yun covertly tapped the Western captive's back with the hilt of his borrowed sword. "Do your job."

Xu Ling didn't have to translate; the man understood Gu Yun's meaning well enough. He flipped up the visor of his light armor with trembling hands, and the familiar tuft of blond hair allayed the guard's suspicions. The man then examined Ge Chen, hanging from his pole, and bared his teeth in a sneer. With a wave of his hand, the cannon muzzles slowly swiveled away, and the garrison opened its gates for them.

"Wait here," said the guard who let them inside. "His Holiness is entertaining an important guest, and the senior officers are all with him. Even if you make your report, there's no one who can do anything about it. Go register yourselves and lock up this pig. We'll roast it later tonight."

No one else could understand a word of this, so none of their party reacted. Xu Ling knew that right now, even Prince Yan couldn't help him. He hastily gulped and calmed himself as much as he could. "Guests from where?"

"The Holy Empire." The guard impatiently scratched at his face. "Don't ask about things that aren't your business. Who knows when they'll let us go home; this war is never going to end—hey, Brother, these useless layabouts from the no-man's-land caught a spy; give them a few bites of meat jerky. This is probably the greatest achievement of their lives."

The Western soldiers laughed. Xu Ling's stuttering heart settled back into a steady rhythm. He led the way, shoving their Western captive in the direction the guard had indicated.

At that moment, the captive jerked to the side, exposing the fuse in Xu Ling's hand. The guard, who had yet to leave, saw it at once. "Wait, what's that on your back?"

Xu Ling was immediately soaked in cold sweat.

Now suspicious, the guard strode up to Xu Ling and looked him up and down. His hand shot to the sword at his waist. "Lift your visor."

Xu Ling's heart pounded in his chest. He froze.

Just then, the shrill cry of an alarm sounded in the distance. The wind swept a burst of flame high into the sky, and countless Western soldiers sprinted past them. While the Western sentry was distracted, Chang Geng stepped forward. A thin needle the length of a man's arm had at some point appeared in his hand, and he jabbed it into the guard's neck like a flash of lightning.

The Western sentry didn't make a sound as he died on his feet. A guard from the Black Iron Battalion plucked off the man's helmet. He cut the rope binding Ge Chen and plunked the helmet onto his head.

When Xu Ling finally caught his breath, he noticed one of Gu Yun's guards was missing.

Gu Yun smoothly snatched the fuse from Xu Ling's hands and strode off with a "Let's go." Before Xu Ling could react, Gu Yun had yanked on the fuse on the captive's back. He flicked something open on the back of the man's light armor with his windslasher and kicked him away. A great white cloud billowed from the captive's back, and Gu Yun's kick sent him flying forward, trailing steam behind him. The man let out an inhuman shriek. At the same time, the garrison soldiers inevitably looked toward the source of the noise. On a signal from Gu Yun, the well-trained Black Iron Battalion guards raised their bows and cannons and unleashed a wave of fire in all directions.

The Western captive's light armor exploded, the force of the blast sending nearby tents and Western soldiers flying. Xu Ling lost his footing, but an armored hand caught him and dragged him into a stumbling run.

They fled in the chaos. Rounding a corner, Gu Yun threw out an arm to halt Xu Ling and Chang Geng, who was still dragging the assistant envoy. "How do you say, 'They went that way, after them'?" he asked, low and quick.

Xu Ling translated it into the Westerners' language before he could give it any conscious thought.

He finished speaking just as the enemy soldiers overtook them. Gu Yun drew the sword that came with the Western light armor. He opened his mouth and perfectly mimicked the words Xu Ling had just taught him, then ran ahead, sword in hand, to personally lead the charge with great vigor.

The soldiers were in identical armor with identical visors; it was impossible to tell who was who. After leading the Black Iron Battalion for so many years, Gu Yun had developed an imperious general's disposition. The Western soldiers couldn't resist running after him at his command.

Xu Ling was speechless. Those who had been the pursued myste-riously became the pursuers.

They ran all the way to the riverbank before Xu Ling saw a dark silhouette peel itself from the crowd in the distance. The man had already removed the Western armor he was using as a disguise, revealing himself to be Gu Yun's missing guard. The Black Iron Battalion soldier let out a piercing whistle, then leapt into the river. Struck by inspiration mid-crisis, Xu Ling yelled in the Westerners' foreign language, "To the ships, after him!"

Gu Yun hadn't expected Commissioner Xu to be corrupted so quickly. He couldn't resist giving him an approving thumbs-up.

Xu Ling didn't have time to be satisfied with himself. Gu Yun unceremoniously hoisted Xu Ling with his several dozen kilograms of light armor and tossed him down from the riverbank onto a Western dragon. A few sailors on the dragon had heard the racket on land and hurried over, only to see several dark silhouettes land in quick succession on their vessel. With a rise and fall of their blades, they mopped up the Western sailors, striking each man down in a single fatal blow without one sloppy move or sound. Before the bodies could fall, their killers deftly supported them so it looked as if they were walking into the cabin side by side.

Shortly thereafter, with the mayhem on the bank still in full swing, a Western dragon slipped out of the garrison's harbor and into the darkness of early dawn.

SUFFERING A BEATING

NOW THAT HE'D GAINED the opportunity to drive this unbelievably swift Western dragon with his own two hands, Ge Chen considered his stint hanging like air-dried pork time well spent. He rubbed his hands all over the control panel with a lascivious look on his face, hungry as a lecher who had spied a peerless beauty. It was a miracle he wasn't drooling.

A strangely colored firework burst from the water of the river—it was Gu Yun's guard, who had drawn everyone's attention before diving into the waters. Ge Chen drove the Western dragon straight for the signal. In short order, an iron cable the thickness of a child's arm shot out from the warship with stunning force, carving through the wind with a shrill whine. As expected of the Black Iron Battalion, not only was the man unafraid of this lethal weapon, he quickly grabbed onto it. Towed along by the iron cable, he swept out in an arc before flipping himself over the cable and onto the deck of the Western dragon.

"Hold on tight!" yelled Ge Chen. "Marshal, the Lingshu Institute has been lusting after these Western dragons for half an age. Now that we've finally gotten our hands on one, if you ask us to wait on you hand and foot or eat your table scraps to show our gratitude, we'll do it gladly!" he finished with a cackle.

Scholar Ge steered the dragon like he was out for a joyride; everyone aboard tumbled this way and that till they could do nothing but cling to the railings for dear life. Gu Yun's ears were filled with the roar of roiling river currents crashing against the flanks of the dragon. He gritted his teeth and thought, *I had him all tied up a second ago; why didn't it occur to me to give him a solid beating?*

The Western dragon shot past the sea monster as if on swift wings. By now, it was too late for the Westerners to give chase even if they wanted to.

The soldiers of the Western garrison on the south bank finally came to their senses and made to pursue them, their faces pale or red with anger. But before any orders could be given, a dark and teeming mass of Great Liang dragons sailed out of their harbor across the river.

Mister Ja lowered his field scope, shocked, and barked out a string of rapid commands. "Hold it! Don't follow, it's a trap! All fleets, fall in line and prepare to engage! Shit! The Central Plains people have huddled in their shells all this time; why have they launched an offensive *today*?"

The pope also had a nasty look on his face. He personally escorted a whiskered man—likely the rumored guest from the Holy Empire—from the tent. The two gazed at each other, apparently in harmony but actually at odds. The pope turned to look at the massive forces of the Jiangbei Garrison encroaching on their perimeter with worried eyes.

The Western dragon scudding across the river vanished into the ranks of the Great Liang dragons in the blink of an eye. Both sides faced off in full battle array. Then, beneath the shocked gazes of their enemy, the Great Liang Navy turned their prows and slowly retreated without doing a single thing, as if they'd merely come to strike a pose.

Never mind the befuddled Western navy they left in their wake; when old General Zhong Chan had received Chang Geng's message via wooden bird, he'd suffered the fright of his life and viciously cursed this madman's deranged behavior under his breath. Still, with Prince Yan and Marshal Gu both gracing the front lines with their presence, Zhong Chan and Yao Zhen, as the military and civil leaders of Jiangbei, were obligated to come greet them.

Zhong Chan made a bow according to the rules of etiquette. "This lower general greets Your Highness Prince Yan and Marshal Gu..."

Both were his former students, so neither would allow him to bow. They immediately strode forward to raise Zhong Chan from his obeisance. Gu Yun's gaze caught on old General Zhong's hand. The back of it was speckled with age spots, his hand so withered it was only skin and bone—the picture of decline and deterioration. Zhong Chan was already past seventy years of age. His back was still straight as an arrow, but his hair had gone white. Even the few dozen kilograms of light-pelt armor were too much for his body to bear; he wore a symbolic suit of thin armor plates in its stead.

Gu Yun looked at him with countless emotions swirling in his heart. He'd once envied old General Zhong to no end and wished he could follow in his teacher's footsteps: lay down his official position and title of nobility, change his name, and roam the jianghu, thwarting all attempts to track him down. How carefree a life would that be? But despite his deep envy, before Gu Yun could manage to lay down his own burdens, old General Zhong had returned to the service of his country in his advanced age. One in the north and one in the south, the two worked themselves to the bone. Gu Yun felt as if he'd seen firsthand the unavoidable cycle of fate.

Zhong Chan leveled Chang Geng with an unreadable look, then scanned Gu Yun from head to toe. "Marshal Gu, you look unwell."

"I received imperial orders to ensure the envoys Prince Yan and Commissioner Xu's safe return to the capital," Gu Yun said with a smile. "But I'd barely started my mission when our ship went down behind enemy lines. I was scared half to death; how can I look well?"

"In that case, let's discuss a welcome banquet for the lords at a later time," Zhong Chan said breezily. "Chongze, make arrangements for our guests to bathe and change; we can continue our conversation after they've had a chance to rest. We are in a state of alert and there are military affairs that require attention; please excuse this lower general's absence."

Zhong Chan gave Prince Yan one last look and cupped his fist at him in a rather lukewarm gesture, then turned on his heel and left without a backward glance. Chang Geng sensed the old general disapproved of his handling of the situation, so he stood aside and held his tongue. At Zhong Chan's age, he had one foot in the grave; he was due to see the late emperor any day now. He'd no need to make nice with anyone, and every one of the high-ranking, powerful figures in court was his junior. Whether it was before Prince Yan or the Marquis of Anding, he never minced words. Xu Ling, fresh from his brush with death, reeled at the old general's attitude.

Yao Zhen was left alone to endure a splitting headache as he strained his weary brain to joke and cajole and smooth things over, all while bustling about arranging tents for everyone so they could rest.

Gu Yun wasted no time freshening up and changing out of his rain-sodden clothes. Before he could do more than that, the fatigue finally hit. After giving orders that he was not to be disturbed, he fell dead asleep in his tent.

When he awoke, it was dark. Gu Yun's sight was blurry, the sounds around him muffled. No sooner had he stirred than a pair of hands reached out and considerately offered him a few sips of tea to wake him, then presented him with a bowl of familiar-smelling medicine.

There was no need to ask to whom these hands belonged.

Gu Yun hadn't much energy in the first place, and his body felt heavier after sleeping. He was in no mood to give Chang Geng attention; he took hold of the bowl and drained it in one draft before collapsing back into his pillow, then focused on resting his eyes as he waited for the medicine to take effect. Chang Geng sat quietly at his side, using his fingers in place of silver needles to apply a perfect amount of pressure along the acupoints at Gu Yun's head and neck. Gu Yun grew drowsy under his ministrations, the bit of alertness in him like the flame of a lamp struggling in the wind, flickering in and out. After a time, the clarity of his hearing and the endless piercing pain in his head swelled simultaneously. Gu Yun was at last roused to full consciousness and unconsciously furrowed his brow.

Chang Geng paused in his movements and dipped to drop a light kiss on the crease between Gu Yun's brows—a brief, experimental touch. Perhaps because Gu Yun didn't react, his courage grew, and he pressed a trail of kisses down the bridge of Gu Yun's nose before coming to land on those faintly medicinal-tasting lips.

Gu Yun had just finished his medicine; his mouth was suffused with bitterness. He didn't much want to kiss Chang Geng just now, so he tilted his head to evade him.

For some reason, this subtle action set Chang Geng off. His tranquil mood evaporated, and his breathing grew rapid as his hands sank into the bed to lock Gu Yun within his arms. He attacked with an indescribable hint of despair, as if he wasn't trying to kiss Gu Yun, but tear at him out of some deep-set grudge.

Gu Yun tried to pinch the back of his neck, but Chang Geng caught his hand and clamped it down to the bed—he was climbing all over him now!

Frowning, Gu Yun twisted and knocked Chang Geng's elbow against the bedframe with moderate force, hitting him right in the funny bone. Chang Geng flinched in pain and reflexively let go—but within an instant, he heedlessly clutched at Gu Yun again.

With a push and a grab, Gu Yun pinned him down in a grappler's hold. "Do you remember where we are? What sort of madness is this?"

Chang Geng's breathing was frighteningly heavy. He clung to Gu Yun as if clinging to life. Even pinned as he was, he wouldn't let go, stubbornly twisting his arm to grab at Gu Yun until the bones of his wrist gave a sharp *crack*. This astonishingly obstinate man would rather injure himself than back down.

Gu Yun obviously didn't want to break his wrist. But the moment he loosened his grip, Chang Geng was on him again, as if he meant to cage him within the narrow confines of the bed. He stared down at Gu Yun from above, his eyes like those of a hungry wolf.

Greedy, yet afraid.

As if he was ready to throw it all away, yet also as if he was constantly anxious and on his guard.

Gu Yun's blurry vision gradually sharpened. He took in his surroundings and realized he had accidentally slept the day away. He'd fallen into bed at dawn and it was already past dusk, the canopy of night descending overhead. In the dim light, he peered into Chang Geng's eyes but failed to find that ominous bloody glow and double pupils. Chang Geng was sensible; he was simply throwing a tantrum.

Who knew how long this standoff lasted. In the end, the viciousness in Chang Geng's eyes faded like a passing tide, the churning water receding to reveal a look of unspeakable imploring. "Zixi, I..."

"You what?" Gu Yun asked, his voice chilly.

Chang Geng shrank back before his gaze and released him. His body was as stiff as a wooden puppet as his eyes slid closed and he sat, defeated, to the side. He was entirely too attuned to Gu Yun's moods—so attuned that Gu Yun didn't need to speak a word. A single glance could leave him stricken.

Silence reigned in the small tent. It was quiet enough to hear a pin drop. At long last, Chang Geng broke the stillness, his voice low. "With this southward expedition, I will force Li Feng to stand on my side and ascertain how much furor the noble families of the court can raise. These people are set in their old ways, and they aren't as united as they seem. If I make too drastic a move in the capital, I risk pushback. It makes more sense to use Jiangbei as a breakthrough point, lure them into lowering their guard, and sow division among them so they'll take the bait. I'll use the opportunity to push new officials into power. Then I can take the next step: eliminating dissent and cleaning up the court."

There seemed to be a hidden current running beneath his terse explanation. "Resettling the refugees" was the one thing he never mentioned, as if he was purposefully avoiding the topic in a fit of pique. He refused to say one positive word about himself and insisted on painting everything in the most sinister, petty, and shameless light.

Who didn't know of Prince Yan's facility for speaking the language of whomever he met? As long as he set his mind to it, his silver tongue could tame even an old porcupine like Zhang Fenghan until he was eating out of the palm of his hand. But before Gu Yun, Chang Geng felt as if he had transformed into a younger version of that same Master Fenghan, saying everything Gu Yun least wanted to hear.

Once he'd opened his mouth, he couldn't stop it all spilling out. He took a pause to breathe and continued: "I gave these newly promoted officials a leg up with the war beacon tickets. If I form them into a party during our national emergency, I won't need to do any more to support them in the future. I'll simply need to give them some attention for everything to fall in place and a major faction to be formed. They'll be champing at the bit to topple the old court and the old system. I'll see to it that the absolute dominion the emperor has held over heaven and earth since the reign of Emperor Wu ends with this generation. As for Li Feng, I care not a whit what happens to him. I won't be satisfied until the entire house of Li is dead."

Gu Yun had put the pieces together by now. This bastard felt guilty, so he was brandishing his claws in a show of false bravado. Only after he'd picked a fight and argued it out would he feel at ease. *Have it your way*, Gu Yun fumed.

"So your surname isn't Li, then? Is it Pig or is it Dog?" Gu Yun snarled back.

"Me?" Chang Geng huffed out a sharp laugh. "I'm much worse than any pig or dog; a mere living puppet of the barbarian shamaness—"

Before he could finish, Gu Yun raised a hand to slap him across the face. Chang Geng instinctively closed his eyes; he forced himself not to dodge by sheer will. Gu Yun's hand whipped through the air but stopped just short of Chang Geng's face, coming to rest beside his neck.

"Merit or misstep are judged by the people of the world. Why throw yourself at me asking for praise or begging for a scolding?" Gu Yun tried to keep his voice low, but with every additional word, sincere anger rose in him. "You're going into conniptions to force me to say you can do anything at all, whatever you do is right,

I'll endorse you with whole heart no matter what disgraceful actions you take—would that satisfy you? Would you sleep well at night? Would your conscience be appeased?"

His voice was like a knife, leaving a bloody gash with every word. Chang Geng sucked in breath after breath of cold air as if in terrible pain. Trembling, he asked, "What does the world have to do with me? It's all the people of the world who've betrayed me. I've never owed this world a thing; what do I care what its people have to say? But everyone needs something worth treasuring. Zixi, in all my life, I've never been able to treasure anything else; it was all you. If you would take this from me, you may as well tell me how to die and I'll go at once."

"Ho, what, Your Highness Prince Yan is going to die for me?" Gu Yun nearly laughed in anger. "If there's one thing I hate the most, it's when other people threaten me."

Chang Geng began to shake, as if he'd fallen into a cellar of ice. Before this row, he hadn't been able to speak to Gu Yun the whole day and had been uneasy in the extreme. He'd very much wanted to strike the perfect balance of words and action, just as when he fooled Xu Ling, and come here to beg for understanding... It would have been no difficult task. But even with a thousand reasons for him to do so, he was perfectly aware that he was simply unwilling and unable.

It seemed that love bewitched the mind; like a double-edged sword without a hilt, it could maim wielder as easily as opponent.

Gu Yun shoved him away. Startled, Chang Geng reached out to grab him in a panic. "Zixi!"

Gu Yun snatched his reaching wrist and forced him to open his hand, then pulled out an object and smacked it hard across Chang Geng's palm. Chang Geng shuddered—His Highness Prince Yan, whose palm had never been slapped by a teacher in his life, was so shocked he forgot to struggle.

Gu Yun had used that white jade flute to smack him. "If you see yourself as a pig or a dog, who will see you as a person? If you don't value yourself, why should anyone spoil you when you throw a fit? How pathetic can you be? How shameless? How wretched?"

He punctuated each reprimand with a strike to Chang Geng's palm. The flute came down three times in the exact same spot, leaving a clean red line across his skin with no blur at the edges.

Gu Yun raised the white jade flute to tilt Chang Geng's chin up. "What does it matter how others treat you? If others respect you, revere you, does that make you invincible? If others disdain you like a pair of tattered shoes, does that make you an actual fucking clod of rotten mud? What can some insignificant barbarian woman who's been dead for about eight hundred years, or some obscure shamanic poison that disturbs one's mind, do to you now? Look at me when you speak!"

Chang Geng could summon no response.

"Everyone says His Highness Prince Yan could fill five carriages with the fruit of his learnings, yet I see he doesn't know what it means to conduct himself with dignity. What exactly do you have in those five carriages? Toilet paper?" Gu Yun tossed his jade flute away and sighed. "You waited all day just to ask for a beating. Well, your wish has been granted. Get out."

Chang Geng stared blankly, sitting on the edge of the bed and clutching his swollen red hand. The sear of pain brought him back to his senses, and he looked up at Gu Yun in disbelief.

Turning back to Chang Geng, Gu Yun poured himself a cup of cold tea and slowly drained it. When the fire of his anger had cooled, he asked, "How long will it take to complete the resettlement of refugees in the Liangjiang area?"

Chang Geng's voice was hoarse. "It'll be the end of the year at the earliest."

Gu Yun asked yet another of Xu Ling's questions: "And when will we have the capability to fight our enemies on the northern border and in Jiangnan?"

Chang Geng closed his eyes. "Their Western nation is not unified in its purpose," he quietly said. "Thanks to this expedition, we know that the pope's position is in peril. They're sure to send an emissary for peace talks within the year. If we play along and use the next year or two to recover our strength, we will be poised to support an all-out assault."

Gu Yun was silent for a beat. "And after the war ends, how long will the peace last?"

"When a nation is rich and strong, its neighbors on all four shores will pledge their allegiance willingly."

"Mm." Gu Yun nodded. "Well then, off you go."

Chang Geng didn't understand at first. "Go... Go where?"

"Weren't you going to investigate Yang Ronggui's corruption and cover-up in Jiangbei with Commissioner Xu? Was I off the mark? Weren't you planning to leave by night, or are you waiting for Zhong-lao to throw you a welcome banquet first?"

Chang Geng stared at him vacantly.

"I have to stay in the Jiangbei Garrison for a few more days," Gu Yun said. "Take the twenty guards with you. Unless the Westerners cross the river with their navy, twenty men'll be enough to deal with any local officials' hired thugs and lackeys. Night is falling now, you mustn't tarry."

Chang Geng stood up without a word and straightened his disheveled clothing.

"Also..." Gu Yun paused. "Put some medicine on your hand when you get a chance."

Chang Geng turned away with difficulty. He seemed to struggle with himself for a time. He quietly said, "Yifu, I want you."

For a moment, Gu Yun thought his ears had acquired some new affliction. "What did you say?"

Chang Geng didn't repeat himself. His ears went red, and he glanced evasively toward Gu Yun, eyes burning with desire as they tried to burrow their way under Gu Yun's snowy white collar.

No matter how much of a playboy Gu Yun might be, he played in the normal way. When it came to *those* kinds of matters, he maintained the decadent customs of noble sons—he was particular about such elegant aesthetics as "amidst flowers and beneath the moon," and "where water flows, a channel forms." He honestly couldn't comprehend such interests as would lead one to insist on calling someone Yifu in bed or to go into heat after receiving a beating. Scalp prickling, he thought to himself, *He really is off his rocker.*

He pointed at the tent's door and said simply, "Out."

Loath to delay his work, Chang Geng suppressed his endless thirst and cast Gu Yun one last secretive and embarrassed look. Then he smoothed his turbulent emotions into calm and fled.

TRUE AND FALSE

WHEN THE STORM that had burst across the coastal region of Liangjiang cleared, it wasn't replaced by a blue sky washed clean of clouds as it would be in the north. Instead, it grew ever hotter and more humid.

The Jiangbei Garrison had started off as a patchwork army, but after a mere year under old General Zhong's command, it had come together into a fit fighting force. If the enemy garrison Gu Yun and the others had infiltrated on the opposing bank had this degree of discipline, it wouldn't have been so easy to turn the place upside down.

Gu Yun and Zhong Chan walked shoulder to shoulder and led their horses. Neither wore armor, and they kept comfortable pace with each other, neither thinking the other too slow.

"I haven't had free time in years," Gu Yun said. "I don't know how long it's been since I last had a conversation with Shifu."

Zhong Chan cared little for formalities and placidly accepted the Marquis of Anding calling him Shifu in private. "The young marquis has been growing much steadier in temperament," he said. "If the old marquis were alive to see your accomplishments, he would surely..."

"Beat me to death," Gu Yun finished for him.

Zhong Chan started, a faint smile appearing on the knife-sharp lines of his face. "There is no need to disparage yourself."

The wind off the river blew from the south, and the moisture in the air made their surroundings feel everywhere damp. Gu Yun brushed his long, unbound hair aside and stared toward the southern shore in silence. Recalling the abandoned village and bleached bones he had witnessed there, the smile slipped from his face. Zhong Chan followed his gaze. He patted Gu Yun's shoulder. "Fate is no easy thing to divine. The greatest sages find it difficult to move against the pull of the world, to say nothing of common men like us. If I may use my advanced age as an excuse to say something rather heretical: never mind the old marquis; even if your grandfather, Emperor Wu, were alive today, he might fare little better than we have. We can only do what is humanly possible. We must leave the rest up to fate, and leave ourselves no regrets."

Gu Yun blinked in surprise. His old teacher was well-versed in the art of war and boasted accomplishments both martial and literary. He had been merciless while instructing Gu Yun all those years ago. His time wandering the jianghu had softened him.

"We have no fear of a land battle," Zhong Chan continued. "The primary issue is that our navy is still lacking. Look at those Westerners: they either sail the seas or stay near the riverbank; they know our navy can't match them. I've gained some insights into the art of naval battle recently, but I'm hardly an expert. You're not going anywhere for a few days. If you have time, let's compare notes."

Gu Yun nodded. "I know. Our sea dragons are inferior to theirs. We were lucky enough to capture a Western dragon this time; I'll have Ge Chen bring it back to the capital and see if the Lingshu Institute has any ideas."

Zhong Chan sighed. "Soldiers can be trained, but when it comes to equipment and violet gold, it's out of this old man's hands. I'm relying on youngsters like you to manage the situation as best you can."

Gu Yun's eyes flickered. He thought he knew where old General Zhong was headed with this. As expected, Zhong Chan continued, "Prince Yan accompanied me for some years in his youth."

"Yes, I know. Thank you for your trouble, Shifu."

"Then you know he holds the Linyuan tablet?"

Gu Yun paused. He wanted to say he didn't, but it would have pricked his conscience, so he relented and told the truth. "He hasn't mentioned it to me, but I've had my guesses... I figured that if not for the Linyuan Pavilion, the God of Wealth and the rest wouldn't have been so quick to support him."

Zhong Chan grunted acknowledgment. "When Prince Yan was young, he displayed no youthful arrogance and was disciplined and calm to a fault. His temperament was a bit stubborn, but not self-pitying or narcissistic. He saw things clearly and knew to put benevolence and justice first—much better than you when you were his age."

Gu Yun held his tongue.

Zhong Chan narrowed his eyes at him, the ghost of a smile flickering across his face. "But the way I see it, sometimes it's good for youth to be a little frivolous. The way he was so mature beyond his years was inhuman—it must be that he suffered too much as a child. That Chen girl told me what the barbarian shamaness did to him. So, what are your plans?"

Gu Yun didn't respond right away, sunk in thought.

"He's not plagued by the wu'ergu of his own volition," Zhong Chang continued. "Sometimes I wonder if my misgivings toward him are unfair. If he were an ordinary child from an ordinary family, I wouldn't have the right to comment. But he is not. He is connected to the fate of the nation. Zixi, in today's imperial court, Prince Yan is the thread that could unravel the whole. The court needs him, but it can't rely wholly on him. Do you understand?"

Gu Yun could hear the unspoken implications in old General Zhong's words. His teacher wanted Gu Yun to have a backup plan. He wanted to make sure Prince Yan didn't grow too powerful. And if necessary, he wanted Gu Yun to use his military might to ensure Chang Geng stepped back when the time came.

Gu Yun didn't pursue this line of conversation. He said simply, "I'll keep an eye on him. Shifu, you needn't worry."

Zhong Chan frowned. "I know he's been with you since he was small, and there are deep bonds of affection between you. But how long can you keep your eye on him really? The Chen family head of this generation is that girl. She's still young; it will probably be another eight to ten years before we can rely on her. Can Prince Yan hold out that long?"

"Every day I'm alive is a day I'll ensure his mind is clear," Gu Yun said. "If he does lose control one day, I can handle it. Tens of thousands of Black Iron Battalion soldiers guard the gates of our nation in the northwest; I won't let him do anything foolish."

Zhong Chan was mildly taken aback. He thought, for an instant, that he detected a different sort of meaning in those words.

As the two generals fretted behind his back, Chang Geng arrived in Yangzhou with Xu Ling, accompanied by the twenty guards Gu Yun had lent them. Disguising their party as refugees would have stretched the imagination, so they had instead impersonated merchants. Their cover story was this: the proprietor of a branch of one of the God of Wealth's pawnshops in Lin'an Prefecture had been forced to flee to Jiangbei because of the war but had no work there. It was commonly known that the chamber of commerce had requested the emperor's authorization to build factories along the canal to give the refugees a place to work. Although the court had yet to approve the request, it seemed to have a good chance of success. Thus, this "proprietor" had been ordered to head north and do some preliminary fieldwork.

The name of the pawnshop in Lin'an and the identity and age of the real proprietor made it a suitable role for Chang Geng to play. Du Wanquan had made all the arrangements; even if someone were to investigate, they wouldn't find any holes.

Secure in their flawless story, they strutted into Yangzhou. Du Wanquan was the entire nation's God of Wealth, and with Chang Geng's support, memorials from his chamber of commerce went directly to the Grand Council. His people had all the grandeur of major imperial merchants, and wielded significantly more power than the minor officials of the region. The local officials had to flock over to greet the God of Wealth's men on principle. Yang Ronggui, being a member of the Lü family, had no affection for Du Wanquan; even so, he had a need to maintain appearances. He held a banquet to welcome Chang Geng and his entourage in Flying Eaves Pavilion.

In the year since the Westerners invaded and turmoil rocked the nation, the New Year's palace banquet had been much reduced in scale. After Kite's Flight Pavilion toppled, it had never been re-erected. It had been a very long time indeed since Xu Ling had looked upon such scenes of opulence. This Flying Eaves Pavilion had an excellent reputation and was known as "Little Kite's Flight." Though it wasn't so grand in scale as Moon-Shot Platform and the Great Yunmeng Outlook had been, its exquisite luxury may have exceeded Kite's Flight Pavilion in its day.

The capital had banned extravagant entertainments long ago, but Jiangbei was remote and the emperor was far; no one cared. The lilting notes of songstresses in Flying Eaves Pavilion could be heard a street away, and gaily dressed men and women streamed in and out without cease.

Xu Ling clicked his tongue in awe at the sight and turned to Chang Geng, eyes wide. "Your High...Proprietor, is your estate this grand?"

Chang Geng shook his head with a smile. "Certainly not. I have just enough to keep me warm and fill my belly. The master of the house spends all his money supporting widows and orphans; he has no head for budgeting. He's going to end up selling his ancestral home someday."

Xu Ling started in surprise, then realized that Chang Geng wasn't talking about the empty Prince Yan Estate, but the estate of the Marquis of Anding. By "supporting widows and orphans," he must have meant bereavement payments. A few years ago, when the nation wasn't at war, the emperor wished to reduce military expenditures because of the sorry state of the national treasury. The meager sum allotted to deceased soldiers' families decreased time and again. Even after countless fights with military representatives, the Ministry of Revenue and the Ministry of War delayed addressing the matter, shirking responsibility at every turn. In the event that the representatives really couldn't get the money, the Marquis of Anding would often go ask for it in person. But Gu Yun returned to the capital once every couple of years; he was too far from the court to be of assistance most of the time. He must have ended up making up the difference himself quite often.

The court had let things slip in times of peace, yet now that war had come, all it took were a few golden words to the tune of "the local garrisons have first access to all the resources of the state" from the emperor's mouth, and these matters became a national priority... In a few years' time, if their lost territory was recovered, the bereaved families filling the cities would probably find themselves patching old clothes by lamplight to get by again.

Xu Ling felt ever more conflicted.

"In a bit, we penniless paupers will probably end up embarrassing ourselves," Chang Geng said quietly, "but it's no matter. They want us to embarrass ourselves so they can have a joke at our expense. As it happens, I've prepared a little joke of my own."

Xu Ling decided he would take Prince Yan as his sole guide. He spoke not a word of objection as he followed Chang Geng inside, bursting with lofty ambitions of scrubbing the filth from society.

The banquet had been hosted in Yang Ronggui's name. Assistant Minister Lü's brother-in-law held the title of Governor of Liangjiang. It sounded impressive enough, but in these extraordinary times, he didn't hold much power. Jiangnan was in the hands of the enemy, and the Jiangbei Garrison governed itself. Most of the Huainan region also wasn't under his control, so his actual sphere of influence was only Yangzhou Prefecture and a handful of its surrounding territories. He had been hastily promoted because the court needed a high-ranking border official who could make arrangements for all the refugees and stabilize the area behind the front lines. If Yang Ronggui showed himself capable, his achievements could certainly earn him a permanent position as one of the eight governors when the lost territory in Jiangnan was recovered.

Unfortunately, it was human nature to imitate the snake that attempted to swallow an elephant. Yang Ronggui had been dissatisfied with the situation in Jiangbei since his appointment. More than once while in his cups he had grumbled to his confidantes that he held the title of governor but was in effect no better than a prefectural magistrate.

As sorry as Governor Yang found himself, he was no less arrogant for it. The Lü family stood behind him, and he naturally held no affection for the newly promoted court officials supported by Du Wanquan. Likewise, he obviously wouldn't lower himself to greet a few merchants in person. He sent some petty officials of Yangzhou to entertain them, who had spent their idle hours honing the gift of gab. The Prefectural Magistrate of Yangzhou, Zheng Kun, deigned to appear partway through the banquet. He sat for less than the duration of a fart, offered a few vapid words, and hadn't even finished speaking those before one of his attendants entered and whispered in his ear. The prefectural magistrate's face paled and he rose to leave then and there.

Xu Ling had assumed the name Zhang Dafu. He was naturally pale, and the way his face flushed when he drank made him appear especially simple and honest. He forced himself to affect drunkenness and tried to make his probing questions seem casual. "We've not yet drunk three rounds of wine; why is Magistrate Zheng leaving so soon?"

A man sitting nearby laughed. "Zhang-xiong, maybe you haven't heard. Governor Yang originally planned to attend this banquet as well; it's too bad you arrived at the wrong time. I hear that guy..." Rather flippantly, he waved his arms like a swan goose flapping its wings and continued quietly, "...is arriving in Yangzhou Prefecture this very day. Governor Yang took a bunch of officials to welcome him in person."

Xu Ling thought he had misunderstood. "Who?" he asked in shock.

"What, Zhang-xiong doesn't know?" Their host had drunk too

much and couldn't quite work his tongue. "Prince Yan, Prince of the First Rank Yan, Yan as in 'Goose,' ever heard of him? The emperor's own brother! I didn't want to mention such an irritating thing, but a while ago, some unruly commoner decided to lodge a complaint against the governor and took it all the way to the capital. The emperor took it seriously and actually sent Prince Yan down here. Now there's a real big shot. If we don't keep him happy, who knows when our heads might roll for all to see."

The man added with exaggerated, unsteady gestures, "We're perfectly innocent; a man who stands up straight needn't worry his shadow will be crooked. The prince can investigate however he likes, ha ha...but it'll be a pain for Governor Yang and the others to keep him company the whole time."

Xu Ling's neck creaked around to gaze at Chang Geng, who was attending this very banquet. The real Prince Yan was right here. Who had Yang Ronggui and the others received?

Prince Yan offered him an enigmatic smile and shoved a crystal dumpling into his mouth without reservation—why let food go to waste?

First they had crashed down behind enemy lines, and now a whole living person had appeared out of thin air. Thank the heavens that even as a scholar, Commissioner Xu was flexible and adept at improvisation. Otherwise, Prince Yan would have frightened him to death with these shocks by now.

It was a meal in which neither guest nor host were happy, and it ended with no one having tasted their food. Xu Ling shooed off a few dancers who had tried to attach themselves to himself and Prince Yan, and the pair rushed back to the inn. After confirming they were completely alone, Xu Ling closed the door and said, "Your Highness, how is there another..."

Chang Geng smiled. "Governor Yang has countless eyes and ears. Surely he knows when the imperial envoy left the capital. If no capital envoy arrives, won't he become paranoid?"

Xu Ling considered the truth of this, but still had his doubts. "But Yang Ronggui has met Your Highness before. What if this person slips up?"

"We've only met once or twice, and we've never spoken at closer than a hundred paces. He's not that familiar with me. My friend knows some jianghu techniques, and if there's one person he can be relied on to impersonate, it's me. So don't worry. Get some rest when you get back to your room; we have plans tonight."

Xu Ling surmised that Prince Yan must intend to investigate the refugee quarters by night, and his spirits perked up.

Around midnight, the pair slipped out of the city in the company of two Black Iron Battalion guards. Their group made straight for the refugee quarters on the city's outskirts. These so-called quarters were in reality little more than a few shacks on the fringes of Yangzhou City. The summer was hot and humid, so the inhabitants wouldn't be cold even if they slept under the open sky. A troop of city guards were stationed nearby to prevent any trouble, and a few large pots stood empty at the side of the road, from which the refugees might claim rations of porridge during the day.

The refugee quarters were silent this late in the night. A Black Iron Battalion guard went ahead to sneak inside, his footfalls so light even the stray cat curled up at the base of a nearby tree didn't stir. Xu Ling said quietly, "Your Highness, something's not right. Places with plague are usually marked with lime, and the ground should be sprinkled with herbal medicine. It shouldn't be so quiet."

Chang Geng's expression remained unchanged. "Yang Ronggui knows we're here; he won't be unprepared. Just watch."

Before he finished speaking, the Black Iron guard returned like a slip of shadow. "Your Highness, there're no more than thirty or so people in this settlement. The majority are young and healthy men and women; there's no sign of plague."

"A hundred thousand refugees in Jiangbei, and there're only thirty people in the refugee quarters outside Yangzhou City?" Xu Ling sneered. "Yang Ronggui takes us for fools. Do the people inside look sleek and shiny—well-fed, warmly dressed, without a care in the world, too? I'd bet they're fake refugees who have been hired."

"Your Highness, what should we do?" the guard asked.

"We can't do anything with our eyes covered," Chang Geng replied softly. "Find a way to contact Great Master Liao Ran. Then have our brothers survey the surrounding area for clues. There's no such thing as a wall that lets in no draft; I refuse to believe Yang Ronggui can maintain total control over this situation."

That night, a swift steed departed Yangzhou City and galloped north to the capital. Its rider carried a secret missive for ambitious individuals great and small: Prince Yan had stepped into their trap.

At the same time, the city defense forces throughout Jiangbei received a middle-of-the-night order from the Governor of Liangjiang. They were to leave their posts in civilian garb and make their way to Yangzhou Prefecture to provide reinforcement. All of Yangzhou was a prosperous scene of song and dance, but it was a relaxed veneer over a tense core.

In the capital city, venomous serpents patiently lay in wait, ready to strike a killing blow. It was unusually quiet, and aside from Old Mister Shen's sudden illness, there was nothing else of note.

Old Mister Shen had been bedridden for days. Imperial physicians streamed in and out of the estate, and even Miracle Doctor

Chen came in person. Seeing that their master's condition was dire, the servants of the Shen Estate made a few visits to the coffin store—it appeared they were making funeral arrangements. No matter how much of a harridan Third Madam Shen might be, she couldn't discuss marriage matches at a time like this. The matter of the engagement had to be dropped.

Shen Yi requested leave to take care of his father and shut the gates of the estate, taking no guests.

At dusk, Miss Chen, who paid a call to the Shen Estate every day, left by carriage as usual, inviting no attention from those who watched from the shadows. When the carriage reached the remote little courtyard Miss Chen occupied when in the capital, the door opened, and out floated a trill of music and a man—it was Shen Yi himself, who should have been performing his filial duties at his father's bedside.

Shen Yi politely cupped his hands toward the open door of the carriage. "Many thanks, Miss Chen."

A guqin lay across Chen Qingxu's lap. With a seated bow, she said, "General, take care. Please let me know if you have further instructions."

Shen Yi looked back at her carefully. He had no knowledge of the Linyuan Pavilion and thought Chen Qingxu merely a woman with no office and no power, an ordinary child of the jianghu. Yet here she was, willing to rough it in the wilderness and eat sand alongside the army, following their every request. He felt sincere gratitude toward her and earnestly said, "Miss Chen is a woman of honor, with the bearing of a famed hero. I truly admire you. A few words of thanks are hardly enough for the assistance you've rendered."

Chen Qingxu seemed to smile—her smiles weren't obvious, and her anger wasn't either. It was as if nothing in the mundane world, no favor nor humiliation, could sway her. She left accompanied by the thrum of plucked strings.

Shen Yi dared not tarry longer. Leaping onto his horse, he rode hard toward the northern outskirts of the capital.

THE STORY CONTINUES IN
Stars of Chaos
VOLUME 4

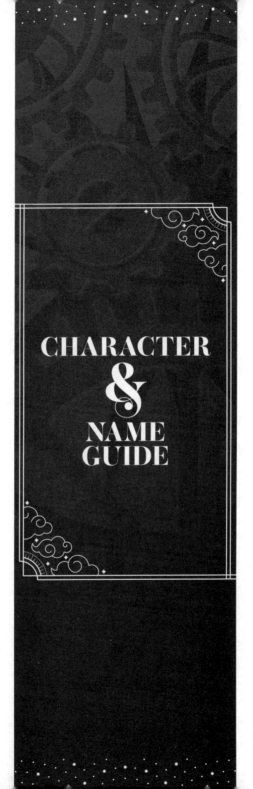

CHARACTER & NAME GUIDE

CHARACTERS

The identity of certain characters may be a spoiler; use this guide with caution on your first read of the novel.

Note on the given name translations: Chinese characters may have many different readings. Each reading here is just one out of several possible readings presented for your reference, and not a definitive translation.

MAIN CHARACTERS

Chang Geng

MILK NAME: Chang Geng (长庚 / "Evening star" or "Evening Venus")

GIVEN NAME: Li Min (李旻 / Surname Li, "Autumn sky")

TITLE: Prince Yan (雁 / "Goose")

Chang Geng spent nearly fourteen years living an uneventful life on the northern border, only for his world to be turned upside down when he learned he was actually the long-lost fourth prince of Great Liang.

Gu Yun

MILK NAME: Shiliu (十六 / "Sixteen")

GIVEN NAME: Gu Yun (顾昀 / Surname Gu, "Sunlight")

COURTESY NAME: Gu Zixi (顾子熹 / Surname Gu; "Daybreak," literary)

TITLE: Marquis of Anding (安定 / "Order")

RANK: Marshal

The fearsome leader of the Black Iron Battalion and Chang Geng's beloved young godfather.

SUPPORTING CHARACTERS

Shen Yi

GIVEN NAME: Shen Yi (沈易 / Surname Shen, "Change" or "Easy")

COURTESY NAME: Shen Jiping (沈季平 / Surname Shen, "Season," "Even" or "Peaceful")

RANK: Commander in Chief of the Southwest Army

Gu Yun's loyal friend and right-hand man.

Ge Pangxiao

MILK NAME: Ge Pangxiao (葛胖小 / Surname Ge, "Chubby youngster")

GIVEN NAME: Ge Chen (葛晨 / Surname Ge, "Dawn")

Chang Geng's childhood tagalong who leaves Yanhui Town with Chang Geng after becoming orphaned. Ge Pangxiao has a fondness for machines.

Cao Niangzi

MILK NAME: Cao Niangzi (曹娘子 / Surname Cao, "Lady")

GIVEN NAME: Cao Chunhua (曹春花 / Surname Cao, "Spring flower")

Chang Geng's childhood admirer, who leaves Yanhui Town with Chang Geng. Cao Niangzi has a fondness for dressing up as both women and men, and is an expert at taking on different roles.

Chen Qingxu

GIVEN NAME: Chen Qingxu (陈轻絮 / Surname Chen, "Gentle," "Silk floss")

A jianghu physician with a cool demeanor whose family specializes in medicine. A member of the Linyuan Pavilion.

Liao Ran

DHARMA NAME: Liao Ran (了然 / "To understand," "To be so")

TITLE: Great Master

A multi-talented monk from the National Temple and member of the Linyuan Pavilion.

THE EIGHTEEN TRIBES

Xiu-niang

ALIAS: Xiu-niang (秀娘 / "Refined lady")

GIVEN NAME: Huge'er (胡格尔 / "The violet gold at the center of the earth")

Chang Geng's "mother," who turns out to be his aunt. She is a member of the Celestial Wolf Tribe and their agent inside Great Liang.

Jialai Yinghuo

GIVEN NAME: Jialai (加莱)

NAME TRANSLATED INTO CHINESE: Yinghuo (荧惑 / "Glimmering deceiver" or "Mars")

TITLE: Wolf King of the Celestial Wolf Tribe

The crown prince and later king of the Celestial Wolf Tribe. He orchestrates the infiltration and attack on Great Liang at the beginning of the story.

THE CAPITAL

Du Wanquan

NAME: Du Wanquan (杜万全 / Surname Du, "Perfectly safe")

A wealthy and powerful merchant known as the "God of Wealth," and a member of the Linyuan Pavilion.

Emperor Wu

The reigning Emperor of Great Liang prior to the Yuanhe Emperor at the start of the story. Gu Yun's maternal grandfather.

Fang Qin

NAME: Fang Qin (方钦 / Surname Fang, "To revere")
TITLE: Minister of Revenue
The leader of a faction of rich and powerful noble families within the imperial court.

Li Feng

GIVEN NAME: Li Feng (李丰 / Surname Li, "Plentiful")
ERA NAME: Longan (隆安 / "Grand Peace")
Chang Geng's elder half-brother, the crown prince, who ascends the throne after the death of his father, the Yuanhe Emperor.

Liao Chi

DHARMA NAME: Liao Chi (了痴, "To understand," "Infatuation")
TITLE: Abbot of the Temple of National Protection
Abbot of the National Temple and Liao Ran's shixiong.

Jiang Chong

GIVEN NAME: Jiang Chong (江充 / Surname Jiang, "Abundance")
COURTESY NAME: Jiang Hanshi (江寒石 / Surname Jiang, "Cold stone")
TITLE: Chief Justice of the Imperial Court of Judicial Review
Shen Yi's senior via the imperial examination system, a friend and ally of Gu Yun, and member of Chang Geng's Grand Council.

Lü Chang

GIVEN NAME: Lü Chang (吕常 / Surname Lü, "Constant/ Unchanging")

COURTESY NAME: Lü Yannian (吕延年 / Surname Lü, "To prolong life")

TITLE: Assistant Minister of Revenue

The head of the well-connected Lü family, and a key player in Fang Qin's faction of nobles.

The Noble Consort

TITLE: Noble Consort

TITLE: Goddess of the Celestial Wolf Tribe

Chang Geng's birth mother. As the goddess of the Celestial Wolf Tribe, she was gifted to Great Liang after their surrender, and became the sole noble consort within the imperial harem.

Prince Wei

TITLE: Prince Wei (魏 / "Kingdom of Wei")

Chang Geng's elder half-brother, the Second Prince. Son of the Yuanhe Emperor. Colluded with Dongying nationals in an unsuccessful plan to overthrow the Longan Emperor by striking the capital from the East Sea.

The Yuanhe Emperor

ERA NAME: Yuanhe (元和 / "Primal," "Harmony")

The reigning emperor of Great Liang at the start of the story. Chang Geng's birth father.

Wang Guo

NAME: Wang Guo (王裹 / Surname Wang, "To enfold")

The Longan Emperor's maternal uncle and the most favored official in the imperial court.

Xu Ling

NAME: Xu Ling (徐令 / Surname Xu, "To command")

TITLE: Right Assistant Supervisory Commissioner of the Department of Supervision

An earnest court official sent to assist Chang Geng on his mission to Jiangbei.

Zhang Fenghan

COURTESY NAME: Zhang Fenghan (张奉函 / Surname Zhang, "To present a letter")

The director of the Lingshu Institute known for his stubbornness. A member of the Linyuan Pavilion.

OTHER

Fu Zhicheng

GIVEN NAME: Fu Zhicheng (傅志诚 / Surname Fu, "Ambition," "Honesty")

RANK: Commander in Chief (of the Southern Border Army)

TITLE: Governor of the Southwest

A military commander in the south who got his start as a bandit. Gu Yun's father, the former Marquis of Anding, supported his military career after defeating him in battle.

Lord Jakobson

ALIAS: Mister Ja

A mysterious operative from the Far West. He is the right hand of the Western pope, who, in the world of Stars of Chaos, is a military leader as well as a religious one.

Tan Hongfei

GIVEN NAME: Tan Hongfei (谭鸿飞 / Surname Tan, "Swan goose," "To fly")

RANK: Commander (of the Northern Camp)

A former member of the Black Iron Battalion who was forced to leave his position after the attack that injured young Gu Yun.

Yang Ronggui

NAME: Yang Ronggui (杨荣桂 / Surname Yang, "Glory," "Osmanthus")

TITLE: Governor of Liangjiang

Governor overseeing the region of Jiangbei, which lies on the front line of the territory occupied by the Far Westerners, and a member of the well-connected Lü family by marriage.

Yao Zhen

GIVEN NAME: Yao Zhen (姚镇 / Surname Yao, "Town")

COURTESY NAME: Yao Chongze (姚重泽 / Surname Yao, "Great favor")

TITLE: Regional Judiciary Commissioner of Yingtian

Gu Yun's longtime acquaintance and a local official in Jiangnan.

Zhong Chan

GIVEN NAME: Zhong Chan (钟蝉 / Surname Zhong, "Cicada")

RANK: General

A general who was dismissed from his post after defying the emperor, and both Gu Yun and Chang Geng's shifu in martial arts.

INSTITUTIONS

The Government of Great Liang

The emperor is the highest authority in Great Liang, an autocratic monarchy. The top-level administrative bodies of the state include a number of departments and ministries, such as the Ministry of Revenue and Ministry of War.

Years ago, the militant Emperor Wu expanded the borders of Great Liang and built the nation to the height of its power. Due to his lack of male heirs, the more compassionate Yuanhe Emperor was selected as his successor from a different branch of the imperial royal family. The Longan Emperor, the son of Yuanhe Emperor, takes after his father in temperament.

The Military of Great Liang and the Black Iron Battalion

The armed forces of Great Liang consist of eight major military branches—the Kite, Carapace, Steed, Pelt, Hawk, Chariot, Cannon, and Dragon Divisions—each of which specializes in a particular type of warfare. Troops are divided between five major garrisons located in five different regions throughout the country.

Chief among these is the Black Iron Battalion, which is presently stationed in the Western Regions. An elite group of soldiers widely considered to be one of the most powerful military forces in the known world, the Black Iron Battalion is currently under the command of Marshal Gu Yun and comprises the Black Hawk, Black Carapace, and Black Steed Divisions.

The Temple of National Protection

The Temple of National Protection, also known as the National Temple, practices Buddhism, the religion of Great Liang's imperial family.

The Lingshu Institute (灵枢 / "Spiritual pivot")

An academy directly under the emperor's authority that develops the equipment of Great Liang's military, as well as other mechanical inventions.

The Linyuan Pavilion (临渊 / "Approaching the abyss")

A mysterious organization of people from all levels of society that emerges to aid parties they find worthy in times of chaos. The decision to intervene in worldly affairs is determined by the formation and bestowment of the Linyuan tablet. In addition to granting its bearer access to the full extent of the Linyuan Pavilion's resources, the tablet also allows for the mobilization of the extrajudicial body responsible for meting out punishments to organization members known as the Daofa Court.

LOCATIONS

GREAT LIANG

The Capital

The capital city of Great Liang.

Dagu Harbor

A naval base in the Beihai region, several days' ride south of Great Liang's capital.

Jiayu Pass

A fortress in the northwest and an important waypoint of the Silk Road.

The Southern Border

The mountainous southernmost region of Great Liang, where bandits run rampant.

Yangzhou City

A city in Jiangbei, north of the Yangtze River.

Yanhui Town (雁回 / "Wild goose's return")

A town on the Northern Border of Great Liang, where Chang Geng grew up.

Yingtian Prefecture

A prefecture in Jiangnan Province, south of the Yangtze River, near the East Sea.

FOREIGN POWERS

The Eighteen Tianlang (Celestial Wolf) Tribes

A people residing in the grasslands north of Great Liang, where violet gold is plentiful. They pay an annual tribute to Great Liang after being defeated in battle by the Black Iron Battalion.

Loulan

A small but prosperous nation in the Western Regions located at the entrance of the Silk Road. They have a friendly relationship with Great Liang.

Qiuci

A tiny nation in the Western Regions that acquired a suspicious number of sand tiger war chariots.

Qiemo

A tiny nation in the Western Regions that came into conflict with Qiuci.

Dongying

An island nation to the east of Great Liang.

The Far West

A region far to the west beyond the Silk Road that excels in seafaring trade and creating violet-gold-powered devices.

NAME GUIDE

NAMES, HONORIFICS, AND TITLES

Courtesy Names versus Given Names

A courtesy name is given to an individual when they come of age. Traditionally, this was at the age of twenty during one's crowning ceremony, but it can also be presented when an elder or teacher deems the recipient worthy. Though generally a male-only tradition, there is historical precedent for women adopting a courtesy name after marriage. Courtesy names were a tradition reserved for the upper class.

It was considered disrespectful for one's peers of the same generation to address someone by their given name, especially in formal or written communication. Use of one's given name was reserved only for elders, close friends, and spouses.

This practice is no longer used in modern China, but is commonly seen in historically-inspired media. As such, many characters have more than one name. Its implementation in novels is irregular and is often treated malleably for the sake of storytelling.

Milk Names

In China, babies are traditionally given their 大名 (literally "big name," or less literally, "given name") one hundred days after their birth. During those first hundred days, parents would refer to the child by their 小名 (lit. "little name") or 乳名 (lit. "milk name"). Milk names might be childish, employing a diminutive like xiao- or doubling a syllable, but they might also be selected to ward off harm to the child, for example Cao Niangzi's milk name meaning "lady." Many parents might continue referring to their children by their milk name long after they have received their given name.

At the beginning of *Stars of Chaos*, Chang Geng is already thirteen or fourteen years old, but has not been given a "big name." Since Yanhui Town is a backwater border town, this is not terribly strange—historically, many rural families have tended to give their children given names much later in life than the hundredth day. This may be because life in the countryside was harsher and it was more difficult to raise children to adulthood.

Diminutives, Nicknames, and Name Tags

A-: Friendly diminutive. Always a prefix. Usually for monosyllabic names, or one syllable out of a disyllabic name.

XIAO-: A diminutive meaning "little." Always a prefix.

-LAO: A suffix attached to the surname of venerated elders. Denotes a particularly high degree of respect.

Family

DAGE: A word meaning "eldest brother." It can also be used to address an unrelated male peer that one respects. When added as a suffix, it becomes an affectionate address for any older male. Can also be used by itself to refer to one's true oldest brother.

DAJIE: A word meaning "eldest sister." It can be used as a casual term of address for an older female.

ERGE: A word meaning "second brother."

JIEJIE: A word meaning "elder sister." It can be attached as a suffix or used independently to address an unrelated female peer.

NIANG: A word meaning "mother" or "lady."

XIONG: A word meaning "elder brother." It can be attached as a suffix to address an unrelated male peer.

YIFU: A word meaning "godfather" or "adoptive father." (*See Godparentage Relationships for more information*)

Martial Arts and Tutelage

SHIDI: Junior male member of one's own school or fellow disciple/apprentice under the same master.

SHIFU: Teacher or master. For one's master in one's own school. Gender-neutral.

SHISHU: The junior fellow disciple of one's master. Gender-neutral.

SHIXIONG: Senior male member of one's own school or fellow disciple/apprentice under the same master.

XIANSHENG: A respectful suffix with several uses, including for someone with a great deal of expertise in their profession or a teacher. Can be used independently.

PRONUNCIATION GUIDE

Mandarin Chinese is the official state language of mainland China, and pinyin is the official system of romanization in which it is written. As Mandarin is a tonal language, pinyin uses diacritical marks (e.g., ā, á, ǎ, à) to indicate these tonal inflections. Most words use one of four tones, though some are a neutral tone. Furthermore, regional variance can change the way native Chinese speakers pronounce the same word. For those reasons and more, please consider the guide below a simplified introduction to pronunciation of select character names and sounds from the world of *Stars of Chaos*.

More resources are available at *sevenseasdanmei.com*

Shā pò láng
Shā as in **shop**
Pò as in **put**
Láng as in **long**

Cháng Gēng
Ch as in **change**, áng as in **long**
G as in **goose**, ēng as in **sung**

Gù Yún
Gù as in **goose**
Y as in **you**, ún as in **bin**, but with lips rounded as for **boon**

GENERAL CONSONANTS

Some Mandarin Chinese consonants sound very similar, such as z/c/s and zh/ch/sh. Audio samples will provide the best opportunity to learn the difference between them.

X: somewhere between the **sh** in **sh**eep and **s** in **s**ilk

Q: a very aspirated **ch** as in **ch**arm

C: **ts** as in pan**ts**

Z: **z** as in **z**oom

S: **s** as in **s**ilk

CH: **ch** as in **ch**arm

ZH: **dg** as in do**dg**e

SH: **sh** as in **sh**ave

G: hard **g** as in **g**allant

GENERAL VOWELS

The pronunciation of a vowel may depend on its preceding consonant. For example, the "i" in "shi" is distinct from the "i" in "di." Vowel pronunciation may also change depending on where the vowel appears in a word, for example the "i" in "shi" versus the "i" in "ting." Finally, compound vowels are often—though not always—pronounced as conjoined but separate vowels. You'll find a few of the trickier compounds below.

IU: **y** as in **y**ou plus **ow** as in sh**ow**

IE: **ye** as in **ye**s

UO: **wa** as in **wa**rm

GLOSSARY

GLOSSARY

While not required reading, this glossary is intended to offer further context to the many concepts and terms utilized throughout this novel and provide a starting point for learning more about the rich Chinese culture from which these stories were written.

TERMINOLOGY

BALD DONKEY: A derogatory epithet used to describe Buddhist monks. It stems from the stereotypical image of a bald monk riding a donkey while begging for alms.

BOWING AND CURTSYING: As is seen in other Asian cultures, standing bows are a traditional greeting and are also used when giving an apology. A deeper bow shows greater respect.

BUDDHISM: The central belief of Buddhism is that life is a cycle of suffering and rebirth, only to be escaped by reaching enlightenment (nirvana). Buddhists believe in karma, that a person's actions will influence their fortune in this life and future lives. The teachings of the Buddha are known as The Middle Way and emphasize a practice that is neither extreme asceticism nor extreme indulgence.

CALLIGRAPHY: Chinese calligraphy is a form of visual art and a central part of Chinese culture. It is considered one of the traditional "four arts" of gentlemen scholars, along with guqin, weiqi, and painting. Calligraphy by notable masters is highly sought-after by collectors. A gift of calligraphy is a great honor for both the giver and the recipient.

CONCUBINES AND THE IMPERIAL HAREM: In ancient China, it was common practice for a wealthy man to possess women as concubines in addition to his wife. They were expected to live with him and bear him children. Generally speaking, a greater number of concubines correlated to higher social status, hence a wealthy merchant might have two or three concubines, while an emperor might have tens or even a hundred.

The imperial harem had its own ranking system. The exact details vary over the course of history, but can generally be divided into three overarching ranks: the empress, consorts, and concubines. The status of a prince or princess's mother is an important factor in their status in the imperial family, in addition to birth order and their own personal merits. Given the patrilineal rules of succession, the birth of a son can also elevate the mother's status, leading to fierce, oftentimes deadly, competition amongst ambitious members of the imperial harem.

CONFUCIANISM: Confucianism is a philosophy based on the teachings of Confucius. Its influence on all aspects of Chinese culture is incalculable. Confucius placed heavy importance on respect for one's elders and family, a concept broadly known as filial piety (孝). The family structure is used in other contexts to urge similar behaviors, such as respect of a student toward a teacher, or people of a country toward their ruler.

COUGHING OR SPITTING BLOOD: A way to show a character is ill, injured, or upset. Despite the very physical nature of the response, it does not necessarily mean that a character has been wounded; their body could simply be reacting to a very strong emotion.

CROWS: An inauspicious symbol in Chinese culture. A person "has the beak of a crow" if they are prone to saying inauspicious things.

CULTIVATION: A practice in Daoism-inspired Chinese myth through which humans can achieve immortality and non-human creatures can acquire higher forms, more humanoid forms, or both.

DHARMA NAME: A name given to new disciples of Buddhism during their initiation ritual.

DAOISM: Daoism is the philosophy of the dao (道 / "the way"). Following the dao involves coming into harmony with the natural order of the universe, which makes someone a "true human," safe from external harm and able to affect the world without intentional action. Cultivation is a concept based on Daoist beliefs.

DRAGONS: There are several kinds of dragons in Chinese mythology. Jiao (蛟) or jiaolong (蛟龙), "flood dragons," are hornless, aquatic dragons that can summon storms and floods. Zhenlong (真龙), "true dragons," also have water-related powers, but are capable of flying through the clouds. "True" dragons are a symbol of the divine and the emperor, hence the translation as "imperial dragons" in this story. According to myth, flood dragons can transform into true, or imperial, dragons by cultivating and passing heavenly tribulations.

ERA NAME: A designation for the years when a given emperor was on the throne (or some part of those years). This title is determined by the emperor when they ascend the throne, and can be used to refer to both the era and the emperor himself.

EYES: Descriptions like "phoenix eyes," "peach-blossom eyes," or "triangular eyes" refer to eye shape. Phoenix eyes have an upturned sweep at their far corners, while peach-blossom eyes have a rounded upper lid with gentle upward tilt at the outer corners and are often considered particularly alluring. Triangular eyes have eyelids which droop at the outer corner and are considered harsh and keen.

FACE: Mianzi (面子), generally translated as "face," is an important concept in Chinese society. It is a metaphor for a person's reputation and can be extended to further descriptive metaphors. For example, "having face" refers to having a good reputation, and "losing face" refers to having one's reputation hurt. Meanwhile, "giving face" means deferring to someone else to help improve their reputation, while "not wanting face" implies that a person is acting so poorly or shamelessly that they clearly don't care about their reputation at all. "Thin face" refers to someone easily embarrassed or prone to offense at perceived slights. Conversely, "thick face" refers to someone not easily embarrassed and immune to insults.

FIRESTARTER: An ancient "lighter" made of easily flammable material inside a bamboo tube. It can be ignited by shaking or blowing on it.

FOOT BINDING : A process used to create artificially small feet, which were seen as an attractive trait for women during certain periods of Chinese history. The process involved breaking and tightly binding the foot to mold its shape. The foot might also be bound with pieces of broken crockery in order to induce necrosis in the broken toes and cause them to fall off, leading to a smaller final result.

GODPARENTAGE RELATIONSHIPS: Similar to the idea of "sworn brothers," gan (干) relationships are nominal familial relationships entered into by non-blood-related parties for a variety of reasons.

In the setting of *Stars of Chaos*, the border towns have a tradition where a debt of gratitude that a person could not repay by other means would be recognized by either the recipient or their descendants naming their benefactor as their godparent. Entering this relationship means that the recipient (or their descendant) now acknowledges filial duties toward their new godparent, such as making sure they are taken care of in their old age.

INCENSE TIME: A common way to tell time in ancient China, referring to how long it takes for a single incense stick to burn. Standardized incense sticks were manufactured and calibrated for specific time measurements: a half hour, an hour, a day, etc. These were available to people of all social classes. "One incense time" is roughly thirty minutes.

IMPERIAL EXAMINATION SYSTEM: The official system of examinations in ancient China that qualified someone for official service. It was a supposedly meritocratic system that allowed students from all backgrounds to rise up in society, but the extent to which this was true varied across time.

An examination mentor presides over the highest level of the imperial examination, with the emperor occasionally proctoring the test himself. The first-, second-, and third-ranked candidates are bestowed the titles Zhuangyuan, Bangyan, and Tanhua, respectively.

JIANGHU: The jianghu (江湖 / "rivers and lakes") describes an underground society of martial artists, monks, rogues, artisans, and merchants who settle disputes between themselves per their own moral codes. For members of the jianghu, these moral codes supersede laws mandated by the government. Thus, the jianghu typically exists outside of or in opposition to mainstream society and its government, with its members customarily avoiding cooperation with government bureaucracy.

The jianghu is a staple of wuxia (武侠 / "martial heroes"), one of the oldest Chinese literary genres, which consists of tales of noble heroes fighting evil and injustice.

LOTUS FLOWER: This flower symbolizes purity of the heart and mind, as lotuses rise untainted from the muddy waters they grow in. It also signifies the holy seat of the Buddha. An extremely rare variety known as the bingdi lian (并蒂莲) or "twin lotus" is considered an auspicious sign and a symbol of marital harmony.

MANDARIN DUCKS: Famous for mating for life, mandarin ducks are a symbol of marital harmony, and are frequently featured in Chinese art.

MOURNING PERIOD: The death of a parent was a major event in historical Chinese culture. Children who survived them would be expected to observe a mourning period during which they wore only plain white clothes, stayed at home, and ceased to partake in entertainment and social events. The exact length of the mourning period varied, and there could be exceptions if, for example, the child had important duties they had to attend to.

SHA PO LANG: Sha Po Lang (杀破狼) is the name of a key star formation in Zi Wei Dou Shu (紫微斗数 / "purple star astrology"), a common system of astrology in Chinese culture. It refers to an element of a natal star chart in which the stars Qi Sha (七杀 / "seven killings"), Tan Lang (贪狼 / "greedy wolf"), and Po Jun (破军 / "vanquisher of armies") appear in four specific "palaces" of the sky.

Sha Po Lang in a natal horoscope foretells change and revolution, a turbulent fate. The fortunate among those with this in their star chart gain talent and fortune amidst chaos, while the less fortunate encounter disaster and destitution. Those with this formation in their natal horoscope will encounter great ups and downs, yet have the potential to make their name in dramatic fashion. Many great generals of ancient times were said to have been born under these stars.

SIX ARTS: The basis of education in ancient China, the six arts comprised the disciplines of rites, music, archery, chariotry, calligraphy, and mathematics.

THREE IMMORTAL SOULS AND SEVEN MORTAL FORMS: Hun (魂) and po (魄) are two types of souls in Chinese philosophy and religion. Hun are immortal souls which represent the spirit and intellect, and leave the body after death. Po are corporeal souls or mortal forms which remain with the body of the deceased. Different traditions claim there are different numbers of each, but three hun and seven po is common in Daoism.

TIGER TALLY: A token used as proof of imperial authorization to deploy and command troops. In *Stars of Chaos*, there are three Black Iron Tiger Tallies total, which can command the eight branches of the Great Liang military in times of emergency. They are held by Gu Yun, the imperial court, and the emperor, respectively.

TITLES OF NOBILITY: Titles of nobility are an important feature of the traditional social structure of Imperial China. While the conferral and organization of specific titles evolved over time, in *Stars of Chaos*, such titles can be either inherited or bestowed by the emperor.

In the world of *Stars of Chaos*, a notable feature of the ranking system with respect to the imperial princes is that monosyllabic titles are reserved for princes of the first rank while disyllabic titles designate princes of the second rank.

Princes of the second rank are also known as commandery princes, so named for the administrative divisions they head. The title of commandery prince is not solely reserved for members of the imperial family, but can also be given to meritorious officials and rulers of vassal states.

TRADITIONAL CHINESE MEDICINE: Traditional medical practices in China are commonly based around the idea that qi, or vital energy, circulates in the body through channels called meridians similarly to how blood flows through the circulatory system. Acupuncture points, or acupoints, are special nodes, most of which lie along the meridians. Stimulating them by massage, acupuncture, or other methods is believed to affect the flow of qi and can be used for healing.

Another central concept in traditional Chinese medicine is that disease arises from an imbalance of elements in the body caused by disharmony in internal functions or environmental factors. For example, an excess of internal heat can cause symptoms such as fever, thirst, insomnia, and redness of the face. Excess internal heat can be treated with the consumption of foods with cooling properties.

QI DEVIATION: A physiological and psychological disorder believed to result from improper spiritual or martial training. Symptoms of qi deviation in fiction include panic, paranoia, sensory hallucinations, and death. Common treatments for qi deviation in fiction include relaxation (voluntary or forced by an external party), massage, meditation, or qi transfer from another individual.

UNBOUND HAIR: Neatly bound hair was historically an important aspect of one's attire. Loose, unbound hair was seen as highly improper, and is used as synecdoche to describe someone who is disheveled in appearance.

WEIQI: Also known by its Japanese name, Go, weiqi is the oldest known board game in human history. The board consists of a nineteen-by-nineteen grid upon which opponents play unmarked black and white stones as game pieces to claim territory.

WILD GEESE: A classic motif in Chinese poetry, the wild goose, or yan (雁), has come to embody a host of different symbolic meanings. As a migratory bird, it can represent seasonal change as well as a loving message sent from afar. Famous for mating for life, a pair of geese can allude to marital bliss, while a lone goose can signify the loss of a loved one.

WUXING THEORY: Wuxing (五行 / "Five Phases") is a concept in Chinese philosophy used for describing interactions and relationships between phenomena. The expression 五行 (literally "five motions") originally refers to the movements of the planets Mars (火星 / "fire star"), Mercury (水星 / "water star"), Jupiter (木星 / "wood star"), Venus (金星 / "metal star"), and Saturn (土星 / "earth star"), which correspond to the phases of fire, water, wood, metal, and earth, respectively. In wuxing cosmology, people are categorized according to the five phases and relationships are described in cycles.

Xiangke (相克 / lit. "mutually overcoming") refers to a cycle in which one phase acts as a restricting (and oftentimes destructive) agent on the other. The phase interactions in the ke (克) cycle are: wood breaks through earth, earth dams up water, water douses fire, fire melts metal, and metal chops through wood. When applied to people, these interactions take the form of karmic consequences, which are oftentimes directed at the children and other family members of the original actor. An example of one such cycle might be: An emperor killed many people to expand the nation → the adverse effects of his great deeds are directed toward his children in the form of early death.

Chinese superstition also holds that, due to their phase categorization, certain people's fate can "suppress" (克) the fates of the people around them. For example, if someone is categorized as metal, they may suppress people who have been categorized as wood. Similarly, if someone's fate is determined to be more tenacious than others, they may bring harm to their familial relations. In the case of Gu Yun's unmarriageable status, people have observed the misfortune that befell his family and concluded that he inherited a similar fate. Thus, any woman who marries him will suffer misfortune as her fate is suppressed by his.

YIN AND YANG ENERGY: The concept of yin and yang in Chinese philosophy that describes the complementary interdependence of opposite or contrary forces. It can be applied to all forms of change and differences. Yang represents the sun, masculinity, and the living, while yin represents the shadows, femininity, and the dead, including spirits and ghosts. In fiction, imbalances between yin and yang energy can do serious harm to the body or act as the driving force for malevolent spirits seeking to replenish themselves of whichever they lack.

THE WORLD OF STARS OF CHAOS

COPPER SQUALL: A horn-shaped device made of copper that amplifies the voice of the speaker when spoken into.

GIANT KITE AND RED-HEADED KITE: A large, amphibious airship, the giant kite is powered by steam and equipped with thousands of wing-like structures called fire pinions, which burn violet gold.

A variation of the giant kite is the red-headed kite. Unlike the giant kite, the red-headed kite is a small pleasure vessel that does not see use in the military.

GREAT CONDOR: An experimental ship which combines the propulsion system of hawk armor with the body of a small kite. This allows it to transport multiple passengers and fly far faster than clumsy giant kites. However, the prototype still suffers from fuel efficiency problems and lacks stability in inclement weather.

HEAVY ARMOR: A class of armor used in the military, heavy armor is powered by violet gold, allowing its wearers to traverse thousands of kilometers in seconds and lift objects weighing hundreds of kilograms. A single suit of heavy armor has the power to annihilate a thousand soldiers.

IRON CUFF: The part of light armor that encircles the wrist. Highly convenient, iron cuffs can be removed from full suits of armor and used on their own. A single iron cuff can conceal three or four silk darts.

LIGHT ARMOR: A class of armor used in the military, light armor is typically worn by the cavalry and can only support a small amount of propulsion. It relies primarily on man- and animal-power, and its primary advantages lie in how light and convenient it is.

LIGHT PELT: The lightest class of armor used in the military, the light pelt is specially designed for riding and weighs less than fifteen kilograms.

PARHELION BOW AND ARROW: A giant mechanical bow that runs on violet gold. When fully powered up, arrows released from such a bow can pierce through a city wall a dozen meters thick.

SILK DART: An extraordinarily thin knife that can be concealed in and fired from wrist cuffs.

VIOLET GOLD: A substance mined from beneath the earth which can be burned as fuel in high-quality mechanical devices. It is of such strategic importance that it is called the "lifeline" of Great Liang.

WINDSLASHER: A weapon used by the Black Iron Battalion. It looks like a staff when at rest, but spinning blades release from hidden incisions in one end when the weapon is spun.

WU'ERGU: A slow-acting poison of northern barbarian origin. It is purported to have the ability to transform someone into a great warrior, but those afflicted with wu'ergu are plagued with nightmares and eventually driven insane with bloodlust.